"My . . . favorite poet was Aeschylus, and he once wrote:
'Even in our sleep, pain which cannot beget falls drop by
drop upon the heart
until in our own despair, against our will,
comes wisdom through the awful grace of God.'"

Senator Robert Francis Kennedy
Indianapolis, 1968
upon announcing the death of Dr. Martin Luther King, Jr.

For Clark Marion Drake, "Papa" (1936-2022)

You didn't know all those questions I asked you about the sixties were for this book. My love of storytelling is only one of the million things I have to thank you for. You were the best of us. Every time I see the train in Colbert, I'll think of you.

and

To my favorite high school teacher, Mr. Dana Richier, whose 11th grade Vietnam War-era class instilled a lifelong interest in Vietnam—and the intersection of class, music, and political upheaval in history—which undoubtedly helped to lead me down this path.

ONE

BOBBI – ATHENS, GEORGIA – MAY 1961

BARBARA Lynn Newton, known to everyone as Bobbi, sat at her dressing table, carefully brushing through her white-blonde hair when the banging on the door started again. "Would you turn that racket down?" Her brother Ed's voice came through the thin wooden door. "There's only so many hours in the day I can listen to that warbling goat! If you don't turn it off, I'm going to break that record in half!"

Bobbi leaned over and turned the knob on the turntable down from nine to eight, then called back, "Like to see you try!"

No answer came, so she resumed brushing, smiling to herself. "Only the Lonely" had been her favorite song for months. She'd driven her family crazy playing it, but Roy Orbison was her favorite and since records were so dear, it was one of only five that she'd bought. *Let Ed try to get his dirty mitts on it*, she thought to herself, running the brush through her hair once more and then setting it back down on the table. *I'll clean his clock.* She took a dollop of cold cream, running it in circles over the apples of her cheeks, playing at being her mother. It was Mom's hairbrush and mirror, and Mom's old cold cream. She wouldn't be missing it now.

The song ended, and just as she was picking up the needle to replay it, Ed's voice came through the door again, angry enough to splinter the wood. "Enough, Bobbi. If you play that damn tune one more time, I swear I'll—"

"You'll what?" she called back defiantly. "Break into my room and take it? If you do that, I might just have to tell Dad that you've been sneaking out to go necking with Pamela Acworth!"

"Turn it *off*, Bobbi. I'm trying to study. If you don't, I won't take you to see your precious Boston boy tomorrow."

Bobbi sat back, and after a moment, switched off the record player. Fine; she'd let Ed win this round. Nothing, and she meant *nothing*, would be stopping her from going to see Robert Kennedy tomorrow. Not even her beloved Roy Orbison was worth the risk. "Suits me fine," she said hotly, getting up from the table and going over to her bed. "I was going to bed, anyway."

"Good. You need your beauty sleep for Ol' Irish Eyes. What if he asks you for a date?" Ed's irritation had given way to bemusement. Bobbi didn't reply, but punched her pillow. "Oh right, he's married. Perhaps he'll bring Ethel along. I hope he doesn't, 'cause you're like to scratch her eyes out!"

Bobbi opened her mouth to retort back that she'd do no such thing, that Bobby Kennedy's wife Ethel was every bit as lovely as Mr. Kennedy himself, and that the charming, laughing young mother reminded her of their own mother, and for that alone she loved her. But she decided against it. Ed would only tease her more mercilessly, and anyway, there was a grain of truth to his ribbing. The sheer volume of black and white, glossy pictures hanging over her school desk gave away the rather large crush she had on John F.

Kennedy's golden-haired, soft-eyed younger brother, so there was no point in trying to deny it.

"Goodnight, Ed," she called gaily, turning off her bedside lamp. "Don't stay up all night, necking with Pamela. Tomorrow's a big day."

"Yeah, yeah," he answered good-naturedly. She heard his footsteps moving down the hall. "For *you*."

Bobbi smiled, her face against the cool pillow, wondering what color Bobby Kennedy's eyes were up close, the chorus of 'Only the Lonely' drifting through her mind as she fell asleep.

The next afternoon, Bobbi stood with Ed in front of the Arch, the famous sloped wrought-iron entrance to the university, impatiently scratching at a mosquito bite on her temple, trying to pull her carefully coiffed hair over to cover up the large red bump, and cursing the unseasonably warm late-spring weather. How could mosquitoes already be out? Her brother, tall and resplendent in his navy-blue suit, was holding a large scoop of ice cream in a sugar cone, lapping at it casually while chatting with a schoolmate. Bobbi sighed impatiently. Mr. Kennedy wasn't set to speak for another hour, but she was eager to get into the law building and take her seat. Ed, maddeningly, did not share her desire to hurry.

"These speeches are a dime a dozen," he'd explained to her from behind the wheel of his blue 1957 Ford Thunderbird as they'd driven into town. "The only thing different about this one is that Kennedy's a celebrity."

"He isn't," Bobbi had argued, unsure why she found the label offensive. "His brother is."

"The whole family is, sugar pie." Ed had laughed, turning onto Broad Street. "They're our version of the Royal Family, you know."

Bobbi thought about that now, still scratching at the welt on her forehead. She didn't know much about the Royal Family in England, though she had a passing interest in their young, sharp, blue-eyed Queen Elizabeth. It was a novel, lovely thing to her, being so young and beautiful and in charge of an entire country, though she knew from her studies that the Queen was little more than a figurehead these days. There was a certain glamour to it, but also a rebellious, delicious sort of power, to be female and in charge of everything, even if it were only pretense. She'd read that the cool and beautiful young queen had served in World War II as a mechanic, a detail that had delighted her.

"You can't tell me you're in love with Robert F. Kennedy just because he makes nice speeches," her brother had continued, teasing her as he maneuvered into a parking spot. "I think it has more to do with that 'aw, shucks' smile of his and his last name."

"*Stop* it, Ed," Bobbi had responded irritably, and her brother had given her a good-natured cuff on the neck and then gone thankfully silent. Her family had indulged her fascination with Kennedy ever since she'd first started following his career, back when he'd been elected Attorney General, though she knew they found it both amusing and perplexing for a twelve-year-old girl to be so enamored with a politician. Daddy, who was very conservative and one of the holdouts who hadn't denounced former Governor Eugene Talmadge, said that Robert F. Kennedy and all his ilk were "rich, yuppie liberals who wouldn't know a hard day's work if it bit 'em on the backside," while her brothers, especially Ed, who was in his second year of law school at UGA, didn't find him liberal *enough*. "I've heard of some of the things going on in Washington," she'd overheard Ed complaining to a law school friend on the phone. "And I'm still not entirely convinced Jack Kennedy is one hundred percent behind the Civil Rights movement. I think it's all tactical." Bobbi didn't fully understand what he'd meant.

It was her secret dream—secret because she hadn't told anyone, not even Ed, or her best friend Amelia, to whom she told everything—to become a lawyer, too. She supposed she'd try for UGA's school of law one day. It was the practical thing to do; she'd be in close proximity to her family and Ed could help her with her studies, since it would be his alma mater—that was, *if* she got in. UGA had desegregated only the year before to allow Black people to join the school, and it wasn't much easier for women to get into certain spaces. Women had been attending UGA since around 1903, but law school was most assuredly considered a 'boys' club.'

"Ed, can't we go in and take our seats?" Bobbi begged her brother, who was still lapping at his vanilla cone, a sly smile on his lips. His friend had departed, but Ed was sneaking a covert glance at a young woman in a tweed skirt that ended just below the knee, seated at the steps in front of the arch, and turning the pages of a textbook with a white-gloved finger. The slit in her skirt revealed a sliver of thigh. Bobbi thumped her brother on the arm. "If you'd stop sneaking inappropriate looks up that girl's skirt."

"Shut up, will you?" Ed hissed, looking at her in irritation. Then

5

he smiled benignly. "If we go in too early, you'll miss seeing Mr. Kennedy enter the building. You want to catch him up close, don't you?" He tossed the remnants of his ice cream in a metal trash can and took her arm. "Besides, we have assigned seats. I always sit in the back row, second seat to the left."

"But what about me?" she said. "I don't have an assigned seat."

"Professor Edwards has saved the seat beside mine for you. Didn't you think I'd take care of that?" Her brother had pulled strings to get her into this speech. Mr. Kennedy was visiting UGA for Law Day, and the speech was reserved for students of the law school only. Ed had gone to his professor and appealed to him to let his little sister listen in. Bobbi wasn't sure how he'd done it, since she'd heard many stories about the old, curmudgeonly professor who made all the students' lives a living hell, but somehow her older brother had managed it. She supposed it had something to do with his 4.0 average and the fact that he was the golden boy of his class, something she thought of with both pride and irritation. Ed was the golden boy in most things, including their home. He was their dad's favorite and had been Mom's, too. He sailed through life on a ship of privilege, and sometimes it galled her. Bobbi and their other brother, Guy, who was in his junior year of high school, had never gotten half the attention or devotion he did. She told herself to mind the ugly jealousy, though, especially on days like this, when Ed had come through for her.

Ed had actually done her two favors without even knowing it. Not only was Bobbi going to see and hear her beloved hero Bobby Kennedy in person, but she was going to visit the law school. She would get to see the great hall that would hopefully one day shape her into a lawyer, too. It was all too much—oh, she could hardly stand it.

Bobbi was so happy she didn't even mind when Ed stopped to say hello to the girl in the tweed skirt, putting them another five minutes behind. She stared out onto Broad Street, pretending not to see as her brother smoothly acquired a telephone number, cupping her hand over her eyes, hoping to catch a glimpse of the motorcade carrying the lovely Mr. Robert F. Kennedy. When her brother finally turned to her, extending his suit-clad arm, she took it eagerly, all smiles. "Finally!" Ed had no smart retort for her; he was in a good mood now, too.

As they approached the building, someone called out to them. "Fancy meeting you here!" Bobbi turned and waved to Landrum Walton, who had been her schoolmate since kindergarten. He lived just a few houses down from theirs, on the west side of Athens near Beech Haven. He was a nice boy, with dishwater blond hair that came over his ears and light gray eyes, and a wide, easy-going smile full of slightly crooked white teeth that lit up his whole face.

"Hi, Landrum," she said, pasting on a smile, though she was positively itching with nerves. Her brother held out a hand respectfully for Landrum to shake. "What are you doing here?"

"Came with my mama," Landrum said, gesturing to a tall woman standing over by the trees, holding a fan in front of her face. "She loves Mr. Kennedy and was hoping to catch a glimpse of him before he went inside."

Bobbi began to tell Landrum that she would be attending the

speech when a loud smattering of applause and excited shrieks filled the air. Bobbi turned to see a smooth black car cruising onto a side street, flanked by several more black cars and the sheriff's cruiser, its lights flashing. The crowd milled as close as they could get to the car, and as they approached, Bobbi noticed with disgust that there were protestors clustered off to the side near the steps. They were holding signs, but she didn't care to read them. Instead, she turned her eyes back to the figure emerging from the sleek black car.

The man inside the fancy car had all the shining brightness of Apollo, with the humble, kind smile of a neighbor: Robert Francis Kennedy, in the flesh. Bobbi's breath caught in her throat as her hero stepped out of the car, full of quiet grace, his smile shy but purposeful. He was a short man, but stood tall, a shock of reddish-blond hair falling over one eye, which he pushed back absently as he touched the shoulder of a security member in thanks. Bobbi watched, riveted, as he adjusted his tapered, dark suit at the collar and glanced over to the crowd of people waiting to see him, gesturing to them with another small, humble wave of hello and a curt nod. He squared his shoulders and centered himself, moving toward the steps and into the law building, seeming to float with a quiet grace. His every movement seemed ornate, genteel, and deliberate; Bobbi now understood why people called the family American royalty. It seemed that sophistication was in his very blood; a second nature. How he managed to appear regal and humble at the same time was nothing short of a magic trick.

A hush came over the crowd as Mr. Kennedy turned one more time, just outside the door, and gave another little wave. "Good afternoon," he called, projecting his reedy, Boston-tinged voice out over the lawn. "Nice to see you all here." *Heah*, Bobbi repeated to herself inwardly, grinning ear to ear. Mr. Kennedy's light-colored eyes seemed to fall on each person clustered there, as though he were committing each face to memory, a ghost of a smile playing over his face, a beam of sunlight illuminating his hair into a golden-reddish hue—and then he disappeared inside the hall.

Bobbi grabbed Ed's arm, her heart fluttering with excitement. "Hurry, let's go. I don't want to miss a moment."

"Yeah, yeah. I'm waiting with bated breath." Ed chuckled, though his bright eyes betrayed his own excitement.

"Oh, hush. Let's *go!*" Bobbi turned to say goodbye to Landrum, but they'd gotten separated in the crowd. She'd find him after and say goodbye; right now, Bobby Kennedy was all she could think of.

She followed her brother breathlessly through the hall and up the stairs to their row of seats. She sat down, her heart beating heavily in her chest. She would never, ever forget the moment out on the lawn. How stately, how majestic he had looked!

Then Mr. Kennedy was on the stage, and Bobbi's breath caught again. As she watched him, his light eyes falling on each person clustered there, she couldn't help but marvel at the way he seemed to make a point to look and truly see each person. For the briefest moment, his eyes met hers, and time stood still. Bobbi struggled to catch a breath and hold it, her eyes memorizing every wrinkle, every strand of hair. Then Kennedy was nodding to the other side of the room and the moment was over.

But Bobbi would never forget any of it, not ever. The shy smile, the way his hair had glowed red in the sunshine outside, the sound of his lovely, unique voice. She knew she would coast on it all her days. She could hardly believe it—she'd stood only feet away from her hero, from American royalty. She, Bobbi Newton!

After a few moments, Mr. Kennedy stood up to the podium to speak, and Bobbi, overwhelmed with joy and pride, covertly wiped a tear from the corner of her eye, ignoring her older brother's snicker.

"For the first time since becoming Attorney General over three months ago, I am making something approaching a formal speech, and I am proud that it is in Georgia," Mr. Kennedy began. Bobbi sat on the edge of her seat, committing every word from her beloved Bobby to memory. There might never be another chance like this again.

⌇

After the speech, Bobbi was breathless and exhilarated as she followed her brother out of the hall. Mr. Kennedy's speech had been a marvel: he had touched on voting rights, the desegregation of UGA, how theirs was a time of change, of equality, with marginalized people all over the globe securing their rights. He had spoken of the future with a fervent hope that was contagious. The speech had invigorated her, and even her opinionated brother had nodded along in agreement several times. They—the young people of Georgia, of the country—had been given their marching orders. She intended to heed them.

When the Attorney General had finished speaking, she wasn't ready to let him go. The crowd had stood, giving him a rousing standing ovation, as Mr. Kennedy stood there, absorbing their energy, returning it to them. The sound of their applause had followed the Attorney General long after he'd exited the stage.

"I suppose we'd better get along home now, sugar pie," Ed said to her as they exited the law school building. "I'd take you to Allen's for a milkshake, but Daddy will be expecting us home for supper." Bobbi sighed in disappointment. Ever since Mama had passed, Daddy was a stickler for everyone attending family supper. You didn't miss the dinner table unless it was something very important. Since Bobbi hadn't been there to do the cooking tonight, they'd likely be having meatloaf that resembled hockey pucks and reheated beans from a tin. She should have accepted an ice cream earlier when Ed had offered. At the time she'd been too twitterpated with nerves to eat.

"But Allen's sounds so good. Couldn't we just phone Daddy and get hamburgers from Allen's to take home?"

"He'd only gripe at me about the money," Ed reminded her as they went down the steps. "He complains enough about my tuition. I don't need a lecture on the luxury that is fast food." He smiled down at her. "A burger does sound mighty good, though."

"Hey, Bobbi!" Her eyes fell on Landrum, standing beside his mother on the lawn. The woman was craning her neck toward the row of shiny black cars, likely hoping to get a glimpse of Mr. Kennedy as he exited the building. The protestors were still there, too, Bobbi noticed with a grimace. Oh, well, she wouldn't pay them any mind, and she hoped the Attorney General wouldn't, either.

Landrum held something out to her—a small banner on a stick, emblazoned with the words "RFK is A-OK."

"Where did you get this?" she asked, admiring it.

"They were selling them for fifty cents apiece in front of Farmer's Hardware," he said with a smile, gesturing to his mother, who was also holding one. "That one's yours. Glad I brought my allowance along so I could snag a couple."

"You shouldn't have," Bobbi said with a smile. "I don't have any money on me to repay you!"

"Don't worry about that," Landrum said good-naturedly, brushing his dirty-blond hair out of his eyes. "I know how much you like him. I don't know who loves him more, you or my mama."

Mrs. Walton had finally come out of her trance and smiled at Bobbi and Ed. "How y'all doin'?" she asked by way of greeting, her face pretty and flushed. Bobbi realized she was wearing one of her best dresses, usually reserved for Sundays, and had on rouge and carefully applied lipstick. Her hair, the same dishwater blonde as her son's, was in a lovely coiffed do. Why, she had done herself up even more than Bobbi had—she really was nuts for Mr. Kennedy! Bobbi wondered what Mr. Walton, who she'd never seen without his signature grimace, must think of all this.

It seemed Bobbi wasn't the only one who had noticed Landrum's mother's altered appearance. Ed leaned forward and pressed his hand into Mrs. Walton's. "Hello, ma'am," he said with his charming grin. "Nice to see you somewhere outside of church. And don't you look pretty as a picture."

Bobbi wanted to elbow him in the side. It wasn't proper to talk to someone's mother that way, and a married woman, to boot, even if they had been neighbors for years. But Mrs. Walton just laughed gaily. "What a good brother you are, to bring Bobbi to catch a glimpse of the fine Mr. Kennedy," she said happily. "Didn't he look so dashing, coming out of that car? The sun shining on all that lovely hair." Her voice had taken on the quality of a love-struck teenager.

"He did," Bobbi agreed excitedly. "I wish you could have heard his speech. It was just wonderful."

"You heard the speech?" Landrum looked at her in surprise.

"Why, yes," Bobbi said. "Ed was able to get me in . . ." Landrum's face fell and she felt guilty. Why had she gone and bragged about that? Of course, Ed wouldn't have been able to get Landrum and his mama in, but that wasn't the point. Both she and Ed had heard their father talk, from time to time, about how the Walton family hadn't had two cents to rub together since Mr. Walton had gotten injured at the sawmill and been forced to take a job as a fry cook at Allen's. Bobbi had never let on to Landrum that she knew about their money troubles. She felt bad about it, especially now, holding the little flag that Landrum had paid for with his meager allowance, knowing that she'd seen the speech and they hadn't. She felt her cheeks flush with shame.

"I didn't realize that's where you'd gone. I don't suppose that silly banner means much to you, then," Landrum said placidly, and her heart gave a little thump.

"Of course it does!" she said with a wide smile. "It's a memento of the best afternoon I've ever had!" Landrum brightened again, and so did his mother, though she did look a bit jealous. "And I'll pay you back first thing Monday at school. I've got a bit of allowance saved up."

"It was my treat, Bobbi," Landrum said. "I won't hear another word."

"They record the speeches, you know, for the students to access later. Transcribe them, too," Ed said to Mrs. Walton with a grin. "Perhaps I can lay my hands on a copy somehow. Bring it by one afternoon for you and Landrum to have a listen."

Bobbi had no idea how her brother would finagle that, but she could have kissed Ed for offering. "We'd love nothing better, would we, Lando?" Mrs. Walton said, her cheeks flushing a pretty pink. Her eyes sparkled as she looked at Ed. "You and Bobbi should stop by for cookies and sweet tea one afternoon and we'll make a party of it. Won't that be nice?"

Gosh, Bobbi thought. *She's coming off a bit desperate, isn't she?*

There was another jeer from the vicinity of Broad Street, and a smattering of applause. Bobbi turned away, hoping to catch another glimpse of Robert F. Kennedy in his resplendent, golden glory.

Landrum Walton, who was wearing his best church suit, took no notice of the flirtation happening between his mother and Bobbi's brother, who was at least fifteen years her junior. Nor did he notice when Robert F. Kennedy exited the building, flanked by his security detail, to cheers and screams from the crowd clustered on the lawn.

Mr. Robert Kennedy gave another wide, toothy smile and small wave before entering his sleek, expensive black motorcar. As the lights from the sheriff's cruiser lit up the afternoon in a cascade of blue and red, the shiny black vehicle carried the beloved politician away from UGA, followed by cheers and the trilling laughter of love-struck young ladies and hero-worshipping young men.

Landrum Walton noticed none of it. He was too busy looking at the pretty flush in Bobbi Newton's cheeks as she watched the motorcade containing her hero drive off down Broad Street, and thinking she was the loveliest girl he'd ever clapped eyes on, even if she *was* the girl next door.

EARLY FALL, 1967

The bell rang and class was dismissed. Bobbi grabbed her knapsack and books and slid out of her seat, waving at Mr. Clark, her history teacher. "Have a nice weekend," he called to her with a smile, wiping down the blackboard. "We'll see you at homecoming."

Bobbi gave him a bright smile in return and edged out into the hall, not bothering to tell Mr. Clark that she wouldn't be at the dance. There was no point in making the poor man feel bad; it certainly wasn't his fault that she and Todd Tatum had broken up a week ago and now she was without a date. Her girlfriends had suggested she go alone, or the four of them as a group. But, Bobbi thought as she walked the long stretch of hallway toward her locker, she couldn't bear the thought of showing up dressed to the nines only to see the boy that had been hers last week getting pawed by Debra Jenkins, head cheerleader and bane of her existence. It was bad enough that Todd was a no-good, filthy cheater, but with Debra? Debra, who had bullied her and made life at Cedar Shoals High School hell on earth for the past two years? What a cad Todd was to throw Bobbi over for her, of all people. The thought of going dateless to the dance and

15

watching them make out all night (and likely be voted in as Prom King and Queen to boot) was too much. So she was planning to stay home with popcorn and the latest Alfred Hitchcock movie with her hair in rollers. To hell with them all.

Bobbi stopped at her locker and turned the dial on the lock absently. It didn't open the first time, because she'd been distracted by thoughts of the dance to the doozy of a fight between Daddy and Ed the night before. It wasn't the first, but this time, it looked like Ed was finally going to move out. It was honestly about time, Bobbi reckoned; Ed was in his mid-twenties and had been a practicing lawyer for almost two years now. He was still the pride and joy of the family, but his popularity with the women of Athens was starting to get tongues wagging, and Ed showed no signs of slowing down. Daddy, who had held his tongue for the past several years, hoping his oldest boy would grow out of his tomcatting, had finally had enough.

"It's bad enough that the folks at church are whispering about what you get up to," he'd seethed to Ed at the dinner table as Bobbi passed the mashed potatoes to her brother Guy, the two of them cutting eyes at each other nervously. "But my boss called me into the office today. Can you guess at why?"

"Can't say I could, Daddy," Ed had said, his eyes respectfully lowered to his roast beef, but Bobbi could see the ghost of a smile at the corner of his lips.

"I think you know good and well what he had to say. And the least you can do is not smile like a tomcat about it," Daddy retorted, slamming his fork down on the table. "'Your son,' he says to me, 'your son is representing the wife of one of our clients. Only he reckons that your son is doing more than representing her, or intends to, anyhow.'" He glared at Ed. "What do you say to that, Edward Newton?"

"I don't say anything to it," Ed had said, stabbing at a carrot with his fork. "It's all idle gossip. And anyhow, you know I can't discuss my work. Client confidentiality. I could lose my job."

"I'd wager that bedding your client could also lose you your job," Daddy had barked, and Bobbi gasped.

"Goodness sakes," Ed had said smoothly, grabbing a roll from the basket in the center of the table. He gave Bobbi a wink. "What an accusation. I'm not stupid, for one, but also, the only female client I currently have is Edith Billings and she's got to be pushing fifty. I suppose she's a handsome woman but she's too old for me, and married, as you say."

"Older married women have been on the menu for you before," Daddy argued, his face like stone. "Haven't they?"

Bobbi stared down at her plate, feeling heat rising to her cheeks. It had been two years since Daddy had gone bowling with his old friend, Mr. Walton, for the last time. Whether that was his doing or Mr. Walton's, she didn't know and was afraid to ask. But her brother's *friendship* with Mrs. Walton was the worst kept secret in Athens. Her handsome, smooth brother was popular with women, to be sure. Too popular. But that Daddy was now saying all this out loud, right in front of her, was shocking. And Bobbi hadn't failed to notice how her brother had surpassed her father's question without really answering it.

"I'll have a word with Mrs. Billings, Dad," Ed replied smoothly. "I'll tell her that her husband is spreading malicious gossip and that if she can't put a stop to it, I'll have to cease being her lawyer. Conflict of interest and all. Satisfied?"

"Too little, too late, son," Daddy had replied, but he'd said no more about it at the dinner table. Bobbi had been wondering all night what would become of the drama. She found out the next morning when, over coffee, Ed announced that he'd be moving out. Dad had already left for work, so he told her and Guy at the kitchen table as he leaned down to tie the laces on his shiny black shoes.

"I've been meaning to go for a long spell," he explained to them, sitting up and tipping his coffee cup to his lips. "Only I get along with both y'all so well, and I wanted to help Daddy raise you. Since Mama's been gone, it's been hard on him." He smiled at them both, reaching out to cuff Guy's hair, getting a scowl in response. "But it'll be better for everybody if I shift on out. I've had my eye on an apartment downtown for a spell and I think I'll go put in the deposit today." He cuffed Guy's hair again. "With Bobbi heading off to UGA this summer and me moving out, you ought to consider making a move, too, little brother. You're not a youngin yourself anymore."

Guy glowered. He had been working as a mechanic on Oak Street ever since graduating, and had made no plans to go to college, which irritated Daddy and Ed to no end. He seemed content to drift through life, doing as little as possible. Bobbi saw no problem with his chosen profession, and sometimes envied him his simple, easy life. Guy did whatever he wanted, whenever he wanted, kept his

18

private life private, and didn't nose into anyone's business. He got along with everyone and kept his nose down—and for that reason, everyone loved him. "I've been working since before I graduated," Guy said, his voice giving no indication of offense. "Just because it's not your type of work doesn't mean it ain't honest work. I help out 'round here just as much as you do."

"If you'd just apply yourself and apply to college—"

"Not everybody cares about college. College don't teach you about the real world," Guy continued, stabbing into his eggs. He faced his brother with an easy smile. "All that fancy learnin' and you can't even change a tire. I'd love to see you out with one of your gals and get a flat—why, you'd have to call me to come rescue you. Then who'd look like the real man?"

"I can change a tire just fine, little brother," Ed grumbled, but his face had turned red. Guy had only grinned wider and continued eating.

For all his vices, Bobbi would miss Ed. He was her doting older brother, and he'd always stepped in to back her up when she needed it. He'd been mentoring her and guiding her all these years, knowing it was her dream to go to law school, giving her every opportunity possible to learn. He had all but raised her himself, given Daddy's long hours, and she would miss going into his bedroom after dinner to talk politics and theory. He was the ideal older brother in *almost* every way; if only he could keep his hands off pretty women.

Ed tousled her hair, reading her thoughts. "I'll still be here for you whenever you need me, little sister. I promise. I'll be just down the road."

"I know." She had a lump in her throat. Now that Ed had decided he was moving out, she suddenly realized she wasn't ready for him to go. Why couldn't he have waited until the summer? Why did he have to always be getting in trouble with this gal or the next?

"You'll do just fine on your own. So will Guy," Ed said reassuringly. "We've all done just fine all these years…since—"

Bobbi waved a hand at him, cutting him off. She didn't want to talk about Mama now, or ever, really. Their mother had died when Bobbi wasn't yet a teenager, and though six years had passed, it still felt fresh and painful. She didn't like to talk about it, preferring to lock the memories of Mama in a box in her mind, shut up tight and safe. When she thought about all the things Mama had missed, the pain in her chest was so great she couldn't breathe.

The doctors had told Mama that she couldn't have another child after Bobbi was born, and she hadn't fallen pregnant again for another ten years. It was only at Bobbi's eleventh birthday, after the guests had gone home and the mess from the piñata was cleaned up, that Alice Newton had sat down on the piano bench and told her children what she said was "happy" news—that she was expecting her fourth child. She and Daddy had always wanted an even four, she'd told them, her cheeks already beginning to flush with a happy, maternal glow. They were over the moon!

Only Ed, who was nineteen by then and full of confident self-possession, had spoken up. "Mama, the doctors told you you ought not to have another child," he'd protested. "And you're close to forty years old!"

Their father had interjected then. "That's enough, young man.

Forty isn't old. Besides, it ain't your place to question."

Ed, tight-lipped and white-faced, had left the room without so much as a congratulations, and Bobbi finally found her voice to speak up. "But Ed's right, isn't he? That it'll be a risk?"

"So they say, baby," Mama had answered, cupping her cheek. "But who are we to say what the Lord blesses us with? And that's what this is, Bobbi. A blessing. Now, how is that for a birthday present?" She'd given Bobbi and Guy one of her sweet smiles, then reached out to clasp her husband's hand. "I'm sure it will all turn out just fine."

Instead, Alice Newton had died and her premature baby—a little brother, James—was gone with her. None of them had ever talked about it. But from time-to-time Bobbi thought back to that fateful birthday party, the ashen look on Ed's face, and the way he'd tried to make Mama see sense. What if she had listened?

It wouldn't have mattered, Bobbi knew. She'd heard the hushed stories and knew places existed where a woman in trouble could go, but those places didn't seem to be anywhere she knew of. And what little she *did* know of such things, she knew Mama and Daddy would've *never* considered what was to them a mortal sin.

Daddy did alright for them. But the truth was, without Ed here to keep everyone together, Bobbi feared they might fall apart. She couldn't talk to Daddy or Guy the way she talked to Ed. He gave her rides to school when she needed them, pocket money when she'd exceeded her allowance, and was always there to chat after dinner about law matters, town gossip or any other old thing, even the boys she liked. He'd even taken Bobbi to buy supplies when she'd started her first period, telling her to "hush up; it's perfectly normal" when she'd blushed to the nines and tittered about a boy taking her to purchase sanitary napkins. He never made her feel small or unimportant, or like a nuisance.

Now, he looked at her with a gleam in his eye, and pulled her into a gruff hug. "It'll take me a few days to get all my stuff packed and to the apartment," he said into her hair. "So don't fret. I'll be here tomorrow night to drive you to the homecoming dance."

"No need," Bobbi said, pulling back from him and grabbing her satchel from the chair. "I'm not going."

"Not going?" Ed sniffed. "Homecoming is the biggest event of the school year, you've got to go. It's your senior year, Bobbi. You won't have another chance."

"Go without a date?" she asked incredulously. Ed had already been filled in on the saga that was Todd Tatum and Debra Hawkins, and she'd politely declined his likely fake but well-meaning offer to go rough him up. "I couldn't bear the embarrassment. Besides, I don't care about these things as much as you did."

"I'm sure there's some boy dying to take you, if only you'd put out a few feelers," Ed said charitably, grabbing his briefcase. "Pretty girl like you? They'd line up to escort you. I can't stand watching you just give up like that, staying home in rollers and watching *The Guiding Light*."

"I wasn't going to watch *The Guiding Light*," she said with a phony wink, wanting the conversation to be over. Feeling like a charity case was too humiliating. "I thought I might watch a Hitchcock film. *The Birds* is on tonight."

"That movie wasn't worth the hype, if you ask me," he said, cuffing her on the ear. "I'm late for work, Bobbi. But you *should* go. It's your homecoming. A memory that'll last a lifetime."

Dinner that night was just Bobbi and Daddy since Guy was putting in a shift at the shop and Ed was staying late at the office—so he said, anyway. Bobbi ate her roasted chicken and potatoes silently, staring at her plate, brooding—on Ed moving out, her lack of a homecoming date, and she was having awful cramps, to boot, which meant her period was coming soon—and she didn't feel much like talking. Daddy was staring at the newspaper; he didn't often get time in the mornings to read the headlines with his coffee, being a man who never stopped for breakfast, so he chose to catch up on the news with dinner, occasionally reading out headlines to his family. Bobbi watched as he scanned a page, then flipped it over with a little more force than was necessary. He was brooding, too, likely upset about Ed's leaving, though he'd never say it.

Bobbi took another bite of chicken and washed it down with sweet tea. The silence in the dining room was thick and she wondered how she and Daddy would endure it, with Ed gone and Guy never around. She worried for her old man, how he'd cope when they were all out of the house. She supposed it'd be easier for him to make ends meet without two grown men to feed, but she knew he'd be lonely, too. And who would cook for him, do the ironing, make his sweet tea? He was capable of all those things, but he wasn't *good* at them. He'd never had to be. And Bobbi would be damned if she stepped into that role for the foreseeable future, just because she was the girl. She had *dreams*.

Seeming to notice that her worrying had shifted to him, Daddy put his paper down and cleared his throat. "What are you getting up to this evening, dear?"

"Just some studying, I guess, Daddy," she replied, pushing her plate to the side. "Why?"

"Your boy is supposed to be on Merv Griffin's show tonight. Thought you might want to stay up and watch."

"My boy?"

"Oh yes, I suppose you have several of them. I didn't think." Daddy winked. "Your beloved Bobby Kennedy."

Bobbi smiled. Daddy hadn't invited her to stay up and watch Merv Griffin with him in a long time. She was surprised he'd asked her tonight with that particular guest—her father disliked Bobby Kennedy as much as always, if not more so. Ever since the Senator had begun protesting the Vietnam War in earnest, he'd been a bad word in the Newton household. Not to mention that heated debate with Ronald Reagan a few months back—it was one of the few times Bobbi had seen her father curse at a TV screen. Ed and Guy had bitten back laughter, Ed hiding his expression behind a cupped hand, but Bobbi had been horrified by the ever-widening political gulf between her father, who she still wanted to idolize, and herself.

She wasn't sure she wanted to watch Bobby Kennedy with Daddy. Discussing political matters with him was liable to start a disagreement, and there had been enough of those at home of late. She tried to avoid hot-button topics with him as much as possible to keep the peace. Still, it was Bobby Kennedy, and she didn't want to miss it; she probably would have snuck back down after bed to watch it anyhow. After all this time, the young, handsome senator was still her hero. And Daddy was clearly making an effort.

Bobbi smiled. "I'd like that a lot. I'll just run up and finish my homework now."

"Good girl. I'll make us a treat to enjoy while we watch if you'll take out the trash when you come back down. Popcorn or ginger snaps?"

"Popcorn," she said with a grin. Daddy's ginger snaps were awful.

Bobbi went upstairs and worked on her math and science assignments, her mind on everything but her work. There were too many thoughts doing battle for her attention, and she couldn't concentrate. Her older brother leaving, her first real relationship ending—how was she supposed to focus on math when her entire world seemed to be turning upside down? Bobbi felt totally lost. If only things would be calm for a time, if only...

After fifteen minutes, she slammed her math textbook shut in frustration, pulled on her jacket, and headed back downstairs and out the kitchen door to take out the trash. She threw the bag into the metal can, slamming the lid a little harder than she had to. She was angry—angry at Ed for not behaving better, for leaving their family in the lurch. Angry at him for not behaving as an upstanding man should, for not caring more about his family, for being irresponsible and unappreciative when he'd had so many opportunities and privileges. Most of all, she was angry at herself for continuing to make excuses for her older brother when she shouldn't. He'd always been good to her, but how much did that count for when he treated everyone else so carelessly? He was no better than Todd Tatum, a thoughtless, sexist cad who didn't care how many hearts he broke.

Sighing, Bobbi started back toward the house, going the long way to the front door, taking a moment to stop at the mailbox and look up at the stars, a habit she'd had since she was a little girl. When she was small, she'd go out every night after dark to say goodnight to the sky, counting as many stars as she could before tiring and going back in the house. Sometimes, she would lie right down in the grass, looking up into the vast blackness. "You'll catch your death out there," Mama had often called to her from the stoop in winters past, and she'd eventually brush the grass off her pajamas and come inside, feeling weightless and renewed. Bobbi hadn't done that in a long time, but she still loved the stars. They were hidden tonight by a pale wisp of fog that seemed to cover the whole sky, as if cloaked in pale white cotton candy. It was early October, but the seasons hadn't fully clicked over yet; this time of year in Georgia, one never knew if they should take a light jacket or wear short pants. Bobbi wrapped her arms around herself, watching her small puff of breath release into the night air, remembering her childhood, when they had all been happy.

A door slammed across the street, breaking her reverie. Bobbi glanced over to see Landrum Walton emerging from his own house, stomping down the front steps, the glowering expression on his face visible even from a distance. He grabbed a lawn chair from the yard and pulled it over to the side of the house, just out of view of the porch light, his sharp features full of anger. Bobbi watched as he sat down roughly in the chair, pulling something small from his pocket. He pushed a cigarette into his mouth, cupping his hands around it, the blue flame shining brightly in the darkness as he lit it and took a long, slow drag. As he blew the smoke out in a perfect ring, Bobbi made her way down the street.

"Landrum!" she called as she got to his yard, and he looked up in surprise.

"Bobbi," he said, his glowering expression turning to a smile. "Evenin'."

"I didn't know you *smoked*," she said, looking pointedly at his cigarette. "Or is that reefer you've got there?"

"Keep your voice down, Bobbi," he said in a hot whisper, though he didn't look angry. She realized he was laughing. "No, it ain't weed. Wish it was, though."

"You do not," she said, cuffing him on the arm. "Do you?"

He made no reply to this, but his face held the hint of a smirk. "What you all up to tonight?" he asked, gesturing toward her house. "Everybody doin' good?"

"I guess," she answered. "Ed and Guy aren't home. Daddy and I are getting ready to watch Bobby on Merv Griffin."

"Oh, yeah," he said. "Ma told me about that. I reckon she'll make me watch it with her. The old man's already in bed, thank the Lord." A shadow passed over his face, then was gone in a flash. "I suppose you're excited for homecoming tomorrow night."

"Not really."

He looked at her in surprise. "Why not? I thought all you girls couldn't wait. Every afternoon at basketball practice, all I hear you cheerleaders yammering on about is homecoming. What dress, what shoes, what corsage—"

"Todd and I broke up." She blinked, not wanting to cry in front of Landrum. "He cheated on me."

"Damn, Bobbi." Landrum's face filled with genuine sympathy. "That stinks. Who with?"

"Debra Hawkins."

Landrum snorted. "Deb Hawkins has dated just about every guy on the football team and half the guys on the basketball team. I bet she won't be with him for more than a few days." He looked at her, his gaze softening. "Don't sweat it, Bobbi. It's his loss. He'll realize that in short order."

Bobbi smiled at his effort to make her feel better, even though she knew Landrum had been out on a few dates with Debra himself last year. "Even so, I'm not taking him back."

"Good for you," he said, standing up and stubbing out his cigarette with his foot. "You can do a lot better than that joker. Trust me."

"It's just... I can't see going without a date, it's too pathetic for words. But you're right—I was looking forward to it. I just feel so stupid. I used some of my college savings to buy my dress," Bobbi said, embarrassed, not sure why she was telling him. "And now I don't dare go and show my face, and I'm not sure the store will take it back. I already took the tag off."

"Don't take it back," Landrum said. "It's your homecoming, like you said. Why should you miss out because of some jerk? In twenty years, you'll look back and remember a fun time, not that stupid yahoo."

"People keep saying that, but going alone is humiliating. If I see the two of them together, I'm likely to scratch their eyes out." Bobbi shook her head furiously.

"Well, I wouldn't blame you one bit if you did," Landrum said, putting a hand on her shoulder and giving it a squeeze. "But you should go, Bobbi. And you don't have to go alone."

"What, are you offering to be my date?" she asked with a laugh.

"Don't see what's so funny about it," Landrum said in a low voice, playing absently with his Zippo lighter with his other hand. Bobbi watched, surprised, as he flicked the lid up and down, up and down with his thumb. His face was cast in shadow, but she could see a hint of a smile. "I'll take you, if you want."

"I thought you had a date," Bobbi said, puzzled. "Aren't you taking Millie?" Millicent Brown was a cheerleader at their rival high school, Clarke Central, and her cousin Thomas was one of Landrum's friends. Landrum had been going with her for the past several months; Bobbi'd often seen them out on double dates with Thomas and his girlfriend, Liz. Millie was tall and glamorous, with long, dark, flowing hair, and a curvaceous figure that Bobbi secretly envied.

"She's going to her own homecoming," Landrum said by way of reply. It wasn't really an answer, but Bobbi decided not to pry further. He was offering her a chance to go to homecoming, and not alone! Todd could eat his heart out. She gave Landrum a bright smile.

"Well, I'd really like that, Landrum…if you're sure you don't mind."

"Mind?" He grinned, his face lighting up. "The lady asks if I mind taking one of the prettiest girls in my class to a dance."

"Oh, you." She cuffed him on the arm again. "Liar." But her mind was already on everything she had to do. She'd need to put her hair in rollers, iron her dress, go to the store for fresh nylons… She bit her lip excitedly, formulating a plan. "Will you come by the house tomorrow night to pick me up? Do you want to come a little early, so we can take photos? I can ask my brother to use his good camera." Excitement fluttered in her belly, all the forlorn feelings from minutes before now gone.

"I sure will. Let's say 6:30?" He smiled down at her, his gray eyes flashing. "I can't wait to see your dress. You always have something nice on."

"Oh, stop it, Landrum," she admonished him, but she couldn't help the grin on her face. "You've cheered me right up. Thank you so much." She rushed forward and gave him a clumsy hug. He smelled like cigarette smoke and freshly baked bread; his mother must have been baking that afternoon. He bent down to return the hug—he had to, because he was so tall. His cheek was rough with stubble, his hair smelling clean and fresh, and Bobbi felt an odd sensation go through her. It seemed like just yesterday that Landrum was a nine-year-old boy, teaching her to skip rocks. Now he was almost a grown man, his arms around her waist, holding her loosely but somehow tightly at the same time, giving her the strangest feelings. A low hum began in her belly, rushing to her extremities and giving her goosebumps. She pulled away, fixing him with her brightest smile.

"Thank you so much, Landrum. I can't wait till tomorrow."

"Me either, Bobbi," he said, his lips curving upwards. "We'll have a groovy time."

They stared at each other for a few moments under the glow of the streetlamp, and Bobbi felt her cheeks grow hot. "Well. I'd better get back to Daddy. Merv Griffin will be coming on."

"Can't miss that RFK," he said with another grin. "He's A-OK."

She turned and headed back to the house, knowing without having to turn around that Landrum would watch until she got up her porch and safely back inside. Just as she reached the door, he called out.

"Hey, Bobbi? Don't tell my Ma you saw me smoking, okay? Daddy knows, but she don't. It would only upset her."

"Don't blame her," she called back. "It's an awful, nasty habit and I hope you quit." But as she ventured inside and shut the door, hearing him laugh behind her, she thought of how cool, how *dangerous* he had looked putting that cigarette to his mouth, the perfectly formed 'o' as he'd blown the smoke from his lips into the night air. It was as if, in the span of a moment, he'd become a different person from the blond-haired, good-natured boy next door she'd known all her life. Something mysterious, possibly dangerous; something *risky*. All it had taken was one invitation and a cigarette in the moonlight. Bobbi smiled to herself, locking the door behind her. Yes, Landrum Walton would make a mighty fine date to homecoming.

"Our next guest…" Merv Griffin began.

Bobbi sat with her father in the quiet living room in her

nightgown, her hair hastily fixed in rollers, her feet tucked under her on the scratchy brown couch. Normally she'd already be in bed, but she intended to listen to every word the senator had to say tonight. She clutched a throw pillow to her chest and sighed; Bobby Kennedy looked polished and handsome as ever this evening, resplendent in a fitted gray suit and dark tie, his plentiful golden hair slicked to one side. His eyes were calm as he thought for a moment, then responded, his voice thoughtful and measured as he talked about how the war, combined with increasing violence in various parts of the world, and the divide between teens and their parents with their very different worldviews, all combined to make for an apathetic group of young people with no real hope for the future. Robert Kennedy's voice was cool and gentle, like a lapping stream.

"Bah," said Daddy from his easy chair, holding a fistful of popcorn. "There's always been wars. I fought in World War II, and I sure didn't—"

"Daddy. Shhh! I want to hear!" Bobbi whispered hotly.

Kennedy went on to explain that for young people, everything had become impersonal, with youth all over the country, and even the world, feeling powerless to invoke real change without drastic measures; how that feeling of being a small cog in a big, ugly machine, could lead to all sorts of prejudice, violence, and suffering. He explained to Merv Griffin that adults, especially those in positions of power, had a responsibility to make young people feel better about the state of the world. That only then might young people feel some sense of self, which would then lead to positive changes. Bobby listened in rapt attention.

SO LONG, BOBBY

"This joker," Daddy said through another mouthful of popcorn. "Talking and talking and saying nothing. Justifying the dang hippies. Listen to him!"

Bobbi jumped up and turned the TV's volume knob, fixing her father with a "shush." She smiled as she settled back on the couch, watching Mr. Kennedy, who seemed to glow as he sat behind the small, dark desk, looking fresh and fine as always, if a bit tired. She marveled at how soft and calm his voice was, how carefully he chose his words, even when he was chewing over an idea. He was practiced at this, and very, very good. She couldn't help but wonder if even his clumsiness, his boyishness, were part of the effort he made to be likeable, agreeable. She hoped it was genuine.

Merv Griffin tried to interrupt Bobby Kennedy, bringing up booming populations as a counterargument that individualism couldn't possibly be to blame. Bobby, unruffled, continued his thought unabated, not allowing himself to be interrupted so rudely.

"Not this again," her father said with a snort as Kennedy brought up the Civil Rights Movement. "He's already mentioned Black folks twice. I suppose he means to make them his target demographic when he finally admits he's running for president. How fast RFK forgets that he was against our boy Martin less than a decade ago."

"He wasn't *against* him," Bobbi said, knowing she shouldn't rise to the argument, but unable to help herself—and where did Daddy get off calling Martin Luther King, Jr. "our boy," when he'd never supported the man in his life? And besides, it had been years since the Kennedy administration had been outed for wiretapping Dr. Martin Luther King, Jr. "Kennedy was Attorney General at the time; that was his *job*. He's gone on record since then, saying he regrets the wiretapping of Dr. King. And he and Martin have become friends."

"Ain't no politician friends with no other politician," Daddy said, turning in his chair to crane at her. He offered her the popcorn bowl, and she shook her head no.

"Daddy, Martin Luther King, Jr. is not a politician," Bobbi scolded. "He's a man of the Lord. I suppose you could call him an activist, but I think he'd take high offense at someone suggesting he's only—"

"You're a smart gal, you ought to know how all this works by now," Daddy interrupted her, wagging a finger. "It's just business, dear. You'll see when you're older. MLK is as political as the rest of them; more so probably. Why, the man has published entire books. And as for 'Bobby' Kennedy, he's realized the hard-lined, mobster persona isn't serving him anymore. He's shrewd—he knows if he comes across as loveable and naïve, working for the underdog, smelling of roses, that it'll appeal to the young folk. He knows folks like me ain't buying what he's selling. We ain't falling for the liberal nonsense. No more than we fell for his brother."

"I believe he really did have a change of heart, Daddy," Bobbi said, knowing it would do no good. She wanted to retort that she knew Mama had voted for John Kennedy—she'd told her so when Bobbi had asked. Daddy surely knew this, though she'd never heard them discuss politics when Mama had been alive. "After his brother was murdered, it changed him. And then when he went down to Mississippi last year and saw the squalor and hunger"—she ignored

34

Daddy's snort, feeling color rushing to her face—"he began to see injustice for what it was. I think that's when it became about really helping people and not just doing a job. I believe that's when he learned the difference between being a moral person and being truly 'good.' I think he wanted his brother's legacy and death to mean something, for his own life to—to *really* mean something." She felt tears well in her eyes and blinked them back, embarrassed. "I believe that's what he's trying to do."

"You go on believing it then, honey," Daddy replied, grabbing another fistful of popcorn, his voice softer now. "It's admirable to see the best in folks. But when you get older, you'll see, darlin'. Nobody does anything selflessly. Least of all some rich Catholic boy born with a silver spoon on his tongue."

"Privileged or not, you don't believe losing his brother changed him?" Bobbi challenged. "You don't believe grief can touch anyone, regardless of their station?"

Daddy shrugged.

Bobbi's cheeks burned. "I can't believe you'd be so heartless, considering how you lost Mama." Mama and Daddy had made their choice to go through with the pregnancy, and Mama had died for it. Even though she'd known the risks, it hadn't made her death any less heartbreaking.

Still, Bobbi regretted the words as soon as they came out of her mouth. Now she was in for it.

"What's that got to do with a damn thing?" Daddy retorted, his own face a little red. "You can't tell me that I have a thing in common with that…that…rich boy politician, just because—hell,

Bobbi, everybody dies. We ain't all gonna be best buddies just because we lost someone."

Bobbi looked down at the floor, feeling the blood rush to her ears. She was so angry at Daddy, but she felt sorry for him, too.

"I reckon losing her changed all of us," Daddy said, sitting the bowl of popcorn down on the side table. He leveled his gaze at her, his face serious. "I do feel sympathy for Mr. Kennedy. Losing two brothers the way he has. Maybe he's even a nice fella in person. But it doesn't mean I agree with his politics. And it sure don't mean I think he's qualified to lead the country. If anything, the opposite. Grief distracts a person, gets their motives all muddled up. Country needs a man who can lead from a place of rational thinkin', somebody who doesn't blow back and forth with the wind. And I'm not sure I agree with your theory, anyhow. Grief doesn't soften…it hardens. Makes a person double down, become blind."

"Is that what happened to you?" Bobbi pushed, and this time Daddy did get mad.

"You just watch your mouth, young miss," he said, his face going redder. "I'm not going to stand for you sassing me like that in my own house. You'll talk to me with respect. You understand?"

"I'm sorry, Daddy." Her face burned, and she looked down at her lap.

After a few moments of uncomfortable silence, Daddy said, "Show me a politician and I'll show you a crook," wiggling his eyebrows at her the way he had when she was a small child. It used to charm Bobbi, make her giggle. She supposed he felt bad for admonishing her so harshly. She tried to smile, but she'd gone and gotten all upset.

"We're all in for a world of hurt if politics get you this riled up," Daddy said with a chuckle, throwing a piece of popcorn at her. "Next thing you'll be out marching with the women's libbers, burning all those expensive brassieres I shell out for."

"Stop patronizing me," Bobbi said hotly, rising from the couch. Bobby Kennedy was still talking to Merv Griffin, his soft Boston-tinged voice almost too quiet to hear. "Why won't you ever take me serious? Bobby Kennedy's been my hero for years, and—"

"—your hero." Daddy laughed, not unkindly, but it stung all the same. "When you get—"

"Yes, yes, when I get older. That's what you always say. In case you hadn't noticed, I *am* older," she said angrily. "I'm almost eighteen. I'm leaving in the fall to go to college. To become a lawyer, just like Ed. You trust me enough to let me do the washing and the cooking and tend your house when you need help, but then you treat me like a child when it comes to the things I care about. You talk about respect, but shouldn't it go both ways? As if it isn't bad enough that you've run Ed out of here, now you're sporting with me, too. Why did you even want to watch this with me, Daddy? Just so you could poke fun? Make a mockery of my dreams?" Hot tears pricked at her eyelids. She knew she was going too far, was getting bent out of shape for nothing, but she couldn't stop herself.

"Bobbi." Daddy looked down at his lap, his voice pained, rubbing his hands absently on his lounge pants, the popcorn long forgotten. "I invited you to watch the show because I wanted to spend time with you. That's all."

"But all you do is criticize and make a joke of me," she said in a small, angry voice.

"That's just what we do, isn't it? What we've always done." He was right. He had always teased her. They'd always debated and argued good-naturedly about things; it was just their dynamic. Bobbi wasn't sure when that had changed, when she'd stopped finding Daddy charming and started resenting his open, unapologetic airing of his views. When it had stopped being a joke to her: politics, current events, and hell, life in general—and started being a serious matter. Was it because she was a girl, or because she was no longer a child? Was it both? She wiped at her cheeks, shamed but still angry. There was nothing to be done for it—it was different now.

She stood there for a moment, unsure of what to do. Her anger was abating, and she was standing in front of the couch, trying not to look at the father she'd just given a dressing down to, who suddenly looked very thin and sad in his worn lounge pants, the half-eaten bowl of popcorn sitting pitifully beside him. He had stayed up late to watch a politician he disagreed with for her. Even if she disagreed with him a million times over, she could not be mad at Daddy. He was lonely, edging ever closer to alone, and Bobbi was almost all he had left. Yes, she was older now, and that meant being the bigger person. *So this is growing up.*

She cleared her throat, then said, "They've gone to commercial. Bobby's part is probably over. She looked at her father. "I think *Bewitched* is on. Want to watch that?"

"You don't have to, Bobbi," Daddy said, still staring at his lap. "I know you don't care for that show."

"But you do. Come on, don't you want to make eyes at Elizabeth Montgomery?" she said. "Anyway, I wouldn't mind some of that popcorn now."

Daddy passed her the bowl and managed a smile, though he still looked stung. "Sit down, then," he said. "I'll be on my best behavior. Not one comment about hippies, hand to God." She sat back down on the couch, taking the bowl, and tried for a laugh, ashamed of the tears drying in her eyes.

Bobbi heard the knock on the front door from upstairs in her room where she was carefully applying blush to her cheeks. She hoped her side-swept updo would stay in place; she'd used three-fourths of a can of Aquanet and still one tendril kept falling down onto her forehead. Bobbi's hair was fine, always slipping out of barrettes and never holding a curl, much to her chagrin. She remembered, with a pang of sadness, how her mother had always joked about it. "To think, bobby pins are named after you and they don't do a lick of good with this cornsilk you call hair."

"Bobbi. Sounds like your date's here," Guy called from his room.

"Can someone get the door?" she called back, but received no answer. Groaning, she dabbed a bit of opaque pearl-colored gloss on her lips and left the room, grabbing a light shawl to go with her dress. It was pale pink and off the shoulder, a very modest dress by modern standards, but the fabric—a crisp, shiny taffeta—caught the light in a way she loved. The neckline was set with tiny teardrop pearls that matched the barrettes in her hair and the gloss on her lips, and she'd set the knee-length dress off with opaque white tights and white boots. She hoped Daddy wouldn't gripe that it was too short, since she'd foregone the lower necklines that girls were wearing these days. Most of them wore long dresses to homecoming and prom, but Bobbi didn't give a fig what the other girls were doing.

Her heart gave a little thump of anticipation as she made her way downstairs, the excitement giving way to nerves. Ed had answered the door and was now standing awkwardly in the foyer, talking with Landrum, who was with his mother. *Cripes*, Bobbi thought, *why is she here?* Mrs. Walton held onto her son's arm as though he was her escort, and she was smiling through tightly pursed, lipsticked lips, her eyes unnaturally bright. All three of them turned to look at Bobbi as she came down the stairs.

"Bobbi, you look beautiful," Landrum breathed, rushing forward and taking her arm. "That dress is breathtaking on you. Look how it lights up your hair."

Bobbi smiled. She had to give it to the boy next door, he knew how to give a compliment. "Why, thank you, Landrum. You look awfully nice yourself." She looked appreciatively at her date. He was in a nicely fitted black suit with a shiny black tie, and his shoes had been polished to a gleam. His hat, which she thought she'd seen on his father from time to time, was bedecked with a single white rose, matching the one on the corsage that he held out to her.

"I hope this is alright. I went with white because I didn't know what color your dress was."

"It's perfect."

Landrum moved to put the corsage on her dress, frowning with concentration as he tried to avoid pinning her in the chest. Bobbi watched his face as he did so, delighting at the way he bit his lip, taking in his smooth cheeks. He had shaved for her; she remembered how his cheeks had been stubbly the night before when she'd hugged him. His eyes met hers as he stepped back, and she marveled at how beautiful and steely gray they were, and with such long lashes. How had she never noticed how pretty his eyes were?

The moment was broken by the sound of tittering. Bobbi looked up. Mrs. Walton appeared to be on the verge of crying, pretending to laugh at some stupid joke Ed was telling her in hushed tones, though he looked like he'd rather be swallowed into the earth and taken into the bowels of Hell than be standing there. Landrum's eyes met Bobbi's again, and his mouth was set in a hard line. He was protective of his mother, she knew, and he had every right to be angry, though of course he'd try not to show it in their home. The business between her brother and Mrs. Walton had barely missed becoming a scandal, and Bobbi knew her family had gotten off light; her father had lost a bowling partner and friend, but much more had been lost than that. The fact that Mrs. Walton had ventured over— and that her brother had dared to come out and speak to her— was a disrespect on both their parts to the shaky foundation of forgiveness that had been forged between the families.

Bobbi stepped forward, not wanting Landrum to feel another moment of discomfort, and said brightly, "Mrs. Walton, it was so lovely of you to escort Landrum over. I'm afraid my father isn't here to greet you; he's working late tonight." Ed's eyes widened in alarm. Bobbi glanced at him and went on. "My brother Guy's upstairs though if you'd like to say hello. I suppose Landrum and I ought to be getting along."

"Oh, that's alright, dear, no need to fetch your brother." Mrs. Walton dabbed at an eye, managing another merry little laugh. "Goodness, my fall allergies are acting up quite badly. No, darling, I just wanted to see my boy off to his homecoming dance. And if I'm being perfectly honest, I was itching to catch a glimpse of your dress. It's been so long since my own homecoming dance, and you always choose such lovely things to wear." Her eyes were unnaturally bright.

"That's very sweet of you to say, ma'am," Bobbi said. Ed was inching closer and closer to the staircase. She'd never wanted to slap him so badly in her life. Couldn't just one moment of joy be had without his constant philandering spoiling things?

"I suppose you ought to be on home then, Mama, now you've seen her," Landrum said, and Bobbi became aware that he was clutching her arm in his own. "Bobbi and I don't want to be late."

"Of course, of course." Mrs. Walton stepped toward the door, Bobbi and Landrum flanking her. "Your father will be wanting his dessert anyhow." She turned with a wistful, desperate look. "Goodbye, Ed. Always lovely to see you. Regards to your brother and father."

"Of course, Mrs. Walton. Nice to have seen you again." Ed was bounding up the stairs before the three of them could get out the front door. Bobbi never even had the chance to ask him to take their picture. Her face burned with embarrassment and shame. Landrum would probably rather eat glass than attend the dance with her now, seeing his own mother's desperation and how badly Ed had wanted shut of her.

As Landrum escorted her to the family car, she looked over and saw Mrs. Walton walking along their footpath back to her house, hands clasped in front of her. She stumbled over a patch of monkey grass and Bobbi winced. "Is she going to be okay?" she asked in a whisper as Landrum held the car door open for her.

"She's fine," he said, a hint of irritation in his voice. He walked over to the driver's side and got in the car. His hands clutched the steering wheel. "Sorry. I just hate seeing her like that. I wish she'd never come over. She insisted on escorting me. She claimed she just had to see your dress, but I knew she was trying to clap eyes on your brother. She's still mad for him, even now." He bit his lip, his cheeks reddening. "I'm sorry, Bobbi."

"What are you sorry for?"

"For my mother making a spectacle of herself over some guy fifteen years younger than her." He swallowed. "For the way she's... carried on... with him."

It was the first time the affair had been mentioned out loud. "It takes two to tango," Bobbi said after an awkward pause. "I love my brother, but he's no saint. You've got nothing to be sorry for. If anything, *I'm* sorry." She swallowed, then asked, "Does your dad know? About...everything that happened?"

Landrum chuckled joylessly. "He knows. Everyone on our street knows." He looked at her from the corner of his eye, his cheeks growing redder. "Don't they?"

Bobbi didn't know how to answer. He was right, of course. After all, it was one of the reasons her brother was moving out, wasn't it? She watched Landrum's face in the glow of the streetlamp, looking somehow boyish and manly at the same time, his eyes gleaming, cheeks red with embarrassment, and her heart went out to him. She put a hand on his arm. The two of them weren't so different, really. Both idolized a family member who was less than perfect, who was good and kind and wonderful, except for one small flaw. "If anyone's to blame, it's Ed. Please, Landrum, don't think about it another second. Please."

"Alright," he said, but he was still staring out the window, his face gloomy.

"Come on, let's go to the dance," Bobbi pleaded, her hand still on his arm, enjoying his warmth. "Forget the two of them. Plenty of time to worry about it later. As for right now, I'm just dying to get you on the dance floor to see if you've got two left feet or if you're the next Gene Kelly."

He turned to her with a grateful smile and started the car.

Bobbi and Landrum hadn't been at the dance for five minutes before Todd had approached her. "You came," he'd said by way of greeting, holding out a cup of punch to her, as she gritted her teeth, trying, and failing, for a smile. "When we broke up, you said you weren't." His wide grin, which she'd always found endearing, had looked like a leer to her.

"If I want punch, I'll get it myself, or my date will." Bobbi retorted, grateful for Landrum by her side. "Why don't you go find Debra and leave us alone?"

"Yeah, where is Debra, anyway?" Landrum asked. He and Todd were both on the basketball team, and while they weren't close friends, Bobbi wasn't surprised that he was being cordial. After all, it wasn't his battle to fight.

"Didn't you guys already go out?" Todd smirked. "Last year, right? She dumped you, didn't she?" He laughed and took a sip of punch. "Stick with Bobbi, man, Deb's not interested."

"C'mon man, don't be a jerk," Landrum said easily, putting an arm around Bobbi's shoulders. "I'm not the least bit interested in your date. Hope you have a swell time. We're going to go dance."

He led Bobbi away before a retort could be made. Bobbi seethed. "I can't believe he had the *nerve*—"

"Don't let it get to you, Bobbi. He only came over because he's jealous. He saw you with a date and it was galling him so he wanted to rile you up. Don't let him."

"But—"

"Don't let him ruin your dance. *Our* dance." He smiled at her, his gray eyes on hers, and she felt her stomach give a little flip. With a shrug of her shoulders, she acquiesced and stepped into his arms. Landrum was a surprisingly good dancer; there was no woodenness to his steps and his arms around her waist felt natural and easy. He gave her a little twirl, and she laughed, surprised at how effortlessly he moved.

"Who taught you to dance?"

"My ma," he said with a smile, and Bobbi banished sudden unwelcome thoughts of Mrs. Walton twirling around a dance floor with her brother Ed. "She used to make me watch Lawrence Welk when I was a kid and we'd dance around the living room."

"Well, that's adorable."

"It is not," he said, flushing. "It's humiliating."

"No, it's wonderful. She did a good job. You're amazing!" She grinned up at him, enjoying the feel of his arms around her. "When I said that about Gene Kelly in the car, I was just teasing, but gosh, you're good!"

He laughed. "I don't know about that. I may've practiced a little last night to make sure I could give you a proper turn around the gym."

"That's so sweet. Thank you for bringing me," Bobbi gushed. "I heard your mother say that you didn't want to come. I never would have guessed. I'm flattered that you ventured out just so I would have a date."

"It wasn't that I didn't want to come," Landrum said with a sly smile. "It's just that you were the only girl I wanted to go with, and up until two days ago you had a boyfriend."

"That can't be true, Landrum."

"Why can't it?" he asked, pulling her closer to him. His eyes bore down on hers. "Why would I lie about it?"

Bobbi felt heat rise in her cheeks. "But I thought you were dating Millie."

"I did for a while," he said easily. "But that's been over for weeks."

"Oh," she said again, feeling dumb. She was very aware of how his hands felt on the small of her back, warm and delicious. "I didn't know."

"Come on, Bobbi," Landrum said, twirling her again, then pulling her close, his face inches from hers. "You had to have realized that I'm crazy about you. I have been for years."

"I didn't—"

"You knew," he pressed, his eyes imploring hers. "You had to've."

"I thought maybe you—you had a little crush, back when we were younger...but I didn't assume that I was the only girl you were interested in," Bobbi said, aware of how fast her heart was beating. "We haven't hung out as much, and you've dated a lot of girls, so I..." She was rambling. Landrum's bemused smile was making her nervous. "I mean, you could have any girl you want."

It was true, though she herself hadn't ever considered Landrum that way. Oh, of course she'd known that he liked her a little, that had been obvious. He'd always been so kind to her. As kids, they'd played together on the street, rode bicycles, hung out after school. Later, as they got older, he would occasionally bring her gifts like cookies from his mom or the RFK banner he'd given her the day of the UGA lecture, the day that had begun the affair between his mother and her brother. That whole thing had been so embarrassing that she'd avoided Landrum, mainly out of shame. Since then, she'd seen a number of girls drift in and out of Landrum's circle. She had never begrudged him that popularity—he was the sweetest guy in the world, and handsome to boot, and he deserved it. He'd always been nice to her, but she'd wondered how much of it was actual interest and how much was him just being nice because he wanted to avoid causing a scene or unnecessary awkwardness. She didn't really know why; all Bobbi knew was that she'd never really considered him like that. As someone for *her*.

Until now. Landrum dipped her, and she became aware of just how tall he was, how strong, and her heart began to beat even faster. Suddenly Todd seemed like the last guy on earth, and nothing existed for her but Landrum. He pulled her close, the two of them still dancing but slowly, as though they were the only people in the room. His breath fluttered her hair, and his lips brushed up against her ear as he spoke. "You're the one I've always wanted, Bobbi."

She felt her knees go weak. So this was what the romance novelists wrote about. She wrapped her arms around Landrum's neck and pulled him closer, smiling as he nestled his head into her hair. She knew it'd be a matter of seconds before one of the buttoned-up teachers came and told them to break it up—to them, even holding hands was as good as necking—but for now she didn't care. She'd sway in Landrum's arms as long as she could. Whatever cologne he was wearing smelled heavenly—musky and sweet—and there was a hint of cigarette smoke wafting from his hair, wild and dangerous. She rested her head on his shoulder and breathed it in, the familiar repeating lines of "Happy Together" by the Turtles resounding in her ears.

"Well, hello, y'all." A girl's voice cut through her bliss, and she and Landrum both turned.

Debra Hawkins stood there, holding a cup of punch out in front of her. She was wearing a bright red, lacy dress that clung to her curvy frame, like something straight from Sofia Loren's closet, and her auburn hair was in an updo that made her blue eyes appear as wide as saucers. She looked like a glamorous fashion model. Next to her, Bobbi felt like a little girl playing dress-up.

"You look very cute, Bobbi," Debra said with a smile. "You too, Lando."

Bobbi wanted to scratch her fellow cheerleader's eyes out for using the nickname that she'd only ever heard his mother use. But she pasted on a smile and rested a hand on Landrum's arm. "Hey, Debra," she said with saccharine sweetness. "Don't you look beautiful tonight."

Debra shrugged. "This dance is dull as dishwater." She gave a pointed gaze to Bobbi's hairstyle, as though to say and so is your hair. Bobbi bristled. "I can't find my date. Have you seen him?"

"No," Bobbi said, her voice giving away her anger. Landrum put a calming hand on her lower back, and Debra smiled.

"I'm sure he's around someplace." Debra smiled sweetly. "Anyway, I hope all this won't affect our relationship on the cheer squad. Let's not let some stupid guy get between us, okay?" She gave a little wink, and Bobbi's hands curled into a fist.

"You backstabbing little—"

Landrum cut her off. "Come on, Bobbi, let's go get some punch. It's so hot in here." He pulled her toward the refreshment table without a goodbye to Debra.

Bobbi was desperately trying to blink back hot tears as Landrum handed her a drink. "She's just trying to get a rise out of you, Bobbi."

"I just wanted to come to the dance. Not play dodge-the-jerk all night."

"Don't sweat it, Bobbi," Landrum said, reaching up to brush the wayward tendril of hair from her face. "Debra's always been nasty, and Todd is an idiot. The only thing they have in common is they're both jerks. Which is why they're a match made in Hell." He grinned, and his eyes shone with mischievousness. "We could always bail. Debra was right—this dance is dull as dishwater. I know somewhere cool where we could go and talk."

"Is that a euphemism for necking?" Bobbi asked, wiping at her eyes, Todd and Debra suddenly the farthest thing from her mind. She was surprised at the coyness in her own voice.

"And risk the wrath of your older brother, Ed? Not on your life. You might look like Twiggy, but I don't feel like having my nose broken." He laughed.

He thinks I look like Twiggy? Bobbi couldn't stop the grin that broke out on her face. And anyhow, Landrum was right. The dance was turning out to be a big nothing. The punch was watery, the music wasn't that great, and none of her friends had shown up yet. Not to mention the couple of jerks she'd had to deal with. "Okay, I'm game," she said with a smile. "Anyplace has to be cooler than here. Besides—Ed owes you one, wouldn't you say?"

She regretted it the moment she said it, but to her relief, Landrum grinned back at her. "I suppose he does, now that you mention it." He wrapped an arm around her waist and led her off the dance floor.

Then Bobbi was sneaking out of the gym through the back door that was usually locked to students, following Landrum's retreating back as he walked through the staff exit and emerged outside.

"Where are we going?" she whispered. Landrum had taken off his suit coat, and his white sleeves were rolled up to his forearms, his skin pale in the moonlight.

"This trail leads to the back of the stadium," he answered, reaching back to grab her hand. "Some of us on the baseball team have keys for the back exit since we're here for practice so much. I thought we could go out here to talk. But if you want to go back in, we will."

"I don't," she said firmly, following closely behind him. She had no desire to go back into the dance and see any of those people again, to watch that disgusting display of nepotism and cliquey-ness. Her feet sunk into the soft ground. She hoped she wouldn't ruin her white patent leather boots. The night was cool, a little foggy, and the breeze was a sweet relief after the muggy, stifling air in the gym

They meandered through the back of the outside bleachers toward an expanse of lawn, which sloped downhill and into a grove of trees. "Students aren't supposed to be back here," Bobbi said stupidly, still staring at the back of Landrum's head.

"Oh, live a little," he replied with a laugh. "We come back here after practice all the time. Just talk, smoke, sometimes drink a little beer. The coach knows and doesn't care. As long as you don't get caught, it's no big deal."

"Right," she said, thumping him in the back of the head. "Just as long as you don't get caught."

"Bobbi Newton, such a square."

"You just shut up, Landrum Walton."

"Well, if you're going to talk to me like that, I suppose I'll just take you on home." They had reached the grove of trees, and Landrum whirled around, his eyes dancing. "And it's a real shame, because I know you'd love this spot. Too bad you won't see it tonight."

"Come off it, Landrum." She laughed, thumping him in the chest this time.

"Nope. I only show this spot to women who know their place."

She stared at him and he stared back, his mouth pursed in a line, his eyes boring into hers, until he lost his decorum and burst out laughing. "You're going to make someone a formidable wife someday." He thumped her back on the shoulder.

"Who's to say I'm getting married?"

"Good point," he said with a smile, grabbing her arm. "I can't think why any sane man would ever want to marry you. I've had those rocks you call biscuits. Come on, it's just through the trees here."

She ignored his retort, suddenly excited. Always the dutiful student, Bobbi had never dared venture this far behind the football field before. She knew some of her fellow cheerleaders had accompanied their boyfriends back here or gone exploring with their friends with a bottle of cheap wine, but she'd never dared. Her father would tan her hide if she'd gotten caught, and anyway, Ed and Guy had done enough teenage partying for all three of them. Bobbi didn't want to do anything that would mess up her ride to law school.

But tonight was different.

Landrum continued leading her through the trees, only a tiny sliver of moonlight leading their way as she clung to his arm. Luckily, it wasn't too cold out; October was clinging to the last bit of humid heat, and there was a slight breeze in the air. She could hear cicadas and crickets, and the odd bullfrog. Landrum was holding her arm, warm and steady, and she didn't mind the feeling at all. He pulled her along, turning every few seconds to smile at her, and her entire body felt warm.

"Here we are."

Bobbi emerged with him from the woods to find that they were standing on a sandy creek bed, grown up with weeds. A space had been cleared out, undoubtedly by the students who had sought refuge there. The makeshift beach was only a few meters wide, but big enough for two people to sit down and stare into the creek, which was small but clear, with a few smooth rocks for stepping across. Above them was a looming, rickety steel bridge. Bobbi recognized it as part of the old train track just past the school, on the way back to her house.

"I always wondered what was under that bridge," she said. "Now I know."

"It's us," Landrum said with a shy smile, and Bobbi felt her insides turn to liquid.

"How far does the creek go?" she asked, smoothing out her skirt over her legs as they both sat down in the sand.

"It's actually part of the Oconee River," he answered. "So it goes all the way down to Madison or something, I think. Probably farther."

"I can see why you like it here." The "beach" was more dirt than sand, but it was soft under her fingers, and the creek was softly trickling in front of them. The sounds of the night were like music all around them. She felt a twist of nerves in her belly as Landrum turned to look at her, the moonlight illuminating the gray of his eyes. "But just you behave yourself, Landrum Walton. I am a lady, after all."

"Believe me, I know *that*," he said, his eyes twinkling. Bobbi wanted to ask what he meant by that, and whether or not she should be insulted, but she couldn't seem to find the words. How could this be happening? Two days ago, she was nursing a broken heart over Todd Tatum, and now, she was full of jitters because she wondered if Landrum Walton, the boy who'd lived next door to her for seventeen years, would kiss her?

She couldn't bear it if he kissed her. She couldn't bear it if he didn't.

"You have such pretty eyes," Landrum murmured, staring at her. "Sorry if that's too forward. But you do."

"It's not too forward," she said huskily. "You have pretty eyes, too. They look blue from far away, but tonight I've realized they're gray. You don't see gray eyes very often. I think your mama has gray eyes, too, doesn't she?" She was aware that she was babbling. But she'd never been so close to Landrum before, had never been alone with him, and the way he was just staring at her, listening to her every word... "Anyhow, they're beautiful."

"Bobbi," he said, inching toward her, his Adam's apple bobbing in his throat.

"Yes?"

"May I kiss you?" He swallowed. "It's okay if you don't want to."

"No," she said, unable to stop the nervous giggle coming from her mouth. "I do. I mean, I do want you to. Yes, you can."

He smiled, then cupped his hand on the back of her head, gently nudging her forward until her lips met his. He tasted like Doublemint gum, and his cheek was warm and soft beneath her fingers. His breath mingled with hers, his mouth opening against her own, and she felt her blood quicken in her veins, rushing to her face, filling it with heat. She'd been kissed before, had spent plenty of time necking with Todd in the back of his car, but those kisses had been fervent and rushed, full of his demanding need. Nothing like this. Landrum's kiss was full of an almost hungry passion, but also with reverence, tenderness—as though she were a flower he coveted but didn't want to crush. He kissed her gently and slowly, but with a promise of rougher things to come. Her entire body erupted in goosebumps as he ran his hand from the back of her head into her hair, then back down her neck to her shoulders. She thought her heart might stop from the delicious, intoxicating shock that the boy next door could kiss her like that.

She pulled away after a time, gasping for breath, and began to giggle, staring at him with wide eyes. Landrum's cheeks were flushed, as she knew hers no doubt were. He stared back. "Did I get carried away?" he asked. "I'm sorry if I was too forward."

"No, you weren't. You seem awfully worried about being too forward." She gave a short laugh. "For a guy who once dated Debra Hawkins."

He looked embarrassed. "It didn't last long. I wasn't ever serious about her, and she wasn't serious about me, either." He picked up a rock and threw it into the water. "I hope you don't judge me for dating a few girls in the past. I like you so much, Bobbi. I meant what I said before. I guess I'm just being cautious because...well, I don't want to do anything that messes things up with you. I've liked you for so long..." He trailed off, looking at her with a smile that made her stomach do flips. "Todd is a fucking idiot—excuse my language." His smile deepened. "I like you a lot. And I've been wanting to do that for a *really* long time.

She was touched. "I'm just like any other girl, Landrum," she said. "You don't have to tiptoe around me."

"No, you're not just any other girl," he said, brushing her hair away from her face again. "You're Bobbi. The girl next door. Who just happens to be my favorite girl in the universe."

Bobbi's face filled with heat and she pulled Landrum to her, kissing him again with such force that he almost fell into her lap. She could feel his laughter as his lips met hers, but he didn't resist, pulling her close to him and placing a kiss behind her ear, then one on her neck. Bobbi's breath caught in her throat as she felt his lips trail down to her collarbone, his hair slicked back earlier in the evening, now falling down over his forehead, tickling her deliciously. Her brain wouldn't stop taunting her. *Landrum is kissing you, you're kissing Landrum, oh my God, you and Landrum*, but it was a wonderful taunting, full of happy surprise. His mouth found hers again, and she tasted him, uttering a little moan as his hands found her waist. Then she was pulling him down onto the sand with her, gasping a little as his weight fell on top of her, loving the feel of his hands caressing the bodice of her dress. She could feel him holding back, deliberately staying near her waist, her shoulders, her hair; he was trying to be a gentleman and she both loved and hated him for it. She was suddenly filled with white-hot desire, running her hands from his shoulders to his chest, down to his stomach and to his belt buckle. His kiss became more intense as she touched his stomach, his lips hard against her mouth.

"Bobbi," he said in the darkness, his lips kissing her face, her neck, her hair.

A low rumble shook the ground. For a moment Bobbi just assumed it was the force of the kissing rumbling in her veins, her heart. But the ground shook and Landrum pulled back, sitting up, grabbing her arms and helping her to sit, both of them out of breath. She looked at him a little stupidly, her hair falling out of the pins and into her eyes, still wrapped up in his kiss, not wanting him to stop. She stared at him in confusion.

"The train's coming," he said breathlessly, his hands still touching her, caressing her. He pushed her bangs out of her eyes and tucked them behind her ear. His fingers tickled her face.

"Oh," she said dumbly. His hands felt so good. "Should we move?"

"It might get a little loud. Come on." He pulled her to her feet, back toward the trees. Bobbi leaned against an oak tree and listened to the sound of metal clanging against metal, and the train's loud whistle that echoed in the night. She could see a light up on the bridge through the thick trees coming closer. The bridge shook and rumbled as the old metal relic came over the tracks, breaking the solitude of the night, inky black and screeching.

"Beautiful, ugly old thing, isn't it?" she said, watching the black beauty clang heavily down the track and into the night. She hadn't expected it to be so eerily poignant. Goosebumps erupted over her arms as she tore her eyes away from the train and back to her date's eyes.

Landrum didn't answer, only smiled at her softly, then he leaned forward and pressed his hands against the tree she was leaning on and kissed her again. Bobbi closed her eyes and lost herself in the moment—the sound of the train rolling down the heavy track, the breeze rustling through her hair, the feel of the rough bark against her back, and Landrum's soft lips searching her own. His chest thumped against hers, and his leg pressed against her thigh, warm and firm. For a moment, they were all that existed.

The train seemed to go on forever, and when the final horn shrieked into the fall air and the train had rumbled away, Bobbi broke away from Landrum, and stared at him, out of breath and falling in love. She smiled in the darkness, and he smiled back, leaning into her, one arm cradled protectively near her shoulder.

This is it. He's the one. Her teenage heart soared and nearly split with joy.

"It's getting late," Landrum said in a gruff whisper, his lips near her ear. "The dance will be ending soon, and your daddy will be looking for you to come on home."

"Tired of me already?" she teased, letting her lips brush against his.

"No way," he said, staring at her. "Never."

"I'm surprised you're ready for this to end," she said boldly, touching his cheek with a finger. "I know I'm not."

"You and I have plenty of time," he said, his voice deep, thrilling her. He placed a gentle kiss behind her ear. "There will be many more nights like this to come, Bobbi Newton. That's a promise."

He deposited her at home right at curfew, and she checked his visor mirror to make sure her hair, which she'd hurriedly put back up, wasn't mussed, that she didn't have pieces of leaves stuck to her clothing. Landrum's hair was in messy disarray, but she supposed boys didn't have to answer for that sort of thing. She pretended not to see the way he watched her, the smile that lit up his face. Feeling suddenly shy, she gave Landrum a quick peck and thanked him for a lovely evening.

"I had a wonderful time, Bobbi," he said, his voice all politeness and decorum, playing along. "I hope you'll allow me to call on you again."

"We'll see about that," she said, exiting the car. She winked at him, noting the grin that sprung up on his face. "Thank you for escorting me to the dance, Mr. Walton."

"It was my pleasure, Ms. Newton." He returned her wink, and cheeks hot, she sprinted from the car to the house.

Daddy was still waiting up, sitting in his chair, an open package of doughnuts on his lap. "How was it?" he asked as she came in.

"Oh, you know, the usual," she answered, depositing her purse on the coffee table. "Awful. Terrible. Painfully bad."

"So the boy next door showed you a good time, then." He raised his eyebrows, his mouth curling up into a smirk.

"I suppose so," Bobbi said dreamily, drifting up the stairs. "He did his best."

TWO

KASEY - NICHOLSON, GEORGIA - 2018

KASEY held her cracked iPhone to her ear and waited. A quiet pause, then straight to voicemail. It was the tenth time that she had called Caden in the past half-hour. Fallon would be home soon, and the last thing she needed was Caden pulling up just as her sister, who hung around like a bad smell whenever he was around, got home.

Kasey rolled over in bed and sniffed the sheets. They smelled musty, like off-brand body spray and stale cigarettes. She and Caden had both been so broke lately they were forced to smoke the three-dollar soft-pack cigarettes that sat on the very bottom corner of the lowest shelf at the Quikpik where she worked. If you held a pack up to your nose, you could smell the stale biscuit and pork grease from the cheap and quick breakfasts slung a few yards away in the little window that served as a deli. Everything purchased there smelled god awful and tasted worse, but if it was a choice between those or no smokes, there wasn't a choice at all. Quikpik let her run a tab, the balance taken from her paycheck at the end of the week. So Kasey smoked her stale-biscuit smelling cigarettes, which tasted even worse than they smelled, with minimal complaint.

Kasey ran her hands over the dirty bedspread, searching for the pack, cussing when she realized Caden had taken it. She didn't remember him shoving it into the pocket of his faded, tight jeans as he'd sauntered out of the bedroom, but she'd been halfway to dozing. He was a petty thief at heart, always stealing her lighters, cigarettes, filching her coffee mugs for her to find crusted over and molded behind his car seats weeks later. He stole change from her purse and energy drinks from her fridge, and on the few occasions when he was hungry, he ransacked the kitchen. None of these were major exploits, but Kasey was annoyed by it in her more lucid moments.

She had been lying in bed most of the day, having called in sick to work that morning. Her manager, Maggie, was a hard-ass and her voice conveyed every bit of annoyance and judgment that she felt toward her shitty employees (which all of them were, including Kasey), most of whom she couldn't keep on the job for more than a month at a time. They were either fired or quit before consecutively collecting four paychecks, and judging from the sass in her gruff smoker's voice, Maggie was fed up. Kasey was on her fifth paycheck, which she'd get on Friday (god, was Friday tomorrow? It was. *Thank god for the paycheck, but where did the rest of the week go?* she wondered). Standing in the back of the sweaty gas station, which was little more than a closet with a rusted tin roof, frying chicken tenders and sausage patties in hot grease and pounding out slick, yellow-pocked biscuit dough at 6:00 a.m. while dodging roaches was not anybody's idea of a good time. And especially not Kasey's, whose bad leg often began to pain her before hour two rolled around.

Kasey resisted the urge to call Caden again, getting up and

stretching her legs instead. A wave of queasiness settled over her stomach as she stood up too quickly, but she swallowed it down and smoothed her covers, rummaging in the nightstand for the Febreze and spritzing it over her threadbare comforter. Purple and covered in unicorns, she'd had it since she was twelve years old; it was a relic. Mom had bought it for her at a Zayre's, just before the retail outlet had gone belly up and succumbed to the grim reaper that was Walmart. Back when Kasey still idolized her mother's sweet smile, dark-blonde hair and easy laugh. Right around the time when Mom started taking her to Sunday school and began cooking pot roast for Ricky every Sunday. Those times were long gone. So was Mom.

As she stretched her stiff legs, Kasey could hear Maggie's irritated, resigned sigh from earlier. "I ain't got nobody else to come in and cover your shift," she'd said, a faint note of desperation marking her gruff voice. "Which means I gotta go in and get the biscuits ready myself. I told you that my Tessa's got chemo this week. I told you I needed to drive her to the hospital."

"Can't you call Greg?" Kasey had pleaded, ignoring the pang of guilt—a familiar pang, one that reverberated through her like a windchime, playing a familiar refrain. *You're bad. You're bad. You're bad.* "The pain is unbearable today. I really feel like I might puke. I shouldn't handle food when I'm like this."

"Greg quit yesterday."

"I'm sorry, but I really do feel sick. Can't your daughter's husband take her just this—"

"And get fired? He's already missed so many days—" Then Maggie had cut herself off mid-sentence and hung up. Kasey wasn't sure she even still had a job at that point. She felt bad for Maggie—her daughter Tessa, a young mother of three, had breast cancer and Maggie was trying to keep her business afloat and help her pay for the rising medical costs since she didn't have health insurance—but god, her *stomach*. If Caden could have scored yesterday, like he'd promised, then Kasey would have been able to go in. This was Caden's fault. He knew that when the pain got bad, she became physically ill and couldn't function. And those damn doctors, with their self-righteous, self-important bullshit, trying to wean her off the pills when they were the ones who'd insisted she go on "pain management" in the first place, buttoning up their empathy behind their stiff white jackets… Well, fuck them. They were the reason she was in this mess.

Still, she felt bad. Really, really bad. Maggie didn't deserve this, and Kasey couldn't help but wonder how Tessa would get to chemo. The gnawing ache in her leg seemed to thump in time with her guilt.

Kasey was pulling on a green crop top and the same pair of ratty, high-waisted cutoffs she'd been wearing for two days, breathing through the pain and trying to forget about Maggie and Tessa when she heard a bump at the window. She jumped and landed funny on her foot, a fresh spasm going up her leg and into her hip, making her moan in agony.

The window slid open and Caden's hands appeared. "Jesus, Caden, couldn't you have just walked through the door? You scared me half to death!" Kasey massaged her hip absently, glad she'd pulled her shorts up moments earlier. She didn't like anybody, not even Caden, to see her scar. She avoided looking at it herself as much as possible.

"Fallon's parked out front," Caden said, pulling himself through the window and dusting off his tight jeans.

"Why didn't you answer your phone? I called."

"It's dead. Forgot my charger at the house."

"Oh." Kasey was somewhat mollified. "Well, did you get it?"

"Get what?"

"Caden, I swear to god—"

"I got it, I got it. Calm your tits."

"They're calm." A wave of relief flooded through her and she felt suddenly playful, all hints of nausea from the moment before totally gone, the pain in her leg subsiding to a dull ache in anticipation of relief. "Now shut up and gimme." She pulled Caden down on the bed and held out her hand. He stared at her expectantly, a bemused grin on his face.

"Pay up."

"Caden, come on. Fallon will be up here any minute now. My leg is really hurting. I just fell on it a minute ago. We don't have time—"

"Oh, come on. Be a pal." With a grin, he reached out and booped her nose with a finger, and she laughed despite herself.

"When was the last time you showered? When was the last time *I* showered?"

"Hell if I know on both counts, darlin'." He grinned. "I seem to recall seeing your hot, wet, naked body in my shower, oh... yesterday?"

A nagging voice in the back of her head threatened to emerge, the same one that always did when she and Caden were together, but Kasey silenced it, leaning forward to place a gentle kiss on Caden's lips. He responded immediately, pulling her into his lap, devouring her mouth with his own. He was a great kisser; always had been—she still hadn't grown tired of it. They had been dating off and on since Kasey was a junior in high school, and even though they'd tried to dump each other a million times in the past four years, it always seemed to come back to the way he kissed. He made her feel alive. He kissed roughly, and did everything else rough, too. But what Caden lacked in stature, he made up for in chivalry—she couldn't think of a single time she'd ridden in his car when he hadn't opened the door for her, he always called her "darlin'," and he never asked her for a dime for her meds (though she supposed he took out his percentages by stealing her lighters and energy drinks). It was a fucked-up way of judging a Prince Charming, she knew, but Caden *was* a good guy, deep down. Even if he didn't love the Royal Family the way she did, had never watched *Game of Thrones* and rarely ate a vegetable. They had little in common other than shared poverty and pain, but that was enough, wasn't it?

Kasey pressed her hand against his dark blue Wranglers, working her way up to feel the warm, taut skin of his stomach, and he sighed against her mouth. Grinning, her hand meandered to the left, feeling its way into his pocket, and pulled out the little plastic bag.

"Aha!" she said against his mouth, feeling the stubble on his top lip, and retreated, laughing.

"That ain't even a little bit fair, darlin'," Caden said, but he was laughing, too.

"I'll rock your world later," Kasey said, opening the baggie and extracting two pills. She placed one in his palm and the other on her tongue. "You don't want me trying to ravish you with a screaming leg." She swallowed the pill dry, relishing the bitter, sharp taste on her tongue. It was hard to believe just a couple of years ago she'd gagged every time she took one. She'd have to upend an entire bottle of Green Apple Gatorade to wash one down. Now, it was as easy as breathing.

Caden swallowed his own pill and took her face in his hands. She met his eyes, narrow and icy blue, and watched as his thin mouth curved into a mischievous grin.

"You're lucky I love you, you stoned bitch." Caden kissed her roughly once more and then pushed her away playfully. "Once these kick in, let's me and you take a shower and you can rock my world after. How 'bout that?"

"Yes, boss." Kasey sighed against him, a pleasant and familiar thrum coursing through her extremities. She didn't remember falling back against the pillows, still damp with Febreze, the horrible, stabbing twinge in her leg starting to fade, nor did she remember either of them falling asleep. But it was eight hours later and 3:00 a.m. when she woke up with a sour taste in her mouth. The room was silent, she was sober, and Caden was gone with his little baggie of pills—and her cigarettes, *again*.

Kasey rolled over and pounded the pillow, trying to catch the tail end of a dream, but she couldn't sleep now. *The witching hour*, she thought to herself with a shudder. She'd fallen asleep with her clothes on, and her jean shorts were riding up, her crop top resting somewhere near her shoulders. *Classy.* She got up, yawning, pulled on her fuzzy slippers, and reluctantly grabbed her cane, just in case, trudging quietly up the stairs to the attic, the haven where she'd recently been spending all her hours of insomnia alone, digging— for what, she didn't know.

Kasey glanced at the clock as she entered the kitchen. 6:30 a.m. She'd been up, pilfering through the attic like a ghost, since 3:00. She was ready to go back to bed, but she couldn't do that, not with Fallon up. And for once, she wasn't in agony—it was going to be a good day, pain-wise—and she figured she ought to be productive while she could. Kasey poured coffee in her favorite chipped turquoise ceramic mug, the one that had been her mother's, and sat down at the worn kitchen table. Her phone dinged, and she picked it up. A message from Caden. *Sorry I had to bail. You were dead to the world, and I got a text from Clint. Can't turn down $$$. I'll be in Clayton all day, try to stop by to see you tonight. Make 'em last. Love you, darlin'.*

Kasey smiled at her phone. If Caden was working today, that meant he'd have extra cash, which meant more of the stuff. Which meant she could function all weekend. The thought of a respite from sweating and gasping through the pain brightened her outlook considerably.

"Morning, sunshine." Kasey's younger sister, Fallon, was peering in the fridge with a frown on her face. "Where's your other half?"

"He left last night." Kasey wasn't sure when Caden had left, only that he'd gone while she slept. She had started to fire off a groggy, pissed text at him demanding to know where he'd taken her cigarettes and pills when she'd noticed the little baggie under her pillow. He'd left her four. Not enough to get her through the day, but enough for the morning, at least. He *had* stolen her cigarettes, but she could dig some change out of the couch to buy more.

"Skipping work two days in a row?" Fallon asked, instantly deflating Kasey's mood. She'd extracted a cup of Yoplait from the fridge and sat down across from her sister. She peeled off the lid and made a face. "Who bought this? Piña Colada? Gross."

"All that stuff tastes like aspartame anyway and it gives you the shits," Kasey answered, deftly avoiding the first question. "Where's Ricky?" Ricky, her stepfather, was diabetic, and responsible for all the sugar-free food in the house that Fallon and Kasey complained about but ate anyway, as the alternative was buying their own.

"Gone to work. Which is where I'm fixing to go. You should try it sometime." Fallon smiled, but it was a fake, catty smile. "What are folks gon' do without their hotlink biscuits?"

Kasey bit her tongue. "I was sick yesterday."

"Dope sick."

"You don't even know what that means." Kasey rolled her eyes, holding her coffee cup steady. Her hands seemed to always have tremors in them nowadays. Her head pounded, the brief euphoria from moments before dissipating. "Can you go one day without being a judgmental little square? You think you know it all and you don't know jack shit. You learn everything from memes and social media. Just because you heard a few catchphrases—"

"I'd rather be a square than a junkie," Fallon interjected with a self-satisfied smile.

"I'm not a junkie." Kasey set down her cup and leveled her gaze on Fallon, which was hard because her eyes were watering. She'd rather die than let Fallon see how much she'd upset her. Kasey could cuss those talking heads in the media who had started the whole preoccupation with what they deemed the "opioid crisis." Ever since the term became mainstream, her sister, always a nosy, naïve snoop, had been more eagle-eyed than ever. What could she possibly know about it? Fallon, a picture of pretty, fresh-faced innocence, with her white-blonde hair, wide blue eyes, and sweet dotting of freckles on her high cheekbones, was what old southern ladies called a "good girl"—her language and behavior every bit as clean and shiny as her pretty blonde hair, dutifully attending church every Sunday, as sweet as a butter cookie at Bible study. Fallon, who had been in middle school when the shit hit the fan, had emerged from all the ensuing drama smelling like roses. Fallon was the good sister, the sweet sister, the one who never gave anybody a moment's worry. The silver cross around her neck glittered, mocking Kasey, who was tarnished through and through. Kasey had once had a matching cross, but she'd hocked it at the pawnshop months ago and never went back for it. One of very few gifts from Mom, not that it meant anything. "You know how bad the accident was. My leg was *crushed*, Fallon. Or did you forget?"

"I haven't forgotten" —Fallon frowned into her Yoplait, a tendril of light hair falling from her bright pink scrunchie and over her eye— "when our family fell apart."

SO LONG, BOBBY

Kasey resented the guilt that always seemed to fall on her. Christ, she'd only been sixteen. Her memories of the accident were fuzzy. The doctors had told her that was to be expected with head injuries, and that she might never fully recall it all. She supposed that was a small blessing, but why couldn't she have forgotten everything that happened after, too? All she remembered of that fateful night was putting on her cheerleader uniform, giggling and eager to see Caden, whom she was not yet dating exclusively but had a monster-sized crush on. There was a party after the football game, and he was supposed to be there, playing bass with his band. She was going to go and seduce him. That was the plan...but things went awry. She had a hazy memory of drinking Angry Orchards, hidden in Slurpee cups, at the game with her best friend, Amber, then ducking out to the parking lot to blaze a joint with a couple of sophomore goth kids, hopping into Amber's little green Fiesta to head to the party, both of them shitfaced. And that...she didn't remember the crash, though she'd seen pictures. The car had been a twisted heap of metal, like something out of a horror movie, blood on the road, glass everywhere. She didn't remember being in the hospital, though she'd seen pictures of that, too. Four busted ribs, a serious concussion, a broken front tooth, stitches in five different places, including her... and her leg, her poor leg. A broken hip, shattered kneecap, and that was just the worst of it. It had taken several surgeries to rebuild the leg, which would always be shorter than its counterpart. She'd been bruised head to toe, covered in road rash, and had remained unconscious for almost two days. There were pictures of that, too, banished somewhere to the back of Ricky's closet, because Kasey couldn't bear to look at them.

People told her it was a blessing that she didn't remember the accident, but the after. Oh, the after. Those memories would never leave her. She'd never felt such pain. She didn't remember most of it, but one thing she remembered was lying in her hospital bed, praying to God to let her die. Everything Kasey loved and cared about—her friends, her family, church, cheerleading, even Caden, who had shown up every day to hold her hand and brought her an iPod loaded with Foo Fighters and Metallica to help her pass the time (one of the most romantic things anyone had ever done for her; she still remembered it fondly in her darker moments)—paled in comparison to the pain. It was like a living thing, sucking the life right from her lungs. Dying would have been better.

But it had been Amber, Kasey's best friend and the one driving, who had died. They had waited days to tell her, and when they finally had, Kasey had wailed so loud that Fallon had run from the hospital room, her hands over her ears.

It had taken months of physical therapy, casts, crutches, stitches, and pain meds. After a solid year, she'd emerged from the ordeal twenty pounds lighter, equipped with a cane and a wheelchair and a lovely new orange bottle of prescription meds—her "pain management." She'd lost all of her friends in one fell swoop—her now-abandoned Facebook wall told the tale. Many of them blamed her for Amber's death. Others just didn't know what to say, so they stopped talking.

Then, one night when the bruises were fading, Caden had shown up on her doorstep, his ear-length hair slicked back with gel, his scraggly goatee and mustache carefully trimmed, holding carnations. He hadn't given up on her. He didn't blame her. He cared. And Kasey had never looked back.

But the woman Kasey had once called *Mama*, now relegated to the less informal "Mom," had left them—Kasey, Fallon and Ricky— less than a month after the accident. It was almost too hard to bear: a mother abandoning her family mere weeks after her oldest daughter almost died in a car crash, before she'd even close to recovered, but that's exactly what she'd done. There had never been an answer as to why, only clues that Kasey could try and guess at, but she'd never really bothered. By the time Mom had left she was well into a hazy, comfy cocoon of Percocet and sleeping pills, and she drifted on that cloud for a long time. Hell, she was *still* drifting.

Ricky had adopted her when he'd married Mom, and if it wasn't for that, Kasey wondered if he would have kicked her to the curb by now. He'd certainly threatened it. "If you can't stay off them pills," he'd said to her more than once, standing against the fridge with a cold Natty in hand, "I'm gon' have to kick you on out. Enough's enough, Kace." She'd graduated (barely) high school close to four years ago now, and God knew she wasn't doing anything to contribute to the household. Fallon was managing tech school and working part-time at Target, and Ricky was never home; he was always at the shop, tinkering on cars and trying to make ends meet as a mechanic. When he wasn't there, he was making house calls. They both worked hard, and Kasey barely made an effort. At least, that's how it must have looked to them. She couldn't blame them for being frustrated. They simply couldn't understand the kind of pain she was in, the everyday struggle it was just to get out of bed and hobble out into the world.

Ricky loved Kasey, treated her like his own, but he had his limits, too. When Mom had left, it had just about broken him. He worked around the clock, and when he wasn't at work, he sat in his easy chair, despondent and depressed, watching *Jeopardy* and *Wheel of Fortune* with a beer cradled on his lap, combing a shaking hand over and over through his salt-and-pepper beard, which had gotten a lot more white lately. Kasey knew he had a hard time supporting them all, and while he loved her, Kasey wasn't his *real* daughter. And Fallon had a job and was going to college, not to mention *she* was his biological offspring. Fallon, the golden girl, wasn't the one with the lingering pill problem, the immature, shifty boyfriend, and a shitty part-time job at a biscuit barn inside a gas station when she was twenty-two years old and should have more of her life figured out.

Kasey knew it was time for a change. She just couldn't seem to find the motivation to make it. Four years on, she still had headaches, her knee and hip throbbed all the time, and she'd made a handful of new friends—but it all paled in comparison to the secret ache in her heart. The ache that came from losing your best friend, then being abandoned by your own mother when you needed her most.

And knowing that it was all your fault.

Kasey sometimes allowed herself to wonder what her mother was doing, where she was living. There were two versions of the Mom she remembered. There was the red-haired, lipsticked beauty who wore plaid skirts with Mary Janes and tiny tees long after they'd gone out of fashion, who drank wine coolers and blasted Hole and 7 Year Bitch while she cleaned the house. That version of Mom had worn her dyed, bright red hair up in a messy bun, with the underside dyed black, smoked Doral cigarettes and cooked macaroni and cheese with Velveeta 'sauce' the consistency of Play-Doh at least three nights a week. She had been loving and fun, if a bit of a mess. Then, after years of dating, Mom and Ricky had finally made it official and gotten married. Kasey could never understand the transformation, because Ricky certainly hadn't expected Mom to change. He'd been as fun-loving and free-spirited—and broke— as Mom, the two of them a picture of grunge nostalgia in their flannel shirts and Doc Martens, chain-smoking cigarettes together on the porch while Ricky strummed his guitar in those early days. Often, he'd play Pearl Jam or Screaming Trees, even though he was more into the local Athens scene. He'd played grunge for Mom because she'd lived in Seattle for a while and he thought it would make her happy. Kasey remembered those nights, sitting out on the porch, listening to Ricky strum "Black" and watching Mom tilt her unnaturally fuchsia wine cooler back, her pretty, dyed-red hair framing her delicate face.

But then Mom had turned into a holy roller, and soon after she was dragging her daughters, decked out in matching floral dresses in garish shades of pink and purple, to the Baptist church down the road. She dragged Ricky, too, when he was willing, which wasn't often. Mom traded her grungy flannels, worn Chucks and floral babydoll dresses for silky smocks and yoga pants with flared legs, delicate ballet flats and huge, clunky, paisley-print purses. She got her hair cut off in a "speak to the manager" 'do. Soon Sundays weren't enough; she was dragging the family to Wednesday night services and Saturday brunches and cooking round the clock for various funerals, wakes, and bridal showers. Any time anyone brought up Seattle, she bit off the conversation with a frown. "That was my other life," she'd say with an ironic smile that was meant to seem joking, but Kasey knew she meant "when I was a sinner."

Holy Roller Mom had been a hell of a lot less fun than Nineties Mom, but Kasey would have given her eyeteeth to have either of them back. She'd never admit that to anyone, least of all Ricky or Fallon, but she missed her mother terribly. She wasn't religious—after the accident, the idea of God left a shitty taste in her mouth—but she understood on some level why Mom had needed faith. Mom's life before Kasey came along had been hard. She knew that much, if nothing else. Mom had never liked to talk about it. All Kasey knew was that Mom's parents had both died before she was four years old. She'd been raised by her mother's brother and his wife, Ed and Grace, who Mom had called "Aunt Evil." She'd run away to Seattle when she was barely nineteen, supposedly for the music scene, but she played no instruments and Kasey had no clue what she'd done out there. All she knew was that when Mom came back to Georgia with her tail between her legs, she'd been pregnant with Kasey and there was no father in the picture. Rather than go back to live with her aunt and uncle, she'd taken a job at the local Walmart and bummed on Ricky's couch until she could afford a place of her own. Eventually, she and Ricky—friends since high school—had gotten the happy accident that was Fallon, fallen in love and eventually gotten married. "I wore her down," Ricky had always said with a chuckle. For a few short years, they had been a family.

Kasey didn't know much about her mom's life before, but she knew enough to see the pattern. Mom was a runner; she ran away from people and things. From herself, maybe.

Kasey longed to run, too, to go somewhere else, anywhere else. To get away from her small town with its painful memories to somewhere that she might start again, where she could finally put away the pills and get past the pain, somewhere where she felt less like a barnacle on Ricky's back, somewhere where she would have purpose.

It was a futile hope. Where would she go, and how would she get there, when she couldn't even get to work two days in a row? Besides, there was Caden. They were both total messes, but they loved each other. She couldn't imagine a future without him. And there were no prospects, not in this town. Here, everybody rode the struggle bus.

"I'm going in this morning," Kasey said to Fallon dumbly, resenting feeling as if she owed her an explanation. "For once, my leg isn't screaming bloody murder."

Fallon's face softened. "You should get a better job. I'm not saying flake out on this one. But maybe look for something better in the meantime, something that pays more and where you aren't on your feet all day."

"Like what? Name one place in this shitty town that's hiring."

"You could find something in Athens, probably."

"That's gonna be hard, sharing a car with Caden," Kasey argued.

"Not to mention I'd be competing with all the pretty sorostitutes."

"I wish you'd stop calling them that; it's so sexist," Fallon countered. "You're pretty too, if you'd put a little time into your appearance. You used to do such amazing makeup, Kace. And you should save and get yourself a car. I bet Ricky would help fix something up for you. You shouldn't be relying on Caden for rides." She gave her a look. "It gives him too much power, and you're too old to not be driving, sis."

"Forgive me for being a little nervous behind the wheel," Kasey spat. "Considering."

"I know it's scary, but you have to move forward." Fallon spooned up the last bit of yogurt. "It's been years. And you weren't even driving that night."

Kasey sighed. For such a wisp of a thing, her sister was awfully good at tough love. Fallon was a pragmatic sort of person—empathy played second fiddle to good old common sense. To her, it was simple. It was time to get over it. She meant well, but Fallon didn't get what Kasey had been through—such a traumatic accident, so much pain…it had left scars. Not all of them were visible. "Whatever. Yeah. I'll just use my biscuit money to buy a Jaguar."

"You could finance something. Unless you've screwed your credit?" Fallon rinsed out her mug and placed it in the sink. "I'm not saying do everything at once, but baby steps."

"Did Ricky put you up to this?" Kasey asked, suddenly angry.

"What? No. I'm just trying to help." Fallon sighed. "And why aren't you calling him Dad anymore?"

"Does it matter?"

"It hurts his feelings."

"It does not. I doubt he's noticed."

"Do you have to argue with everything I say?"

"Yes," Kasey spat. "Do you have to micromanage me, as if you're doing so much better?"

"If you're going to be a child, I'm going to work. You know, like adults do."

"Like ringing up tampons and leggings for college girls is any better than slinging biscuits," Kasey retorted to Fallon's retreating back. The door slammed and Kasey frowned into her coffee. She hated fighting with Fallon, but it happened most days without fail.

On the way up to her bedroom, Kasey paused, looking at the framed picture of the four of them—she and Fallon in matching glittery pink dresses and leggings, wide smiles pasted on their little faces, and Mom, her hair still long and layered, her arms around Ricky, who had not yet started to go gray, his hair long and brown, without a hint of a beard. They were both laughing. Kasey remembered the photoshoot. The photographer had made a face when Mom and Ricky showed up in band t-shirts and jeans, and had frowned even more when Mom had passed her and Fallon big hunks of cotton candy-flavored Bubblelicious gum. They'd gathered for the photo, and the photographer had waited patiently for Mom to stop blowing in Ricky's ear long enough to get a decent shot. Throughout the shoot, as the photographer got more and more impatient, Ricky and Mom had only giggled more. The silliness had been contagious, with both girls giving way to laughter, and at one point Fallon had reached over and poked Kasey under the armpit, which had sent her into a fit of hysterics. That ended up being the shot Mom chose—all four of them with wide-open laughing mouths, laughing and blowing bubbles. After the shoot was over, Ricky had paid the red-faced photographer, given him a tip "for your troubles," and taken his three girls to Guthrie's where they'd gorged themselves on chicken fingers with special sauce and extra-large Budwines. It had been a really fun day. One of the best memories she had with her family. It had been irretrievably broken for years now. Mom was never coming back, and yet, Ricky still had the framed photo on the wall, in a place of honor.

Kasey sighed and trudged up the stairs to her room to find something clean to wear to work, and take another pill.

THREE

"I'M going to Colbert today," Daddy announced the next morning as he stirred milk into his coffee. "Be nice if you and Guy came with me. It's been a while since they saw y'all."

Bobbi sighed. She loved her grandparents dearly, but she'd planned on going to the library to get some much-needed studying done, and hoped to see what Landrum was getting up to later. The memory of his kisses wouldn't leave her mind, and she couldn't think of the way his lips felt on hers without the blood rushing to her face. The fact that he lived right down the road didn't help—she'd been fantasizing since before she even got out of bed about sneaking into his bedroom and helping herself to more of those kisses. But Daddy was right—she hadn't seen her grandparents in nearly two months.

"I thought Guy was working today," she said, poking her spoon around in her oatmeal. Her brother never ceased to pick up an extra shift when they were offered. "But I'll go. I have some studying to do, though, so I can't stay all day."

"Neither can I," Daddy said, sipping his coffee. "We'll head out around dinner time. Your granny will want to feed us. I reckon we'll be back before supper, so you'll have plenty of time to study." *And plenty of time to go see Landrum,* Bobbi thought.

Bobbi had already run into Ed that morning when she'd passed him in the hall, carrying boxes to his room. He'd been in there ever since, packing up his belongings. When she thought of her older brother leaving, she had a lump in her throat. "Do you want to ask Ed to come?"

"No," Daddy answered with a firm look. "He has a car. If he wants to visit his grandparents, he can drive himself over. Besides, he's busy—he's got that entire room to pack up if he means to move into his apartment by Monday."

Bobbi sighed but said nothing. She wondered if Daddy and Ed had talked since their big fight. She didn't like the idea of the two of them waging war; it would only put her and Guy in the middle like always, and she had enough to contend with without them making her their mediator, which they inevitably would, since she was the girl. Bobbi wanted no part of it, and resolved to remain neutral, even if it did tie her stomach into knots.

Just before lunch, she met Daddy outside and the two of them headed toward Colbert in his old gray sedan. It was a bright, sunny day, if a bit cool, and Bobbi stared out the window as the city scenes began to give way to trees full of autumn leaves. She'd always liked Colbert; time seemed to stand still there. The people always smiled, and her grandparents lived on what she assumed had to be the prettiest land in all of Madison County. The two had been operating their farm there for decades, since back when the town was still known as "Five Forks," providing fresh eggs and milk to several nearby families as well as a few markets. But they were getting up in age, and both their sons—Daddy and her uncle Ned—were busy with families of their own, and both lived in Athens. Bobbi had lost count of the times Granny had cornered Daddy to insist he move back home.

"I can't uproot my kids," he'd argue with an apologetic smile. "They're used to living in town; they wouldn't know what to do out in the country. Besides, I've got my job, and the house..."

But her grandparents had never stopped pushing. There had been a few times, after Mama had died, that Bobbi had wondered if Daddy might cave and move them all to Colbert, but he never had. Bobbi couldn't imagine she and her siblings growing up in farm country, not being near the university or town.

But she did have a soft spot for the old place, and had to admit it seemed like time stood still a little when she was there—she felt at peace. As the family Oldsmobile rumbled down Highway 29 toward Madison County, Bobbi leaned her head against the window and let the colors of the turning leaves in the trees lining the road blur in front of her eyes. She could still hardly believe what had happened the night before between her and Landrum. *Those kisses...* She closed her eyes and allowed herself to daydream, the sun coming in through the windows of the car warming her.

If only they could just enjoy things without the glaring elephant in the room.

For years, Bobbi had pretended not to notice her brother sneaking down the street in the middle of the afternoon, then emerging with his suit rumpled an hour later. She'd pretended not to see Mrs. Walton cutting her eyes at Ed at the store, at church, and everywhere else. She'd ignored the pointed, red-faced looks Daddy had given Ed when he'd catch him watching Mrs. Walton watering her roses, her skirt riding up her shapely calves. And she'd pretended not to notice the anger on Landrum's face whenever her brother was around. Bobbi felt guilty, thinking of all the times she'd sat right beside his family at church, noticing Mr. Walton's pursed lips out of the corner of her eye, feeling the embarrassment coming off Landrum's tense, fidgeting shoulders. And she'd never once considered telling her brother to knock it off. Bobbi was ashamed now of the blind eye she'd turned.

Maybe it *was* a good thing that Ed was moving. Bobbi didn't want anything to sully the burgeoning feelings between her and Landrum. Not when he was so handsome, so sweet... Remembering the feel of his mouth on hers, she ran a finger over her bottom lip and smiled to herself. She couldn't wait to see him again, to get lost in his eyes, to feel his arms around her, and taste his kisses... She shook her head, trying to clear it of the delicious thoughts taking over her brain.

When they pulled up at the Newton family farm, Granny and Papaw were standing out on the porch to greet them. Their scruffy sheepdog, Wayne, was standing at attention, and Bobbi rushed to greet him. She'd loved the dog ever since she was a child—he had to be going on fourteen years old, at least. He was nearly blind, but always had a happy, wagging tail and a sloppy kiss for anyone who gave him pats.

"Get y'all on inside." Granny beamed, pulling Bobbi in for a kiss, then doing the same to her father. "I've got biscuits just out the oven, and fatback and turnip greens and okra and hot buttered rice." Bobbi's mouth watered. Granny's food, full of love and tradition, and plenty of grease, was reason enough to come visit her more often.

At the table, Daddy filled her grandparents in on what was happening at home. "Ed's finally flown the coop," he said, pasting on a smile as he passed the chow chow to Bobbi. "We'll miss him, but he'll be thirty before long, and he makes good at the firm. It was high time he got on with it."

"And high time he settled down with a nice young lady," Granny said, putting a buttered biscuit on Bobbi's plate. "He seein' anyone nice?"

"Actually, yes," Daddy answered, taking a sip of sweet tea. "Name of Grace Stockton. They've been seeing each other for a few months. It started to get serious late in the summer. He met her at church. She teaches Sunday School there."

Bobbi hid her smile. Grace was the type of woman Bobbi had always known her brother would marry. In looks, she resembled their mother a bit, though her hair was darker. She had wide, ice-blue eyes, a trim figure, and a guarded smile, prim and proper and every inch the lady—and she meant business. She would run a household like a tight ship. Ed needed that. But being with a stern woman meant that he'd have to be more careful, and with Grace having finally come to family dinner last week, making things even more official, a dalliance with the older married woman next door wasn't going to fly. Bobbi worried Mrs. Walton wouldn't let Ed go that easily, though, fiancée or not. In many ways, Daddy had been right to push Ed out of the nest—things were getting crowded and tense in more ways than one. The scene between the two former lovers the night before in Bobbi's foyer proved that.

"Well, I reckon that's good news." Granny was a southern Baptist and had always had misgivings about Daddy converting to Methodism when he'd married Bobbi's mother. She didn't say anything, but her deep, pained sighs weren't lost on anyone. Bobbi supposed the old woman was just glad they all still went to church. "Maybe he'll settle down, then. I'd love to see a great-grandchild before I leave this world."

"You've got a long time for that yet, Ma," Daddy said with a grin, winking at Bobbi. Granny loved to pepper any conversation with talk about her impending death, or that of her husband, who never said anything, but grunted into his plate.

"Garden making anything, or is it all dried up now?" Daddy asked, changing the subject.

"We've still got a few turnip greens, and a few pods of okra, both of which are on your plate, Keith," Granny said with a pleased look. "Tomatoes are long since gone, and so is the corn and the beans. Deer got into the tomato plants; we barely got one juicy tomato out of the entire mess. I like to cried."

"That's a shame, Granny." Granny's tomatoes were the best in several counties, and Bobbi could practically taste one now, sliced thick and placed between two slices of white bread, slathered with Duke's mayo and black pepper. The chow chow, which she'd heaped on top of her rice, must have come from last year's canned tomatoes. "Can hardly blame the does, though, good as them tomatoes are.

Maybe next year."

"If these old bones hold out long enough."

"Don't talk that way, Granny."

"And did you go to your homecoming dance, my dear? With your beau? What did you say his name was?"

"Todd, Granny. But we broke up." Bobbi considered telling her about Todd cheating with Debra and decided against it. No sense in worrying Granny's old-fashioned sensibilities. Instead, she said, "I took a friend, or rather he took me. You remember that nice family who lives by us, the Waltons? Their son, Landrum, is in my class at school. We went along together." She flushed, a flashback of leaning against the tree by the bridge filling her senses, and tried to shake it off.

Her grandfather's eyes sharpened when she mentioned the Waltons, and she thought she caught a look passing between him and Daddy. Ah, so Papaw knew about the business with Ed, then. She cleared her throat. "He's a nice boy. We've been friends since we were little."

"The Waltons, huh. Like on the TV show. Just see that you don't get serious. About anybody." Granny wagged a finger at her. "You're too young. Take the time to get to know him. Girls are in such a screaming hurry these days to get hitched and get a youngin on 'em. Take your time."

Bobbi smiled. "I plan to, Granny. I don't plan to get married until I've finished college." She wasn't sure she wanted to marry at all, but telling her old-fashioned Granny, who had come of age in the 1930s, would give her a heart attack. She had told her grandparents her plan before, about going to UGA Law School, but neither had given it much attention. It wasn't that they didn't take her seriously, only that they seemed to assume that she'd change her mind, or perhaps that she wouldn't get in. It seemed a pie-in-the-sky dream to them. A lot had changed in thirty years.

"Mmm," Granny said, splitting open a steaming biscuit and topping it with soft butter. "You'll have to work very hard, and it'll cost a lot of money. Law school is dear."

"Ed managed," Bobbi began, but Granny cut her off.

"Your daddy isn't a rich man, honey. You may have to work, or perhaps your future husband will support—"

"I'll pay for Bobbi's school," Daddy interrupted in a firm tone, and he gave Bobbi a wink. "Same as I did for Ed. If it's what she wants."

Bobbi almost cried with relief. It wasn't a topic they'd discussed, and Granny's bringing it up had rekindled an old fear in her heart. Part of her had always wondered if Daddy even *had* the money to send her to school; or worse, if he had it, but might refuse to give it to her because she was a girl.

"Things might be a little tight," he went on, taking a bite of fatback. "But with Ed out of the house, the grocery bill will be cut in half."

Granny smiled. "I hope you appreciate how generous your father is, darlin'."

"I do," Bobbi said, remembering the fight she'd had with Daddy during the Bobby Kennedy interview, feeling ashamed. "Of course I do." Daddy gave her another wink, pushing the basket of okra her way. She grabbed a piece, the cornmeal still hot, and crunched it in her mouth.

"Now if only Guy would apply to school."

"Aw, Guy's happy doing what he's doing," Papaw cut in. "Nothing wrong with doing an honest man's work. He works hard, don't he? Sets a little by?"

"He does, yeah," Daddy answered thoughtfully. "Takes every shift he can get. He just used his savings to buy him that Mustang. He helps out at the house, and all. I'm grateful. But he blows more on beer than I'd like. Ed, too. Young men these days drink too much."

"Ought not to allow it in the house," Granny advised.

"If I didn't let them drink in the house, they'd just do it elsewhere," Daddy argued. "I'd rather them be safe at home."

"Does that mean I can have a bottle of wine while I'm watching Petticoat Junction?" Bobbi teased.

"That old show," Granny snorted. "I can't stand the sight of them girls, harlots, the lot of 'em. What they lack in clothes they make up for in face paint."

"Bobbi's a modern girl of the world, Ma," Daddy teased. "You should have seen her the other night. She like to have kicked my tail, arguing for Bobby Kennedy. The love of her life."

"You're pinin' for that sucker?" Papaw asked, setting down his fork. "What on earth for? He's short and prissy and got more money than he does sense."

"I'd hardly call him prissy, Pa," Bobbi said, trying not to get riled. "I think he can hang with the best of them. He's tougher than he looks. He's had to be—he went up against Jimmy Hoffa, didn't he?"

"I reckon so." Papaw's face said that he did not reckon at all, but he knew better than to argue with a teenage girl.

"He's a handsome devil, I'll give you that," Granny said with a wink. "Those pretty blue eyes and that dimple in his chin. I was always partial to a man with blue eyes." She looked over at Papaw, whose eyes were brown. "I'd let him park his shiny shoes under my bed, yes sirree, I suppose I would."

"If it got you out of my bed, Belle, the way you snore like the dickens," Papaw said, sitting back in his chair and burping, "it'd suit me just fine. I reckon I could do with a night off from seeing that tatty ol' yeller nightgown of yours and smellin' that Oil of Olay cold cream that stinks of fartin' roses." He smiled. "And maybe I'd invite that sister-in-law of his over, Missus Jackie, to get into the dickens with *me*. Now that woman is a looker.*"

"You just hush your mouth, Grady." Granny wagged a finger at Papaw, and he snorted.

Daddy pushed his plate back and stood up. "I think I'll go outside and have a smoke," he said with a laugh, "before I lose all the dinner I just ate."

Daddy had gone with Granny and Papaw to see what was left of the garden, though most of it had shriveled up to nothing in the late-summer humidity, and Bobbi had gone off on her own toward the bridge. Her grandparents lived just half a mile from the Broad River Bridge, which sat above the rushing, powerful Broad River, tinged orange with red Georgia clay and peppered with big, flat, moss-covered stones. As a girl, she'd joined her grandfather, dad, and brothers down at the water to fish, wade, and go camping. She'd spent more time at the river than she had at Granny and Pa's house, especially in the summer. Over the past couple of years, her granny had discouraged her from coming out here alone. She said that traffic just got faster and busier with every passing month, and after losing her precious cat Whiskers to a speeding motorist, she was afraid somebody might hit Bobbi. Bobbi, who had spent her entire life navigating the stretch of road and who knew every pathway and trail, had always assumed this was a fib on Granny's part. The truth was, she didn't like Bobbi coming out here because of the business that had happened in 1964.

The grass was all grown up around the bridge, and Bobbi wondered when the county would come and mow. Papaw's land ceased at the trees, and this belonged to Madison County; he said he *could* mow around here, but why would he? "The government don't do nothin' for my land, so why should I tend theirs?" Bobbi hitched up her skirt, glad of the fact that she'd worn boots.

The water was low under the bridge, proof of that summer's drought, but it still had a powerful current. She watched the muddy reddish-orange water rush over the rocks for a time, then decided it wouldn't be worth making her way down the dusty, dried-up Georgia clay to the rocks below, especially not in a skirt and boots with little tread left. Besides, she thought she caught a glimpse of a makeshift tent a few yards away, perched on a rock directly under the highest part of the bridge. If there was someone down there, she wouldn't care to disturb them.

She smiled to herself, thinking of the bridge she'd been under with Landrum for the hundredth time. She decided she'd tell him about this place and what it meant to her, that maybe he'd understand. She hoped he would. Landrum was a good guy, and if his mother's love for Bobby Kennedy was any indication, he'd understand on a deep level why she had to come here and pay her respects. He'd also appreciate the quiet reverence of nature here, the poignancy of this spot.

As Bobbi made her way onto the bridge, squeezing herself into the narrow ledge between the rail and the road, a car raced past, so close she could feel the heat from the engine. Bobbi stepped back quickly, the wind making her skirt fly. She almost hadn't seen it in time and certainly had not heard it. Her heart raced with the realization that she'd almost gotten hit by the car, and she raised her fist in anger at the retreating vehicle. Maybe Granny hadn't been fibbing after all. Bobbi's heart racing and her hands shaking, she stepped back onto the bridge, careful to stay close to the guardrail. The memorial was on the opposite side, so she walked slowly, her hands caressing the concrete, breathing the trees and the water in deeply, a kind of prayer. The expanse above her was bejeweled with leaves in every beautiful color: rust, burgundy, yellow-green, chocolate brown. A breeze kicked up, and several of those leaves took flight, slowly landing in the water below. This place had always been so beautiful to her; that it was also a place of death made her feel a little haunted.

The sign was small, having already been vandalized and replaced several times in only three years, and the average person driving past wasn't likely to even notice it. Bobbi placed her hands on the plaque and ran her hands over the letters. "In Memory of Lemuel Penn," it read. Brief, just as Mr. Penn's life had been, and sad.

It was hard to believe it had only happened three years ago. Bobbi had thought of Lemuel Penn so many times in those three years it was a defining moment for her, almost as big as the death of her own mother, though it seemed like most everybody else around these parts had done their best to forget it. Right here, on the Broad River Bridge, Lemuel Penn, a World War II veteran who had been passing through town with some Army friends on his way back up north, had been apprehended by three Klan members. The men had followed Penn's vehicle all the way from Athens, waiting until they had the car on the bridge, then pulled into the opposite lane and fired their gun into the driver's side window, killing Penn instantly. The courts were still hung up on appeal after appeal, and so far, none of the men responsible had served any jail time. The sheriff of Madison County had turned out to be as crooked as the murderers themselves, and the locals had turned the entire thing into a spectacle befitting a television soap opera. And yet, nobody seemed to really care about serving up justice to the three men who had killed a Black man just passing through their town. Bobbi and Ed had stayed up several nights talking about the logistics of the case. Watching the horror unfold, seeing the prejudice and violence on her own grandparents' doorstep firsthand, had only solidified her fervent desire to become a lawyer. "People like you and me, we have to work even harder for people like Lemuel Penn," she'd said to her brother. "We have to use our voice to fight for their rights."

"Yes," Ed had agreed, his face sad. "To the fullest extent that they'll let us, anyhow."

Bobbi ran her hands over the sign, tracing each letter. Over the years, he'd become a heroic figure to her, a symbol of struggle, a martyr for a cause. His specter loomed over her, a reminder of the deep injustice of racial hatred. Bobbi didn't know how her grandparents could carry on, knowing that a man had been murdered by the Klan so close to their home. And yet, that seemed to be the way most people lived, just carrying on in the face of horrible injustice, closing their eyes to it so that they might survive with a semblance of comfort. She didn't always see eye to eye with her grandparents, but they were good people, gentle, kind people. It was hard for her to accept that there were folks right here in their neck of the woods—and in her own, too, back in Athens—who were filled with such hatred and violence. She found herself wondering, who were these masked men? She could be standing next to one of them at the grocery, or sitting beside one at church. One might work with Ed at the firm, or attend Daddy's poker night. Guy might fix one of their cars, or the daughter of one of the Klan might be on the cheer squad with her at school.

"Best thing you can do to fight this sort of thing," Ed had told her recently, "is to vote. Always, always vote, little sister." Bobbi couldn't wait until next November when she would be eighteen and could vote for the first time. She was resolved not only to vote in the big elections, but in the small, seemingly inconsequential ones, too. She would make her mark; she would be heard.

The rushing water ran over the rocks, cleansing them, wiping the slate clean…but it was never *really* clean. The past, the violent, bloody history…it was all there, just under the surface, if you cared to see it. Penn's death wasn't even the first lynching in the small town of Colbert. Lent Shaw had been murdered by an angry mob just a few miles away at Mills Shoal Creek back in 1936. Despite the lynching making national headlines and with at least a dozen participants and onlookers proudly posing for pictures, not a single perpetrator of the violent, barbarous crime had ever been arrested or even identified, and Lent Shaw had never even been given a memorial, his family run out of town afterward. In fact, most of the current residents of Colbert had never even heard of the man, if they were to be believed.

More leaves fell into the water, riding the rapids, disappearing from sight, and Bobbi sighed as she watched them, a heaviness in her chest.

She'd once read that Robert F. Kennedy had covertly paid for Lemuel Penn's funeral costs and set up the family. She wondered if—and hoped—that rumor was true.

Bobbi let her hand rest on the plaque for another moment, then mouthed *goodbye* and made her way back off the bridge. As she crested the hill toward her grandparent's farm, another car raced by, thundering over the bridge, and Bobbi shuddered.

Her grandparents and Daddy were no longer at the garden, so she went back inside the house, where she found them sitting in the living room, the television blaring *As the World Turns,* Granny's favorite daytime program. Daddy was leaned up against the couch cushions, his face a little green.

"You don't look so good, Daddy," Bobbi said, sitting down beside him. "Something you ate?"

"Reckon so," he said, putting a hand to his midsection. "I knew I shouldn't have had that fatback; it plays hell on my digestion."

"I got some Tums in the cabinet," Granny offered, her eyes on the television.

"Nah, Mama, I'm alright. I do think Bobbi and I will get on down the road, though." They both stood. "Thank you for dinner. Next time I come, I'll try to bring the boys with me, if they ain't stayin' too busy."

"You all got to leave so soon?" Papaw asked.

"Bobbi's got homework and all," Daddy said. "Big test she's studyin' for. And I need to change out the oil in my truck. Been puttin' it off for weeks."

"Oughtn't Guy to do that for you?" Granny sniffed. "He's a mechanic, and all, seems like he could fix his own daddy's truck."

"He said he would, but he stays so busy at that shop he never has the time to look at it. By the time he gets home, it's late, and I don't want him fiddlin' around with my truck in the garage after dark," Daddy answered. "My jack ain't worth a lick, and we don't have no lift. I suppose I could take it into his shop, but I don't want his boss thinkin' he's playing favorites. Might as well do it on my own."

"Ought to go home and get yourself in bed if you're feeling poorly, Keith," she argued. "Save the truck for tomorrow."

"I ain't feelin' poorly," Daddy insisted. "Just ate too much."

Bobbi smiled as Granny ran off to the kitchen to pack a bag of leftovers and produce to send home with them. Any time they visited

Granny, they came home with an assortment of cakes, cookies, and other baked goods, half the garden, several tins of leftovers, and a wad of one-dollar bills Granny advised Bobbi to "put away for a rainy day." After half an hour of Granny rustling around, gathering up gifts for everybody, plus some goodbye hugs and kisses, she and Daddy were back on the road, headed toward Athens.

Landrum and his parents were outside in the yard when they pulled into the drive. Bobbi fidgeted with her hair before getting out of the car, hoping there wasn't mud on her skirt. The Waltons were doing yard work, Mrs. Walton tending to her roses, and Mr. Walton tinkering with his mower. Landrum's shirt sleeves were pushed up and he was covered with a sheen of sweat.

"Afternoon," her daddy called over to them as they walked toward their front porch. Mrs. Walton said a soft hello, but Mr. Walton just nodded in their direction, barely turning his head. He hadn't had much to say to their family in a long time, thanks to Ed. Landrum wiped at his face with his handkerchief and walked over to them with a friendly smile.

"Good afternoon, Mr. Newton," he said to Bobbi's father. Landrum hadn't spoken to anyone but Bobbi in a long time, either, and she was touched, knowing this effort was for her. "Hi, Bobbi."

"Hey," she said, feeling suddenly shy, unable to keep her eyes from his mouth, remembering the way those lips had felt on hers. God, she'd known Landrum a million years; how could he be making her so nervous?

"I been planning to call you," he said by way of apology, wiping sweat from his brow, watching Bobbi's dad retreat into the house, "but my folks have kept me busy all day. Ma's been cleaning out all the closets in the house, and Daddy wanted me to mow the lawn" — he gestured at his father— "and I got halfway done before the dang mower quit. Anyway, I didn't want you to think I was ignoring you."

"That's okay," Bobbi said. "I've been at my grandparents for most of the day anyhow."

"The ones who live in Madison County?" he asked.

Bobbi was pleased that he remembered. "Yeah." Even though her father had already gone inside, she lowered her voice and said, "I had fun last night. Thanks for taking me."

"I had fun, too." He reached out and touched her arm lightly. "So much fun that, well, I was planning on asking you for a date when I called you later." His cheeks were pink. Bobbi couldn't tell if it was from the sun or if he was blushing. "Do you have plans tonight?"

She had planned to study for her test all evening, but before she could stop herself, she said, "No, I don't. What did you have in mind?"

"Can I take you downtown for a burger and a shake?"

"I'd love that." She beamed at him. She could study all afternoon and have time to go. That was if Daddy let her. She'd beg him if she had to.

"I won't keep you out late," he said, seeming to read her mind. "I've got to study for that chemistry test we've got Monday morning."

"So do I."

"I'll call you in an hour or so and work out the details," he said, wiping at his face again. "I've got to finish the mowing first. Is that okay?"

"Sure." She turned to go into the house, throwing him one more cursory smile as she did.

"Bobbi." She turned around. "You look awfully pretty today. I like that skirt." He grinned. "Even if it does have mud all over the back of it."

She flushed, and he laughed. "I'll explain later," she said.

"Looking forward to it."

"I'll have an order of fries and a frosted orange," Bobbi said as she stood at The Varsity's long, high counter with Landrum, who had ordered a cheeseburger and Cherry Coke.

"Don't you want a burger?" he asked, reaching for his wallet.

"Let me go Dutch," she said. "And no, I just want fries. They're my favorite thing here."

"Why do I suspect you're calling me poor?" he teased, then turned to the cashier. "Make her strings a double." He pulled out a ten-dollar bill and laid it on the counter, Bobbi inwardly swooning at how cool he sounded using The Varsity lingo.

"I'm not, but I happen to know Rachel is stealing all your shifts," she said to him. Landrum worked part-time at Hawthorne's Drugs, a local pharmacy. Bobbi knew that he'd been getting fewer and fewer shifts lately, because Rachel, one of her fellow cheerleaders, had been working more since her widowed mother had lost her job at Westclox.

"I don't mind," he said, leading Bobbi to a table in the corner.

"Rachel's nice. And anyway, I can still afford to treat you to some fries and a drink."

"Only if you let me pay next time."

"There's gonna be a next time?" His eyes sparkled as they settled into their booth. His foot brushed against hers; she wasn't sure if it was an accident or on purpose, but her heartbeat quickened.

"If you play your cards right."

"Just tell me what I need to do, and I'll do it, Ms. Newton." Their eyes met, and she found it hard to look away. She fidgeted with her jacket.

The waitress brought her frosted orange over and she took a long sip, savoring the sweetness on her tongue. Orange-flavored anything was her favorite. She dug in her spoon and stirred up the ice. "So, like I told you, I went to my grandparents' today."

"They live in Colbert, right?" Landrum asked, sipping his Coke.

"Just past Colbert, on the way to Bowman," she answered. "Their house is just up the way from the Broad River bridge. I pay a visit every time I go." Landrum listened intently, his pretty eyes meeting hers. "I usually go out there alone, but it occurred to me that you might like to go sometime." She paused, then added, "I'd like to take somebody...show somebody. I'm not sure why...just... because. It seems like the kinda place you might...I dunno, that you might understand."

"Intriguing. What's so special about it?" he asked.

"Well...it'll sound weird but...it's where Lemuel Penn was murdered," she said quietly.

Landrum nodded. "I remember when he was killed." He took

another sip of his Coke, then said seriously, "I've never been so angry than when those jokers were acquitted. I wanted to put my fist through a wall. Cold-blooded murder, that's what it was. It just ain't right."

"I've never gotten over it, either," Bobbi said.

"I can see why. You've always been into social justice," he said, and her heart soared. He knew her, really knew her, and the things she cared about. "And with that happening right up the road from your kin… Well, it makes sense that it'd be a hard thing to let go." He looked at her curiously. "But why go to the bridge? Seems like that'd only make you feel worse."

"I just… I don't know…go to pay my respects," Bobbi said. "Just to say hello to him. His people all up north and all, I worry he's alone." Her cheeks reddened as she stirred her drink, which had already turned to slush. "It's just so brutally unfair what happened to him. And I think about how my grandparents were just up the hill, sound asleep, never knowing a thing that went on. Did you know Penn's car passed right by a police officer when they headed into Colbert? The officer said he thought about stopping them, because they were speeding, and decided to give them a break." She shook her head. "The one time a police officer gives a Black man a break. If he'd pulled them over, it would have saved Penn's life."

"Talk about some rotten luck," Landrum agreed, shaking his head. "Damn."

The waitress brought their food, setting the platter of hot, salted fries in front of Bobbi. She inhaled the grease, her stomach rumbling. As the waitress departed, she said, "I'm sorry to bring up such a sad subject. It's only that, and it occurred to me that you might be the one person I could bring along. Who might" —she shrugged— "understand. I don't know why," she rushed to say. "But if you don't want to, I totally get it."

"Of course I'll go along, Bobbi," Landrum said, biting into his burger. "I'd be glad to. It'd be nice to pay my respects."

"Okay. Well, good." She smiled, popping a fry into her mouth.

"Anyhow, I'd follow you anywhere."

"Oh, stop it."

"I would, though." His voice turned soft, and his eyes were dreamy.

"You're sweet." His foot brushed against hers again and she pushed hers back at him.

"I wish to hell they had a jukebox in here. I'd play you a tune. Who's your favorite these days? I remember it used to be Roy Orbison."

"You're certainly laying it on thick," she said with a laugh. "Did you do research before our date?"

"Say I did. Is it working? Making you fall in love with me?"

"I suppose we'll see," Bobbi retorted, though the truth was she was already well on her way. She grinned, spotting her best friend Amelia entering The Varsity, on the arm of her on-and-off-again boyfriend, Sam. As the two joined their table, Amelia's eyebrows raised when she saw who Bobbi was with. Her friend was only able to get her alone to grill her after they were done eating, as the guys walked across Milledge to the gas station to buy a pack of smokes.

"Are you two getting serious?" Amelia asked, as they stood on the curb together. Her face was full of naked curiosity.

"It's only our second date," Bobbi said, rolling her eyes.

"You disappeared from homecoming after being there ten minutes," Amelia retorted. "I saw you rushing out the back right as I was walking in. I'm not stupid, Bobbi. You two are obviously grooving on each other." She glared at Bobbi in mock anger. "And you didn't even call me to give me the dirty details."

"There's nothing dirty to tell. We were just in back of the gym," Bobbi answered, which wasn't technically a lie. "Todd and Debra got me all upset, and he was just trying to be a gentleman. You know he's a nice guy."

"Even nice guys try to get up your skirt if they can," Amelia said knowingly. "And Landrum's seen a lot of action."

"He didn't try to get up my skirt," Bobbi said, annoyed at her friend for trying to rain on her parade. "But I think I might let him if he did. He's so cute, Amelia."

"You can do better than him," Amelia continued with a sniff. "He's been around. And his parents—"

"I don't care if he's had girlfriends before. I've known him my whole life, and he's a doll. And I know what his parents are like. It's not like my family is that much better." After all, Ed was the reason for most of the gossip that surrounded them. "Worse, probably." She didn't like the note of judgment in her friend's tone, the way she looked at Landrum like he was a speck of dirt, or the implication that he might try it on with her. She knew Landrum wasn't that type of boy.

"He's been with Debra," Amelia countered.

"So has Sam," Bobbi spat, feeling her ears burning red. It was beginning to chafe at her, thinking about all the girls Landrum had dated before her, and Amelia certainly wasn't helping. She supposed the brewing seed of jealousy meant that she really *was* starting to like Landrum. A whole lot.

"Touché. Okay, Bobbi, I fold, you win. I don't want to fight." Amelia laughed, throwing up her hands in surrender. "He's cute as a button, I'll admit, always has been." Her friend grinned, watching the two boys approach them. "And he's always been into *you*. He's been making eyes at you through the azaleas since middle school. I just wonder what suddenly changed to make you notice when all these years you barely knew he was alive."

"I did so. I just…didn't really *see* him, I guess," Bobbi answered honestly, watching Landrum walk toward her, one hand stuffed in his dark blue jeans, the other holding a cigarette up to his lips. "He's so sexy when he smokes. Is that terrible?"

"Yes," Amelia said with a laugh, threading her arm through Bobbi's. "Sam does, too. I swear, something about a guy holding a cigarette…it's so James Dean. Irresistible."

"And Amelia…he's the most amazing kisser," Bobbi confided in a whisper, feeling the blood rush to her face. Amelia gave a squeal of delight.

"What are you two whispering about?" Landrum asked, the two of them having reached the girls. He put out his cigarette with his black boot, then picked up the butt, throwing it into the trash. "All good, I hope, and not idle gossip."

"Can't it be both?" Amelia asked, taking Sam's arm and winking at Bobbi.

"Where are you two headed?" Landrum asked them as they walked toward the parking deck.

"Thelma and Thomas Brown are having a party," Sam said. "Y'all want to come along?"

Bobbi was opening her mouth to say no, that she had to go home and study, when Landrum answered for her. "Y'all go on ahead. Me and Bobbi have a bridge to go see."

"You didn't have to drive all this way tonight!" Bobbi said in the dark of Landrum's car as they headed down 29 toward Colbert. She looked at her watch. It was only 8:30, but if she wasn't back home in exactly two hours, Daddy would have a fit. "When I suggested it before, I didn't mean it had to be right now!"

"I want to see it," Landrum said, looking over at her. "We won't stay long, and I'll park a ways away so your grandparents don't notice the car. We'll just hop out and pay our respects and head on home."

"Okay." Bobbi leaned back into the seat happily. What a sweetheart Landrum was. And so handsome. She snuck a glance at his profile, admiring his high cheekbones and long eyelashes.

"I've just got to stop off and get a tank of gas," he said, looking at the gauge. "Not sure if I've got enough to make it halfway to Bowman and back. Won't take but a minute."

They pulled into the service station and Bobbi leaned against the window, smiling as she watched Landrum hop out of the car, pulling on his hat before walking over to pay for the gas. He made a handsome figure in his pressed dark jeans and white shirt, with the black jacket with rolled-up sleeves. She knew Mrs. Walton probably pressed his clothes, but that didn't make it any less attractive; the effort had been made for *her*. She reckoned Mama, wherever she was, would tell her that that sort of thing—carefully pressing your clothes before a date—meant Landrum was a keeper. Todd had always come around wearing wrinkled, slouchy clothes, not having bothered to go home and shower or change after football practice. And he certainly wouldn't have doubled her fries, used terms like "social justice," or drove her all the way out to the boonies to look at a bridge.

A knock on the car window startled her. Bobbi rolled down the window, smiling when she saw it was Hank Jarrett, another neighbor from down the street. "Why, hello, Hank," she said with a grin. Hank went to church with them and was good friends with her brother Guy. "Nice evenin', huh?"

Hank's normally jovial face was grim. "Hey there, Barbara. You all on your way back to the house, I reckon?"

"Not just yet. We've got somewhere to stop off first," she said affably. Hank was a notoriously nosy neighbor, but he meant well.

"I only asked on account of your father," Hank said, his face still drawn. "I figured you'd be in a rush to get to him."

"My father?" Bobbi's brow furrowed in confusion.

"You mean you don't know?"

"Know what?"

Landrum stepped back over to the car and tipped his hat at Hank as he pulled the nozzle from the pump. "What about her father,

Hank? Everything alright?"

"Gosh, Barbara, I hate to be the one to tell you," Hank said, though his excited face seemed to say the opposite. "And I don't got no details. Only that I was leaving about an hour ago, and as I was pulling out of the driveway, I saw the ambulance pull up at your house."

Bobbi felt the color drain from her face. An hour ago, she'd been sitting in a booth at Allen's shoving fries into her mouth and laughing with her friends, and there had been an ambulance at her place? "Are you sure it was my father? It wasn't Guy or—"

"No." Hank swallowed, now looking like he wished he was anywhere else. "I saw him, Barbara. Your daddy. They put him in the ambulance." Noting the panic on her face, he rushed to say, "He wasn't on no stretcher—he was walkin' along. But he didn't look so good. They left—without the lights or sirens on, mind—in a right hurry."

"Hank—" She couldn't form any more words.

"I'm sorry to be the one to tell you," Hank said again, looking mightily uncomfortable. The excitement of being the bearer of big news had undoubtedly left him now. "I'll let y'all go, now. I reckon you'll be wantin' to get to the hospital."

"Yes, of course," Landrum said, finishing pumping the gas, his face grave. "I'll take you right now, Bobbi." Tipping his hat again to Hank, he jumped in the car and started the ignition. "We'll head right back into town. Don't worry, Bobbi, it'll be alright."

"He didn't say which hospital!" Bobbi cried frantically as Landrum put the car into drive. She looked frantically around the parking lot, but Hank was already gone. "Landrum, which one? Athens Regional or St. Mary's?"

"Don't worry, darlin'. I'll take you to both. We'll start with Athens Regional since it's closer. If he ain't there, then St. Mary's. Just don't you worry. We'll find him and everything is going to be just fine." Landrum's voice was calm and soothing, but his face gave away his worry. He drove over the speed limit all the way back to Athens.

Bobbi had torn the tissue in her hands to ribbons. The little pieces were falling to the floor around her feet, and she knew she should pick them up and not use the waiting room as a trash can. But she couldn't seem to make herself move. They'd found her father at St. Mary's, and now she was waiting for the doctors to come out and tell her what was going on. All the receptionists had been able to tell her was that her father had called the ambulance himself because he'd been feeling poorly, and that he'd been responsive when they'd transported him. She knew nothing else. She'd been waiting a half-hour already, and her father had been admitted almost an hour before she'd arrived. She ripped at the tissue some more, cursing herself for going out with Landrum. If she'd stayed home to study as she'd planned, she would have been there when it happened; she might've been able to help. Daddy had dismissed their concerns earlier at Granny and Papaw's, saying it was indigestion, but they'd all known he was lying. She'd known he had felt ill, and she'd gone out, anyway.

Landrum appeared, his black jacket folded over one arm, holding a steaming cup. He handed it to her and took the chair beside her. "It's coffee," he said needlessly, gingerly brushing the tissue pieces off her lap, placing a fresh napkin in their place. "They were out of tea. I called your house, trying to find Guy, and he wasn't there— luckily, I was able to get hold of him at the shop. He's on his way. I couldn't find Ed, and he wasn't at the firm. But I've called my mama, and she's on the way, too. She said she'd stop at Ed's apartment and let him know. She said she'd bring him along with her if he's there."

Bobbi smiled gratefully, ignoring that Mrs. Walton already knew where Ed's apartment was only a few days after he'd gotten it. Funny, that. She took a sip of the coffee, which was scalding, but fresh and surprisingly strong. "Thank you, Landrum," she said, managing a grateful smile. "Thank you so much. For bringing me, and for doing all of this for me." She looked at her lap. "I'm falling to pieces. They haven't told me anything. I don't even know what happened to him."

Landrum leaned down, picking up the pieces of tissue that she'd ripped and scattered everywhere. Bobbi watched as he placed them in a nearby trash can. "I didn't mind at all, Bobbi. I wish they'd come out and tell you something soon."

"You should get home and get some rest," she said. "You spent all day doing yard work, and then driving me around..." She swallowed. "And your mother...it wasn't necessary for her to..."

"You just shush," he said, wagging a finger at her. "We care about y'all. I'm not going anywhere. I'm here as long as you need me. As long as you want me here, anyway." He brushed her hair out of her eyes, his expression full of kindness and worry.

Bobbi put her head on Landrum's shoulder, and he placed a kiss on her temple. His lips felt good on her skin; comforting and already familiar. It was hard to believe just an hour ago they were leaving The Varsity, getting ready to take a trip to Colbert to look at a bridge. Now they were in the hospital, waiting to find out what was wrong with her father. Bobbi tried to blink back the tears that were threatening to fall.

The door flew open and Ed walked in, his eyes wild. Mrs. Walton was behind him. "Bobbi? What's going on? What's happened to Daddy?"

Bobbi jumped up and rushed into her brother's arms. "Ed, thank God. I don't know anything. I wouldn't have even known he was here if we hadn't run into Hank—"

"Where is he? They haven't told you anything?"

"Nothing. All I know is that he called an ambulance, and they brought him here. They said he was conscious on the way over, but they can't tell me anything else until the doctor comes out." Bobbi wiped her eyes. "It's been almost an hour and nobody has told me a thing."

"I'm going to remedy that right now," Ed said angrily. "I'll be right back." He stormed out of the waiting room.

"Oh, Bobbi, honey. I'm so sorry." Mrs. Walton came over and gave Bobbi a gentle hug. "Can I do anything?"

"No. Thank you, Mrs. Walton," Bobbi said, looking down at the floor.

"Thanks for finding Ed, Mama," Landrum said, sensing Bobbi's discomfort. "I'll wait here with Bobbi if you want to go on home.

No sense in a bunch of folks crowding around the waiting room."

"I'll wait until Ed gets back," Mrs. Walton said, settling into a chair. "Just to see if he needs anything."

"Mama—" Landrum began, but the door opened and a man in a white coat came walking through.

"Miss Newton?" Bobbi nodded. "I'm sorry for the delay; I understand you're needing an update on your father?"

"An update? She hasn't even been told why he's here," Landrum spoke up.

"I'm terribly sorry about that, truly. We've been very busy this evening," the doctor said. "Miss Newton, it appears that your father had a heart attack at his home this evening. He recognized the signs and called us right away. Our EMTs were able to get him checked out and into the ambulance, where he was conscious and responding, but then he suffered another heart attack shortly after arrival. I'm afraid he's unconscious right now. We're doing all we can for him, I assure you."

"He had two heart attacks?" Bobbi felt like she might faint. She reached out to the air, and Landrum caught her by the arm. Ed had reappeared in the room and was flanking her other arm.

"What do we do?" Ed asked, his face ashen.

"Just wait. Pray, if you like. We're doing everything we can for your father, Mr. Newton," the doctor said calmly. "If you're more comfortable waiting at home, we can take down your number and have someone ring you once we've got an update."

"No," Bobbi said firmly. "Guy hasn't even gotten here yet. I'm staying."

"I'll stay with you," Landrum offered, just as Ed was saying, "I'm going to stay, too."

The doctor politely exited the room and Bobbi slumped in a chair, her blood rushing in her ears. "I can't believe it," she said quietly. "Daddy's so healthy."

"He's been under a lot of stress," Ed said, his face gray and guilty. "And he eats like shit."

"I'm sure it's going to be okay," Landrum said, his hand clasping Bobbi's. She squeezed it gratefully.

"Perhaps you should go on home, Irene," Ed said to Mrs. Walton, whose eyes were filled with tears. "No sense in all of us standing around here waiting for updates."

"I'd like to stay," Mrs. Walton said in a small voice. "With the rest of you." Her eyes were focused on Ed, and she reached out to touch his arm. Ed stiffened at her touch, seemingly aware of their eyes on him.

"If I hadn't argued with him…" he said, staring at a spot on the wall.

"Let's go downstairs, Mama," Landrum said, taking his mother by the elbow. "Go get everybody something to eat from the cafeteria. Give them a few minutes to talk." Bobbi was grateful as he led his mother out of the room. Ed slumped in the chair beside her, looking much older than his years.

"What's keeping Guy?" he demanded, bringing his fist down on his leg. "Irene said Landrum called him at the shop before she left the house. It's been at least an hour."

"I'm sure he'll be here any minute," Bobbi said, but she

wondered. The repair shop where Guy worked was only about ten minutes away from the hospital, even in traffic. "We could call the shop again, see when he left?"

"If he's not here in ten minutes, I'll do just that," Ed replied. "Christ. I knew Daddy was stressed out lately, getting worked up about me, but...he's so young, Bobbi. How could this happen?"

"He doesn't take care of himself like he should," she said, staring at the floor. "He eats too much fried stuff, junk food, like you said. He doesn't exercise. He's too busy taking care of all of us. Worrying about this and that."

"Micromanaging us, more like," Ed said bitterly.

Bobbi looked at him sharply. "He's just trying to help," she said angrily. "He's trying to keep us from making mistakes."

"Why do I get the feeling you're talking about me more than you and Guy?"

"Oh, I don't know." Bobbi looked at him pointedly. "Maybe because Mrs. Walton is here, ready to tend to your every need, and your actual girlfriend isn't? How does she know where your apartment is already, Ed, when me and Guy haven't even seen it?" She shook her head. "Is it any wonder Daddy is worried sick? Don't you learn, Ed?" She'd never talked to her brother in such a way before, but she couldn't help it.

"I called Grace before I came," Ed said defensively. "She wanted to come, but I told her there was no sense in it. Her parents are elderly and she would've woken up her whole house getting ready."

"Mighty big of you." Bobbi sneered, and Ed winced.

"Christ, Bobbi, it isn't like I called Irene. Landrum did. I didn't ask her to come."

"Does Grace know about Mrs. Walton?" Bobbi asked.

Ed sighed. "What's there to know?"

"Seriously?"

"Look, Bobbi. There's nothing going on, honest. Not anymore. Irene—Mrs. Walton—she's our neighbor, a friend, and she came to help. Just like Landrum did. That's all."

Bobbi was opening her mouth to argue that it certainly didn't seem like that was all when Ed cut her off. "I'm going to go call Guy's shop, see what's keeping him. We'll discuss this later—or better yet, we won't. I don't ask you about your personal life, so leave off asking about mine." His voice sounded near to tears. Ed was just as worried as she was, so why was she raking him over the coals now, of all times?

Bobbi watched her brother leave the waiting room, his shoulders drooping. She didn't want to fight with Ed. Things were just tense. Daddy was too healthy for this, too young and strong. She thought back to a few nights before, how angry she'd gotten with him over the Bobby Kennedy interview, and bit the inside of her cheek. She'd been so mean to him over something so silly, and now he was lying in a hospital bed, fighting for his life.

Ed came back into the room, and the look on his face was fierce. Seeing his red cheeks and wild eyes, Bobbi decided to make peace. "Ed, look, I'm sorry," she said, "I'm just worried about Daddy. I didn't mean to pry in your business. You're a grown man and it's your choice what you—"

"Bobbi, it doesn't matter." Ed cut her off. "I found Guy, he just

114

got here. He's outside in the hall. You'd better come along."

"What do you mean?" Bobbi stood, dread rising in her belly. "Why?"

"I just saw the doctor again. He was coming to find us." Ed took Bobbi's hands in his own. He squeezed them too hard, and Bobbi winced. "Sugar pie…Daddy's gone. He had another heart attack and he died. Just now."

Bobbi remembered nothing else but hitting the floor and her world going black.

Bobbi awoke several hours later with a crick in her neck, the hard, wooden chair digging into her face where she'd curled up. A puddle of drool had pooled on the wood, and she wiped at it with a sleeve, stretching into a sitting position. The waiting room was quiet and empty. After seeing their father for themselves and knowing it was really real, Bobbi had refused to leave the hospital. The hospital staff had urged her to go home and rest, saying that there was nothing she could do here now, but she'd wanted to stay, at least until her brothers had signed the papers they needed to and made arrangements for her father. She'd leave when they left.

She'd fallen asleep in the uncomfortable chair, though she had no idea how. Her mouth tasted like stale coffee and sleep. She'd kill for a glass of water, but there was none in the room and she wasn't sure she wanted to emerge from the safe cocoon of the empty room with its whirring air conditioner and stiff-backed chairs. This little space, with its worn, dog-eared magazines and mustard-colored carpet, was a welcome hiding place.

Still, not only was she thirsty, she also had to pee. She stood, stretching her stiff, jelly-filled legs, and walked to the door, opening it silently. Voices immediately trailed in from just outside the door and she stopped, listening.

"Go on home to your husband, Irene. You've done all you can, and I appreciate it."

"I want to help, Ed. I want to be here for you. For Bobbi, too."

"It's not appropriate for you to be here, Irene. People will talk."

"Landrum's here, ain't he? He's my son. I'm just here supporting him…and supporting you." Her voice was full of pleading tenderness.

"I can't control him, but I'm telling *you* to go on home. Your husband is going to wonder what in the devil kept you—"

"Oh, to hell with Johnny. I don't give a flip what he thinks." There was a silence, and Bobbi imagined Mrs. Walton had stepped closer to her brother. "Ed, I love you. I don't want to be with Johnny anymore. Can't we stop playing around and just—"

Ed gave a deep, ragged sigh. "Irene…you know I care for you. But we've talked about this. You're *married*. Even if y'all got a divorce, there's the age difference… People know how we got started…and now your son is dating my baby sister. It can't work."

A choked sob escaped from Mrs. Walton.

"We agreed that we'd move on. You know I'm going steady with Grace. If we up and took off together, I'd be ruined in this town. Not to mention your husband will never let you go; he'd never stop looking for us."

"To hell with all of it, Ed. We love each other. What's between us is—"

116

"If you loved me at all you'd know that now is not the time to try and sway me from what we've already agreed upon." Ed's voice turned to ice. "My father is dead in the morgue, my brother wrecked and totaled his car on the way here he was so worried, and my little sister is distraught. The audacity, Irene, trying to talk about *love* when—"

Bobbi held her hand to her mouth. Guy had been in an accident?

"You forget, Ed Newton, that you're the one who pursued me. Running after me, begging me for the time of day when I—"

"And I'm sorry I did." Ed's voice was still cold. "Now, for the last time, Irene, go on and get out of here. I've got more important things to think on just now. My goddamn daddy just died. *Goodbye.*"

There was a choked sob and the sound of high heels clacking down the hall. Ed did not return to the waiting room. Bobbi could hear him pacing outside, muttering to himself under his breath.

At that moment, Landrum pushed through the opposite door, holding two plastic cups, almost knocking into Bobbi. When he saw her standing there, his eyes widened. "You're awake! I thought you were snoozing. I snuck out for a quick smoke. I brought you some water. I thought you might be thirsty for something other than that lava they call coffee." He walked over and held the cup out to her, and Bobbi crept away from the door, grateful that he hadn't heard the exchange between Ed and his mother.

She took the water gratefully and downed the entire cup in a gulp. Landrum's gray eyes were wide and full of tender concern. He handed her the other cup, and she waved it away. Her eyes filled with tears. "Landrum…I appreciate you coming here and being with me…bringing me drinks and all, but…I think you ought to go on home."

"I want to stay and help you in any way I can—" he began.

"I know, and you're a dear, but…" She lowered her voice to a whisper. "Your mother and Ed…they just had a fuss, and I heard it, and honestly… Landrum, I just can't handle it right now. I think you both ought to go."

His eyes narrowed. "What did she do now?"

"Nothing, Landrum. But you ought to see her home. She's upset. We all are."

He nodded, his expression grave. "Alright, Bobbi, if that's what you need, that's what I'll do." He sat the cup of water down on the table and headed toward the door, stopping to put a hand on her shoulder. "You need anything at all, you holler. Call me, no matter what time it is. I'll come by your house and check on you tomorrow, okay?"

"Thank you, Lando," she said, calling him by his family nickname.

He smiled, leaning in to give her a gentle kiss on the cheek. Then he was gone, leaving her to her grief.

FOUR

KASEY - NICHOLSON, GEORGIA - 2018

KASEY couldn't sleep. It had been two days since she'd had a pill, and she was in pain, plus she was worried. She'd been fired the day before from her job at the Quikpik—it had come as no surprise to her, after the way she'd done Maggie—and while she hadn't had a chance to talk to Ricky about it yet, she knew Fallon had probably already told him. She was trying hard not to do anything else to upset the household, staying clean and telling Caden not to come over. She knew that the goodwill Ricky felt toward her was just about dried up, and she couldn't be thrown out, not now. Not without any money, no car, no job, and no way to get by.

Kasey stared at the ceiling, trying to ignore the pain in her back and legs. Whether it was phantom pain or real had long ago ceased to matter—pain was pain—and prayed to the god she didn't believe in to deliver her from herself. She knew she couldn't go on like this, but how in the fuck was she going to get out of it? She'd burned every bridge she had that might've helped her. It was only a matter of time before she was sent packing.

She sat up in bed, throwing the covers off, and pulled on her robe. No sense in lying in bed, just staring at the walls.

She silently crept up the stairs to the attic, gripping the banister tightly, like she did so many nights, to rummage around and kill time. She never found anything much up there, just useless old school papers of hers and Fallon's, the occasional discarded toy, but it was better than lying in a sweaty bed marinating in her past failures. And it made her feel better, surrounded by all that nostalgia. Plus, Ricky had a treasure trove of old books and papers about the history of Jackson County that she found fascinating. He had once been into genealogy, researching the history of his family, who were among the first settlers of the county. The downstairs shelves were once filled with weather-beaten books about the Native American tribes in the area, the history of trade in the county, and catalogs of land shares, old Farmer's Almanacs, and yearbooks. Now, all those books were packed away and collecting dust in the attic, and she loved to pore through them, absorbing the history and the memories.

Had she not thrown her life away after the accident, Kasey thought to herself sometimes, she might have enjoyed becoming a historian, or perhaps a history professor. Oh well, too late now. Even if she found the motivation to go to college, she had no money to pay for it, and her grades in high school had been total shit, nowhere near good enough to get into a decent university like UGA. No, for her, it was tech school all the way—*if* she could pass the entrance tests and find a way to pay tuition, which was next to impossible without a job. And neither a job nor college could be obtained without a reliable vehicle. That wasn't possible without money… and on and on it went.

The attic door opened with a tiny creak that Kasey hoped wouldn't wake the house. She tiptoed over to her favorite spot in the corner, just by the window, where Ricky had stacked all his boxes of books and papers. The last time she'd been up here, she'd found a box full of old piano sheet music dated from the early 1900s, signed at the bottom by Ricky's great-great-grandmother, who had written a few lines about each song and its significance to the family. "Daughter Janice learned to play this for 10th birthday party" read one. "Learned Tchaikovsky piece for Christmas 1898" read another. That same piano now sat in Ricky's garage, dreadfully out of tune and splintering at the bottom. She'd been bugging him to get it fixed up, but he said the repairs and tuning would cost far more than the piano was worth.

"Some things are worth more than money," she'd argued.

He'd laughed, a dry, bitter sound. "The money to fix up that piano goes to your food and cigarettes, Kasey." She'd said no more after that.

She eased herself slowly onto the attic floor and opened the box, shuffling through the papers, gingerly running her fingers over each piece of music, one by one, until the box was empty. Then she moved on to the next box. She'd never bothered with it before, mainly because it was taped shut tightly with super strong industrial tape, plus it was heavy. Today, Kasey had decided to bring Ricky's box cutter with her, which she used to slide through the thick tape. She pried the box open with excitement, sitting cross-legged in front of it to enjoy its treasure, hoping it might be full of old history books. The barest sliver of moonlight showed through the thick-paned window for her to see by.

Once it was open, Kasey stared inside, frowning at its contents.

It wasn't full of books, but what appeared to be old dresses. But this clothing was not as old as the items in the other nearby boxes. Rather than turn of the century, Kasey could swear this fabric looked to be newer, likely from the sixties or seventies. She gingerly pulled out a dress, which appeared to be a silky, pale-pink taffeta, and held it out. The tag was a brand she'd heard of before: Mary Quant. She'd once read that Mary Quant was the "it girl" brand in the sixties. More dresses were folded in the box, the next one in the pile an olive-green polyester A-line number, sleeveless, with a scooped white collar. There were several more dresses in the same style, in various colors—tomato red, plum, navy blue, mustard—all of them bright and loud, and below them there was a pair of folded up patent leather white boots with a scuff on one toe. Kasey grinned, pulling them out of the box. She'd hit a treasure trove of sixties nostalgia— these clothes could have been worn by Twiggy herself! They looked like every dress on every heavy-eyelashed girl in all the videos she'd seen on TV from that decade. Kasey slipped a boot over her bare foot, not bothering to worry about cobwebs or mice, and was pleased to find that it slid on easily. A perfect fit, even though the zipper was broken.

She supposed this box must have belonged to Ricky's mother. She did the math in her head. Ricky was in his mid-forties, so his mother would have been a teenager in the sixties. Ricky had never talked about his mother being a stylish go-go, but as a buttoned up, prissy matriarch who had forced them to attend church four days a week and rapped their knuckles with a ruler when they misbehaved. Kasey had only met her once, on a childhood visit to the nursing home where she later died, and the lady had been severe and quiet, nothing like the type of woman these dresses conjured up.

Below the dresses and shoes was a cigar box, and Kasey gave a little squeal as she pulled it out, assuming it was filled with costume jewelry, or maybe even *real* jewelry. *Fallon would die if she knew this was up here*, she thought to herself, unsuccessfully banishing thoughts of how she might hock some of it for money if there was anything of worth. But when she opened the little box, Kasey's face scrunched up in confusion. It was not filled with costume jewelry at all, but with what appeared to be political memorabilia. Dozens of buttons and pins, a few handheld banners, political flyers and cards, maps, faded bus tickets, and an ancient pack of Pall Malls. Kasey held the pack up to her face and was surprised to find that the cellophane pack, worn with age and slightly folded at the top, still contained two cigarettes. *Christ,* they must be at least fifty years old. There was a faded business card, too, that Ricky might find interesting.

Kasey grabbed her phone and turned on the flashlight app, propping it up against the box so she could see better, and held up a button. Rusted on the back, the front was emblazoned with a picture of RFK, brother of President Kennedy, former Attorney General, senator and onetime presidential candidate. Kasey didn't know much about the man beyond that, having mainly studied his brother in school. As she rummaged through the buttons, she realized that almost all of them were emblazoned with Robert Kennedy's visage, though there were a handful of MLK, and one or two others Bobbi didn't recognize but assumed were notable figures. The banners were for RFK, too, one which read in big bold type: "*RFK is A-OK*" and there was a cut-out from the Athens Banner Herald dated 1961 with the headline "Robert Kennedy visits UGA Law School." There were other newspaper clippings, as well as a booklet about Fred Hampton and his feed-the-children program, but Kasey didn't take the time to read them. The cigar box held a pair of cufflinks, engraved with the initials "LW," and a few black-and-white pictures of a handsome young couple, the woman tall and waiflike with light hair, big eyes and a longing smile, and a man, also tall and lanky but muscular, with wavy dark-blond hair and his arm around her, looking at her like there was nothing better he loved in the world. In the second picture, the same couple had just finished feeding each other cake from the looks of it, the woman laughing with frosting smeared on her chin, the man looking away into the distance, his face wistful. Kasey's brow furrowed. She knew Ricky's mother had had dark hair; she'd seen many pictures. And Ricky's father had been fat, with a large, bushy beard. Who were these people?

She looked in the bottom of the box, pulling out a weathered envelope stuck to the cardboard. She pulled it out, her brow furrowing further as she realized it was addressed to her mother. *Ella Walton-Jones, P.O. Box 82, Nicholson, GA.* The postmark said 2012—just a few years ago, right around the time of her accident. She didn't recognize the return address in California or the senders' names.

Kasey's heart was suddenly beating hard in her chest. She turned off her phone's harsh flashlight and leaned back against the wall. With shaking fingers, she gingerly pulled the folded letter out of the envelope, opened it, and began to read by the moonlight, her heart in her throat.

A little after daybreak, Kasey smelled coffee percolating in the kitchen and tied her robe tightly around herself, emerging from the dingy attic where she'd spent the past two hours. She pressed the letter into the folds of her robe and padded downstairs, bracing herself.

Ricky had his back to her, frying an egg in a skillet. He was whistling "Sweet Home Alabama," tufts of his graying hair peeking out from his work cap. Kasey almost hated to break up his reverie, but she might as well get it over with.

"Morning," she said, and he turned around with a wary smile.

"Good morning, Kace." He turned back to his egg without saying anything more.

She poured herself a cup of coffee and sat down at the kitchen bar. "I know you're in a hurry to get to work," she began, hating the tremor in her voice, "but I was hoping to set up a time that you and me could talk."

"Do we need to?" he asked, flipping the fried egg onto a plate and turning around with a sigh. "Fallon told me you lost your job."

"I figured." *Thanks, sis.* Kasey swallowed a sip of coffee. "I'm sorry, Ricky. I don't have any excuses. But that's actually not what I need to talk about."

To her surprise, he put the egg in front of her and handed her a fork. "Eat that. You're too damn skinny and you don't eat." He put the skillet in the sink and faced her. "If you're going to try to segue losing your job into asking me for a car or a loan or something, forget it, Kasey. Even if I wanted to help, I don't have anything to spare. I'm barely getting by as it is. Fallon's doing all she can, but it's not enough, and you know it."

"I wasn't going to ask that," Kasey insisted, her cheeks burning. Why did he always have to assume the worst? Why did he treat her like a wayward child, the prodigal daughter, or more accurately, stepdaughter? She never ceased to be reminded that she wasn't really his every time he pointed out her failings and propped them up with Fallon's do-gooding. Ricky had never once referred to her as anything but his daughter, but the implication was wrapped up in his disappointment.

"What is it, then?"

She stared down at her plate, not at all hungry. "Do we have any cheese for this?"

"For Christ's sake, Kace." He went to the fridge and pulled it open, staring in the cheese drawer. "We have American and cheddar. Which one?"

"American." She fiddled with her coffee cup, then added, "Please."

He pressed a cellophane-wrapped slice into her hand and folded his arms over his chest. "I've got a few minutes before I need to head out. What did you want to talk about?"

"Morning!" Fallon came into the kitchen, freshly showered, her wet hair in a braid. She poured herself a cup of coffee and gave Ricky a kiss on the cheek before turning to notice Kasey. "You're up early. Aren't you usually going to bed around this time?"

SO LONG, BOBBY

Kasey swallowed and fingered the letter in her pocket, losing her nerve. "We can talk later," she said.

"What is it?" Fallon asked, nosy as ever, rummaging in the fridge for a cup of yogurt, then changing her mind and grabbing an orange from the basket on the kitchen island. "If it's about your job, he already knows."

"Yes, thank you. I know you told Ricky that I'm a deadbeat with no job," Kasey snapped, throwing her fork down on the plate. "Jesus Christ!"

"What's got you so angry, hon?" Ricky asked, peering at her. His face had softened a bit. "Fallon's your sister. You can tell her whatever it is you want to tell me. We love you. We'll take care of it, whatever it is, as a family." Fallon came over to stand beside him, holding her orange in front of her unpeeled, snark forgotten, her pretty face lined with worry. Kasey knew she was being unkind, but in that moment, she hated her sister more than ever. Always around, hovering, buzzing in her father's ear before anybody else had a chance.

Of course, they both thought that she was in trouble. She could see the way they'd both braced their shoulders, how they were waiting for her to drop the gauntlet.

Kasey sighed; she didn't want to do this in front of Fallon. Just for once, she wanted to have something that was just hers for a while. But that wasn't going to be an option; nobody let her breathe in this house. "Calm down. I'm not pregnant or going to jail." She pulled the letter and the ancient pack of cigarettes out of her robe pocket, sliding them toward Ricky. "I was just hoping you could

127

explain this."

"Look at that ancient pack of Pall Malls!" he marveled, pronouncing it *Pail-Mails*. Fallon wrinkled her nose in disgust. Ricky had only quit smoking a couple of years ago, mainly due to Fallon's nagging. He'd always been a Marlboro Man, in more ways than one.

Kasey handed him the business card and his eyes widened. "I'll be damned," Ricky exclaimed, running his large fingers over the faded lettering that read *Grant's Garage and Tire*. "I been working at Grant's for over twenty years and I ain't never seen this logo. This must be real old, maybe from when they opened. Where'd you find these things, Kace?"

"In the attic. Along with this letter." Kasey nudged it forward, her heart pounding.

"What is it?" Ricky stared down at the envelope. Fallon put down her half-peeled orange and picked up the letter, scanned the address, and looked at her.

"It's made out to Mom, but who's it from?"

"No idea." Whoever the sender was, it appeared Ricky didn't know them. He stared at the envelope, his brow crinkling.

"It was at the bottom of a box, buried under a bunch of sixties clothes and pictures and memorabilia that belonged to a woman I've never seen in my life," Kasey explained. "It's not any of your family, is it, Ricky?" She passed the picture of the couple with the wedding cake over to Ricky.

Realization dawned on his face. "Gosh, I didn't realize that box was up there. I thought Ella had taken it." He sighed. "I don't know about the letter, Kace, other than it's clearly addressed to your mom, but…I'm pretty sure I know who these folks in the picture are."

"Who?"

"Don't you see the resemblance?" He passed the photo to Fallon. "You look like her, a bit. Those are your mom's folks."

"You mean Aunt and Uncle Newton?" Kasey asked, grabbing the photo back from Fallon. "No, it can't be. I've seen pictures of them from when Mom was a kid. Ed was taller than this, and he had dark hair and eyes. And Aunt Grace was a teeny thing, less than five feet tall with curly hair."

"Not your great aunt and uncle," Ricky corrected her. "Your grandparents."

"But Mom never knew her parents," Kasey said, confused.

"No, she didn't. But she had a few photos. I assume her uncle Ed gave them to her. Or someone else in the family. She didn't look at them much, just kept 'em shut up in a box. She found all that stuff painful. It was hard on her, growing up without them."

"Did she tell you that?"

"Didn't have to," Ricky said gruffly. "I know my wife." His face was so pained that Kasey felt sorry that she'd brought it up. Ricky was usually a good sport about her pawing around in the attic, but when it came to memories of Mom, she knew he'd rather forget. It was part of the reason he drank. He'd never gotten over her.

"Growing up without a parent. Wonder what that's like," Kasey said, unable to stop herself, full of bitterness for Ricky's sake as well as her own, and Fallon's, too. How could Ella have left them the way she did, so unceremoniously, without warning, at the time when they needed her the most? Kasey didn't care how painful her mom's childhood had been, how lonely she'd been without her parents. It was no excuse to abandon her own kids and husband, who loved her.

He placed a gruff hand on her shoulder as if he sensed her guilt. "Don't worry about it, sugar booger," he said, calling her by her old nickname. He hadn't called her that since she was eight years old, and Kasey smiled.

She dug into her egg, suddenly ravenous, the picture staring up at her from the counter. So these were her grandparents. "Do you know their names?" she asked Ricky.

"I can't remember right off, hon," Ricky answered, pouring himself another coffee. "I could dig around a little tonight and find out. Probably written in a Bible somewhere around here." He took a sip, thinking. "Obviously, your grandmother's maiden name was Newton, and I feel like her first name was a boy's name, some nickname or something. As for your grandfather, no idea. If your mom ever told me, I forgot. But I doubt she did. She didn't talk about them hardly at all. They both died when she was a baby. She preferred to keep it in the past."

"I suppose that's why she never told me—or you—about this letter?" Kasey dug the letter out of the envelope, which Ricky still hadn't touched—almost as if he were afraid of it—and handed it to him. He took it warily and scanned it over, Fallon reading over his shoulder.

"What on earth does this even mean?" Fallon asked, looking at Kasey, who shrugged. She took another bite. "Who is this from and why would Mom have stuffed it in with a bunch of her dead mother's stuff?"

"I assume it's all related somehow," Kasey answered, draining her coffee, wishing there were more eggs. She couldn't remember the last time she'd felt hungry. "I just don't know how. But I'm going to try to find out."

"I'll help you, if you want," Fallon said, brightening. "It could be like an adventure."

"That's okay," Kasey said, noticing her sister's face fall out of the corner of her eye, but paying it no attention. "I know you're busy."

"It sure doesn't make any sense," Ricky murmured, handing the letter back to her. "Shoot, I'm going to be late for work." He shoved his wallet into his back pocket, adjusted his cap, and leaned over to give her a hug. "Wow, you ate it all. A little mystery is good for your appetite, evidently."

"Oh that," Kasey said absently, staring at the letter. "I haven't had a pain pill in two days. I guess they suppressed my appetite or something."

Ricky surprised her with a sloppy kiss on the cheek. "Keep it up, hon." He headed toward the door. "We'll talk more about this when I get home. Until then, please put in a few job applications today."

8/10/2012

Dear Ella,

I hope this letter gets to you. I've had a hell of a time finding you. I've searched for you online for years. I finally caved and called your aunt. She was still listed! She sounded about a thousand years old, and meaner than hell. She didn't want to help me and refused to give me your phone number, but eventually broke down and agreed to give me your P.O. Box so I could write—on the condition that I left her alone from now on. All those stories you used to tell us about her being an evil old hag must be true.

I think about you every day, Ella, and I am writing to you now just to tell you that, so you'll know. That even after all this time, you are loved. You were just a girl, and we were all so young, so it shouldn't have mattered... Yet, after all these years, I still miss you and I still wonder what it was that made you run away. Was it me and Louie? Things happened, and we hurt each other, but you felt the love that was there. I know you did.

There's so much I want to catch you up on, and I want to catch up on you. For the sake of our parents if nothing else (but there's so much else). I want to know that you're okay. If you have a family. If you're happy. I don't know if you care, but I'm very happy. I'm a mom—imagine that. I have a son and a daughter. They are the loves of my life.

I'm still in touch with Louie, too (just friends). He misses you to this day.

So do I.

Ella, please get back to me. Whatever happened, whatever you felt or feel, we are FAMILY. Our parents sealed that deal for us, and I intend to honor it. I won't stop trying to find you so I can hug your neck and tell you I love you.

I always have, and I always will.

Please get in touch.

Always,
Janelle xxoo

FIVE

BOBBI - 1967

BOBBI woke to the sun streaming through her bedroom window, hurting her eyes, which were halfway crusted shut. She'd cried herself to sleep. She looked at her bedside clock, groaning when she saw it was after 10:00 a.m. She, Ed, and Guy had to make funeral arrangements, and she was probably keeping her brothers waiting. As she sat up, stretching and putting her feet on the floor, she became aware that her entire body ached——every single muscle. The pain seemed fitting. She slipped into her dressing gown, slid her feet into her slippers, and headed downstairs, pulling her tangled hair into a ponytail as she went.

The smell of coffee hit her nose and immediately made her stomach turn, bringing back memories of the boiling hot coffee she'd drank by the cupful the night before as she waited for news. As she entered the kitchen, Ed handed her a cup, but she waved it away.

"I think I'd better have tea this morning," she said, reaching for the tea bags on the top shelf. She turned to look at her brother, who looked every bit as worn out and upset as she felt. "I'm sorry you had to stay here last night, away from your own bed. And just as you finally moved into your own apartment."

"Forget it, Bobbi," he said, flicking the kettle on for her tea. "I'll be giving it up. With Dad gone, somebody needs to be here to take care of things and to help you and Guy along. There's no sense in me living across town when there's enough room here. Besides, I'll need to pay the mortgage."

Bobbi didn't argue, though the thought horrified her. Ed was a grown man, and he was successful, but the thought of him having to take over the mortgage was too much. She wondered what her father would say about it—only two days after pushing Ed out of the house, here he was planning to come back in. But there was no way around it. Ed was right. Guy didn't make enough money at the garage to pay the mortgage on his own, and Bobbi had high school to finish. And she knew if Daddy had a will, which she was certain he did, Ed was probably getting the house anyway. The thought of having her big brother there to watch over her, and help out, was a comfort. She'd lain awake the night before, between bouts of crying, wondering what would happen to her and Guy, and if they would have to move.

"How is Guy?"

"He's alright. He's lying down on the sofa in the den." Ed poured the boiling water over the teabag in Bobbi's cup. "I think he's still in shock."

"Me, too," she said, her eyes welling up with tears again. She was surprised she had any tears left. "Why didn't you tell me he was in an accident?"

Ed looked at her sharply. "He wasn't hurt… It seemed foolish to worry you unnecessarily when Dad…" He trailed off, his eyes bright with tears. He evidently was not going to reproach her for listening in on his conversation the night before.

"He loves that Mustang…"

"He'll get another," Ed said, his voice gruff. "It doesn't matter now."

Bobbi swallowed. "So, what do we do now? I suppose we have to go to the funeral home, make arrangements and everything."

He nodded. "They were supposed to pick up Dad from the morgue this morning." They both winced as he said the words. "I've called them and they said to come in around noon. So we've got a couple of hours before we need to go." He looked at her sympathetically. "Honestly, Bobbi, nobody expects you to go. There isn't any need—Guy and I can handle it on our own. No sense in you going along and becoming upset."

"I'm going," she said firmly. "You'll need a woman to pick out the flowers. If you and Guy do it, Daddy'll end up with carnations."

"Bobbi!" Mrs. Walton exclaimed in surprise, holding the door open. Bobbi stood on the stoop, drenched to the bone. She wasn't sure at this point where her tears ended and the rain began. Both had started steadily falling as they'd left for the funeral home, and neither had stopped since. She should have listened to her brother and stayed home. Standing in the cold funeral parlor, smelling of potpourri and chemicals, had been bad enough, but the process of picking out a casket, a box made of wood and lined with too-clean velvet, had been too much for her. When the kind funeral director had asked her if she'd like to see the body, to say a private goodbye before the wake, she had fled to the car, claiming a sudden migraine.

As soon as they'd pulled back up at the house, she'd come here, though she had no idea why and no real memory of deciding to do it.

"Is Landrum home?"

"Of course, dear. I'll just go and get him—" Mrs. Walton began, but Bobbi stopped her.

"I'll just go up, if that's okay." She didn't wait for an answer, but walked inside the warm house and started up the stairs. It had been a couple of years since she'd been beyond the Walton's foyer, but she remembered where Landrum's room was. She was being rude, but she didn't care. She just needed to be somewhere neutral, somewhere safe, out of the rain, and away from people's curious eyes for a minute.

"Are your brothers alright?" Mrs. Walton called faintly after her, but Bobbi didn't pay any attention. She bounded up the stairs and down the hall, knocking on the closed door she remembered as Landrum's. She could hear the faint sounds of the Rolling Stones' "Let it Bleed" drifting through the door.

"Just a minute, Mama."

Bobbi could smell smoke, too, and it didn't smell like cigarettes. Paper, her foot.

She knocked again. "It's not your mother, Landrum. It's me."

"Bobbi?" he exclaimed in surprise, then he threw the door open, his eyes wide. He stood there in a white V-neck t-shirt, green plaid pajama bottoms, and white crew socks. "Christ, I didn't know you were coming over or I would have gotten out of my nightclothes." He saw the look on her face, her drenched hair and splotchy complexion, and appeared to forget about his own embarrassment.

"Come in, come on." He ushered her inside his room and shut the door.

Landrum's bedroom was messy, strewn with empty glass Pepsi bottles, dirty socks, and wadded-up papers. Bobbi couldn't help but smile as she watched him frantically clear a spot on the bed for her to sit, trying to covertly pick up the trash as he did so. He waved his hands by the window, dispelling the smoke that she was now certain was pot. "I can't believe my mom let you up here," he said sheepishly, and came to sit down beside her on his unmade bed.

"I didn't exactly ask her," Bobbi said, and dissolved into a flood of tears, putting her head in her hands.

"Shh, shh, Bobbi. It's okay. It's going to be okay." Landrum's arms were around her, pulling her close, resting her head on his shoulder. He stroked her hair and let her cry. Her hand came to rest on his leg, comforted by how soft and worn his pants felt. He was so warm. She sat there and cried, letting him hold her, letting him warm her up, Mick Jagger's twangy, dulcet tones in the background. Landrum murmured softly, still playing with her hair, holding her tight.

After a few minutes, she pulled away and looked into his gray eyes. "I'm sorry I barged in on you like this," she said, wiping at her face. "I must look a total fright. I should have waited downstairs like a normal person. It's just that I—"

"No, I get it," he said softly, silencing her. "Don't apologize. You're always welcome here. I'm just sorry it's such a mess."

"It reeks," she said, managing a laugh. "Your parents will bust a gasket if they find out you're smoking reefer."

He shrugged.

"I imagine you've had lots of girls up here."

"No, actually," he admitted. "My folks are kind of prudes about that sort of thing, so I never tried." He added, "Not that there's been anybody worth bringing up here."

"I don't want to get you in trouble," she said, aware that his arms were still around her, his lips just inches from hers.

"I don't want you to, either," he said softly, pulling her close. He leaned forward and gave her a gentle kiss on the lips. "But it'll be worth it if you do. I'm so sorry about my Ma, Bobbi. God, it's so embarrassing, the way she is around Ed, the way she follows him around like a puppy…and my dad will make her pay if he finds out." He pushed his hair out of his eyes. "I'm going to try and sort her out, I promise."

"I'll sort Ed out, too," she said, wiping at her eyes, having no real idea how either of them could accomplish such a thing. "Could I get you to do something for me, Landrum?"

"What is it?"

"My brothers are going to my grandparents' house this afternoon. It was so late last night, we decided not to call. They don't know yet." She swallowed back a sob, thinking of how they would break such awful news to Granny and Papaw, that their son was dead. They'd only just seen him yesterday. "They've got to tell them in person. They're old and frail and…" She swallowed. "They told me not to come. I went along to the funeral home and it turned out to be…more difficult than I expected. They don't think I should go to Granny and Papaw's." She wiped at her eyes, feeling tears starting again. "I wondered if you might…if you might want to come and sit with me at the house, just so I'm not alone."

He gave her a tender smile. "Of course I will."

"It's okay if you're busy—"

"Shut that pretty mouth."

The next thing she knew, she was pulling his face to hers, kissing him hungrily, her arms going around his neck, her hands in his hair, his mouth against hers, rough and eager. He tasted faintly of pot smoke and coffee, and he smelled so good, freshly showered and sweet. She leaned back against his pillows, pulling him on top of her, their legs tangled together in the sheets of the unmade bed, the thin cloth of his pajama pants soft against her skin. She sighed against his mouth, and he gave a soft moan in response, lighting her blood on fire.

A knock at the door broke them apart. "Landrum? Are you two all right?"

His face inches from Bobbi's, Landrum called out, "Yes, Mama, we're fine. We're coming downstairs!" He waited until they heard her retreating steps, then got off the bed, offering Bobbi his arm. He pulled her up and brushed the hair from her face, his own face bright red.

"I'm sorry," she said, embarrassed at the way she'd thrown herself at him.

"Don't be sorry." He leaned forward and placed a light kiss on her lips. "I probably ought to get dressed, go down and face the arsenal. Can I meet you at your house in a little bit?"

"Sure." She adjusted her dress, pushed her hair back, and wiped at her eyes.

She left him in his room, and trudged back down the stairs, passing Mrs. Walton in the foyer. She gave her a small smile, ignoring the look on Mrs. Walton's face—equal parts pity and suspicion. A few days ago, she would have been eaten up with shame at the way she'd marched up to Landrum's room and fooled around with him, right there on his bed. But she figured, as she walked out of the house and heard the door shut behind her, that Mrs. Walton had no business judging *her* for a single thing she did.

The house was silent as a tomb when Landrum rang the bell an hour later, and Bobbi felt the tears begin all over again. She wondered if Granny and Papaw were holding up okay, and hoped that Guy and Ed would bring them back to the house. They shouldn't be alone, any of them.

It felt so empty here now without Daddy. Daddy, who would never greet her at the doorway again, asking where she'd been and how her day had gone. Never again would she smell his popcorn popping in his ancient old red popper, or his hockey puck meatloaf, or the industrial-strength coffee he brewed in the mornings. It was no longer Daddy's house; now it would be Ed's, or, she supposed, all of theirs. It felt like anything but.

She was barely aware of letting Landrum in; him guiding her toward the living room to sit down, offering cups of tea, her stopping in the hallway abruptly. She couldn't go in the living room, couldn't bear to see the empty room with the threadbare easy chair that Daddy always sat in, the afghan her mother had crocheted that he wrapped up in on cold nights, thrown over the arm. She couldn't face the emptiness of it, the fact that he'd never sit there again, one leg crossed over the other, watching his afternoon shows. She couldn't bear to be in that room. Instead, she took Landrum by the arm and pulled him up the stairs, down the narrow hallway to her room, shutting the door and locking it behind her. Her room was the only room that felt safe right now, that felt open to anything other than crushing grief.

"Bobbi—" Landrum began, his voice carrying a note of concern, but she stopped him by pulling him close and pressing her lips to his. She was suddenly eager to finish what they'd started earlier in his bedroom, needing to feel him close to her, needing to feel his warm, firm body holding her tight. She wrapped her arms around his neck and moaned softly, but he put his arms on her shoulders and pushed her away.

"I...I can't," he said, his eyes searching hers. "This isn't right. I don't feel good fooling around with you like this when you're grieving."

"What?"

"You're in shock. I bet you haven't slept at all. I don't feel right taking advantage of you, that's all." He ran a hand through his hair, sheepish. "It isn't that I don't want to—you know I do—but I don't want to do anything that you'll regret later."

"Who says I'll regret it?" She was aware that she was pouting, but his rejection hurt.

"Maybe you wouldn't, but how can I know? I care about you, Bobbi," he said, sitting down on her bed, pulling her down next to him. "I told you—it's different with you. Christ, you've known me since I was some dumb kindergartner who picked his nose. I don't want to do anything to mess this up, you understand? Your family, your friendship—you, Bobbi—mean too much to me." He chuckled. "My mama's made enough of a mess for the both of us. I want to do this right, you know?"

She did, but she didn't want to know. Her heart clenched; he was too sweet. Much too sweet. She didn't deserve him. How had she been so blind all this time to how much he meant to her? What a good friend he'd been all these years? How perfect they were for each other? It had been right under her nose the whole time.

She grabbed his hand, pulling him closer to her. "You're not going to mess anything up, Landrum," she said in a whisper, leaning forward to place a kiss behind his ear. "You couldn't. You've been so good to me the past couple of days. It's been so wonderful, being with you…" She let her lips trail down his neck, toward his collarbone. His entire body had tensed up, but he didn't pull away or let go of her hand. Her other hand trailed up his thigh as she nuzzled into his chest. "I appreciate you trying to take care of me, but I'm a grown woman and I can decide for myself. And right now, I just want to forget… I just want to feel good, you know? To feel loved." She placed a gentle kiss on his mouth, tentatively, to see if he'd kiss her back or pull away. His lips moved just barely under hers. She kissed him harder this time, opening her mouth to his, tasting him, and he took her in his arms, relenting, "I think you're the guy to do that… I want you, Landrum…if you want me…"

"If I want you? Are you nuts?" He pushed her back and looked into her eyes. His face was flushed, and he swallowed hard. "I like you so much, Bobbi. But you're hurting…"

"Yes, I'm hurting now and I'll still be hurting later, but for right now, would you just kiss me?"

"Yes." He took her face in his hands and kissed her passionately, more passionately than he ever had before, almost taking her breath away. His hands on her face were warm, and he tasted so good. They moved as one person, leaning back on her bed much as they had on his bed hours earlier, against the cushions, legs tangled, getting lost in each other. Landrum's hands caressed her all over, and she fumbled with his jacket, pulling it off and throwing it on the floor, then his shirt, running her hands up his chest and into his hair. He kissed her neck, her chin, her ears, her collarbone, and she sighed against him, becoming weightless, a blessed forgetting. She fumbled with his belt buckle, and he let out a small gasp, then let her continue.

His weight pressed down on her as he lifted his head and looked into her eyes. "Are you sure about this?"

"I'm sure."

He continued to stare at her, his eyes flashing in the room's dim light. "Really sure?"

"Oh my gosh, Landrum, shut up."

Finally silenced, he bent down and kissed her, his hands pulling at her shirt, making contact with her bare skin. Her skirt zipped up in the back, so she leaned up, pressing against him, and reached back to unzip it. His dark blond hair fell over his eyes. As she shimmied beneath him, trying to gracefully remove her skirt, he shrugged out of his pants and came to rest on top of her again, supporting his weight on his arms, just staring down, looking at her. They were both out of breath, and Bobbi felt that she'd remember this forever. The way he looked, staring down at her with his hair in his wild eyes, his mouth open, a hint of stubble on his chin because he hadn't had a chance to shave that day. Her whole world was crumbling, but at this moment it didn't matter, because she had a handsome, sweet boy in her bed, one who cared about her, who wanted her. To hell with everything else, with other people's expectations, with decorum, with propriety—none of it meant a thing when people died all around you, when you were alone.

"Do you have...um..." she whispered.

He stared at her for a moment, then recognition dawned. "I do, um...yeah. In my wallet." He reached over and fumbled with his pants, drawing his black leather wallet out of the back pocket.

She smiled, watching him, taking in the muscles in his arms and chest as he leaned over the bed. The skin there was smooth, taut, and tanned. "You *were* prepared for this, then?" She winked as he sat up, ripping the wrapper.

His brow furrowed, and he frowned. "What, no. I mean, I wasn't trying to—" He put down the condom and looked at her. "I always keep one in my wallet. My dad drilled that into my head when I turned fourteen. I didn't—"

She giggled. "I was just teasing. I'm glad," she said, running a hand up his arm, "that you thought of it."

With a wary smile, he took out the condom and rolled it on, his cheeks turning a little red as she watched him. She pulled him close, and as he positioned himself on top of her, his face was serious. "I want to tell you something," he said.

"What is it?"

He brushed her hair from her eyes. "I love you, Barbara Newton," he said softly, his gray eyes seeming to contain a storm within them. "It's probably too soon to say, but I've loved you for years, since we were kids. I just wanted you to know that." He was so sincere, so innocent. Bobbi felt tears spring to her eyes.

She didn't know what to say. She felt her heart might burst. She wrapped her arms around Landrum's warm shoulders and pulled him down to her, pressing her lips to his neck and saying a silent prayer.

SIX

ELLA - SEATTLE, WASHINGTON - 1995

ELLA couldn't do anything but stand there, staring up at the Space Needle in a state of disbelief. Before now, she'd never left Georgia, and she'd never been on a bus trip by herself. She'd never even driven a car. Now she was here all on her own, in the city of her dreams, holding a coffee that she'd purchased from a café (another first, as her aunt and uncle didn't believe in frivolous spending at places like the new Starbucks on the corner in downtown Athens), listening to the music of a busker sitting over by the corner of a building. Ella stood silently, listening to him as he leaned up against the brick, holding a turquoise guitar that looked hand-painted, strumming the lines of a song that was familiar and beloved to her. She craned her neck, picking out lyrics she knew by heart; lyrics about leaving your wife and kids for the army, bullets screaming by out of nowhere.

She tore her eyes away from the Space Needle, telling herself she'd see it dozens of times a day and could take photos later (when she'd bought a camera), and walked over to the busker, digging a few quarters out of her pocket. She was curious to see if he'd try the yodel in the chorus, and resolved that if he pulled it off, she'd turn the two quarters into a full dollar.

The man winked, the sliver of sun peeking through an otherwise overcast sky, alighting for a moment on his salt-and-pepper hair, which was cut into a gentle mullet. Ella grinned as he strummed, his soft voice rising into a pretty decent, if a bit scratchy, yodel.

Ella pulled out her tiny wallet, pink and emblazoned with hearts, a childish relic she'd need to replace immediately, and grabbed a crumpled dollar. She tossed it into the man's guitar case with a smile, and he paused to say "thanks" and resumed playing.

"Alice in Chains," Ella said approvingly. "Great song."

The man nodded absently, still playing. Realizing that she was bothering him, Ella moved to walk off. She had plenty of city to explore and she supposed she ought to get started finding a place to stay.

"It's about his father in Vietnam," the man called after her, still strumming. Ella turned back in surprise. "Jerry's. They called him Rooster, did you know that?"

"I didn't, actually," Ella said. Jerry Cantrell was her favorite member of the band, but she'd never read the story behind that particular song. She wouldn't tell the busker, but she had a fairly huge crush on Jerry Cantrell; so cute with his long, straight blond hair and cupid's bow mouth. She had a poster of him that her aunt wouldn't allow her to put on the wall, so she'd kept it folded under her bed and brought it out to look at from time to time. She was sad she'd left it back home.

"Yeah, it's about Jerry's dad, but damned if Layne didn't make it his own," the busker said, propping his guitar against his leg. "The pain in that man's voice, my god. He stretches it out and weaves a blanket with it, don't he?"

"He sure does," Ella agreed.

"It's just a shame," the busker said, resting his chin on his acoustic guitar. He drew his knees up a little, and Ella noticed the holes in his jeans. "Fighting in that shitty war like that, to never be the same again." Ella inferred he was no longer talking about Layne or Jerry, or his father, but something…someone…else entirely. "And then on top of it, your kid having to grow up without a father. It's sad, isn't it? Vietnam orphaned a lot of kids, and not just the Vietnamese ones, you dig?"

"Yes," Ella said, feeling a sudden, strange chill go up her neck. She eased a little further down the sidewalk, suddenly desiring to be away from the man. "It's very sad."

"Pain," the busker said with a sad smile, positioning his guitar back in his lap and strumming the familiar opening bars of "All Apologies." As he hit the strings, his faded denim shirt sleeve crept up his arm and Ella saw the lined scars there, long-healed but shiny. Her own arm, under her worn black hoodie, throbbed in muscle memory. "No wonder we all die from it, one way or the other." He began to hum the first verse of the song, his voice low and sad.

"No wonder," Ella agreed, a weight in her chest. She didn't want to hear that song or talk about such sad things anymore. Not when the city beckoned. "Have a nice day, sir." She practically sprinted down the road.

The backpacker's hostel Ella was staying in had no other Americans. Ella found this bizarre, though admittedly, until the helpful person in the coffee shop had suggested it to her, Ella didn't even know what a hostel was. To her thinking, tourists and visitors stayed in hotels and motels, or bed and breakfasts. This average-sized house on a corner right on Pike Street, each room decked out with one, two, sometimes even three twin-sized beds to be shared by various people, was a novelty to her. So far, she'd been greeted by an Australian, two English people on their honeymoon, a man from the United Arab Emirates who wore a black leather jacket with various grunge band patches all over it, and a deaf woman from Sweden; she'd gestured to see if Ella spoke ASL, and when she shook her head no, the man from Austria had translated for her. Everyone was friendly, but Ella felt weird. All these people were interesting, had lived *lives*—and who the hell was she? The shared community space was filled with threadbare but comfy couches, and everyone was gathered in the little room watching a heavy documentary about heroin. The entire bottom floor of the house smelled like scorched popcorn and cheap wine. Ella had excused herself politely and gone upstairs to the room she soon found she'd be sharing with another young woman, only slightly older than her, who quickly introduced herself as Anita from Vancouver.

"So what brings you to Seattle?" Anita asked, pulling her curly black hair into a bun on top of her head. Her fingernails were painted bright green to match the plastic-looking Doc Martens on her feet. "The usual, I assume. Staking out the old haunts of Kurt Cobain? Or are you one of the purists, all about the old original Sub Pop lineup?"

"Both, I guess." Ella laughed nervously. "I'm a big grunge fan in general. But I admit I don't know as much about it as other folks do."

"Oh?"

"I grew up kind of sheltered. My aunt and uncle—well, it was mainly my aunt—didn't like me listening to secular music, so I had to smuggle my CDs and keep them hidden. They didn't let me go on AOL very much, so what little research I've done has come from friend's magazines and the library." She flushed, realizing she was rambling. "And I'd sneak to Wuxtry, this little record store in downtown Athens, whenever I spent the night with friends. They gave me some good stuff. We have our own music scene, you know."

Anita didn't seem phased by this, and Ella deflated. She'd thought her hometown might have more street cred here. "So go on, then," she said with a wink. "Which one do you fancy?"

"What do you mean?"

"Which grunge god is your cup of tea?" Anita giggled, taking a sip of Josta. She called them "grunge gods," too. Ella had to smile. "Do you love Kurt because he was pretty and tortured, or Layne because he's tortured and less obviously pretty? Chris Cornell with all his sexy curly hair and that voice, or Eddie Vedder, the beautiful and damaged little engine who could? Or are you really hardcore and want to bang Dark Mark Lanegan?"

Ella smiled wanly. "None of the above, or all of the above, I guess, depending on the day."

"Oh, come on. You've got to choose one. Everybody has a favorite."

Ella hesitated. "Jerry Cantrell."

Anita snorted. "Oh honey, I've heard *rumors*. If you can track him down, I'd say you have a shot."

"Seriously?" Ella scoffed. "He's like ten years older than me, at least."

"Like that makes a difference," Anita said. "Hell, that's a plus. He loves his groupies. That's like his thing. I've got a friend back home who used to live here, like, five years ago, right before everybody hit it big. She knew the guys from AIC really well, and Krist Novoselic a little bit, and she hung around with Andy Wood before he died, too." Her eyes turned dreamy. "He's *my* personal favorite, by the way."

"Who's Andy Wood?"

"Oh, Jesus Christ. I thought you were a *grunge fan.*" Anita looked at her pityingly. "You can't say that out loud in Seattle, hon, you just can't." She leaned forward conspiratorially, pulling a magazine out of her army green duffel bag. She handed it to Ella. "Andy Wood was the lead singer of Mother Love Bone. He basically gave birth to the whole grunge movement. Their music wasn't really grungy, but he was the first, so he gets the credit." Ella looked down at the magazine, which was one of those 'in memoriam' glossies that the rock and pop mags liked to put out; commemorative editions that pulled three times the price. The man on the cover was blond, his big eyes lined in heavy black eyeliner, with a sexy pout that seemed to propel him off the page. Ella stared at him, transfixed. "When he died, it just about killed all those guys. Cornell, Lanegan, all of 'em. He was their god, mentor, hero."

"I can see why," Ella said, still staring down at the page. "I have heard of Mother Love Bone, of course, but I didn't realize…"

"Shame, huh," Anita said, taking the magazine back. "He was a beauty. He would have been famous as fuck if he'd lived." She sighed. "Fucking heroin, man. It'll get us all in the end."

Ella didn't know what to say to that. "So, what brings *you* to Seattle?" she asked, uncomfortable. "Other than your love of grunge, I mean."

"That's pretty much it," Anita said. "I got tired of listening to Amy brag about having lived here, and all the roadies she banged along the way. I saved up my summer job money and cashed in my inheritance when my dad died and came here after graduation. I stayed all summer and then went back home to work in the cold months. I missed it so much, though." She smiled. "So I came back about a week ago, this time with a view of staying. I've been looking for jobs—I'm running out of money, so if I don't find something soon, I'm going to have to go back home to Vancouver and live with my *mother.*"

"I'm sure you will," Ella said. "You're so pretty, I'm sure some guy would be glad to hire you to tend bar or do some waitressing."

"I may have to resort to that. But I was hoping to get a job at a studio or even a record shop, something related to music. I want to be a producer."

"Oh, wow!" Ella was impressed. "That's really cool. You're in the right city for it."

"That's the idea," Anita said with a proud smile. "So what's your story, love? Other than the overprotective guardians."

Ella shrugged, embarrassed. "I, uh…I kind of ran away from

155

home. Cliche, right?" She rushed to explain. "I'm over eighteen, so it's not like anybody can stop me. I was already tired of their endless rules and I had nowhere else to go…but then…" She shrugged again. "I've always dreamed of going to Seattle—" she swallowed, then rushed on "—so I bought a bus ticket with my savings, and here I am. But now that I'm here, I have no idea what to do."

"Holy shit," Anita exclaimed in delight. "Our stories are so similar! Both of us with a home we don't want to go back to, we both love grunge…" She grinned. "And neither of us with a clue what we're going to do next, not even knowing anybody in this crazy town."

"Well, I do sort of know someone here," Ella said, regretting it the moment she'd said it. "I've never met them in person, but…my godparents live in Seattle. They used to, anyway."

"For real?" Anita looked interested, and Ella really wished she hadn't said anything. Anita might urge her to contact them, and she wasn't sure she had the courage to do it.

"Yeah. My parents are both dead. My godparents were friends of my mother's, apparently. I've never met them in person and they didn't get along with my aunt and uncle, so. They wrote me a few letters when I was a kid, but I never responded. Didn't care because I didn't know them, and my aunt and uncle never encouraged it because they didn't like them, anyway. They gave up eventually. But the last letter they ever sent me, the return address was here in Seattle." Ella had brought the letter along with her, tucked away in the bottom of her bag. "I know they were really eager to meet me when I was a child, even invited me out here, but who knows how they feel now. It's been a long time."

"You should like, totally contact them," Anita said. "You can't *not* contact them after you came all the way out here!"

"I'm still thinking about it," Ella said quietly.

The truth was, she had already pretty much decided against it. When she'd first booked the bus ticket, she'd dreamed of defying her aunt and uncle by going to Seattle and accepting her godparents' hospitality. She remembered the impassioned letters they'd sent her, snuck out of her aunt's top bureau drawer, that she'd read over and over as a child. How risky it had felt to pore over those letters, tracing the looping scrawl, knowing if her aunt caught her she'd be in huge trouble. When she was little, she had no idea why her aunt hid the letters, why it mattered. As she got older, it became apparent that her guardians were afraid that her godparents might try to step in and take her, though why they worried about that, Ella would never know, since she seemed to be a burden to them in every sense of the word. Eventually, Ella had put it behind her and stopped caring—or tried to. But after the *incident*—when Ella decided she'd finally had enough—her godparents and their letters were the first thing she'd thought of. She had one letter—stolen from the bureau drawer and stashed in the pages of a crumbling copy of *Ramona and Beezus* that she'd had forever—that bore their address, but now that she was here, she wasn't so sure. She didn't know them. And they didn't know her, no matter how much they might've loved her mother.

Even if she was curious. After all, they knew her mother, and Ella knew nothing about her...

No, she said to herself, biting the thought off before it began. *Better to know nothing.* It had been her mantra for a very long time. The less she knew about her parents, the better.

But hadn't Ella picked this particular area of Seattle for a reason? She had done a little research over the past few months. She didn't know much, and she might not have the courage to reach out to her illusive godparents, but she *did* know where someone connected to them lived and worked. And Ella just happened to be staying right around the corner from them.

Just in case.

It had been easy to forget about growing up. Her uncle had been so devastated by the premature death of his sister that he preferred not to talk about her at all, and his wife was only too happy to oblige under the guise of empathy. The truth was that she'd hated her sister-in-law and most of the rest of their family. Ella sensed that her mother's memory sparked other memories, memories of things that were painful to her aunt, some faint whiff of scandal or betrayal. Nobody ever talked about it, but it was there all the same. Whenever her mother's name was mentioned, which was rare, Aunt Grace's lips would purse into a grimace disguised as a smile, and she'd often leave the room. She would make cutting remarks disguised under compliments, passive-aggressive comments.

Ella remembered getting ready for a dance in ninth grade, standing at the bathroom sink, carefully trying to apply eyeshadow without much luck. Aunt Grace had never taught her the ins and outs of makeup, thinking it sinful for a young girl to wear it. When Ella had gotten a small makeup set for Christmas from one of the families at church, her aunt Grace could hardly take it back, but she hadn't been happy about it. Ella was only allowed to use the four colors at the bottom of the palette—a pale pink, opal, taupe, and a muted mauve. As she'd dabbed on the mauve near her eyelash line with no idea what she was doing, inspecting her dark-blonde hair for strays falling from her upsweep, her aunt had stood behind her, inspecting her critically in the mirror. "You look rather lovely," she'd said in a pinched voice. "You look like the Newton side of the family, thank the good Lord. The Waltons..." She'd trailed off, her disapproval and disgust plain in her voice. "Well, the less said about *them,* the better."

That was the first time Ella had ever heard anyone speak of her father or his family. And it had been the last.

Anita was digging through her duffel bag again. "I think I have a picture of Jerry Cantrell somewhere," she said. "There's a bunch of pictures from that gig they did in '91 at the Moore, the one that made them famous. Have you seen it?"

"Yeah," Ella responded, though she wasn't sure she actually had. She wasn't allowed online much, and what little she'd read and seen of her favorite bands had been done by swiping the odd magazine from the library, or covertly printing out articles at the school computer lab. She'd seen some concert footage once at her boyfriend's house, but he wasn't a fan and had turned it off after fifteen minutes, preferring to blast 311 and No Doubt from his disc-changer while they made out.

Ella yawned and stared at the twin bed pointedly. Anita was nice, but she was tired and wanted to go to bed. The bus trip had worn her out, and now that she was here, she felt overwhelmed.

"I'll find it later," Anita said, as if sensing her mood. "I'm going to go down and get a beer. Want to come?"

"I'm not old enough," Ella said stupidly, and Anita grinned.

"Nobody cares about that shit here," she said with a laugh. "You're in Seattle, bitch. I thought about going to a show tonight, but I'm broke. I've had to limit myself to just going out to see live music on the weekends, otherwise I'll blow the rest of my money. So; you want?"

"I'm good," Ella said. "Thanks. Honestly, I'm really tired and I might try to get some sleep."

"You're no fun," Anita teased. "Give me a couple of days, and I'll have you out of your shell in no time. You'll be backstage with Pearl Jam before you know it."

"Don't I wish," Ella said, lying down on the twin bed, listening to the gentle rain that had started on the roof. *Anything's better than what I just came from.*

"Alright, no excuses," Anita said, giving Ella a gentle thwap with a pillow. "It's Friday night, you've been in Seattle two days, and you haven't been to ONE club to see a band play! We're going, and I don't want to hear your bullshit!"

Ella laughed, reaching for her bag to pick out an outfit. Nothing she had was remotely suitable—her clothes from back home were various shades of pastel, boot cut jeans, and sensible Adidas tennis shoes, all of it paid for and, therefore, picked out by Aunt Grace. "Fine, fine. I wouldn't mind getting out of this room for a while. But

I have nothing to wear unless you count this." She held up a tiny tee—the only one she owned—emblazoned with the words "Girls Kick Butt." Just the word "butt" had ignited a hell of a fight with Grace when she'd bought it.

"Oh god, honey, no." Anita grimaced. "Borrow something of mine. Just go through my bag. I don't care." She was standing in the corner by their only mirror, gliding coal-black eyeliner along her eyes. "I'll do your makeup when I'm done with mine."

"Cool beans." Ella pulled out a floral slip dress, black with red roses, a slinky material that felt like silk. It was a bit low cut, but she could put it over a white fitted t-shirt and it'd look okay. "Can I borrow this and your black tights?" she asked. "And maybe your black boots with the heel?"

"The Georgia boots?" Anita turned to look at her. "I guess, but if you scuff them, I'll beat you up. Those cost me a fortune, and they're my favorite." She turned back to the mirror. "You'll be cold in that, though."

"I thought I'd wear a white tiny tee—"

"No way," Anita commanded. "You're not in high school anymore, sweetie. Just borrow my black hoodie. It'll keep you warm, and the whole grunge-meets-princess look is very in right now. Just look at Courtney Love. She doesn't even brush her hair and all the guys want to fuck her."

"Now there's a woman whose makeup I could actually pull off." She shrugged out of her clothes and into the dress. It left very little to the imagination, and she was grateful that the gray lacy bra she wore underneath was at least cute. She'd feel a lot less self-conscious once she had on the tights and the hoodie. The dress was incredibly short, coming to mid-thigh, and she wouldn't be able to bend over without flashing her underwear. "So where are we going, anyway?"

"O.K. Hotel," Anita said, dabbing chocolate-brown lip gloss from a pot on her perfect pout. It was two shades lighter than the lip liner she'd thickly applied around her lips. "It's a pretty happening place. Every major grunge band has played there, and a few of them still do. Tad, Bikini Kill, they still come back for shows all the time. I forget the name of the band playing tonight, but I was talking to Evan downstairs, and he said the lead singer is cute as fuck."

Evan Jackson had taken a room downstairs as of yesterday and had already made an impression on the girls. He was twenty-one and fresh from Texas, with a boisterous drawl and wide-set brown eyes. His dad and stepmother had kicked him out of the house when he'd come out as bisexual, so he'd come to Seattle, where he'd been visiting his mother every summer since he was a kid. "Sounds like Evan's got dibs," Ella said with a smile.

"Only if the guy's gay, or bi," Anita said. "If not, he's all mine." She winked at Ella in the mirror. "Or yours, maybe."

"Ha. I'm not here looking for love," Ella assured her. "That's the last thing I need, to fall for some guy who screws me over. I just need to be on my own for a while."

"Who said anything about love?" Anita said with a wink. "I'm talking about sex."

"I haven't had much opportunity for that," Ella admitted. "Not in the house of Jesus."

"You've had boyfriends, though, right?" Anita asked. "Did you leave some guy high and dry when you left Podunk?"

"Not really," Ella answered blithely. She'd dumped Harrison Davis, her high school boyfriend, just before she'd come out west. Ending things with him had been one of her proudest achievements; she'd never forget the look of shock on his face when she'd told him it was over. Not because he'd been heartbroken, but because it was the first time he had ever been dumped.

Harrison's father had worked at the same firm as Uncle Ed for years, and his mother and her aunt Grace had been close friends. He and Ella had been flung together more than anything. Harrison was nice enough, handsome and popular with his thick, wavy brown hair, large blue eyes, and athletic frame. He played football, tennis, and basketball and played in the marching band, and had been valedictorian of their class. Even his name dripped money. Ella had often thought, walking hand in hand with him down the hall, that their classmates must wonder what on earth he saw in her. Him, the most popular guy in school, wildly handsome, universally liked— and Ella, a boring chunk of nothing. Despite being a judge's niece, Ella had faded into the background all four years of high school. Harrison had teased her many times about the way she'd flitted in and out of the various cliques in the school, from the stoner kids to the nerds to the "special eds," as he rudely called them, never settling down anywhere. He claimed it was what he loved about her, but she suspected it had been a backhanded compliment.

"I had a high school boyfriend, but we weren't serious. I'm sure he was glad to get rid of me, honestly."

"Why would you say that?"

"We were a set-up." Ella found herself telling Anita about Harrison. "His dad's a lawyer and they've got tons of money. They live in this crazy-huge house on the edge of Athens. Like, they have actual servants. His parents are what they call 'progressive.' They do a lot of volunteering and stuff in the community, so everybody loves them. They champion a lot of important social causes and hold dinners and charity functions and stuff every other week." She didn't mention that her aunt and uncle often did the same and ran in the very same circles. "But all their servants are Latino, and they ripped Harrison a new one once for bringing home a black guy from the basketball team. They're hypocrites."

"Ew," Anita said. "Well, fuck them."

"They're holy rollers, just like my aunt. Big church-goers. For all their liberal talk, they made Harrison participate in a chastity ceremony." Ella didn't add that she'd been made to participate in the same ceremony. She planned to hock her chastity ring as soon as she could find a pawnshop. "He wore that ring so proudly…and then every time we were alone, he was begging me for BJs. It wasn't *actually* having sex, he said."

"Did he at least offer to return the favor?" Anita asked, looking at her with interest.

"Yeah, right. He probably wouldn't even know what to do." Ella laughed. "I'm sure he would have thought *that* was a mortal sin. He was really kind of awful. Like, he was nice to me, but I don't think he really *liked* me. We just dated because our families wanted us to. I think they had this dream that we'd end up together. My uncle and his dad were chummy at the same law firm, before my uncle moved on."

"Moved on to what?"

"Oh," Ella said absently, tying up the boots, which were a smidge too big for her. "He's a judge."

"A judge! No way! You didn't tell me your family are big wigs!"

"We're not, really," Ella said, embarrassed. "I mean, my aunt and uncle are well known in the community, but it's not like I am. I'm an embarrassment. I didn't turn out at all like they hoped I would."

"You don't seem all that bad to me," Anita said, peering at her. "I mean, considering how you *could* have rebelled, they really lucked out."

"Tell them that," Ella said with a bitter laugh, not sure if she'd been complimented or insulted. "Well, it's really my aunt more than anything. She hates me. As long as I look like my dead parents, I'm just a reminder of everything she loathes."

"Yikes," Anita said, coming over and handing Ella her hoodie. "I'm sorry. Here, let me do your makeup. I'm thinking of smoky eyes and purple lipstick. How do you feel about going bold?"

"Why not?" Ella said, staring into the compact mirror Anita had handed her. "First time for everything."

Ella handed the bearded bouncer her ID and grimaced as he stamped the back of her hand with a bright purple M for minor. "Hey, at least you got in," Anita said with a laugh, pulling her into the club. "Half the places in town don't even let you through the door if you're under twenty-one. You'll have to get creative."

The bar was bursting with people, standing room just barely, and Ella immediately started to feel claustrophobic. The band on stage sounded like a mix between Nirvana and Alice in Chains, with a warbling lead singer and crunchy guitar. Every single member was wearing a flannel shirt.

"Who are they?" she asked over the crowd as she and Anita waited for the bartender to notice them.

Anita craned her neck to look at the flyer posted over the bar. "Um…looks like their name is War Hero. Never heard of 'em." She grinned. "They kinda suck."

"They don't suck…exactly," Ella argued. "They're definitely leaning in to the Nirvana thing hard, but the lead singer has a great voice. Good vibrato."

"Oh god, don't tell me you were one of those chorus nerds." Anita laughed, and Ella blushed, because she had been.

The bartender came over, and Anita ordered herself a shot of Jack Daniels and a gin and tonic. Ella raised an eyebrow at her, then pointed to the stamp on the back of her hand. "Just a Coke, please," she said with a smile. After they'd paid for their drinks, they milled into the crowd to get a closer look at the band. "Should you be mixing gin and whiskey?" she asked Anita, feeling like a mother hen.

Anita shrugged. "Wouldn't hurt me, but this isn't mine, anyway." She leaned toward Ella and covertly dumped the shot into her drink. "Now you've got a Jack and Coke."

"Anita!"

"If anybody asks, you ordered Coke, and you're drinking Coke."

Anita winked. "At no point have you lied."

"Yeah, unless I get caught and thrown out."

"I guess you'd better drink it quick, then."

Ella tipped the drink back, enjoying its warmth as it went down her throat. Anita pulled her closer to the stage. Ella found herself swaying along, unable to stay still as the music washed over her. It was loud and chaotic in the little bar, but she couldn't help grinning. This was a far cry from anything she'd ever experienced back home. Oh, Athens had a tremendous music scene, one that would rival Seattle, according to who you asked—but her aunt had never allowed her to go to shows, and most of the kids at her school hadn't been into it, anyway. They were an even mix of preppy jocks and ag kids, and the few kids into the scene—affectionately known as "townies" and "gutter punks"—weren't the type of kids Ella had been allowed to mix with. They could usually be found playing hacky sack downtown in front of The Grill, but most of them didn't go in. They were either too young or too broke. "Your uncle has a reputation in this town," Aunt Grace had said to her more than once. "You won't be bringing potheads and hippies into this house."

She'd always said "hippie" like a dirty word, ignoring the snorting laughter from Ella, who equated the word with the bell-bottom wearing, sign-toting kids from the 1960s. Suddenly though, standing in the cramped bar, listening to the guitarist play an angsty, fuzzy solo, she sort of got it. These kids, kids like her, in their flannels and stompy boots, smelling of weed and incense and cheap beer, were simply another evolution of the hippies. They were their own decade's version of the same thing. In their heart of hearts, all young people in their idealism and rebellion were hippies of a kind. And it wasn't a bad word, no matter what Aunt Evil had thought.

Ella drained the rest of her drink and let herself be propelled right up to the front, standing directly in front of the stage. The band's lead singer looked down, giving Anita an obvious wink. Ella looked over at her friend, who was clearly pleased with herself. "I guess you regret saying he sucks now, huh?" she said in her ear.

"No," Anita said with a laugh. "I still think they kinda do, but there's room for improvement. Maybe I can give him a few pointers."

"Do you play?"

"No." Anita laughed again. "I wasn't talking about music. Hey, you're empty! So am I. Hold our spots and I'll go get us refills."

"Just straight Coke this time!" Ella yelled over the music, and Anita held a hand up to her ear as though she hadn't caught that, and retreated back to the bar, still laughing. Ella focused back on the band, trying to make out the lyrics, curious about what they were about. The music was pretty, but gritty too, and she loved the singer's gravelly, emotive voice. She closed her eyes, letting the sounds wash in and out of her ears, swaying with the rhythm.

She was in a state of bliss until someone crashed into her right shoulder, sending her sprawling, her cup falling and spilling ice all over the floor. "Hey!" she yelled, picking herself up and wincing; she'd hit her knee pretty hard. She scrambled to pick up the ice and put it back into the cup; she didn't want someone slipping and falling. A young man leaned down to help her, and she glanced at him in irritation.

"I'm sorry. I didn't mean to knock into you like that," he yelled over the music. "Some fucking idiot decided to crowd surf and kicked me right in the face—"

"It's okay," Ella said, still irritated, but not wanting to argue about it. She'd had her eyes closed anyway, which had been stupid. "Don't worry about it."

She stood, brushing her borrowed dress off and looking down at her knee, which was bleeding. She took the cup of dirty ice and held it to the scrape, knowing how stupid she must look. The band must have seen everything. She felt her cheeks flood with embarrassment.

The guy was still standing beside her. "I really am sorry," the guy said again as the band finished the song and the bar got momentarily quieter. "Can I buy you a drink to make up for it? Or run across to the pharmacy to get you a Band-Aid?"

"No, it's fine," she said, turning to look at him. She immediately regretted being irritable—this dude was the cutest guy she'd ever seen. He was just an inch or two taller than her, with curly brown hair that fell just below his ears, hidden under a blue knitted cap, dark, sapphire-blue eyes, and a full mouth, below which was a tiny patch of hair above his chin and a scruffy goatee.

"Speaking of Band-Aids...this band sure could use some aid, huh?" He gestured at the stage and waited for her to get the joke. When she chuckled, he held out a hand. "I'm Louis." Ella shook his hand and looked him over. He was wearing a brown denim jacket with a fleece hood, dark blue JNCOs, black combat boots, and a Patti Smith t-shirt. "You can call me Louie if you want, all my friends do, but if you call me 'Lou,' I'll never talk to you again."

"Sure thing, Lou."

"Okay, so you're either yanking my chain, or that was a creative way to get me to leave you alone." He grinned, craning his head toward her. "I'm a little slow on the uptake, so you might have to tell me which."

"I'm Ella," she replied, giving him a bright smile. This guy was cute, and he seemed nice, so what was the harm? She could always get Anita to rescue her if he turned out to be a creep.

"It's nice to meet you, Ella," Louie said, tipping his beer at her. "And again, I'm sorry that I tackled you. I was just joking about the band, by the way. Have you seen them play before?"

Ella glanced at the stage. One of the guitarists had broken a string, but it worked out well for her, since the lull was giving her a chance to chat up a cute guy. "No, I haven't. I'm new to Seattle; I've only been here a couple of days. You?"

"Oh yeah, more times than I can count. The drummer's my cousin. I try to come to all their shows. If I ever get my own band off the ground, I'll need them to return the favor."

"Who's your band?" she asked.

"Horsehair." He grinned. "Yes, that's really the name. Right now, it just consists of me and my friend Buster, who shows up for practice once a month and plays the shittiest bass you ever heard."

"And you?"

He looked down at his feet. "I compose and I sing…and I play guitar."

"You'll have to play for me sometime," Ella said, surprised at her own gall. Where had that come from? She didn't know this guy from Adam. And he looked older than her. But he was so cute and had the friendliest eyes. Bright and blue and piercing.

"You bet," he said with a sweet smile, and her heart gave a little flip. "Where are you from, Ella?"

"Athens, Georgia," she said, and his eyes lit up.

"Home of Pylon!" he said with a huge grin, and Ella nodded excitedly. She had never really listened to the local band, who were from before her time, though she'd die before she ever let Louie know that.

"Here's your boring-ass Coke, bitch," Anita said, pressing in on them and handing Ella a new cup. "Who's your friend?"

"Louie," he said, extending a hand, and Anita shook it, looking him over with interest.

"I've seen you here before," she said. "With Janelle, right?" Ella's heart came back down to the ground with a thud at the sound of a familiar name. "Is she here?"

"Not tonight," Louie said, swigging his beer. "She'll probably be at the show tomorrow, though."

"Who's playing tomorrow night?" Ella asked, trying not to show her disappointment. He should have disclosed that he had a girlfriend, but she supposed he hadn't done or said anything inappropriate. Still, it bugged her. Cute as he was, she shouldn't be surprised to find he was dating someone.

"Mother Love Bone Tribute," he said. "A bunch of awesome bands are opening, and then there's an actual tribute band, Stargazer, that'll cap off the night. They do it every year, raise a bunch of money for Andy Wood's charity. You should definitely come."

"I might," Ella said. It sounded like something she'd love, but she didn't want to seem too eager. Ever since Anita had shown her the glossy picture of Andy Wood, she'd had a hankering to dive deep into the band and find out more about them.

"Well, I'm definitely going," he said. "Where do you guys live? I can pick you up if you want."

"That'd be great," Anita answered for both of them. "Fucking cab fares in this city are about to kill me, and I hate taking the bus. We're at the hostel on Pike Street."

"That's only about a mile from my apartment," Louie said to Anita, but he was looking at Ella. She took another sip of her drink, noticing that Anita had managed to dump another shot in it. She was already feeling pleasantly buzzed, despite her deflated ego at the revelation that Louie had a girlfriend. She supposed this Janelle would be along for the ride tomorrow, too. Was it possible that… Oh well, it didn't matter. She was in Seattle!

"I can't wait," she said to Louie, her beaming smile genuine.

"Change of plans," Anita said, entering the little room the two of them shared and dumping her shopping bags on her bed. "I met up with an old friend this afternoon. Chris. We dated a couple of times last summer. He looked, like, *ridiculously* good. He's got a beard now, and he's been working out…" She raised her perfectly arched eyebrows. "Anyway. He's going to the show tonight, too, so I'm gonna ride with him." She winked. "Get while the getting's good, you know."

"But what about…" Ella was flustered. She'd spent all afternoon finding the perfect outfit and carefully applying her makeup, and less than an hour before Louie was set to pick them up, Anita was flaking? "That guy Louie said he'd give us a ride."

"You can just hitch with him alone. I'm sure he's cool," Anita said. "It's not a big deal. I'll just meet up with you at the bar. Okay?"

Ella slumped down on the bed. She didn't relish the prospect of riding alone in a car with Louie, cute as he was. He was still a stranger, and she'd been taught all her life not to go off with strangers. And what if he brought his girlfriend? How awkward. But she supposed it was either that or take the bus, and she didn't feel much like doing that either, dressed in her black babydoll dress, thigh-high knit socks, and Mary Janes. Ella fingered the thick velvet choker around her neck and managed a smile. "I guess. Here's hoping he's not a murderer. They still haven't caught Mia Zapata's killer, have they?" The tragic death of the Gits enigmatic frontwoman, right here in Seattle, had not missed Ella's radar back home; she'd read everything she could get her hands on about the case.

"No. I'm beginning to think they never will." Anita looked at her with a sad smile. "I think Louie's okay, though. I've seen him around a lot. And I know Janelle. I can vouch that you'll be safe."

Ella nodded, though she still felt iffy about it. "Do I look okay?"

"You look gorgeous," Anita said, rummaging through her shopping bags. "Are you going to wear your hair down like that? I like it."

Ella had pulled her dark-blonde hair out of its usual sloppy ponytail and let it fall into its naturally soft, layered waves. She'd grown it out enough from last summer's regretful "Rachel" haircut, and she was dying to put some color in it. "Thanks." She had to admit, she felt good. Grown-up and pretty for the first time. It was so nice being out from under her aunt's watchful eye.

Downstairs, Ella waited on the porch for Louie to arrive. Evan joined her, lighting up an American Spirit. "Anita said you're going to the Mother Love Bone tribute show," he said, offering her a smoke. She waved it away. "Be okay if I tag along with you?"

"This guy is picking me up," she said, relief washing over her. She'd feel a lot less nervous with a friend. "Louie. I can ask him."

A black Ford Explorer pulled up a few minutes later, with Louie behind the wheel. A beautiful girl with dark skin and glossy-looking dreads was sitting in the passenger seat. As Ella got in the car, she said, "Would it be okay if my friend came with us? He's going to the show, too."

Louie turned around to look at her, seeming surprised, but he smiled. "Yeah, no problem. Where's Anita?"

"She's riding with someone else. A date," Ella said, scooting over to make room for Evan. She buckled her seatbelt.

"I'm Janelle," the woman said, turning around to shake her hand.

Ella took her hand, hoping the girl didn't notice the tremble in hers. "I'm Ella, and this is Evan." Janelle was gorgeous with high cheekbones, beautiful dark brown eyes lined with thick black eyeliner, and full lips, the bottom studded with a silver hoop. Her hands were soft and smelled like Bath & Body Works' Sun-Ripened Raspberry. couldn't know it, but it immediately took Ella back to tenth grade, and how inadequate she'd felt next to the glamorous, more popular girls. "Thanks for picking us up, you guys. You really saved us on cab fare."

"Don't worry about it," Louie said, his eyes on the road. He fiddled with the remote on his CD changer and soon a melodic, bluesy voice filled the car. "This is my favorite Mother Love Bone song," he said, catching Ella's eyes in the rearview mirror. "Everybody else loves Crown of Thorns, but I always thought this one really showed who Andy Wood was, deep down inside."

Janelle rolled her eyes, but her laugh was friendly. "He'll write you a dissertation on Andy Wood if you let him."

Evan piped up. "I'm more into Malfunkshun, to be honest, but Mother Love Bone was solid. I can't wait to hear this tribute band. I hear they're really good."

"They remind me of the Black Crowes," Ella said, and everybody fell silent. Had she made a faux pas? She tried to recover. "I mean… obviously the Crowes ripped them off big time."

"So, I hear that you're new to Seattle by way of Georgia, Ella," Janelle said, craning around to look at her, her voice full of friendly laughter. "Which is why I'll forgive the Black Crowes thing. Are you planning on staying, or is this just a visit?"

"Staying," Ella said, then added, "that is, if I can find a job and an apartment."

"What kind of work do you do?"

"Anything? As long as it pays, and doesn't involve stripping, I'll take it." She laughed despite herself. "And that's only because I can't dance."

"We might have an opening at the store," Janelle said. "One of the girls is leaving at the end of next week, moving back to Nebraska.

I'm not sure about the hours, though. Let me check on Monday."

"Where do you work?" Ella asked casually, picking at a thread on her jacket nervously.

"Janelle runs an organic co-op," Louie explained, catching Ella's eyes in the mirror again. "How do you feel about slinging vegetables to rich hippies?"

"I'm from Athens. I've known my share of rich hippies. I lived just around the corner from Boulevard." Ella swallowed. She wasn't sure this was a good idea—for starters, what would it be like working for the girlfriend of the guy she was developing a massive crush on? But there was something else, too, about Janelle... "You own a store? I'm impressed."

"Oh no, I don't own it," Janelle said easily, dabbing on dark brown lip stain with a finger in the visor mirror. "My parents do. I grew up watching them run the shop and when I graduated from high school, I wanted to stay. They live in California part-time, but they come back for the summer every year. In the meantime, I co-run the store for them. Me and the manager, Dustin, who's been there since I was a kid." She shrugged. "I can't complain. It pays the bills and I'm able to hire my friends from time to time, help them out."

"Your parents sound cool." Ella couldn't imagine Grace and Ed owning something like an organic food co-op, much less trusting someone fresh out of high school to run the place in their absence. If only she'd grown up with parents like that, how different her life might have been.

"They're legit," Janelle said with a laugh. "Like, my mom still wears bell-bottoms. She's been rockin' the same natural hair since the sixties. They're amazing."

"They're amazing," Louie piped up, and Ella felt her belly clench with envy. "Seriously, she's downplaying it. Her parents were big-time activists in the late sixties; part of the Freedom Riders, The Black Panthers, all of that. They went up and down the east coast, protesting injustice and helping people register to vote. They knew," he said, turning to look at Janelle with pride, "MLK *and* Robert F. Kennedy."

"They didn't *know* them," Janelle corrected him. "They just met them a couple of times." She turned to look at Ella. "They *do* know Congressman John Lewis, though. Still send his office a Christmas card every year, though I don't know that he still gets them. He's a bigwig in Atlanta now." She smiled. "I suppose you've heard of him if you're from Georgia?"

"Oh, of course!" Ella exclaimed. She'd heard her uncle talk about John Lewis plenty of times; he was a local hero and had been ever since getting elected to the 5th district in Atlanta. There was a framed picture of him standing with a group of democratic judges and lawmakers from a Capital gathering a few years ago in the foyer of her aunt and uncle's house. She had been invited to go to that gathering and had declined. She'd never been particularly interested in her uncle's work, a fact which now brought her some shame. "My uncle actually knows him, too."

"Who is your uncle?" Janelle asked with interest.

"Edward Newton. He's a judge," Ella said, then added hastily, "a Democrat."

"Oh, okay," Janelle said, nonplussed. She turned back to the mirror to apply more makeup.

Ella stared at her lap, embarrassed. She felt like such a backwoods yokel around these cool, beautiful people.

"We're here," Louie said, navigating into a parking space. The street was brightly lit and sparkling with rain. "Gonna have to walk in the rain, though. At least it's just a drizzle. Sorry I couldn't get any closer." They all got out and, as they started to run toward the bar, Janelle pulled out a cigarette. Evan rushed forward to light it for her, and as the two began talking about Andy Wood's first band, Malfunkshun, Louie fell behind to walk with Ella.

"Tonight will be fun," he said, smiling at her, and the sincerity of his voice made her immediately believe it. The collar of his brown jacket was pulled up near his ears, and droplets of rain were in his curly, soft brown hair. He looked impossibly cute, and Ella felt like screaming in frustration. Why was he taken? It wasn't fair.

She glanced in front of her at the impossibly beautiful girl holding onto Evan's arm as though she'd known him her whole life, her glossy black hair shiny under the streetlights. Was it any wonder that a guy like Louie would be in love with someone who ran a co-op, knew John Lewis and looked like *that?* There was no competition at all; Janelle was a living goddess, and small-town Ella would just have to get over it.

Midway through the show, Ella retreated outside to get some air. It was still raining, but only a light drizzle, and she decided to brave it. The bar was so crowded there was hardly standing room, and with hundreds of people's body heat combined with the mingling smells of pot smoke, body odor, stale beer, and cigarettes, it was stifling. She stood near the balcony under a little alcove, trying to keep her hair from getting the brunt of the drizzle. Her breath came out in little puffs in front of her; the night was turning cold. She hadn't seen the first sign of Anita. She wondered how her impromptu date was going.

She'd spent much of the night trying not to look at her new crush. The four of them—she, Evan, Janelle and Louie—had spent the majority of the show standing together near the back, listening to the music. Evan had bought them all a round of drinks, and Janelle had gotten a little tipsy. She'd managed to part the crowd and get out into the middle of the floor, where she'd danced all by herself, totally unselfconscious, her gauzy, patterned burgundy skirt swirling around her shapely calves. Her dance movements were jerky and awkward, but it lent her an ethereal, clumsy beauty. On anyone else, it would have been ridiculous, but by the time Janelle had retreated, stumbling and laughing from the dance floor, several people were cheering her on. Then she'd pulled both Evan and Ella out onto the floor, forcing them to dance with her. Ella had tried her best, but it had resulted in mainly just swaying around Janelle like a planet orbiting the sun. When she'd become aware that Louie was standing by the stage, watching them all with an amused look on his face, she'd stopped, embarrassed, and decided to go outside.

It had been days since she left Athens. She had not called home and didn't plan to. She wasn't sure how long it would be before her rage simmered and cooled enough for her to speak to Aunt Evil again. She would call eventually. She'd have to, but it was going to take time. She loved her uncle, and she had to reluctantly admit that she missed him a little—but it was hard to face what he'd done. As for Aunt Grace, well, Ella didn't miss her much at all. So many years she'd tried to be the daughter Grace wanted, to be close to her, and for what? She was a miserable woman who pushed away happiness with both hands. Why, after all these years of misery, had they not divorced? She knew why, of course; he was a judge, his reputation dependent on having a structured, respectable family life—but the rumors had swirled about him for years. Everybody in Athens, hell—probably even the esteemed John Lewis in Atlanta knew he cheated on his wife. It seemed to Ella that cutting his losses with a quiet divorce and a handsome payout to Grace would have been a much better option for her uncle than staying married to the shrill, mean-spirited woman and banging everything that moved—especially when, as Ella now knew, some of those girls were far too young to reasonably give consent.

She'd wondered sometimes what Aunt Grace had been like before getting married. There had been times, growing up, when a flicker of the woman she must have once been would shine through; the rare occasions she'd ruffle Ella's hair with a feather-light touch; how she'd laugh during *Hee Haw,* loud and uproariously; the shy smile that showed on her face when Ed brought her flowers one Valentine's Day. But those moments were few and far between. Most of the time, Grace was a joyless, shriveled-up old prune.

"Mind if I join you?" Ella jumped, then turned to see Louie lurking by the doorway. She nodded with a smile, her stomach flipping over.

"It's raining out here," he said, stating the obvious. He shrugged off his brown corduroy jacket, revealing an Iggy Pop t-shirt underneath, and placed the jacket around her shoulders before she could protest.

"You'll be cold," she said, and he shrugged.

"Nah. I'm used to Seattle weather. You, on the other hand, look like you're about to melt into a puddle or turn into an icicle, one or the other."

"Thank you," she said awkwardly, the warm jacket enveloping her with the pleasant scent of CK One. She'd recognize it anywhere—she'd scratched off a dozen *Sassy* inserts and rubbed them on her arms over the years. She'd always wanted her own bottle and never managed to get one. When she'd asked for one a few Christmases back, her aunt had said, "Vanity is a sin, to say nothing of androgyny." Apparently, a non-gendered fragrance was the devil's work.

"What do you think of the band?" Louie asked after a moment, settling in beside her, his arms resting on the railing. The deck looked out over an expanse of the parking lot, which was empty of people and rapidly filling up with puddles. The drizzle had settled again in his hair, resting in the brown curls. Ella liked the way it made his hair almost glisten, like he was covered in silver glitter.

"I like them a lot," she said honestly, leaning on the rail, aware that their shoulders were touching. "I think I'm going to have to explore more Mother Love Bone, and Malfunkshun, too. I feel so stupid that I've never listened to them much."

"I can imagine that Athens has no shortage of good shit. I gotta tell you, I know people say they sold out, or they're too mainstream now or whatever, but I love REM's stuff, and the B-52's are solid, too, even if they are mainstream now. I love how avantgarde they are. That's one thing the grunge scene doesn't have, or doesn't anymore, now that Andy's gone. That sort of brazen, over-the-top, kitschy stuff. Camp. You need a little of that, some lightness. You know?"

"If you like the avant-garde," Ella said shyly, "you might like the Elephant Six stuff."

"I've heard of it," Louie said. "Isn't that a record label?"

"Yeah, but it's also kind of a whole movement," Ella replied, glad to have a little knowledge on the subject for once. "Several Athens bands… Elf Power, Olivia Tremor Control, and my favorite, Neutral Milk Hotel." She knew a dreamy smile had erupted on her face, but she couldn't stop it with the way Louie was staring at her. "They're amazing, really amazing. The lead singer…he's like something from another world. You'd never guess it to look at him—he's just this nerdy-looking dude with a bowl cut" —she hugged Louie's jacket to herself— "but the voice that comes out of him is like something from the heavens. The music is so weird, like a depressed circus, but he literally has the voice of an angel. And they've got a singing saw player! I've never heard anything like them."

"Have you seen them live?"

"I wish," Ella admitted. "I never got to many shows back home. Actually," she corrected herself, unable to be dishonest with Louie,

"I never got to go to any. My home life was—well, strict. That's the reason I came out here, actually."

"Well, show or no show, they sound awesome, and I can't wait for you to play them for me," Louie said with an understanding smile.

"Okay." She smiled at him, their eyes locking. He was so cute. She had to remind herself that he was off-limits. "Janelle is really nice. And wow, she's beautiful. I like her."

"Yeah, she's great." Louie laughed. "She's shitfaced, though. I've got to sober her up before she gets back in my car. I'm tired of cleaning her puke out of my seats."

Ella giggled. "I don't envy you that. How long have you guys been dating?"

Louie's eyes widened, his dark brows furrowing. "Oh, Janelle isn't my girlfriend," he said quickly. "I mean, we dated before, like a long time ago, but we broke up. We're just friends."

"Oh," Ella said, feeling her pulse quicken. "I'm sorry, I just assumed…"

"No, it's okay," he rushed to explain. "We're still really close, so I guess people assume…" He looked at her, his eyes bright. "But no… I'm single. I guess I didn't do a very good job of making that clear, huh?"

Ella shrugged. "Why should you?"

"Because I'm into *you*," he said, inching closer to her. "I thought you could tell."

"I thought maybe…" Ella's brain whirled, and she hugged the coat around herself tighter, feeling nervous. He was so close to her, his eyes so bright. "But I mean, it's Seattle, who knows…"

Louie laughed, his eyes still locked on hers. He inched just a little closer. "And this guy, Evan," he said, his voice suddenly low. "Just a friend, or more?"

"A friend, and barely that," Ella said softly. They were almost touching. She watched a drop of water fall from his brown curls and land on the bare skin of his collarbone. She swallowed. "I just met him myself two days ago." She started to add that he was bi, then decided that the information was irrelevant. Small-town Ella would have felt the need to note it, but Seattle Ella was more mature.

"I'm glad to hear that." Louie reached out and touched her hand lightly. His hand was damp from the rain, but warm. Electric shocks went through Ella's skin at the contact. "So, Ella… Can I kiss you, then?"

"Yes," she said without hesitation, swallowing hard and looking up into his dark blue eyes.

Louie leaned forward and gently pressed his lips to hers. His hand was still touching hers, and the drizzle was falling, getting steadily heavier, making her hair stick to her face. Ella didn't care. The feel of Louie's lips on hers was like nothing she'd ever experienced. She leaned into him, enjoying the way he smelled, the way his warm, soft coat felt around her shoulders, the tickle of his damp, curly hair on her face. His lips were soft and sweet, the patch of hair above his chin pleasantly prickly against her mouth. When he pulled away, Ella couldn't help but giggle.

"What?" he asked playfully, his mouth still inches from hers.

"The hair on your chin, it tickles," Ella said, leaning forward to kiss him again, surprised at her own boldness. "I like it."

"You like my flavor saver?" Louie murmured, and she erupted in giggles again.

"If you two are done sucking face," a laughing voice said behind them, "I've lost my purse and I need somebody to help me fucking find it."

Anita had arrived.

SEVEN

KASEY - 2018

KASEY was jonesing. She had picked up her phone no less than ten times with the intention of calling Caden, but every time, she'd put it back down, determined not to cave. She missed him, and she knew he was confused as to why she'd gone silent. His last text had betrayed his suspicion: *"Why don't you want me to come over? Got another guy over there?"* He'd been joking, but there was likely some real worry there, too. They'd been dating for years, and she'd never stayed away from him for more than a day or two.

Sharp chinned with pockmarked skin leftover from teen acne, mousy brown hair and crooked teeth, coming in at 5'9" even in the thick-soled work boots that seemed too big for his feet, at face value Caden wouldn't be considered a catch, but he had a certain something…a playful, cocky swagger backed by genuine good-old-boy charm that coasted him through. It didn't hurt that his skin was tanned, his arms and chest taut and muscular from working out in the sun, and that his smile, while crooked, was bright and real. The old Kasey—popular, on-trend high school Kasey—never would have guessed that Caden, who had been a full-on prep in pastel polo shirts and slide-on loafers, would have turned into a full-on *ag boy*, nor that she would have ever found it attractive. Then, she'd been the type to spend a full hour in the bathroom contouring and following makeup tutorials on YouTube. Now she wasn't sure if she still owned a tube of mascara. They had both changed so much.

In many different ways, and many of them not good.

Was it bad, Kasey wondered, idly twirling her cheap birthstone necklace between a thumb and forefinger, that she'd almost rather have Caden worry she was cheating than tell him the truth? She had no idea how to begin. *Caden, I'm trying to get clean. I want to reclaim my life.* She knew it was understandable, admirable even— but Caden was an addict too, and her sobriety was tied up in his. It could be a make-or-break for their relationship. Either Caden would be forced to try and get clean too, a thing he might succeed at, but might fail—or, if he wasn't ready, they would be forced to break up. She could hear his coaxing tones, knew exactly what he'd say: "I'll keep it away from you, I'll make sure it's never around"—and he'd mean it sincerely. But just the knowledge that he *had* them, could get them, would be enough to throw her right off the wagon. Even now, as she sat in the easy chair in the living room, waiting for Ricky to get home, she could feel a deep pain starting to throb in her hip. Her stomach was queasy and acid crept up her throat. She was sweaty, too. She wondered momentarily if she was getting the flu, but she knew, deep down, that it was the pain she'd been living with for the past six years—just uncloaked.

It was bullshit, was what it was. The more she thought about it clear-headed, the angrier she felt. After her accident, her doctors had all but shoved opioids down her throat; she'd never been asked which ones she'd prefer to take, or if she wanted to take them at all.

Her doctors just assumed that she'd need them, that without pain management, the agony of recovery would be unbearable. Kasey was grateful that she'd had access to medication that made her life somewhat more manageable back then—as if there was anything about having a shattered body and a dead best friend that could be *managed*—but she wished she had been told then how excruciating it would be to come back down. Perhaps knowing what to expect would have made it more bearable. If only someone would have told her naïve sixteen-year-old self that after a year or two, the doctors would unceremoniously abandon her treatment, leaving her to her own pitifully equipped devices, expecting her to wean herself off strong, addictive medication on her own, with no support or care, before her body had even fully healed. No warning given, just: you're done.

Kasey would never forget the day she'd gone to the pharmacy inside Kroger, holding her tattered script in her hand, and approached the consultation window, presenting the slip of paper to the tired-and-bored looking pharmacist. The woman had held the paper in front of her, tapped a few keys on her computer, then pushed the script back to Kasey, never once meeting her eyes.

"Sorry," she'd said. "There's no more refills on this."

"What?" Kasey had been confused. "Of course there is. He always writes the prescription for two refills, because I don't go for regular appointments anymore."

"The refill you got…let's see…two weeks ago, was the last one," the pharmacist said, "I'm sorry ma'am. I can't help you."

"Call my doctor, then," Kasey had insisted. "There's a mistake, obviously. He'll tell you to refill it or have his receptionist call in another prescription. He's done that once or twice before."

"I'm sorry," the pharmacist repeated, her voice growing firm, irritation evident on her face. "We can't just call in scripts for opioids. You'll have to go in and see the doctor for that. Get a written prescription."

"But why?" Kasey was confused. Her hip was screaming blue murder. "This *is* a written prescription." She pushed the paper back toward the pharmacist, who didn't bother to take it.

"This is expired. You need a new one. People commit fraud, fake scripts, scam the system." The pharmacist lowered her voice and smirked. "You could be drug-seeking." She was looking at her like she was an idiot. A woman standing behind her, with a huge buggy of groceries, made a "harrumph" noise, and Kasey's face burned with embarrassment and anger.

Drug-seeking. Kasey had left the pharmacy after going several more rounds with the rude pharmacist, tears rolling down her face, her fists clenched tightly at her sides. All she'd tried to do was fill the same prescription her doctor had been writing for her for over two years now. He'd made a brief mention at her last appointment of wanting to wean her off the pain meds, but he'd never told her to ration them or that he was scaling back her prescription, much less that he was cutting her off cold turkey. He'd thrown her into the deep end without so much as a lifejacket. When she'd called him, he had been apologetic, but firm. "You're healing nicely," he'd said in an overly patient voice, one she knew he reserved for trying patients. "Come in and I'll write you a short script, but you'll need to start rationing them. Get some Tylenol 3s to help in the meantime."

"Don't you think you should have told me you were stopping my medication, given me some kind of warning?" she'd demanded through her tears, her leg throbbing.

"I'm certain that I did, Kasey," he'd said in a calm, logical voice. Kasey knew he hadn't, but what good would it do to argue with a doctor?

The doc had no free appointments for another two weeks, and Kasey had suffered in agonizing pain, until then. Tylenol 3s did nothing. Caden, unable to bear seeing her in so much pain, had called a friend who moonlighted selling Percocets. He'd bought her a handful, and she'd broken down and taken them. By the time she saw the doctor, and he'd written her a measly script for less than half the usual dosage of pain meds, shrugging with apology, she'd resigned herself to not going back. She could get the medication she needed on her own, without the shaming pharmacy and the doctor who had set her up for this drug dependency and then unceremoniously abandoned her to it. Screw 'em. Kasey would take care of herself.

And she had, with Caden's help, up until recently. But now she needed a change. She knew it wasn't fair that the doctor had done her dirty, or that the people in her life, even Fallon and Ricky, who knew the pain she was constantly in, judged her dependency and looked at her like she was a useless addict. It wasn't fair at all... but they weren't the reason that Kasey was ready to make some changes. She wasn't doing it for them.

Ignoring the constant pain in her legs, that old, nagging friend, she'd dragged the box down from the attic and it was now sitting open in front of her by her feet. When she'd talked to Ricky earlier, he'd told her to wait for him, that he'd grab a couple of pizzas from Little Caesars and they'd go through the contents together. He was already half an hour late, though. Kasey couldn't fault him; he had texted to say that a customer had come in at the last minute needing an oil change, and he couldn't turn down an easy fifty bucks. She got it, but damn, she was itching to go through the stuff. If nothing else, for the distraction it would offer.

She grabbed the tattered copy of *Sassy* magazine off the side table and flipped through it absently; it was one of the things she'd found in the box of her mother's stuff. She'd already read it cover to cover twice, but she couldn't stop looking at the thing. This edition, from April 1992, boasted a sex survey and featured two cover models: Kurt Cobain and Courtney Love, both fresh-faced with messy hair, beautiful and impossibly tragic all at once. The way Kurt's eyes met the camera, slightly mistrustful, made Kasey feel sad. The caption, in a quirky, lowercase font, read "Ain't Love Grand?"

"Yep, fucking grand," Kasey muttered to herself, peering at the feature article again. God, Kurt Cobain had been hot as hell with fuchsia hair. Who knew? Frustrated, she threw the magazine down and stared at the clock.

She was willing to bet money that Ricky had emailed her mother. He didn't talk about it much, but he had contact with her. Kasey knew from snooping that Ricky emailed her every couple of months, just to give updates on how the girls were doing. He always sugar-coated Kasey's life, telling her mother all about how

Kasey was working, how she and Caden were so happy together, how Kasey's injuries were giving her much less pain these days. He never mentioned the pills, how dependent she was on them, or how she often stubbornly refused to use her wheelchair or her cane on bad days. He never told her about Kasey jumping from job to job or how Caden practically lived at their house, or how she sponged off everyone for her cigarettes and barely ate and had no friends left.

From what she could see, her mother rarely wrote back. She'd seen only two emails from her in Ricky's inbox in the past eight months. One had been a simple smiley face, obviously fired off quickly from her phone, and the second had been a Bible verse, some maudlin crap that Kasey couldn't quite remember, about men and their families. She supposed it was her mother's way of praising Ricky for all he was doing in her absence. In her abandonment. Throwing him scraps.

She wondered if her mother would respond to the email Ricky had undoubtedly sent. "Kasey's found the box of stuff you left behind," she imagined the email saying, "And she has questions. Come home and answer them." No, Ricky wouldn't be that firm, that commanding. He never talked to her mother that way, and issuing orders would do no good. Mom did what she wanted— always had, always would. And she spooked worse than a horse in a thunderstorm.

Unable to wait any longer, Kasey reached into the box and rummaged. Folded in among the silky vintage dresses was a hat she hadn't paid much attention to the first go-round. She pulled it out, running her fingers along the felt, admiring the olive-green hue so

193

synonymous with the military. It was clean, unbothered by moths or cobwebs, and emblazoned with a couple of shining pins and medals. Kasey had no idea what any of them meant. She supposed it must have come from Vietnam; it had that sort of look about it. And everything else in the box was from that era, so it made sense. She turned the hat over, looking at the inside, hoping to find a stray hair or perhaps something tucked inside, some kind of clue, but there was nothing. Then, just as she moved to put the hat back, her finger caught on something metal inside the brim. She pushed at the top of the hat with her fingers, forcing the stiff inner material outward, and found a tiny pin attached to the inside of the brim. It took her a minute to get the clasp undone, as it had been pinned to the hat for so long, but finally she forced the rusted metal free and managed to get the pin loose without pricking herself. She held the shiny metal up to the light and scanned the letters there, reading them aloud.

"Private Landrum Walton," she read, liking the feel of the name in her mouth. Landrum. That was a pretty cool, old-fashioned name. "Now who on earth are you?"

"Ella's daddy," a voice said behind her, and she turned to see Ricky hovering in the doorway, a cardboard pizza box in his hands. "I couldn't remember his name when you asked me, but hearing you say it aloud... Yep, that was him."

"My grandfather," Kasey said, holding the hat in her hands like a precious jewel. "My grandfather fought in Vietnam?"

"Sure did. Was a P.O.W., too."

"Did Mom tell you that?"

Ricky laughed. "Shoot, no. She never said much of nothin'

about 'em. I think it was your great aunt Grace who told me that once, at some family reunion or something." He grimaced. "She was a miserable old bat, Grace, wasn't she? I remember her telling me that like it was something to be ashamed of, him bein' captured. She was implying he was weak. I always remembered it 'cause that right offended me; I seen enough of folks mockin' P.O.W.s just lately."

Kasey wrinkled her nose. Great Aunt Grace had been dead for almost ten years, and uncle Ed years before her—he'd died of a heart attack when she was two years old, so she had no memories of him at all—but she'd never forget the old woman who had lived alone in a huge house near Boulevard. Just before her death, Mama would drag her and Fallon, in their best Sunday dresses, to go and sing songs to the old woman. Aunt Grace had been hateful and dissatisfied with everything and had always yelled at the girls when she wasn't busy yelling out commands at her mother. She had a dish of buttermints in the foyer that nobody was allowed to touch. Once Kasey had dared to sneak one, and she'd gotten her hand lashed with a fly swatter for her troubles. "Was Landrum Aunt Grace's brother?"

Ricky sat the pizza box down and frowned as he settled into a chair. "Gosh, I wish your mama was here to tell you. Lemme see…um… No, your aunt Grace isn't your aunt by blood. She was married to your uncle Ed, who was your grandmother's brother. Now shoot if I can't remember your grandmother's name. And your mama never talked about any of 'em. Other than Ed and Grace, of course, and things between them were…strained."

"And now they're all dead," Kasey said glumly, staring at the hat. "How did they die, anyway? Mama never said." She knew her mother's parents had died when she was a baby, but she'd never heard how. Once she'd worked up the courage to ask her mother when she was ten or so. In response, she'd been given a ferocious, "It doesn't matter, now don't ask about it again." And she never had.

"She never told me outright," Ricky admitted, cracking open a beer and selecting a slice of pizza. He'd gotten mushroom, pineapple, and onion, her favorite. Kasey felt a surge of love for him, this man who had taken her in even though she wasn't his and continued to care for her even after her mother had split, who ordered her favorite pizza even when nobody else in the house—and probably the world—would eat such a concoction. "With your grandmother, it was an accident, but that's all I know."

"Like a car accident?" she asked, grabbing a slice for herself, suppressing a shudder at the thought. Her leg pinged with a sympathy pain. "I'm guessing my grandfather died in the war?"

Ricky shook his head. "Nope. He was captured and M.I.A. for a while, but if I remember right from what Grace said, he came back stateside in '69. But he wasn't quite right after that. Who would be, I reckon."

"That sucks," Kasey said. Her poor grandfather. "So, he came home, and they pretty much shacked up immediately, I guess."

"That's the way it usually goes," Ricky said with a chuckle. "Ain't you heard of the Baby Boomers? But yeah, they were together a while before your mama was born—that was in '75. After that, I got no idea. And your great uncle Ed was around for a lot of years—he and Grace raised your mama." He chewed thoughtfully, then swallowed. "Though he died a lot of years before Grace did."

Kasey chewed her own pizza, thinking, staring down at the hat mixed in with the gauzy, brightly colored dresses.

"Speaking of your mom and all of this," Ricky said, his face brightening, "I took that business card you gave me to work and asked about it. I found out that a man used to work there years ago, back in the sixties. His name was Guy Newton. Now, I reckon that was your mom's uncle. Ain't that a neat coincidence? Me and him working in the same spot, fifty years apart?"

Kasey nodded, though to her, it felt more eerie than neat.

"Are you sure you should be focusing on this right now?" Ricky asked her, noting her expression, and she looked up, surprised.

"Why shouldn't I?"

"If you mean what you said about quitting the" —he gestured, miming opening a bottle of pills, reluctant to speak it aloud— "it seems like digging into the past, a past that was real painful for your mama, might make it hard for you to uh…you know, stay on the…"

"Finding this stuff helped me decide," Kasey said, touched by his concern. "I realized I had a whole life out there, maybe even some family, and I thought about what it might be like to meet them. She hoped admitting that wouldn't hurt Ricky's feelings, hoped he would understand. "I think having this to focus on might actually help me, if you can believe it." To her horror, tears welled up in her eyes. "If you can believe a word I say, after everything I've put you through over the years."

"Don't you start that," Ricky said gruffly. "Just see that you mean it, Kasey, that's all I ask. You've always got a home here, unconditionally. If I kick you in the ass from time to time, it's only because I'm trying to see you succeed, to do better. But I'm your dad and I'll always be your dad, no matter who you find out there in the big wide world, and no matter how much you fuck up, got it?"

Kasey wiped at her eye. She had needed to hear that; wished she could have allowed herself to hear it years ago. "Thank you."

"And hey, it ain't just the pills that's the problem," Ricky said. "You take too many of 'em, but I know it's because you're in pain, and I know you didn't have no say in takin' 'em in the first place. But if you ask me, it's not the medication that's the main problem. It's you, bein' too stubborn to use your cane, choosing crappy paying jobs where you're always on your feet, and wasting too much time lazing around with that boy. I'd love to see you get back in school or find a job that actually challenges you. I get that you want to ease off the meds, but Kasey… It won't amount to a hill of beans if you don't change the rest of the stuff in your head, you know?"

"I know," she said in a small voice. Ricky was right. "I'm working on it." She almost bit her tongue, but the words came out in a flood. "You could stop drinking, you know. It's a crutch of its own, isn't it?"

"You're right," Ricky said quickly, staring her straight in the eye. "You're absolutely right. Why don't I see what I can do about that? Why don't we have us a little deal?"

Kasey stared at him in surprise.

"It might be hard, but I'll give it my best try," Ricky assured her. "As for you… It's only been a few days," he said. "You're not in the clear. I feel like you could use some help. There's a place nearby… I researched the prices on my lunch break. I could send you—"

She was a little hurt, but also oddly touched. "Let's see how I do on my own first," she said with a nervous laugh. "And we'll cross that bridge when we get to it."

The doorbell rang, and she looked at Ricky quizzically. "Is it the police? Or my doctor?" she asked with a hollow laugh. "You had them on standby?"

Ricky laughed and shook his head, craning his neck and looking out the window. "I'm not quite ready to send you off yet. Looks like it's Caden," he said. "Since when did he ever ring the doorbell? He usually just lets himself in. Half the time through the window."

"I haven't talked to him for a couple of days," Kasey admitted, looking down at her feet. "I think he's worried."

"You haven't told him about…"

"Not yet," Kasey said. "Was trying to figure out how to."

"Wow," Ricky said. "You *are* serious, then." He stood, grabbing his beer and another slice of pizza from the carton. "I'll head on upstairs and watch TV," he said. "Let you sort that out. After I pour this down the sink."

Kasey smiled at her stepfather's retreating back. She knew Ricky had always liked Caden, though he was wary about the two of them together, and for good reason. While Fallon treated Caden like a roach she'd like to squish, Ricky was always nice to him. She thought that deep down, he hoped the two of them would straighten themselves out before settling in too deep. To Kasey, that possibility seemed like something light-years away, if it was even possible at all. She had friends she'd gone to high school with who were already getting married, having kids—Caden's sister was only twenty-one and already had two of her own—but Kasey could barely take care of herself, much less anyone else.

She sighed and stood up to answer the door. No use putting it off. Caden was here and wouldn't be going anywhere until she gave him some answers.

She let him in silently, and he followed her into the living room. His hands were shoved down in the pockets of his jeans, which were tucked into his work boots. He was wearing a black and red flannel that was rolled up at the forearms, and a black beanie. He must have just come off the job. He looked flushed and out of breath, and she wondered if that was from a hard day's work, or something else.

"Hey," she said absently, plopping back down on the couch, gesturing to the pizza box. "Ricky brought dinner if you want some."

"Not hungry," he said, still standing, looking at her.

"You gonna sit down?"

"Do you want me to?"

"I asked, didn't I?" Kasey said. "Are you okay? You look upset."

"You haven't talked to me hardly at all in days," Caden said, his brows furrowing. "You've been blowing me off. I heard you lost your job. I went by to get smokes and asked where you were and your boss told me. I felt like a fuckin' idiot; you'd think I'd know when my own girlfriend got fired. But you've been making excuses not to see me and rushing me off the phone for a week." His cheeks were red. "What's going on, Kace? You seein' somebody else?"

"Of course not!" Kasey knew he was serious, but she had to laugh. "Like I could get away with something like that in this town. Somebody would race to tell you within five minutes."

"You score big or something and don't want to share, then?"

"No. Definitely not," she said quietly.

"Then why are you avoiding me?"

"There is a reason," she said, feeling her stomach flip-flop. "And it's not your fault, doesn't have anything to do with you, really." She swallowed. "The truth is, I'm trying to wean myself off the pills. See if I can go without them. It's only been a few days, but I was afraid if I saw you, I'd..." She trailed off, wringing her hands. "...cave."

His eyebrows raised. "Are you for real?"

"Yes," Kasey said. "I haven't had one in close to a week."

"Damn." Caden sat up, surprise etched on his face. "We've been dating what, four years? And this entire time you've been—"

"I know," she said. "I can't do it anymore, Caden. If I keep this up, I'm gonna die." She rubbed at her painful shoulder absently. "At first I needed them, and the way the doctor threw me to the wolves and I was in so much pain..." She swallowed. "But it stopped being about pain management a long time ago, and we both know that. I've got to try. I hope you can understand that."

"Of course I understand it," he said, his face breaking into a smile. He was suddenly that boy again, the one who had come to her hospital room every day and sat there holding her hand, ignoring the ribbing from her parents about his long hair, his baggy jeans. The boy who had played her Foo Fighters acoustic 'Everlong' as she lay in her bed, hurting, because he knew it helped her fall asleep. Kasey's heart clenched. "Shit, Kace, that's great. I'm really proud of you. You're a fuck of a lot stronger than I am, just deciding like that. Hell, I always said I'd quit at some point or another, but I guess

I was waiting for some sign from the heavens or something to *make* me quit. I never thought I was strong enough to just say, 'fuck it, I'm done', but look at you... You've gone and done it. That's awesome, Kasey. Really awesome." He came over to the couch and took her in his arms, enveloping her in a warm hug.

Kasey hugged him back, breathing in the familiar smell of cigarette smoke on his jacket and the deodorant spray he wore, her heart filling with love and gratitude. "Thanks. I guess I'm a little surprised, too. I thought you might...be mad."

"Fuck no." Caden pulled back and kissed her on the cheek. She was shocked to find his eyes were bright with tears. "I'm crazy fucking proud of you. And you know what? We'll kick 'em together. If you're done, so am I."

"It might not be that easy—"

"If you can do it, why can't I?" he answered. "You had a damn good reason for getting on the things in the first place. That accident... God, they practically had to glue you back together piece by piece. You had real pain. Me, I was just doing the shit for fun. I can kick it."

Kasey hoped he was right, but she wondered. She smiled and squeezed his shoulder. "Only if you really want to. It's going to be hard. For both of us. Don't let me make the decision for you, Caden."

"Nope, it's my decision," he said, brushing her hair back from her face. "It's worth it if it means it helps *you*. You're everything to me, Kasey. Always have been. I love you." His face was bright and hopeful. "Maybe this can be a fresh start for us both, get our lives back on track, and start looking toward the future."

"I hope so," she said, and as he pulled her into another hug, her eyes caught on the cardboard box full of her mother's discarded past.

"What's that stuff?" he asked, catching her glance.

"Just some crap of my mom's bound for the attic," she said, kissing him on the lips, not sure why she didn't want to tell him. "Nothing important."

EIGHT

BOBBI - 1967

BOBBI made her way through the heavy throng of people gathered on the steps in front of the Arch, most of them holding signs and placards, and onto the expanse of lawn that comprised UGA's campus. She put a hand over her eyebrows, squinting in the late sun, looking for Amelia, who was nowhere to be found. It was already half-past five, and the sun would start going down soon. They were supposed to meet Landrum and Sam at dusk out by the Greenway. Instead, Amelia appeared to have run off.

It wouldn't be the first time, Bobbi thought to herself bitterly, rummaging through her handbag for a pot of gloss to dab on her lips, which were dry from being outside all afternoon; it was unseasonably cold for October. Her friend was always disappearing on her these days. The weather felt more like a drab day in January, the day after a snowfall, somehow both damp and dry. She pulled her black tweed jacket around herself tighter and cursed herself for wearing an A-line dress and tights. She loved the olive-green polyester number that hugged her frame in just the right places, and so did Landrum, but it itched her skin, and her feet were screaming in pain after standing on the steps for the past two hours. In Amelia's absence, she'd done all the work.

Even as she complained inwardly of her aches and pains and dry lips, to say nothing of her missing friend, who was more than likely flirting with some guy, Bobbi was glad she had come. This was her third draft protest, and every time she left one, she felt more energized, hopeful, and inspired. She was certain the tides were ready to turn, that LBJ would reverse the awful draft. Public opinion of Vietnam had been steadily declining over the past few years, and things had hit a fever pitch this past year. With Julian Bond and other legislators kicking up a fuss in the Georgia House of Representatives, and guys like dear Bobby Kennedy becoming more outspoken in their opposition to the war in Washington, it seemed a foregone conclusion that something had to give, and soon. The newspapers said that LBJ was considering pulling troops out of the Asian country, and Bobbi prayed every night that he would.

Julian Bond and Lester Maddox, being seated earlier in the year, had invigorated the young and disenfranchised people of Georgia; every day they attended rallies, marches, and political meetings to organize with renewed energy and hope. Bobbi was among those who had renewed faith that these young, impassioned, moral men and women would lead the way and they might just all make it to the "promised land" that the handsome, enigmatic MLK, Jr., who she and her father had argued so fervently over, liked to talk about.

Still, she lived in fear of the men she loved being shipped overseas to spill blood for what she knew in her heart was an immoral war. Since he was pushing thirty, Ed might be able to dodge it, especially considering his status as an in-demand lawyer, but Guy, in his early twenties, was young enough, and Landrum would be considered a prime candidate—just-turned-eighteen, able-bodied, and almost out of high school. Every time the draft came up, Bobbi held her breath, hoping against hope he wouldn't be called up. Landrum was cavalier about it. "Don't worry, hon, I'm colorblind," he'd said to her once with a chuckle. Another time, "Oh, forget it. I inherited the crazy from my mama's side. They don't want me." But she knew he was putting on a brave face for her. Landrum *had* to be, like every other man in the United States under twenty-seven, utterly terrified.

Landrum had not come with her today. "You want me to avoid the draft? Seems like the least I can do is not show my face anywhere that draws attention to it," he'd joked, but there was a grain of truth to it. Bobbi agreed that he probably *shouldn't* come, though she knew he felt bad about not doing his part for the anti-war effort. She was content to show up for the both of them. And bless his heart, Landrum had been planning the dinner picnic at the Oconee River for the past week and a half as a reward for all the hard work she'd been doing, both at school and in her free time. She'd been cramming like mad for the SATs, desperate to get as perfect a score as she possibly could, and the test had finally come and gone yesterday. She'd barely had time to rest, because she'd been immediately back to work, making signs and placards for the protest.

Tired though she was, it felt good to be useful, to work hard. It kept Bobbi's mind from the increasing loneliness in the house she shared with her brothers, both of whom were always gone, and the emptiness she felt without her father. Though it had been a month, the grief had not lessened. She'd been out to visit Granny and Papaw twice, but things were bad there…it was as though her robust, lively grandparents had shrunken into themselves overnight. They had barely even got up off the couch at her last visit, and there had been no hot lunch on the table, nor to-go bag like usual. Bobbi had overheard Ed talking to her uncle on the phone, in murmured tones, about what to do about them.

Bobbi often woke up crying after dreadful nightmares that both her parents were dying. Sometimes she dreamed they were on the Broad River Bridge, shot by a lone gunman. Other times they were both in hospital beds, dried up with tubes sticking out, dying slow, agonizing deaths. No matter the outcome, she always woke up sobbing, her hair clinging to her sweaty face. Often, she would roll over into the comfort of Landrum's waiting arms and cry herself back to sleep.

Most nights, Landrum would sneak into the house after her brother Guy was asleep to be with her. It was improper, and both families would hit the roof if they knew they had begun a sexual relationship, that the two unmarried teens shared a bed more often than not. But for Bobbi, it was more about comfort, safety. She just needed to be able to sleep, and she couldn't do it alone. The grief and the terror were too great. She needed Landrum's dependable warmth, his sweet arms around her, to lull her to comfort. She knew, without him having to say it, that she was comforting Landrum, too. Together, they found safety and security that they no longer felt within their families. They had each other, and that was all they needed.

Though it was true, Bobbi thought to herself, a ghost of a smile on her lips as she walked among the trees, her tall boots sinking into the soft grass, that she and Landrum had an amazing physical connection, one that spoke a lot louder than any safety or security did. Maybe it *was* improper, but Bobbi didn't care. When Landrum touched her, her whole body erupted in electric shocks. They'd been dating for over a month, and she still hadn't tired of his kisses; she was addicted to the way they began tender and turned rough, then gave way to his hands on her skin, making every cell of her body come alive. Bobbi was already in love with Landrum; she had been from the onset. Amelia told her she was moving too fast, but Bobbi knew in her heart he was the one—it wasn't like she'd just picked him up off the street a month ago. She'd known him her entire life. She knew him inside and out, and he knew her, too. What they had was lightning in a bottle; the kind of love that didn't just happen every day to anyone. What they had was *special.*

Bobbi glanced at her watch, irritated. Landrum and Sam were undoubtedly already at the river, spreading out their blankets by the riverbed, putting out the lemonade and sandwiches and cookies she knew Landrum had prepared. She'd offered to help that morning, and he'd swatted her hand and said agreeably, "Nope, you ain't lifting a finger. But don't worry, my mama helped me with the cookies." She wondered what treats Sam had in store for Amelia. Things had cooled between the two of them, and Bobbi suspected Amelia was getting ready to flee, if her constant flirting with other boys and flaking out on plans was any indication. Bobbi wondered if she just wasn't saying because she didn't want to hurt Bobbi's feelings. The four of them had turned into a happy little group in the past month, and she figured Amelia probably felt guilty about abandoning it.

Finally, she spotted Amelia off near a large magnolia tree, clipboard pressed to her chest, a pen tucked behind her ear, talking to a young man in a dark navy-blue suit. This conversation was definitely not a flirtation. Amelia's face was red and impassioned, and as Bobbi approached, she could tell that her best friend was angry. The young man was leaning up against the tree as if he owned it, a bemused expression on his pale face.

"Julian Bond is right—the draft is inhumane," Amelia was saying furiously. "I don't care what that crooked Lester Maddox has to say about it. They can fight that among themselves all day long at the Capitol for all I care. What I *do* care about are our boys right here at UGA. Good, kind, smart boys just trying to get an education at a fine college, trying to take charge of their futures. Boys who just want to start families and have careers. Why should they go off to fight in some immoral war and come home in a box because some rich bigwig in Washington—"

"This your friend?" the man said to Bobbi as he saw her approach, still smirking. "You might want to get her in hand. She's gotten herself all worked up." He reached out and cuffed Amelia under the chin. "That time of the month, doll?"

Bobbi shot him a withering, disgusted look, then wrenched Amelia away before the smarmy man's chin bore the brunt of Amelia's anger. "Come on, we're late for the picnic. The guys are waiting," she whispered.

"Did you hear that—" Amelia sputtered, her face red. "The

nerve of him. Bobbi, I swear —"

"Oh, I heard him," Bobbi said evenly, leading her friend to where her car was parked on Broad Street. "They're a dime a dozen, all of them the same. They show up in their pressed little suits and their perfectly pomaded hair and they stand around looking bored and wait for someone to start talking to them, and then they say things to get us all riled up. Then they wait for somebody to come along and take a photo, and the next thing you know, your picture is in the paper under a headline about aggressive, rowdy anti-war activists who don't know how to be polite." She opened the door for Amelia, who got in angrily and slammed it in response. She got into the driver's side and smiled at her friend. "They do it to me all the time. You've just got to stay calm. Don't engage them if it's not worth it, and for God's sake, just smile. If you can't think of a good retort, or you're so angry you might punch someone, just stand there and smile."

"Stand there and smile," Amelia said sullenly, looking at her lap. "Stand there and fucking *smile.*" Her chin jutted out in fury. "Aren't you tired of being told to smile, Bobbi?"

"Yes," Bobbi said sympathetically, backing out onto the street and heading toward North Avenue. "Of course I am. It's hard for me, too. But that's what they all say to do—all the peace activists, every last one of them, they say to take the path of least violence, to remain calm, to stay peaceful and silent. Don't ever let them egg you on. It's not worth it."

"I know you love your MLK and your John Lewis and everything," Amelia said with a grimace. "And I do, too, but sometimes I can't help but wonder if those cats at the SNCC don't have the better idea. I think we need to be angry, get loud, and start demanding some action. Not just about the draft, but about everything else, too. Things are just getting worse, aren't they, Bobbi?"

"I suppose they are." Bobbi had no choice but to agree. Deep down inside, she was just as angry as Amelia was, but the fear ran stronger. The fear kept her cautious. "Remember that the repercussions of us losing our heads often get taken out on our Black friends and neighbors, and not us. That's why we've got to stay calm and cool. We lose our tempers, and our friends bear the brunt."

"I know, I know. But how long are we supposed to just smile in the face of injustice?" Amelia demanded, and Bobbi had no answer. In her rearview, she could see two police cars pulling in where they'd just left. They'd just managed to miss them; good. They didn't need a kerfuffle today.

Amelia was still fuming as they pulled into the parking space under the little canopy of trees by the Greenway, a popular walking and bike trail about a mile from campus. This time of year, it was usually deserted, especially in the evenings, with affluent college students citing fear of the people living in the nearby community. What they didn't say, but was implied, was that the people who lived on the surrounding streets were largely Black, and they didn't feel safe among them at night. Bobbi and Landrum had come here together several times since they'd been dating, and it had quickly become a refuge for her. She loved to walk along the river, listening to the moving water and the leaves crunching beneath her feet.

Landrum's truck was parked nearby, but the boys were nowhere to be found. Bobbi and Amelia exited the car and walked toward where the picnic tables were. "They must have gone off walking since we were late," Bobbi assumed. "Should we sit here and wait?"

Amelia still hadn't gotten over her anger. Her face was red as she sat down absently at a table. "Do you know what that annoying jerk told me?"

"Who?"

"The guy back at the Arch, the one you dragged me away from." Amelia leaned forward, her green eyes flashing. "He was crowing about next year's election, saying that the White House will be under a Republican again before we know it. He claimed to know who was running on the Democratic ticket, and he said he doesn't have a shot in hell of winning."

"Who'd he think was running?" Bobbi asked. "Herbert Humphrey, I suppose. Everybody says he's running. Or McCarthy."

"Nope," Amelia said, her eyes flashing with sudden playfulness rather than anger. "You'll like this one. He reckons it's Robert F. Kennedy."

Bobbi stared at her dubiously. "Bobby for President? I mean, there've been rumors, but he's always insisted he didn't want..."

Amelia shrugged. "I think it's kinda plausible, actually. He *is* a Kennedy, after all."

Before Bobbi could counter, a flash of white caught her eye, and she heard a twig snapping in the distance. "What was that?" she whispered, whirling to Amelia. "Is someone in the woods?"

"I heard footsteps," Amelia whispered back, looking frightened. "I think there's a guy out there. Maybe we should go back to the car."

Before they had a chance to get up, two figures came running out of the woods toward them at full speed. Bobbi screamed and jumped up, and Amelia followed suit. As they moved to dash to the car, one of the figures grabbed Bobbi around the waist.

"Gotcha!" he exclaimed, and Bobbi wrenched her arms, trying to free herself and elbow the person in the ribs, when she realized she recognized the voice.

"Landrum, you creep!" His arms immediately released her, and she realized he was laughing. She whirled around angrily to see his hat pulled down low over his face, Sam beside him. Both were laughing hysterically.

"What on earth?" she exclaimed angrily. "What the hell, Landrum? You two are out here traipsing in the woods, trying to scare us? We thought we were about to be kidnapped and raped!"

"Hey now," Landrum said, giving her a sheepish grin. "We weren't trying to scare y'all *that* bad. You were just late, and we thought it'd be funny…"

"It's okay," Bobbi said, feeling embarrassed at overreacting. "Still, that was mean. You can't scare two women like that out in the middle of nowhere! You should've known what we'd think!"

"I didn't think, Bobbi," he said, looking embarrassed himself. "We just thought we'd have some fun."

Bobbi leaned forward, mollified, to give him a kiss. "I forgive you. This time."

"Yeah, well, *I* don't," Amelia said, pouting. She fixed a pointed, angry stare on Sam, who looked chagrined. "After where we just were…all those counter-protestors…"

Landrum still had a funny expression on his face. "I'm sorry, y'all," he said in a small voice. "I didn't even think about… Shit. I'm sorry."

"I guess we've got to start thinking about stuff like that, I guess," Sam said thoughtfully. "The world isn't the same as it was, and we're not kids anymore, huh?"

"No," Amelia said glumly, linking her arm through his, her face grim. "We aren't."

Bobbi pulled up at her house around ten o'clock, glad to see her brother Guy's car in the drive. Both he and Ed worked so late these days, she barely got to see either of them. She smiled as she watched Landrum's truck pull into the drive next door and blew him a kiss as she walked into the house. He'd be sneaking into her room in a couple of hours, as they had pre-arranged, but she still felt the need to bid him a good night.

The house was dark as she let herself in, barring one light in the kitchen. She put her purse down on the hall table and followed the smell of tomato sauce. Her brother Guy was sitting at the kitchen table, a piece of paper folded out in front of him, a largely untouched plate of canned spaghetti sitting beside him.

"Ed here?" she asked as she came into the room.

"No," Guy said. "He took some flowers over to Grace's. They got in a fuss and he wanted to make it up with her before she went to bed. You know how that goes."

"Ugh." The less said about her brother's tumultuous relationship with Grace, the better. "Any of that left?" she asked, sitting across from him and pulling off her jacket. "I haven't eaten since breakfast and I'm starving." After the boys had scared her and Amelia in the woods, it had started to rain, and none of them had felt hungry after the joke that had gone awry. The four of them had loaded into their cars and headed toward Allen's, but the line was out the door. Tired and hungry, they'd all decided to go home. It just hadn't been their day.

"It's just Chef Boyardee," Guy said, pushing the plate toward her. "There was only the one can, but I'm not hungry. If you want to reheat it, you can have it."

"What's that?" Bobbi asked, gesturing toward the piece of paper with a sigh, assuming it was a bill. Guy made decent money at the garage, and Ed made good money, but it still hurt her heart to see her two older brothers paying all the family's bills. It seemed so wrong to her, both of her parents dead and everything falling into her brothers' hands. She couldn't wait to get a job and help out. She just hoped she could find something that worked around her school schedule. How she would pay for college was a new but constant worry. Daddy had said he'd pay for it, but now Daddy was gone. Bobbi hadn't worked up the courage to ask Ed what the plan was, or if there still was one.

Guy was still staring off into space, so Bobbi asked again. "What's that paper, Guy?"

"Oh. This. My number's up," he said casually, meeting her eyes with a matter-of-fact smile.

"What do you mean?" Bobbi asked, not comprehending. He slid

the paper over to her, his face eerily calm. Bobbi felt all the breath leave her body as she read over the paper, fighting the urge to rip it into a million pieces and fling them into the stove. "No," she said, her voice sounding strange and shrill to her own ears. "No." She shook her head. "Guy, *no*."

"I knew I'd get called up," Guy said, taking the paper back and folding it, his fingers trembling slightly. "It was just a matter of when. It's alright, Bobbi."

"It most certainly is *not*—" she began, but he cut her off.

"I ain't political like you and Ed. I don't like the war, but I'm not opposed to going and lending a hand if they need me. That's my duty, right? I'm young and healthy and I don't have a wife or kids. Makes sense. It'll all work out."

"You don't know that, Guy," Bobbi said, choking back tears. "You have no idea what it's like over there. How many young men never come home—"

"Ain't no sense in dwelling on that," Guy responded. "They're gonna send me over there no matter how I feel about it. And if what they say in the papers is true, the war isn't gonna last much longer. Maybe I'll luck out and get sent home before I even see any action." He put a hand on Bobbi's and gave it a squeeze. "It'll all work out," he said again.

"Does Ed know?" Bobbi tried to beat back tears.

"Nah. Not yet. I was gonna tell him, but him and Grace were fighting and all, and I didn't want to make his night any worse." He grinned. How Guy could remain so calm, so unfazed, at a time like this, Bobbi couldn't understand. "I'll tell him in the morning."

Bobbi was no longer hungry. She took her brother's plate to the sink and ran the garbage disposal, still trying to blink back tears. "I want to be there when you do," she said, coming over to give her brother a hug. He squeezed her in return, then patted her on the back. Her stomach rolled; she felt like she might throw up. Her brother couldn't go off to war, he just *couldn't*.

"You look tired," Guy said, still patting her back. "You go on up to bed, get some rest. It'll all work out, Bobbi."

Why did he keep saying that? He couldn't possibly believe it was true. "I won't be able to sleep," she argued. "Are you sure you don't want me to wait up with you?"

"Nope," Guy said with a smile. "I'm going to turn in soon, too."

Guy's latest check from the garage sat on the table, one of his business cards stapled to the paystub. Bobbi grabbed the card on impulse, ripping it from the paper and shoving it in her pocket. Then she trudged up the stairs, letting the tears come. She hadn't wanted to leave her brother alone in the kitchen, but she didn't want him to see her cry, either. The tears silently rolled down her face as she walked up the stairs. She thought she heard a small *sniff* behind her in the kitchen, but then all was quiet, so she continued to her room.

Bobbi changed into her pajamas, willing herself to calm down, to breathe slowly, then flicked on the little black-and-white TV. It would be over an hour before Landrum came over and she could pour her heart out to him, tell him the bad news. God, he must be sick of all her bad news by now. She might as well kill some time, and besides, it would help calm her. The television set had once sat in her parent's room, and she remembered them watching the nightly news before bed every night, Mom with her hair in curlers and cold cream on her face, and Daddy with a book on his lap. Sometimes she and her brothers would pile into the room to watch television, all five of them curled up in the bed, usually with one of her brother's feet in her face. After Daddy had passed, she'd dragged the set into her room. Neither of her brothers had protested. Bobbi stared at the TV blankly, watching the news, the images blurring through the tears in her eyes.

"Rumors of a presidential run have followed the former Attorney General, now senator, ever since his brother's untimely death in 1963," the newscaster was saying, and Bobbi felt her ears perk up despite how desolate she felt. This was what Amelia had been talking about earlier. She turned the volume up and began to brush her hair with a trembling hand. "Senator Kennedy will appear on next week's 'Face the Nation,' where perhaps he can shed some light on the latest batch of rumors in Washington: that he is considering following his late brother, President John F. Kennedy's footsteps, and throwing his hat into the ring for the 1968 presidential election."

The anchor turned to his newscaster, who sat with him at a large mahogany desk. "And what do you think, Gary?" he asked, shuffling the papers in front of him. "Do you think Senator Robert Kennedy has designs on the White House, and if so, does he have a real chance at the presidency?"

"Well, he certainly has the political know-how," his fellow anchor answered with a polished smile, "and the work ethic. But perhaps most importantly, he's got the Kennedy political dynasty behind him, and he's popular with the people. Perhaps he wasn't so much as a young man, but tragedy has befallen him so many times—losing two brothers, his parents in ill health, a sister with mental struggles—look at all he's lost, and maintained a brave face throughout. In fact, it seems that loss has made him kinder, with more of a moral compass—I dare say that losing so many loved ones has turned Bobby Kennedy downright presidential." He turned to his colleague. "The question is, do the American people hold with such a man for president, or might they prefer someone with a bit more steel in his spine?"

"I can't imagine losing so much so quickly," the anchor agreed with a sympathetic expression. "I suppose it makes or breaks one, doesn't it?"

"And it's made him," the co-anchor said assuredly. "It's made him a man; a good man, and perhaps our future president."

"Real progress sometimes requires sacrifice," the anchor agreed. Bobbi flipped the TV off and resumed brushing her hair in bitter silence.

NINE

HER first day on the job at the co-op, Ella found herself stuck in the back with crates of oranges. "I know it's the worst, but it'll go quick," Janelle had said to her, sipping from a Starbucks coffee cup. "Aaron is going to help you. You guys just sort through them—no need to take them all out one by one, just kinda rummage through—and take out any that are spotty, shriveled, or too squishy and look like they're about to rot. The boxes you've sorted go over here by the door, and we'll come get them to put out for the customers."

Ella groaned internally but pasted on a bright smile for her new boss. She'd managed to come to terms with the fact that said new boss was only three years older than her, looked like a cross between Lisa Bonet and Iman, and had dated the guy she was currently smitten with. Ella supposed she could make her peace with anything if it meant making money and being able to shift from the backpackers'. Much as she liked Anita, sharing a room with another girl and sleeping in a rickety twin bed was starting to get really old. The place was never quiet, a steady influx of guests always coming in and out at all hours of the morning, reeking of cigarette smoke and being as loud as possible.

She ought to be grateful for the experience, Ella knew, and not be so nitpicky about everything. She was too young to be worrying about getting enough sleep, to be dissatisfied with a job, to be so down and out. But the more she thought about the life she'd left behind, the more upset she became. There were pieces missing… pieces from the past she'd always allowed her aunt and uncle to bury, and she knew without a doubt that no place—not even glorious, drizzly Seattle—would feel like a true home until she knew exactly who she was.

She sorted through the boxes of oranges with Aaron, a ponytailed guy with a lip ring and bright blue eyes who sang Temple of the Dog songs the entire time they worked for the next two hours. He took frequent smoke breaks and sounded nothing like Chris Cornell, but Ella found him pleasant enough. And she had to admit, mindless busywork was a welcome distraction from the chaos of her thoughts.

When it was time for her lunch break, she sat outside behind the building and opened a bag of Doritos, a room-temperature Fruitopia by her feet.

"Please tell me that isn't your lunch." Janelle crouched down beside her, clutching another coffee. In her other hand was a paper cup filled with cut fruit.

"I'm poor," Ella said, reaching into the bag and pulling out a chip. "And I've never had this kind."

"They come out with a new flavor every other day, and they all taste the same." Janelle made a face. "You're gonna be bad for business, people seeing an employee eating all that chemical dust. Want some fruit?"

"I'm good," Ella said. "I'll get some later."

"How are you liking it so far?" Janelle asked, reaching behind her to pull her locs back from her face. "I know shuffling through oranges is boring as hell. It won't always be like that, though. We just got a huge shipment in and I needed to get through them fast before half of them rot. Did you put the janky ones in that gallon bucket?"

"I did, yeah," Ella responded, giggling at Janelle's use of the word *janky*. "I was wondering about that. Why didn't you have us throw them away?"

"I'm going to use them," Janelle responded. "I wouldn't dare waste anything, not if I don't have to. Whatever we don't sell at the end of the day goes to the homeless shelter. And if I have any fruit that is dead-ripe or not presentable, I use that, too. If I can't donate it outright, I'll try to whip something up with it. I thought I might make some orange spice cakes and donate for the Thanksgiving meal that's coming up."

It had never even occurred to Ella that the oranges might be salvageable. And Janelle would be going home to strain the juice and bake cakes for the homeless? Now she felt even more inadequate next to the beautiful girl. "I'm impressed," she admitted. "You're a certified do-gooder."

Janelle laughed. "I try. It's mainly down to my parents; they've led by example my whole life. Never let me slip up. They're in California now and I can't look into that box of oranges without thinking of the fucking *Grapes of Wrath*. You know, the part with all the fallen fruit that they make the workers cover over with dirt? Sprinkle it with poison so nobody's tempted to take one. All that fruit could have fed somebody, but they'd shoot anyone on sight who tried to steal even a piece. They'd rather it rot than anybody get an orange for free."

"I haven't read it," Ella admitted.

"You should." Janelle took a sip of her coffee. She put a hand to her heart and sang out a few lines of a song in a bright, clear voice. *Of course, she has the voice of an angel, too.* "What's that?"

"Springsteen. 'The Ghost of Tom Joad.'" Janelle smiled. "Don't tell anybody I listen to him."

"Scout's honor." Ella smiled back shyly.

Janelle popped a strawberry in her mouth. "Listen, don't go thinking of me as some kind of saint. This coffee here represents the capitalist side of me. I'm addicted to them. I don't even have a coffee pot at home."

"How dare you!" Ella giggled.

"Louie loves to tease me about what a hypocrite I am," Janelle said with a grin.

At the mention of his name, Ella felt herself flush. Before she could stop herself, she was asking, "So, the two of you... There's really nothing there?" Louie had already told her the story, but she needed to hear it from Janelle. After all, she was her boss now, and she hoped, maybe, her friend.

"Nope. We dated on and off for a couple of years, but we make better friends." Janelle grinned. "Don't get me wrong, he's a great guy, and I'd murder anybody who ever hurt him, but it just didn't work between us."

"Why not?"

"Well, for starters, I'm more into women than I am into men." Janelle's lips curved into a bigger smile, and Ella felt her stomach do a weird flip, "And that got to be a problem for him, as you can imagine." She chuckled and took a sip of her coffee. "But it's not because I'm bi. Louie was always cool. He's a very open-minded guy. We're the best of friends. But when we try to date, it's like... he gets all crazy jealous and possessive, which is not like him at all, and I get all bitter and resentful, which isn't like *me,* and it's like oil and water. Every time we've ever tried it, it ended up a mess." She shook her head. "The last time we broke up, I threw a glass vase at his head. Barely missed him. Knocked a hole in his wall."

"Jesus," Ella said, her eyes wide. She thought back to the sweet, gentle kiss on the deck at the bar, and couldn't imagine such a lovely guy ever making her so angry.

"It was a bad scene. After that, we decided that friends it is. The sex might be great, but it's not worth the—" Janelle's eyes widened, and she made an awkward face. "Shit. Forget I said that last part. I know you guys are like...whatever. I know he likes you. If he finds out, I said that—"

"I won't say anything," Ella said quickly, feeling her cheeks turn even redder. "It's not like I didn't know."

"He likes you," Janelle said again, trying to reassure her. "A lot. I can tell."

Ella shrugged, feeling uncomfortable. "I don't know. I don't want to get in the middle of anything..."

"Girl, I'm telling you the truth. He and I *do not work.* Anyway, you met him before you met me. You don't owe me shit."

I kinda do, Ella thought to herself, anxious butterflies in her stomach. *You gave me a job, after all.* She planned to start looking at apartments this weekend. She'd already found a few want ads for roommates. At this point, she'd have to choose between paying the backpackers' or making a deposit on something, and she was dreading it. The first paycheck from Janelle would be welcome, but not a solution. That was, unless Janelle was willing to give her overtime or perhaps an advance on her pay, but Ella *really* didn't want to ask. The matter of Louie, Janelle's ex-boyfriend, seemed like it would only complicate matters, no matter how much Janelle said they were over, and it didn't matter. Ella knew from her own meager experience with guys that what you said and how you felt could often be at odds with each other. Janelle might feel different once she saw the two of them together.

And that would happen soon enough, since Louie had called Ella the night before and asked her out. He was going to pick her up from the co-op tomorrow and take her out to dinner and to a show. Ella felt butterflies in her stomach thinking about it; it was her first real date. Harrison didn't count. He was just a high school boyfriend and the only dates he ever took her on were to a couple of football games and one late-night showing of Pet Sematary—and he'd only done that because half his friends from the football team were going and bringing dates.

Ella had already picked out an outfit to wear, borrowing yet another ensemble from Anita, and she planned to stop on the way home to buy some makeup and maybe, if she could muster up the courage, a pack of condoms.

SO LONG, BOBBY

This was Seattle, after all, and she was an adult now. Going on a date with a super-hot guy, a guy who was older than her and had more experience and apparently really good at sex, if Janelle was to be believed.

Finding out her new friend was bi had put a weird feeling over her. Now she had *two* friends who weren't straight. Ella had been so sheltered, she'd never known anyone who was gay or bi back home, which was a disgrace, really, since her uncle was so liberal. Aunt Evil had been decidedly less so. Ella had never much considered same-sex relationships one way or the other because they hadn't been around her. Now, watching Janelle sip her coffee, unaware of how effortlessly gorgeous she looked, Ella wondered what it might be like to be with someone like her, to really *be with* her. She swallowed down the churning feeling in her gut, imagining the great chemistry between Louie and Janelle, wondering who she was more jealous of, and felt herself blush. She quickly dismissed those thoughts. As if her life wasn't complicated *enough.*

Ella had been so sheltered, so *censored*. She should have some of these feelings sorted out by now; she was beyond old enough. Her uncle was, by all accounts, a progressive guy, open-minded, liberal—he supported LGBT organizations and always voted on the side of women's autonomy over their own bodies. He supported a woman's right to abortion and the home Ella grew up in had been egged more than once by pro-life activists. When Ella turned sixteen, he had taken her aside and, after wishing her a happy birthday, had told her he planned to take her to get birth control. "Your aunt is funny about these things," he'd said in a whisper. "So I'll just take you after school. It'll be our secret. OK?" Ella had nodded eagerly—she was happy to get on birth control, to control her awful periods and acne if nothing else. Guys weren't on her radar yet, at least not sexually. It was kind of hard to find someone to lust after when your free time was relegated to color guard practice and church. But still, it seemed a rite of passage, and one she welcomed. She'd walked around with the happy secret for two days, feeling herself blossoming into womanhood with the secret knowledge, like she was joining an exclusive club. Until it had all fallen apart.

She'd come home from school two days later, excited about her impending trip to the health department, and heard raised voices from upstairs. Grace was yelling. She had found out about the plan.

"Why on earth would you take her to that filthy clinic and get on those pills? Are you trying to *encourage* her to be promiscuous? To go out and have sex with any old body?"

"Grace, lots of girls her age are on them. I've read they help with other issues beyond just preventing pregnancy, and honestly, at this point it's just responsible—"

Grace laughed loudly. "How so? Teaching young people that it's okay to sleep around before they're married?"

"Grace, I've long tolerated your religious views; let her go along with that silly chastity ceremony to make you happy. But this is *my* niece, and I think this is the right thing to do for her. It's what my sister would have wanted. It has nothing to do with being sexually active so much as teaching her responsibility over her own body and choices. That's important for a young girl."

"Oh, so now she's suddenly *your* niece," Grace had seethed. "After I've raised her practically on my own since she was three. You were busy working late every night—or at least that's the official story. I've busted my back trying to give her everything while you've barely been here, and now you swoop in and decide major life decisions for her as if she's only yours, and not mine at all!"

"I didn't say that, Grace. I know how much you've given Ella—"

"And what would you know about responsibility of choices? What's right for a young woman?" she interrupted. "What would you know about what's moral? You might be a judge in town, but you aren't in this house. I think I have a better idea what kind of things a young woman will face if she—you have no idea the kind of pressure boys—well, just remember your own track record, Ed Newton. Or have you forgotten?"

"I haven't forgotten. How could I, with you, throwing it in my face every day? But it's not the sixties anymore, Grace," he'd countered angrily. "I'd rather not see my niece pregnant at eighteen. Do you want another child to care for that isn't yours?" Ella had winced at that.

"Of course I don't," Grace had snapped back. "Which is why I don't let her out of my sight. Oh, don't give me that look. She's a good kid, but she *is* a Newton, isn't she? To say nothing of the Waltons."

"Careful," Ed had begun, but she'd cut him off.

"As if it isn't bad enough, you tomcatting around, making a fool of yourself and of me, all these years, and before we were even married," Grace had hissed, "but that sister of yours was fooling with that Walton boy before she was even out of high school…and, of course, he learned his ways from his mother Irene—"

An awful sound had sliced through the air and cut her off mid-sentence; a sharp *thwack,* followed by a cry of pain, that sent Ella running into the kitchen to get away from the sound, hot tears springing to her eyes. She had pulled a paper towel off the wall and wiped at her face, taking a few deep breaths, her feelings in a jumble. After a few moments, she coughed loudly to let them know she was home, hoping it would put a stop to things. She couldn't bear to hear anymore. After a moment, her uncle's steps thundered on the stairs.

Uncle Ed had entered the kitchen, red-faced and flustered. "Hey, sugar pie," he said to her with a smile that didn't reach his eyes. "You're home a little early. You about ready to go to the clinic?"

Ella hesitated. She thought of her aunt, sniffling upstairs, whom she hated and pitied. She smiled. "If it's okay, Uncle Ed, I think I want to wait a little longer."

His brow furrowed. "Are you sure? Because I don't mind taking you." He'd sniffed, his eyes darting to the stairs for the briefest second. "And it's your right to have them, regardless of how anyone *else* feels on the matter."

"I know," Ella had said with a wistful smile. "I guess I'm just not ready to grow up yet, that's all."

"I can understand that," he had said with a smile, and reached up to tousle her hair. "You sure look like your mom today," he said with a wink, and retreated to the fridge to grab a glass of sweet tea.

SO LONG, BOBBY

As he drank, Ella had regarded him, her head tingling where he'd tousled her hair. Her uncle was tall and handsome, with an attractive, squarish face, a strong, solid jaw that seemed to be etched out of stone. There were just some men who looked the part, and Ed did. Looking at him, you couldn't mistake him for anything but what he was—a high-falutin', preppy southern lawyer-turned-judge. He made an imposing figure when decked out in his fancy suits and shiny black shoes, and Ella had seen more than one client shrink in his presence. He had a wolflike smile that could turn kind if he really liked you; Ella had seen it often, but she rarely saw it directed at her aunt. Almost never, in fact.

Her uncle Ed was such a mystery to her. He was kind, devoted to important causes, generous and fair to a fault—he fought for the underdog, believed in what was right and just, and he'd told her stories about being called a "commie" and a "socialist" when he was a younger man just starting out practicing law. He had a shelf full of awards in both his office and in the library at home, and he rubbed shoulders with some of the most powerful figures in the state. There were framed pictures of him with the likes of Zell Miller, and even President Jimmy Carter. Ella had never had to ask him for anything he didn't automatically give to her, and she often caught him staring at her wistfully, understanding instinctively that he was thinking of his dead sister, her mother. He didn't talk about her often, but the few times her mother's name had come up, her uncle's eyes would often glisten with tears.

And yet, that same kind, open-minded man who championed women's rights and believed in showing kindness to the most

231

marginalized in society, had a reputation for cheating on his wife with anything that moved, and when he wasn't being unfaithful to Grace, he was cruel to her in other ways. It had been going on for years, with Ella stuck in the middle, hating and loving them both.

"Well, if you're sure you don't want to go, I suppose I'll head back to the office and do a bit of work," Uncle Ed had said finally, peering at her from the top of his tea glass.

"I'm sure," she'd said. "I'm going to go start my homework."

"Good girl," he had said with a smile. "Keep up those grades. We'll get you into law school yet."

Ella made no reply. She had no interest in law school. She wanted to be a painter. Under her bed, hidden from sight, were several stacked canvases of her art, paintings she had never shown anyone. She painted in the dead of night or when nobody was home, let the paintings dry in the closet and then she'd hide them under her bed. They were just for her, at least for now. Whether she'd ever do anything with them, or her talent, she didn't know and didn't allow herself to care.

Ella waited for her uncle's car to back out of the driveway before getting up from the table and going upstairs, mainly to give Grace time to compose herself. As much as she hated the severity of her rules, Ella hated seeing Grace vulnerable and undone even more. There was something *delicate* about her, almost weak, that she tried so desperately to hide. And yet her uncle always seemed to root it out easily.

It wasn't Grace's delicacy that was the real issue between Ed and Grace Newton in recent years, though. The real issue was Chastain.

SO LONG, BOBBY

Chastain Jackson had been on the color guard team with Ella a few years before—she was a senior when Ella was a freshman. Her mother and Aunt Grace had once been close friends, co-chairing events together and teaching with each other at Sunday School. Chastain was sweet, pretty and fresh-faced; a wholesome girl who attended church regularly and had been one of the senior superlatives when she'd graduated. They'd never been close friends, but Ella knew Chastain had planned to go off to a Christian college after getting her diploma. But it seemed that Chastain had either come back or never left, because suddenly her name was being whispered hotly at church and around the neighborhood, peppered in with words like *ruined* and *disgrace*. Chastain Jackson was pregnant, and even though her parents had threatened to disown her or send her off somewhere, she refused to say who the father was.

A teen pregnancy wasn't any big shock, not in Athens. The "epidemic" teachers talked about in health class was now the norm since adults stubbornly clung to abstinence-only education and it was hard for young, broke kids to find birth control. But for a girl like Chastain, who'd been raised in abstinence culture and who had planned a life of Christian service, it *was* a big deal. The fact that she wouldn't throw some poor teenage boy accomplice under the bus was an even bigger deal. And Ella was pretty sure why—the father of the baby wasn't some hapless young guy Chastain had given into in the heat of the moment—he was an older man, and a distinguished one in the community.

A judge, perhaps.

Ella had tried to ignore the rumors at school, but she'd been forced to confront the truth when Chastain Jackson had shown up at their house one day.

She had looked different than Ella remembered. Blonde-haired and blue-eyed, Chastain had always possessed the pretty Barbie-doll-next-door looks that made girls like Ella jealous; easy beauty, effortless. She'd always been thin and graceful, immaculately groomed, and sparkling. In school, she had been friendly and sweet, yet still one of the popular girls, and therefore somewhat untouchable. The girl who had stood on Ella's front stoop was a cheap knockoff of that—her blonde hair, pulled back into a messy ponytail, was greasy, and her once smooth skin was covered in a couple of angry red pimples. She wore a black oversized hoodie that dwarfed her, baggy cargo jeans, and a pair of scuffed Airwalks. She could have easily fit in with the stoners, if not for the sad look in her eyes—the hacky sack playing townies were always happy, because they were stoned.

Ella didn't know exactly what to say. "Hi, Chastain," she had said by way of greeting, leaning awkwardly against the door. "Gosh, it's been forever. How long has it been since I saw you?"

"I don't know," Chastain had said, not bothering to feign cheerfulness. "Look, is your uncle Ed here by chance? I need to talk to him."

Ella had stepped onto the porch, shutting the door behind her. "He's in Atlanta today for a meeting. Can I help with something?" Chastain looked a wreck, and Ella felt bad for her. She tried not to look at the swollen roundness of the girl's belly, badly hidden under her baggy hoodie.

Chastain hesitated, then her jaw jutted forward, and she said, "Grace, then. Go get her."

What had transpired after that had been a bad scene. Aunt Grace, summoned to the front stoop, had stood with all the dignity of haughty royalty, and banished Ella upstairs; Ella wasn't going to be kept out of the loop on this, though. She'd craned her ear to her bedroom window, which was over the front porch, and could just make out bits and pieces.

"This is supposed to *help*, is it?"

The steely voice of Aunt Grace, full of fury. "It's all he's authorized me to give you. Take it and be grateful."

"This isn't enough for…for anything. How am I supposed to…" Ella could hear Chastain's voice giving way to tears. "He promised me he'd take care of us, that he'd…"

"Men promise a lot of things in bed," Grace had seethed, and Ella had flinched.

"This money isn't for the *baby*," Chastain said, her voice accusing, "is it?"

"What you do with it isn't my concern," Grace had said. "Though I'd suggest, for the good of all of us—for your poor mother's sake, and the rest of your family, and mine—that you use it wisely."

Ella had gasped at that. The meaning was plain. Grace was so religious, so stern in her views. So steadfast in her faith that she hadn't even wanted her own niece to go on birth control. She'd made her participate in a chastity ceremony, and talked endlessly of how marriage was for procreation, how raising children was women's divine mission in life. And yet here she was…clearly urging Chastain to get rid of a baby that was her husband's. The hypocrisy almost bowled Ella over; her stomach clenched with nausea.

What was worse, Ella knew the family crack would push Chastain over the edge. Chastain's mother had stage four breast cancer; her second bout with the disease. Grace and Chastain's mother were the best of friends or had been. To use Chastain's worry and guilt about her mother was truly evil. She inched toward the wall, wishing she could shrink into it, but unable to wrench herself away.

"Thanks to you, Grace Newton, Athens' most pious Christian, for your generous check," Chastain had sneered, and Ella heard her bounding off the porch, the ignition starting, and the car squealing out of their quiet street. After a moment, she'd heard the front door shut and Grace's footsteps meandering into the kitchen. She heard pots and pans clanging and the sizzling of oil. Life was carrying on as normal.

But not for Ella. Hearing that conversation had been the final straw. She'd known for years that her uncle was unfaithful, that he had a roving eye for women of "all types and stripes," as she'd once heard Grace throw at him during an argument. She'd known that Grace was damaged beyond repair; whatever had once been good about her was now shrouded in a cloak of bitterness and fervent faith.

But now Ella could no longer ignore that Ed and Grace's toxicity, their hypocrisy, was hurting other people. People outside of their family, innocent people who had done nothing to deserve such pain. Thinking of poor Chastain, abandoned to an impossible decision, left to fend for herself and her baby, when her aunt and uncle had plenty of money and all the resources in the world to help, made her feel sick to her stomach. She couldn't imagine spending another night in their home, pretending that everything was just fine, participating in the delusion they'd created.

That night, after Grace had gone to sleep, Ella had packed her bookbag with clothes, toiletries, and a few random items. The next morning, she'd said a casual goodbye, grabbing an apple from the fruit bowl, and headed out the door. But instead of showing up for class at Clarke Central, she'd walked down to the bank. She'd been there once or twice over the years, and now that she was over eighteen, she had access to the savings account her uncle had started for her as a child. What little money her parents had left her was there, combined with all those holiday checks that her uncle had made her save rather than spend throughout her childhood. She'd been angry at the time, but now she was glad. Somewhere, she knew there was a separate college fund that uncle Ed had started for her, intending to send her to law school, but Ella would never ask for that. The savings account, hers and hers alone, would be enough.

Ella had twiddled her thumbs nervously in the lobby as the teller closed out the account and pushed a check toward her. It wasn't a ton of money, but the few thousand dollars was more than Ella had ever seen before. She'd signed the check with a shaking hand and had it cashed right there at the bank. When she was finished, she'd taken a few bills off the top of the pile, pushing them gingerly into her wallet with the pink hearts, and tucked the rest into an envelope. Her hand still shaking, she'd written *Chastain* in firm, dark script, tucked the envelope into her pocket, and headed out of the bank toward the bus station. Once she bought her ticket, she'd have only one last stop to make—the Jackson household, where she'd do what her aunt and uncle hadn't the decency to—and then Ella would be gone, baby, gone.

∞

And now she was.

Gone.

Ella crunched another chip, wiping the orange dust on her jeans and strengthening her resolve. She missed her aunt and uncle, and it galled her. After all they'd put her through, she was ashamed of her own weakness.

This was her new home, and she'd build a new family, a better one. A family where being bi or queer wasn't a dirty word, where it was okay to have sex with your boyfriend, and where music wasn't just allowed—it was celebrated. It was *life*.

Ella crumpled the bag of chips and stood up. Time to get moving.

TEN

KASEY - 2018

FIVE days. Kasey felt like her skin was melting, and when it wasn't melting, it itched. She couldn't stop going to the bathroom, and every extremity in her body was screaming in pain. She'd gone through almost an entire bottle of ibuprofen in two days, but nothing touched the ache that seemed to come from deep within her bones.

"I can't tell what's my injury and what's withdrawal," she confessed to Caden as they lay together on her bed, both staring without really looking at the TV in front of them. It was turned to MTV Classic, old music videos from the '90s. Pearl Jam's Eddie Vedder was staring into the camera, his soft-brown curls falling down his shoulders, singing about the angst of the murderous Jeremy. "To think there was once a time when people tried to empathize with school shooters," she said absently, rubbing at her neck, which was also aching. "Now we can't even keep them all straight."

Caden made no reply but grabbed another fistful of Skittles from the nightstand. He'd eaten so many Skittles in the past few days, he told her, that he had a blister on his tongue. "I'm going to crawl right out of my fuckin' skin if I don't get out of this room, Kace," he said, turning to her. "Isn't there anywhere we can go?"

"We're broke, and we're both sweating like pigs," she said.

"What would you suggest?"

"The park, maybe?" Caden asked. "Why don't we go for a walk? It doesn't cost any money to walk trails and we could use some fresh air."

"I guess," Kasey said reluctantly, not relishing the thought of dragging her aching limbs out into the cool afternoon, hiking through trails full of fresh-faced young women out for runs in their tight-fitting leggings. She would have to take her cane, and god, she hated using the thing. Sometimes it bothered her how other people could casually get up and go out for a run, or a hike, without stopping to think about the logistics. Without pain. She didn't begrudge Caden or anyone else being able-bodied, but she envied them their thoughtlessness when it came to accessibility.

Kasey had to begrudgingly admit though, it would probably do her some good to get some fresh air, vitamin D, and sweat a little. And she wanted to encourage Caden, who was trying so hard. So far, he'd stuck to his word and really was trying to kick the pills right along with her. She felt guilty at how surprised she was. He loved her and would support her, but Caden had never been one to say no to a drug, no matter the flavor.

"Let me just run upstairs and get my running shoes. I'll be back in a minute." Kasey ventured upstairs, rummaging through the hall closet for her tennis shoes. As she passed by Ricky's room, the glow of his computer caught her eye. He was one of the few people left in the world who still checked his email on an actual computer, and he'd never even owned a laptop. Kasey giggled as she passed by, picturing Ricky's ancient Nokia that he used instead of a smartphone.

Then she turned back around, peeking her head into his doorway and staring at the screen. Gmail was open, and there were several new messages waiting there. Kasey had been wondering ever since their conversation a few days ago, when he had tried to help her find out more about her family, if Ricky had contacted her mother. Well, now she could find out.

On impulse, Kasey sat down at his desk and scrolled through the email, looking for a familiar name among the spam. Just as she was getting ready to give up, a message from the previous day caught her eye. It was marked as already read, and so far, Ricky had not sent a reply.

To: RickyMechanic54321@gmail
From: EllaVayTor@gmail

Yes. I got your text. Fine, I'll do it. Just give me some time. This isn't exactly my idea of a pleasant conversation. I need to think.

I'm glad to hear she's off the pills. I mean it, Ricky. I know they helped at first, but I was in Seattle in the '90s and I know all about the link between heroin and opioids. I could kill those doctors, prescribing that stuff to her for so long and then just cutting her off like that. What else could she have done? I always regretted that I passed that on to her. Bad genes, I guess. I can hear you in my head right now— you're wondering how long I'm going to coast on that. Forever, probably.

She didn't find that portrait I did, did she? Please, please throw that damned thing away. I know you always said it's

too good to chuck it, but I'd rather her not see it.
I know you weren't asking, but I'll send you some cash as
soon as I have it. Things are tight.

Talk to you later, hubby (it is not snowing)

Kasey stared at the email, feeling a mixture of disgust and surprise. To think her mother had the gall to still refer to Ricky as her hubby and to talk to him in such a casual manner. To talk about Kasey so maternally, as though she hadn't just abandoned her to him, abandoned the entire life they had together. And what had she meant, "passed it on to her"? Had her mother had a pill problem or some other kind of addiction? If she had, she'd never told Kasey about it. And what portrait? What on earth was that about? Unable to quell her curiosity, Kasey clicked on the "see more" tab to read the email Ricky had originally sent to her mother.

Ell,

Kasey found the box you stowed away in the attic, that stuff of your parents'. I thought you'd took that with you, wished you had. She has a lot of questions that I can't answer.

She's off the pills. She told me she's quitting, and I believe she's sincere this time. I saw a light in her eyes when she was looking in that box that I hadn't seen since before the accident. Maybe this is a good thing for her to focus on, finding out her family. But she's going to ask me about her real dad, Ella. I can feel it brewing, and I don't have shit to tell her. You're gonna have to step in. You're gonna have to field this one.

You left her for me to raise, and I've done it. I love her like she's my own. I've never asked you for a dime, and I never will. And I'm not asking you for anything now. Other than for you to call your daughter and fill in those blanks. She needs this. You owe it to her, and to Fallon, too.

All my love, always. Wish you'd come on home.
Rick

P.S. Dawgs won the last game. You said it'd be a cold day in hell before they beat Florida, so tell me, is it snowing where you are? :P

Kasey felt tears prickling at her eyelids. Dear, dear Ricky.

BOBBI - DECEMBER 1967

"Senator Robert F. Kennedy delivered a toast to the citizens of New York yesterday…" Bobbi listened as she applied the thick black eyeliner to her lids, "Rumors continue to plague the senator about his alleged affair with his sister-in-law Jackie, widow of Mr. Kennedy's late brother, President John F. Kennedy…"

Bobbi snorted as she carefully drew an upward slash on her left lid with a steady hand. "The nerve," she said, digging through her makeup bag for her opaque pink lipstick, "to suggest that Bobby'd do such a thing. With his own brother's widow. Those vultures will make up any old thing for ratings these days."

"I don't know, there might be something to it," Landrum argued from behind her, where he was propped up against the pillows on her bed. He was clutching the old teddy bear that she'd had since she was a kid—Clarence—to his chest, and it made him look impossibly boyish. He was long overdue for a haircut; it was growing down over his ears, making him look like Stephen Stills. "I know he's got this wholesome image and you love him, but those rumors about Marilyn Monroe, and now this…"

"Oh, stop," Bobbi said dismissively, turning from the dressing table to give him a look. "Rumors have always plagued the Kennedys. Always have, always will. I'm not saying he's a Boy Scout, but I imagine most of it is a whole lot of nonsense. How much of a dummy would he have to be to have an affair with his brother's widow when his brother was the most famous man in the world? And Jackie as visible as she is… He'd have to be a complete and utter fool." She shook her head. "And have you seen his family? I reckon by 1970 he'll have a baker's dozen of mini-Kennedys with Ethel. I can't see how he has the time to play around with anybody else; he clearly can't keep his paws off her."

"They're Catholic." Landrum laughed. "That's all the explanation you need."

"Or maybe he just really loves his wife," Bobbi argued. "Some men actually *do,* you know."

"Yikes! Calm down! RFK kinda is a fool, though," Landrum said easily, still chuckling. "I mean, he's an idealist, kinda boyish… maybe he just never grew up. Doesn't think about the risks. He does have that quality like he's invincible or something. Not in an arrogant way, but kind of an ignorant way; naïve. Like he doesn't notice that he's got enemies. He believes people are more good than they are, and he thinks he's invincible to any kind of malice." He frowned. "Look at what happened to his brother Jack. He ought to be more cautious, is all I'm saying."

"That's ridiculous." Bobbi was affronted. "Bobby was Attorney General, for God's sake. I'd say the man is pretty well aware of who his enemies are, and what the risks are, too. I don't think he's naïve—I think he's courageous." She finished applying her lipstick and got up from the table, putting her hands on her hips. "He knows what he's up against every day, and he still gets up and does what he thinks is right. I just don't believe a man as good as him, as *moral* as him, would ever stoop so low."

"All right, all right," Landrum said, throwing up his hands in mock surrender. "Don't get sore. I shouldn't have insulted your knight in shining armor." He winked at her. "You look pretty. Why don't you come over here and give your old man a kiss?"

"I hate it when you call yourself 'old man,'" Bobbi said with a mock pout. "We're still teenagers, for goodness' sake, and you're playing like we're middle-aged and married."

"Well, we have been playing house for a while," he said, blowing her a kiss. "And anyway, we will be one day," he said, his gray eyes sparkling. "Won't we? Middle-aged, married, and happy?"

Bobbi didn't answer, turning to look in the mirror one more time. It was the first time Landrum had said anything about them getting married, and she wanted to screech with happiness. Getting into law school and marrying Landrum Walton were her two biggest dreams. She went to bed every night fantasizing about the life they'd lead together—she a lawyer, him opening the landscaping business he always talked about, with a few beautiful tow-headed babies and a big, beautiful house. She wanted to run to Landrum, tackle him and smother him with kisses, and say, *yes, yes, of course, let's do it!*

Instead, she inspected herself in the mirror, buying time. She needed to look perfect. It wasn't every day she was a bridesmaid—and at the church where her own parents were married. It wouldn't do to start making plans with Landrum about any impending nuptials until this particular set of nuptials was complete. She hoped things wouldn't be complicated today. Bobbi smoothed out her pale-pink dress, a confection with a skirt that came to mid-shin, in shiny taffeta with big roses on the bodice. She hadn't picked it out, but she didn't hate it. Pink was a nice color on her; it reminded her of her homecoming dress. And she loved the heels she was wearing—dyed pale pink to match the dress, and every bit as shiny, they gave a satisfying clack as she crossed the room and yanked the teddy bear out of her boyfriend's hands, inwardly cursing her brother for the millionth time for making her life complicated.

"Let's daydream another time, lover boy; we're late. Now get up before you mess up your suit. You can't go to a wedding all wrinkled."

"It's already wrinkled," he said, standing up with a shrug. "I'm useless with the iron. Every time I've ever used it, I've burned something."

"Couldn't you have asked your…" Bobbi regretted the words as soon as they left her lips. "Sorry, I didn't think. Would you like me to iron it?" She reached out and touched his lapel, admiring his tie, which was a lovely shade of burgundy. She'd worried it would clash with her dress, but it actually looked quite nice and would look even better once she was holding her bouquet, which was a mixture of white and pink roses and deep red carnations. He had always been so good at matching her. It was one of the things she loved about him; men didn't often think of things like that, but Landrum did.

"No, that's alright, Bobbi. I don't think I need it, do I?"

"No. I suppose not."

As they ventured downstairs, Bobbi mentally kicked herself for almost bringing up Mrs. Walton. She'd hoped they might get through this day without thinking of *the affair*, or at the very least, without having to discuss the things that had transpired over the past few weeks, resulting in an impromptu and very rushed wedding.

Bobbi had known for a while that her brother had resumed seeing Mrs. Walton on occasion. He was living right next door to her, for goodness' sake, and any fool with eyes could see that Mrs. Walton's passion for Ed ran hot. And ever since their father's death and Guy getting drafted soon after, Ed had been a ball of misery and stress, and he'd never had self-control when it came to attractive women. It was no surprise he'd seek comfort in Mrs. Walton's arms. That might have gone on unabated if the two had been discreet and Ed had behaved with even a sliver of decorum. The problem was, he'd continued to court Grace at the same time, supposing he could have his cake and eat it, too. Bobbi didn't know if Ed had been outright trying to get caught, or if his arrogance had blinded him, but there had been a series of blunders that finally resulted in the big one: Grace coming over to watch *Hee Haw*, a piping homemade casserole in hand, and as she let herself in, running smack into Mrs. Walton, who was rushing to get out the door, still pulling her dress over her lacy black slip. The fight that had ensued had been a doozy; Bobbi and Landrum had come home in the middle of it to find Ed standing in the foyer, his face red with anger, covered head to toe in tuna casserole. Grace, holding one trembling hand to her cheek, had screamed that it was over, that he was a cad, that she should have listened to the rumors and she never wanted to see his face again. She'd yelled, "And that goes for you, too" to Bobbi and Landrum before slamming out of the house, a bedraggled and crying Mrs. Walton in the corner, still trying to cover her revealing slip, muttering tear-soaked apologies.

Bobbi was ashamed of her brother's affair, always had been, but she hadn't been terribly heartbroken to see the back of Grace, who had always been rigid and prudish and oddly evangelical, considering how liberal her brother was. She'd pulled Landrum into the kitchen, hoping to avoid a further scene. But Ed had followed them, sitting down at the kitchen table and putting his head in his hands.

"I'm so sorry," he'd said, and Bobbi had been shocked. Her easy-going, confident brother had never apologized for anything. "To both of you. Especially you, Landrum. I know it must...I know how you must hate me."

Landrum had said nothing, his face tight with barely contained anger.

"The truth is, I love her. I love your mother," Ed said, a pleading look in his eyes, made all the more ridiculous because his face was covered in casserole. "I honestly do. But we can't get married, we can't be together out in the open. For obvious reasons. And I've thought that going around with Grace provided a cover. She didn't— she doesn't believe in sex before marriage, so I thought it'd be fine, that she wouldn't notice that my affections were—"

"You don't have to tell us this, Ed," Bobbi said, wishing he'd just be quiet. Landrum surely didn't want to hear any of this, and the last thing she wanted was to see her boyfriend deck her brother.

"I need to tell someone," he said desperately. "Irene and I have tried to be discreet." Landrum's eyes narrowed at Ed using his mother's first name. "But I know the rumors have been following us. I didn't want to listen to Daddy when he warned me, or when you did, and I should have. I should have known Grace would hear things. She confronted me a while back, asked me if I was seeing her. I said no. She pretended to believe me, but she warned me that if she ever caught me with Irene, she'd go to my boss and tell him I'm sleeping with a married woman. Get me kicked off the firm. And then she'd go to everybody in town and tell them the same."

"Do you think she'll actually do that?" Bobbi asked.

"I wish I could say no," Ed said sadly, looking up at her. He wiped at his face with the napkin she handed him. "But I think she would. Yes, I think she would."

"You can't let her drag my mama's name through the mud," Landrum said, his voice tight and strained. "My mom's got...she has a hard time, she gets depressed. My dad is already so hard on her. If he finds out about this—"

"I know." The two men exchanged a glance. "I've got to protect her," Ed said, and Bobbi felt a brief rush of tenderness toward him, though it was quickly stalled by the memory of Grace cupping her reddened cheek. "And I will. I'm going to have to go after Grace, make this right somehow."

"But how?" Bobbi asked. "She saw you, Ed. She saw Mrs. Walton—"

"She'd be willing to overlook it," Ed said, still wiping casserole off himself, "just like she did before. If I made enough of a gesture. But I won't be able to see Irene anymore. For real this time. I'm sure you two are glad of that." He laughed joylessly and stood up. "But I just hope that she'll take it alright, that she'll be okay. I don't want to hurt her. I swear I don't." For a moment, it looked as though his eyes were full of tears. "Jesus, I've made such a mess of this. I guess I'd better not waste any more time. I'll just go change my shirt and go propose to a woman I hate." He left the room, his shoulders downcast.

Landrum said quietly, "I love you, Bobbi. You know I do. But I fucking hate that son of a bitch."

"I know," Bobbi said in a whisper. Sometimes, she hated him, too. Hated him and loved him.

"If it weren't for you, I'd tear him limb from limb and, by god, I'd enjoy it," Landrum said, one hand curled into a fist. Bobbi said nothing; there was nothing to say.

Ed had come home later that night and unceremoniously announced to Bobbi, as she sat on the couch curled up in an afghan, that he was engaged. The wedding would be in three weeks at the family church. Grace had forgiven everything—provided he called things off with Mrs. Walton immediately and never saw her again— and was thrilled at the thought of being a Christmas bride. She was to have white and pink roses, and they were ring shopping tomorrow. Bobbi had accepted this news with lukewarm congratulations and given her brother a hug, noting that his shoulders were shaking when she wrapped her arms around him.

"I'll only say this once," she said as he sat down on the couch beside her. "And then I won't say anything else. You don't have to do this, Ed. You've made a mess of things, to be sure. But let's be honest. Grace can expose you, but it won't reveal anything more than what people already know. Tongues will wag just as they've always done. The scandal could blow over. In time, people would forget, if you just kept your nose clean from now on. It wouldn't have to mean your job. You don't have to marry Grace just to save face."

"It's not my face I'm trying to save, sis," he'd said sadly. "It's everyone else's. Yours, and Landrum's, and our family name...and Irene's. Hers most of all. I can't let her be hurt by all this. Not if I can fix it."

"But she'll be hurt anyway if you marry someone else," Bobbi said.

"I can't marry *her*, can I?" he said bitterly. "She's already married."

"Ed, you know you can't keep seeing her, not after this. It's different this time. Grace will make sure of it."

"Oh, I know she will," Ed said with a dry laugh. "No, it's over with Irene. But better her be heartbroken than the entire community shun her for a harlot. Or for her husband to break her nose again." He looked at Bobbi, his face unreadable. "But you don't see anybody gossiping about *him*, no. Johnny's a pillar of the community. Landrum can hate me all he wants; I don't blame him. But you should know what it's like in that house, what Irene has to deal with. And I hope you both know that I *do* love her, Bobbi. I do."

"I know it enough for the both of us, I guess," Bobbi said. And even though she hated Grace, she added, "I just hope you'll treat *your* wife better than Mr. Walton treats his."

"I will," Ed said firmly, but his eyes didn't meet hers.

ELEVEN

KASEY - 2018

KASEY had been tossing and turning for the past hour, and she was finally starting to drift off when her phone's shrill text alert sounded. With a groan, she picked it up, blinking at the screen in the dark of the room. It was 11:58; what kind of asshole texted so late? She unlocked her phone, sat up, and peered at the screen, not recognizing the number.

Hey hon. It's Mom. I have some information for you. Not much, but it's something.

Kasey's heart pounded in her throat. Her mother! A flurry of feelings went through her in the span of a moment: anxiety, excitement, joy; but most of all, white-hot anger. How long had it been since she had heard from Mom? Close to a year, at least since the last text, which had been a simple, joyless "Merry Christmas." She poised her finger over the letter keys, fighting the urge to write back with "fuck off." And she hadn't even *called. No,* she was using a cop-out text. At least she'd actually listened to Ricky and gotten in touch. That was something, she supposed.

The little dots on the screen were blinking, which meant her mother was writing more, so Kasey held off. However angry she was, she *did* want information. She'd been up in the attic several times since discovering the box, but had found nothing else. She'd gone through every item, but hadn't unearthed any additional information about her mysterious grandparents, and she found herself dying to know more. For most of her life, she'd never given her mom's people a second thought, but now she found herself wanting to know everything about them. It consumed her, this need. To know not only their story, but her mom's, and by proxy, her biological father's, and her own. It felt crucial somehow, important not only to her recovery, but to her identity going forward, her hopes and dreams. She had the sense that she couldn't start her new life if she didn't know how it began. Who she came from. Why her mother was the way she was.

It was obvious that her grandmother had been political, though Kasey had always assumed that everybody in the sixties was in one way or another—you were either a hippie or a diehard conservative, and it was still the same these days, the way she saw it. Kasey had never cared. She'd never even voted. What was the point when everything always remained the same?

Kasey *had* found the mysterious portrait her mother had asked Ricky to dispose of—she'd made a point to go and look for it— hidden in the back of the garage behind a stack of paints and cleaning supplies, wrapped in a black Hefty garbage bag. She'd taken it out gingerly, sitting down on the cement floor to look at it, perplexed. It was a beautiful painting—displaying far more skill than she'd ever known her mother possessed—of a gorgeous woman. In the portrait, the subject had her back to the viewer, but was turning around, craning her neck, her eyes seemingly focused on a subject just outside the frame with an expression stark and raw; a gaze that could strip a person bare. The woman was undeniably beautiful: dark-skinned, with wide, expressive brown eyes, curly black hair, and a soft mouth curled into the faintest ghost of a smile. She held an orange in her hand up by her face, the fingers graceful and long. It was a strange picture, Kasey thought as she looked at it—why was she holding an orange, for example—but it was undeniably good. Her mother had been crafty when she was a kid. She remembered her drawing cartoons for her and Fallon, and she'd sent out hand-sketched Christmas cards for a few years when she'd first married Ricky…but she'd never known that her mother had such a talent for painting. Unsatisfied, she'd put the painting back in the garbage bag and hid it in the closet to look at later, secretly glad that Ricky had ignored her mom's wishes.

After five minutes, another text pinged through. *My parents died when I was a toddler. I don't remember them. I was raised by my uncle Ed and aunt Grace, who you remember. They never talked about my parents much and I didn't ask. But when I was grown, I was given a box of their stuff by some family friends who had kept it for me over the years. My godparents.*

Kasey read over this, swallowing. What did these people have to do with the letter from Janelle?

Another text. *I've chosen not to remain in contact with them or with anybody else in their family for personal reasons. But I know if you decide to reach out, they will accept you. In fact, they would probably be thrilled to hear from you.*

Kasey felt the weight of her mother's typed words, could feel the dread behind them. The unspoken message was, *I wish you'd just leave it alone.*

Kasey didn't want to reply, but she had to. She had to know more. She typed out a short response. *Okay?*

More dots. Another message appeared. *Ricky said you found the letter from Janelle. You can probably write to her there. That's her business address, so it'll get to her eventually, even if she's moved.* Kasey had to smile. This was downright chatty for her mother. *She can tell you everything—she knows about your grandparents, and she knows your dad. She can explain it all.*

Kasey stared at the phone, confused. Who was this *Janelle*, this all-knowing sage who not only knew all about her long-dead maternal grandparents, but knew her father, too, who Kasey had never even met? How was it possible that someone so important to her parents could exist and Kasey never knew her? Her heart pounded in her throat as she waited for the next message to appear.

If she doesn't respond, there's one more option you can try. I'd save it as a last resort, though. It'll be a shock hearing from you. He doesn't know— There was a break in the text, then another one popped up—*about you. His name is Louis Bradenton. Seattle. If you enter the name in the FB search bar, his is the first that comes up. I don't think he uses his account, but I checked it out before I texted you, and you can probably get in touch with him that way. But try Janelle first.* Then, after a pause: *They're still in touch. Of course.*

Kasey took a deep breath and responded, *What on earth do I say?*

She waited for over an hour, but her mother never responded. Desperate, Kasey pressed "call" and held the phone to her ear, her hands shaking. The call went straight to voicemail. Her mother, it seemed, was done talking.

The next morning, Kasey headed to Ricky's computer as soon as he'd left for work. She felt guilty, not telling him she'd heard from her mother, but for now, she wanted it to be a secret that was hers alone. At least until she found out more. Her mother's messages had only made her more confused, but at least she had a couple of names and an address to go on.

"Dear Janelle, she typed, *I found a letter from you to my mother, Ella, in the attic. She has given me her blessing to contact you. I'm sorry for writing you out of the blue like this, but I'm hoping to get some information. I was told that you also know my father and that you have info about my grandparents. I haven't seen my mother in several years. We have minimal contact, and I know next to nothing about either side of my family. She doesn't like to talk about any of this stuff. But I need to know. Any and all info you could give me would be greatly appreciated. Thank you, Kasey Newton.*

Her finger hovered over the mouse for a moment before she hit "print" and folded up the paper, stuffing it in the pre-addressed envelope, ignoring the pounding of her heart. She affixed the stamp and sealed the envelope without looking it over again, lest she lose her nerve.

Kasey moved to get up from the desk and then stopped. She'd already come this far. Why not? She opened another tab and logged into Facebook. With shaking hands, she typed "Louis Bradenton" into the search tab. The first result showed a thumbnail picture of a handsome man holding a guitar, with curly brown hair obscuring half his face. She clicked on the profile and was dejected to find it was set to private. All she could see was the profile photo and the cover photo; even the location was hidden. She clicked on the cover photo and stared. In this picture, the man, who looked around her mom's age, was standing on a rocky beach, holding up a fishing pole. He was dressed in ragged flannel and torn jeans, black Chucks on his feet and a brown beanie on his head. He could have stepped right out of 1994, from the looks of it, Kasey thought to herself. The sky was overcast and gray, but the man was laughing, and her heart clenched a little as she tried to memorize his handsome face, his kind smile. Beside him in the picture was a young man, holding a fishing pole of his own, his other arm around the older guy's waist. Despite the fact that the younger man had much darker skin, and was almost a foot taller, it was clear that they were father and son. Kasey swallowed, and moved her mouse around, letting the arrow hover over the picture to see the tags. "Louis Bradenton," she read aloud, then hovered the cursor over the younger man, who had the laughing smile. "Andy Bradenton."

Without thinking, she clicked on the young man's name and was taken to another profile. The picture was a close-up of Andy Bradenton's face, and Kasey gasped, her hand flying to her own face. She recognized those almond-shaped brown eyes. The color might be different, but they were *her* eyes.

She skimmed over the "About Me" section, her hands trembling harder now. Andy Ramon Bradenton. Twenty-one years old. Student at University of Seattle. Musician, surfer, and day manager at The

SO LONG, BOBBY

Co-Op-Erative. Relationship status: It's Complicated.

Fortunately, his profile was public. Kasey knew she should just wait, send off the letter to this Janelle, and see what would come of it. But her hand moved as if independent from her, as though someone else were controlling her every movement. She clicked "message," and before she could stop herself, she'd drafted out a note.

Dear Andy,

My name is Kasey Newton. This will sound really strange but...I think I'm your sister.

TWELVE

BOBBI - VIRGINIA - FEBRUARY 1968

THE bus came to a screeching halt several yards from the bus station. Bobbi stood, hoisting her knapsack over her shoulder, and sighed. She could see out the window that the streets were waterlogged, the grass flooded, and she'd have to step through the mud just to get inside to the ticket window. Her black boots were already worn down to nothing; there was a hole in the toe of the left one and the sole on the right was starting to come apart from the shoe at the heel. When she'd just packed the one pair, she'd assumed traveling light would be her best bet, but now that she was several states from home with almost no money, she wished she'd at least thought to bring her sneakers.

The bus doors swooshed open and Bobbi stepped out, doing her best to avoid the massive oil-slicked puddle on her right, choosing instead to squish through the muddy grass and toward the bus station. The bus had been filled with people like her, young people—activists and hippies and marchers—and someone had started up a portable radio to play Joan Baez and Bobby Dylan, and people had sung along in an impossible state of glee until the bus driver had asked them to quiet. Several times during the nine-hour ride she had wanted to chime in on people's conversations, but she hadn't known how, and she was afraid her grief would show on her face, stark and wild, and would scare people away. She was still so raw, so angry, from all that had happened. She supposed she'd have time to get to know these people soon enough before they arrived at their final destination, as it were.

Bobbi was on her way to Washington, D.C. Mainly because she didn't know what else to do.

It had been three weeks since Landrum stepped on a bus of his own, and she'd heard nothing from him since. Three short weeks was all it took for everything to fall spectacularly apart. Bobbi hadn't willingly left Athens so much as fled as fast as her legs could take her.

When Landrum had gotten his draft card right after Christmas, just a couple of months after Guy had been called up, just two weeks after Ed and Grace's wedding, he and Bobbi sat huddled in her room, arms around each other, Bobbi's face streaked with tears and Landrum's full of eerie calm. The same unsettling calm her brother Guy had shown. They had briefly discussed burning the card and hightailing it to Canada, which was what Bobbi wanted. That proved a pipe dream, as Landrum's pickup likely wouldn't have made it. Neither of them had any money to set them up once they got there, and Landrum was certain his father would give him up. "Besides," he'd said to her gravely, "if I go to Canada, I can't ever come back. I couldn't do that to my ma."

Bobbi could understand that, even though she didn't feel either of Landrum's parents deserved his loyalty, not after the way things had been lately. "What do we do?" she'd asked, her voice wavering with fear. Her brother Guy had just finished boot camp and was set to be deployed within the week. She'd only had one letter from him since he'd gone, and she lay awake nights worrying about him. And now Landrum, her love, her rock, her everything, was leaving, too. It was too much.

About a week before he was set to leave for boot camp, Bobbi raised a question that had been on her heart. "You mentioned... us getting married," she said, her voice small. "I put you off then, but now... Landrum, I think we should do it. I think we should get married before you go."

"Aw, honey," Landrum had said, pulling her onto his lap and ruffling her hair. "I know you're not ready to get married yet. I wasn't sore about it when you put me off; I understand. We got time. We should wait till we've got the money to have a nice wedding. We shouldn't shotgun it just because I'm getting shipped off."

"But..." She was afraid to say the words they both knew she was thinking. *We should get married before you go, in case you don't come back.* "Don't you want to marry me?"

"Of course I do," he'd said, placing a tender kiss on her temple. "When it's right."

"But what if now is right?" she'd murmured in his ear, placing kisses up and down his neck. He sighed with pleasure, but then he pulled away, putting his hands over hers, staring into her eyes.

Then Landrum had dropped the bombshell that had broken her heart in half. "Actually Bobbi... I...I think we should break up."

"What?" she managed to croak out, the tears already beginning to well up in her eyes. He stared at her calmly, his own eyes clear and sad. "But why?"

"It's not that I don't love you," he rushed to explain, putting a hand up to tousle her hair again. Bobbi pulled away. "It's because I *do* love you. I can't have you waiting around, wondering when I'll come back, if I ever come back… You've got law school to think of, colleges to apply for… It's too much to ask of you. You're young and you deserve a life without so much uncertainty." He paused, then added, "You've already had too much pain as it is, and it's not fair. That's all."

"Don't you think I get to decide what I can bear and what I can't?" she asked savagely, wiping tears from her cheeks.

"Yes, of course. But this is about me, too," he said with a sigh. "If I'm out there worrying about my girlfriend back home, I'm liable to get my head blown off. It's going to be bad enough worrying about Mama, home with Daddy without me to look after her."

Bobbi hadn't laid eyes on Mrs. Walton since the night she'd seen her rushing out of their house, the night Ed had gone and proposed to Grace, but she knew that Mrs. Walton wasn't coping so well with her former affair and his new wife living on the same street. Landrum hadn't told her many details, but Bobbi knew that Mrs. Walton had come clean to her husband, afraid of Grace doing it first, and that there had been a terrible row. Bobbi may not have had much love for either of the women in her brother's life, but she felt a great deal of pity for the both of them, for very different reasons. Mrs. Walton especially. She had to be a good woman, despite her failings, Bobbi'd often thought, if she raised a boy like Landrum.

Except at that moment, she hated Landrum. "I can't believe you would do this," she said hotly, her face coloring, trying to swallow back tears. "Break up with me right before you ship off to war. You *just* said you wanted to marry me! I might never see you again; is this how you want to leave things?"

"No," Landrum said, then added, "And yes." He took her hands in his and she tried to snatch them away. "Bobbi, stop. This is hard for me. I laid awake half the night worrying about it. I don't want you to put your life on hold if I'm gone for years. And I could be. This damned war is like a cancer. I'm beginning to think it'll never end. And god knows what it'll be like when I do come back...*if* I come back... You've seen the footage on the news of those guys, what they look like..."

"Shut up," she said, stricken. "Stop it."

"We've got to face this, darlin'. I don't want to leave you. That's the last thing I want to do." Landrum's voice broke. "You have to know I love you. I was...I was planning to propose to you again at New Year's. But I can't do that, not in good faith when I'm leaving for god knows how long. You deserve happiness, to go to school and travel and meet folks without my specter hanging over your head, that's all." He wiped at his eyes. "If I come back, and you still want me... Well, we can talk about marriage then. When it's right."

"I can't believe you'd tell me this. That you were going to propose and then decided to break up with me instead."

"It's the last thing I want to do," Landrum said dumbly, his face imploring.

"And yet here you are doing it."

"Yeah," he had said softly, turning his face to the wall.

He hadn't spent the night that night. Bobbi had secretly yearned for him to, but she was still so angry, and also afraid. Afraid if she asked him to, he'd refuse, begin putting distance between the two of them, and afraid if he said yes, she wouldn't be able to let him go in the morning. She'd spent that night alone, cold in her bed, tense and crying, her pillow damp. In the next room, she could hear the muffled voices of Grace and Ed, raised in a heated argument; they did that all the time, and the house was always rife with tension. This week, it was fighting over money: specifically, the cost of the nursing home Ed was scouring for Granny and Papaw.

Bobbi's beloved grandparents had only continued to decline, and after briefly moving back in to help them, her uncle Ned had quickly found himself snowed under and unable to care for them both. Bobbi and Ed had tried their best to chip in, but Granny and Papaw were stubborn and listless, now that their eldest son was gone. There was nothing for it, according to Ed… It was time to send them somewhere they could be cared for in their old age. It broke Bobbi's heart. She knew her father wouldn't have wanted such a fate for his parents, but he wasn't here to protest. And as if it wasn't hard enough, Grace was constantly harping about the cost.

In short order, Grace had turned their once warm, casual home into a pristine, cold museum, full of knick-knacks and embroidered cushions that gave the pretense of warmth to hide the coolness beneath. And now her Landrum, Bobbi's only source of light and warmth, was gone, too. And soon Bobbi found that even law school, the thing she'd been dreaming of for years, no longer had any appeal to her. She just wanted to get *out*.

SO LONG, BOBBY

Well, Bobbi now thought to herself as she made her way into the bus station, sighing with relief as the warm current of air hit her from the industrial-strength heaters: I'm gone now, too. Ed's on his own. For better or worse.

"Got a light, hon?" Bobbi jumped from the hard plastic seat in which she'd been dozing and stared, startled, at the pretty young black woman who sat across from her. For a moment, she had forgotten where she was, then it hit her with a tumbling realization. The bus station. She was halfway to Washington, D.C.

The young woman was beautiful, with wide-set, deep brown eyes that sparkled and dimples in her dark cheeks. Her hair was curly and wild, piled atop her head and held in place with multiple barrettes. She was wearing a large paisley peacoat that dwarfed her, like something Bobbi would imagine a displaced vampire might wear. It almost looked baroque, threaded with gold and burgundy throughout. She had sleek black boots like Bobbi's, but hers had no holes.

"Sorry, what?"

"I just asked if you had a light," the girl said with a smile. "I'm dying for a cig, and I used my last match at the last stop. You got the fire, I got the smoke."

"I don't smoke," Bobbi said, and the girl's face fell. "Sorry."

Bobbi maneuvered in the uncomfortable plastic chair, trying to find some semblance of rest again, then she sat up. "Wait," she said aloud, rummaging in her bag. "I do actually have a lighter... Landrum's..." She had taken a bag full of his things with her for comfort, and wasn't his engraved silver Zippo among them? "Let's see… Yes, here it is!"

"Oh, thank God," the girl said, standing up and producing a package of cigarettes. "You just saved my life." Bobbi handed over the lighter, and the girl said, "Sure you don't want to come out for some air? I know you don't smoke, but that guy in the corner has been eyeing you ever since you came in, and I bet he'll hit on you the second I leave."

"In that case," Bobbi said, offering the girl a grateful smile, "I'd love a smoke."

"Us gals gotta stick together," she said with a grin, and Bobbi got up to follow her.

Outside, Bobbi again declined the offered cigarette and pulled her coat tighter around herself. "I'm Bobbi," she said as she watched the girl inhale, then exhale smoke in a long stream.

"Kat," the girl replied, extending her free hand to shake Bobbi's. "Where you from?"

"Athens, Georgia," Bobbi said, and was surprised to see the girl nod.

"I've been there," Kat said, flicking ash onto the ground. "I'm from Auburn. Alabama. Your rival."

Bobbi stared at her blankly, and the girl smiled. "Not a football fan, huh?"

"Not really," Bobbi said. "My boyfriend watched the games. He always said he was going to take me to one, but he never got the chance to…" She trailed off, fighting the tears that started in her eyes. She couldn't do this every time she thought of Landrum or said his name. It was too embarrassing, not to mention childish.

"He die?" Kat's face was full of sympathy.

"Oh, no," Bobbi rushed to explain, embarrassed, watching as another load of young people got off a second bus, only half of them dodging the huge muddy puddle on the grass. She held back a laugh as a young man stepped foot-first into the muck and let out a stream of cuss words. "He just got sent over there. A few weeks ago." She didn't elaborate; the girl would know what she meant.

"Oh," Kat replied, staring in the direction of the bus. "Well, I'm sorry. Shit sucks. I know a couple of guys over there, too. But at least he's not dead, right? At least he's got a fighting chance. And that's what we're doing this for, right?"

"Yeah." Bobbi nodded. "I guess so." The truth was, she didn't have the first clue what she was doing here, why she was going. The idea had just come to her, fully formed, and she'd packed her bag and been out the door before she could second-guess herself. It had been as much about getting away from Ed and Grace and that empty shell of a house as it had been about protesting the war. "My brother is over there, too," she added. "My middle brother."

"Damn. Well, I'm sorry," Kat said again, stubbing out her cigarette. "But it's gonna be okay, hon. I promise. You've got us, now."

Bobbi assumed she was referring to the motley crew of people she'd got off the bus with, who she'd no doubt resume traveling with until they reached Washington. But as the young man she'd just seen fall into the puddle came up beside them, resting an easy arm over Kat's shoulders, she realized what the girl had meant. Her cheeks colored slightly as the man's narrow, dark-brown eyes worked over her face, taking in her clothes, her hair. He smiled, an easy thing, lighting him up all the way to his eyebrows. "Hey. I'm Leon."

"Ramon," Kat said, giving him a pouty, flirty look, and leaned forward for a kiss. "His name is Ramon." She pronounced it with a bit of a lilt, like *Ramone*.

"Leon Ramon Hawks," the man said, extending a hand with long, tapered fingers. Bobbi was surprised to find, as she shook it, that the hand was calloused and rough. She wondered if he played guitar, or if he was a laborer of some kind. "But as you can see, my woman likes me to go by Ramon." He rolled his eyes.

Bobbi didn't follow. They both laughed. "He's Black and Puerto Rican," Kat explained, pulling her jacket tighter around her shoulders. A cool breeze had lifted in the air. "He teases me that I want a man from an exotic locale. But that's not it. I had a handsy uncle named Leon. I just don't like the name."

"So, should I call you Leon or Ramon?" Bobbi asked, and they both laughed again.

"Whatever you want, chick," he said with another easy smile. "Gonna go in and check on the next bus," he said, giving Kat another loud smooch. "Nice to meet you..."

"Bobbi," she said, feeling herself flush again and suddenly hating her annoyingly pale, embarrassing whiteness. "Bobbi Newton."

"I like that," he called from over his shoulder as he walked into the building. "Like Bobby Kennedy and Huey Newton, huh? Now that's a legacy. You keep that." Bobbi's brow furrowed as he sauntered inside.

Kat laughed. "My man, ever the politico. He's a writer, too." Her face beamed with pride. "He's always thinking in terms of pen names and stuff like that. All that arguing we do over Leon or Ramon... Give him another few weeks and he'll be going by D'artagnan or something, just to spite me." She rolled her eyes, but her face was aglow. She'd brightened up like a gemstone the moment he'd stepped next to her. "I sure do love that man, though, Lord."

Bobbi said nothing, falling in lockstep with Kat as they went back inside, hiding her smile with the back of her hand. She knew that feeling. And for the first time in weeks, she could think of it without crying.

It turned out that Ramon—Bobbi decided she'd call him that for the time being, since that's what her new friend Kat preferred—*did* play guitar, which she discovered as they sat back down in the bench seats to wait for the next bus, and he pulled a beautiful black Les Paul out of his bag and began to strum. "Ain't nobody's fault..." he began crooning the opening lyrics to Blind Willie Johnson's *Nobody's Fault but Mine* in a velvety smooth voice with a hint of cracked concrete.

As it happened, he was also a laborer. Kat talked incessantly for the next hour, and most of what she had to say was about Ramon. Ramon occasionally piped up with his own recollections, but mainly, he just strummed his guitar as Kat told his story.

Ramon had worked as part of a road crew with his cousin, Kat explained, back home in Alabama since he was thirteen years old.

"Nobody ever even asked him his age," she'd said in a low voice to Bobbi. She went on to tell Bobbi about how, during his time on the crew, Ramon had witnessed a white woman veer off the road, drunk, hitting his cousin Elmer and breaking his leg. Rather than charge the woman, the police had tried to place the blame on Elmer, accusing him of stumbling into the road as the woman drove past. Elmer had pushed for consequences for the woman—she'd been drinking, after all, and hurt him badly—and the town had riled up against him violently as a consequence. Kat didn't go into details, but Bobbi could imagine what types of things had happened next. She'd seen the same types of racist behaviors in Athens, and, remembering Lent Shaw and Lemuel Penn, was relieved when Kat said Elmer was alive and well.

"That's how Ramon got started as an activist," Kat said, recounting the story to Bobbi, who felt deep shame, even though she hadn't been there. Ramon was still plucking at his guitar, his face grim. "He couldn't go back to the road crew after that. Not seeing what he'd seen. He wanted to speak out, to do something. So he took off that same month for Selma. He wanted to meet folks, get organized, join their ranks." Kat's face beamed with pride. "It was about six months after that that I met him. He was passing through with young Mr. Lewis in one of their demonstrations. I was sitting up inside the soda shop with my friend Claire, drinking a malted. And I saw the handsomest men I'd ever seen breezing on by the window, decked out in tan trench coats and shiny black shoes... They were heading on down to the department store to sit at the counter and protest. I swallowed the rest of my malted and followed them." She smiled. "Tell the truth, at first I only joined because I wanted to get to know Ramon. He was so handsome. I was dying to know how a half Puerto Rican man ended up in Alabama." Bobbi snuck a glance at Ramon, who had a ghost of a smile on his face. "But as I took up time with the group, I began to see the importance of their work. I began to wake up myself."

"You know John Lewis?" Bobbi asked, feeling a little awestruck. She'd been fascinated by the young activist ever since Bloody Sunday, when he'd become famous for the violent beating he'd taken on the Edmund Pettus Bridge, three years before. Bobbi and her friends had been following his movements within the SNCC and with Reverend Dr. Martin Luther King ever since. She'd seen his face in plenty of newspapers and felt she knew the sensitive, intelligent young man. He was destined for amazing things; she just felt it.

"I do, a little," Kat said, her smile deepening. "Ramon knows him better than I do. If you keep with us, you'll probably meet him at some point."

"Gosh, I'd love to," Bobbi said, aware that she was gushing. "The only person I'd love to meet more is maybe Bobby Kennedy."

"That one might be a little harder," Kat said with a laugh. "But I'll see what I can do."

Bobbi couldn't help but notice how Kat's eyes didn't stay off of Ramon for long; clearly, the young man meant a lot to her. And she could see why. Ramon's long, thin fingers flew over the guitar strings as he tapped a boot-clad foot in time. A bit of mud from the puddle was still crusted there, but he appeared not to have noticed; it flaked off little by little as he tapped along to the song. When they'd first sat down in the cluster of bench seats closest to the doors, it'd just been the three of them. But over the course of Kat telling the story, Bobbi noticed that four other young people had come to sit down near them. A tall guy with large Coke-bottle glasses and olive-green corduroy pants sat down beside her, tapping along to the tune. He nodded to her with a smile.

Ramon was a natural leader, Bobbi thought, smiling over at the man, noting how Kat's eyes followed his every move. He had that quality about him. *I see why she's so taken with him. I bet people would follow him anywhere,* she thought to herself as she watched him.

As it turned out, Bobbi was one of them.

THIRTEEN

ELLA - 1995

"**AMERICA** has always celebrated its *potential* as though it were the *reality*," Ella heard herself saying as she helped herself to another dinner roll. She was blissfully drunk.

"Fuck, that's deep," Anita said with a laugh, taking the platter of rolls from Ella's outstretched hand. "I didn't know we were getting a political philosophy lecture along with our Thanksgiving dinner."

"She's right, though," Louie said, looking up from his plate, which held the same clump of untouched tofu glop as everyone else's. Ella had tried—and failed—at making a healthy alternative to turkey this year. So far, everyone had been politely pretending it didn't exist. "All the pomp and circumstance, all the 'America the Great' stuff we celebrate on the Fourth of July, our anthems and fireworks and all that red, white, and blue... It's not real, it's not who we actually are, or ever have been. It's all just a celebration of what we aspire to be. What we pretend we are. And never will be, because nobody is willing to stop worshipping guns and dollar bills."

"Hear, hear," Janelle said boisterously, leaning over to refill Ella's glass with mead. She'd brought several bottles from the co-op, sickly sweet and delicious. Ella was certain she'd drunk almost a whole bottle herself. "Here's to our brilliant, politically-minded friends and this delicious meal. Especially that scrumptious fucking tofu meatloaf."

"Hey," Ella slurred, her face growing hot. "If you hadn't been plying me with mead all afternoon, maybe I would've—"

"I'm not sure she even glanced at the recipe again after glass number two," she heard Anita whisper to Tad, her date, the two of them collapsing into drunken giggles.

"In my defense, I've never *seen* tofu before, much less cooked with it, before today," Ella began hotly, then dissolved into laughter herself. "Okay, fine, it's trash. Don't eat it."

"It's okay, Ell," Janelle said, raising her glass in a toast. "None of us like tofu anyway, so we were bound to hate it, regardless of your cooking prowess. And you know, it's like you said. We're celebrating your potential as a vegan...not your reality. As a person who lives off Doritos and Cherry Coke."

Ella had been trying, and failing miserably, at going vegan for the past month. Everyone at the co-op was vegan, vegetarian, or pescatarian, whatever that meant, and she felt like the odd one out, standing around shoveling junk food in her face all the time. Not to mention, she wanted to look hot and thin for Louie. She knew that gaining weight was the last thing she should care about, and Janelle and Anita would revoke her feminist card if they knew she felt that way, but she couldn't seem to stop herself from hearing Aunt Grace's voice in her head. *You eat too much junk; you're getting chunky.* She'd heard that refrain all throughout her adolescence.

Ella had managed to stave off a few bad habits—one of the

biggest being that she'd stopped scratching at her arms until they bled, something she'd done for years—but worrying about her weight was one she'd yet to shake.

Not that Louie would care if she *did* gain weight. Louie was the sweetest, most easy-going guy she'd ever met. He didn't have a shallow bone in his body. Ella could still hardly believe his interest in her. What could he possibly see in her, the anxious, depressed, moody southern mess she was? Especially with women like Janelle and Anita around, who exuded confidence, sexuality, both of whom had amazing figures and could apply winged eyeliner in their sleep.

"You might have a thundercloud over your head," Louie had said to her one night, the two of them sharing a pillow in his little apartment, "but I can see the sun breaking out from underneath it." She'd kissed him then. It was the sweetest thing anyone had ever said to her.

As much as she loved him and his friends, being among Louie and Janelle seemed to be a never-ending political conversation, for which Ella felt unequipped. They were both fascinated with her thoughts on various issues, being from the South and having a high-profile judge for an uncle. They were shocked when Ella had told them she didn't care about politics and didn't have many opinions one way or the other. Since then, the pair had gone out of their way to call her on it as often as possible, determined to pull her out of her ignorant slumber and get her involved. Evidently, the conversation was still on the table.

"I'll give you that about America...but, Ella. How can you not be engaged in the world around you?" Janelle asked. "Don't you want to vote? I just can't understand that."

"I'm not interested in what President Clinton does in the oval office, sexual or otherwise," Ella said, going for a laugh. She dutifully took a bite of her broccoli rice casserole, which Janelle had spent an hour making; the kitchen looked like a bomb site, but she was certain it was the most delicious thing she'd ever tasted. "Why anyone else would care is beyond me."

"It's about more than that. All that shit with Clinton...it's just a distraction. I'm not talking about the scandals, the gossip. I'm talking about the issues. Your right to an abortion, for one thing. Don't you care? The AIDS crisis. Let's face it, any one of us could get—"

"Let's not get too heavy here," Tad interjected, and Janelle shot him a look.

"I think that ship sailed a while ago," Ella said, poking at her tofu, wondering if it might poke back. "Of course I care, but...I guess I just don't feel educated enough to have a real opinion. If I felt I was really up on the issues, then yes, I'd vote."

"So educate yourself, then," Janelle said with a pointed look. "What's your next excuse?"

Louie broke in with an apologetic smile. "You have to remember that Janelle is the daughter of Freedom Riders. She's been on a steady diet of politics since she was in diapers. She doesn't mean to throw the hammer down on you."

"They weren't Freedom Riders," Janelle said irritably, but her face softened. "They started later than that...the Freedom Rides were in '65. Don't you guys know anything?" She blotted her mouth with a napkin, then smirked proudly. "They do *know* a few Freedom Riders, though. By the way, speaking of my folks" —she looked over at Ella— "I think they might drop in for dessert."

Ella's stomach dropped. She'd heard so much about Janelle's parents, so much that she was beginning to feel like they were famous, in a way. The way Louie hero-worshipped them and the pride that touched Janelle's voice as she talked about them always filled Ella with a nervous anxiety, as though they were living legends, the type of folks that one aspired to be but never could. Definitely far too sophisticated, cool and intelligent to hang out with the likes of her, some nobody niece of a southern-fried judge. Ella immediately began to regret all the mead she'd drunk. Politics and activism aside, she thought the world of Janelle—she worshipped her, if she was being honest—and meeting her parents filled her with dread. What if they didn't like her? She couldn't meet these two infamous people—who had made someone as wonderful and maddening as Janelle—while shitfaced drunk. With her dried-out, flavorless tofu meatloaf still gracing the table.

Especially considering the secret Ella had been keeping from Janelle.

A secret that might change everything—including the way Janelle felt about her—forever.

"Relax," Janelle said, noticing her discomfort. "My parents are super chill. They'll love you."

"They don't love *me*," Louie said with a chuckle.

"They like you fine," Janelle argued. "Though that was pretty stupid of you, asking my dad what it was like to meet George

Wallace. Of all the fucking people to ask about—"

"It wasn't like I was hero-worshiping the guy; I was wondering if he's as awful in person as you hear, that's all."

"Yeah, but you were a spoon-fed white boy from Seattle dating their Black daughter, asking what a noted southern white supremacist is like in person," Janelle said, rolling her eyes. "Not your best look."

Louie made an "oops," face, meeting Ella's eyes. "She's right. It wasn't my best day. In my defense, she brought them around unannounced, and I was high as a fucking kite."

"Oh god," Ella said, her stomach rolling over. "So this is a pattern with you, then." Janelle just grinned and tipped her glass. The girl really did have a totally different existence than the rest of the mortals. Ella was certain of it.

"Why didn't you invite your parents to join us for dinner?" Anita asked.

"I did," Janelle answered. "But they'd already accepted an invite at a friend's house. They have friends all over Seattle, hell, all over everywhere. It's like pulling teeth to get them to visit me when they're here. Not because they don't want to, but because they stay so busy, meeting up with all their different friends and connections. Their social life puts mine to shame."

Ella was feeling more and more dread by the second. She poked at her casserole.

"Stop stressing," Janelle said, putting her hand on Ella's arm. "They're just people, for the love of dog."

"They sound so intimidating from the way you talk about them,"

Ella admitted. "Like royalty."

Janelle snorted. "If they heard you say that, they'd laugh their asses off. The only royal my folks approve of is Princess Di. They're cool, I promise. Don't make it a big deal and it won't be, sweets."

"They aren't vegan, are they?" Evan asked with horror from his corner seat. He had been the first to get lit up on the mead and hadn't spoken two words through dinner. "I made lemon meringue pie. Anita said it wouldn't matter if the dessert was vegan."

"They aren't vegan," Janelle said with a smile. "My dad loves bacon double cheeseburgers more than he loves me."

"So they aren't Muslim then," Tad said from beside Anita, and the table fell suddenly, awkwardly silent.

"They were born and bred in Alabama, good southern Baptists," Janelle said after a long pause, looking at Tad steadily. "Well, actually, they're both agnostic these days. But raised Christian. I'm curious why you would think they were Muslim."

"Black Panthers... You know, all the political Black people... A lot of them, like you guys..." Tad floundered, looking at Janelle and Anita for confirmation, his face turning red. "They're Muslim, right?" He threw up his hands in mock surrender, turning to Louie and Ella. "You guys know what I'm trying to say, right?"

"Dude." Louie looked down at his plate, and Ella took another long drag of mead, well aware that she'd had quite enough. But damn, even she knew better than to say something so utterly ignorant.

Janelle's voice was calm. "Let's just finish eating and get the table cleared for dessert." Ella knew Tad would not be back at their table, judging from the horrified, embarrassed look on Anita's face.

"I can't believe he said that," Ella whispered, wiping down the wet dishes and placing them back in the cabinet. She and Janelle were doing the washing while Evan and Anita set up for coffee and dessert. Louie was in the back, rolling a few joints. Janelle's parents had just called to confirm they were on their way, and the house had taken on an excited frenzy. Ella was still half-drunk. "I just can't."

"I can," Janelle said, washing a bowl and handing it over without looking. "It's just run-of-the-mill ignorance. Dime a dozen. He means well, but you can't fight that internalized racism."

"But I'm from the South and even I know better than to…"

"Yeah, but you were raised in a political family," Janelle said. "Your uncle was obviously savvy enough to keep you from showing your ass like that, regardless of whatever his private opinions were."

"That's true," Ella agreed. "I doubt Anita will bother to try and school him. From the look she was giving him, he's probably being dumped as we speak."

"I don't blame her," Janelle said, handing her another plate. "Why waste her time trying to educate him? Even if she gets him right on that issue, another one will crop up later. I'm telling you, Ella, women spend way too much emotional labor trying to teach men how to act—especially Black women like me and Anita—and where does it get us?"

"Nowhere," Ella agreed. Janelle was right. Ella had seen how Uncle Ed called on the Black community, especially the Black women elders, when it was politically advantageous to do so. They always showed up for him, always. Her uncle, for his part, made all the right declarations and showed up at the right photo ops. But what Janelle was talking about—sticking your neck out for the good of your friends—no, Uncle Ed would not have done that. Not if it would cost him.

As she dried a plate, it dawned on Ella that that was racism, too, as much as any other kind. It was just more insidious, cloaked beneath good intentions and pretense.

She was so grateful for what she was learning—but also terribly ashamed.

Not knowing what else to say, she confessed, "I'm so nervous to meet your parents."

"Don't be silly. Smoke some weed; that'll even you out," Janelle said, emptying the soapy water from the sink and wiping her hands on a dishtowel. "Always works for me."

"I'm tempted to just run on home," Ella confessed, feeling her cheeks redden. She and Anita had recently put down a deposit on a small two-bedroom apartment. There were still boxes everywhere. "I'm afraid I'll—"

"Say something dumb like Tad did?" Janelle laughed. "Don't worry. I spotted that guy for a jackoff the moment I saw him; we all did. And anyway, you can't go. My parents are dying to meet you."

"Me? Why?" Ella asked.

"Well, because you're an employee at their co-op, for starters," Janelle said with a smile. She poured herself another glug of mead and chuckled when Ella waved away her attempt to pour more in her glass. "And I've talked their ears off about you."

"Janelle…" Ella's stomach rolled over. It was now or never. She couldn't *not* tell her. "There's something you should know. Before your parents get here."

"What is it?" Janelle asked. She put down her glass and met Ella's gaze. Ella stared for a moment, noticing the pretty flecks of green in her friend's warm brown eyes, wishing she could bypass this entire conversation and go back to the easy friendship from before.

"Well…" Ella took a deep breath. "There's a reason I'm so nervous to meet your parents. This is gonna sound crazy, but…I already know—knew—who they are. Before I even came to Seattle. In fact…they're the reason I came here in the first place."

Janelle's brow furrowed. "What? How?"

"I didn't make the connection when we first met, but then…I connected the dots after you and I met, and I realized…" Ella swallowed, realizing she needed to back up. "Janelle…I grew up knowing that I had godparents, friends of my mother's who lived out in Seattle. It seemed like a far-off land to me when I was a kid, like Narnia or something… My mom died when I was a baby, so I never heard much about my godparents, but I had this one letter from them I looked at sometimes when things felt bad. I liked to think of them, out in the world, wondering what had become of me. And I daydreamed about finding them one day. So when I split from my uncle's house, the first place I thought to go was Seattle."

Janelle looked at her intently, and Ella went on in a shaky voice.

"Once I actually got here, though, I lost all my nerve. I decided not to contact them after all, to not disrupt their lives after so many years. I decided to just strike out on my own and see what happened. Then I met you…and something just sort of clicked for me. It felt like destiny. And then when you began talking about your folks, I realized they sounded an awful lot like the godparents I'd spent my childhood daydreaming about. I thought it couldn't be real, but then when we signed the papers at the co-op and I saw their names on the contract, I knew for sure." Ella opened her eyes and looked at her friend. "Fate must have brought us together, Janelle. Your parents are my godparents."

She expected Janelle to be gobsmacked, to stare at her in confusion, to deny that was possible. At the very least, a shocked "What?" But Janelle just looked at her for a moment, then said, "You're telling me that you're Bobbi Newton's baby?"

"Yes. I am." Ella said, then her own brow furrowed. "Wait, you knew my mother?"

"No. But I grew up hearing about her. Mom talked about her all the time, about Bobbi's baby girl who was supposed to come live with us, but her stupid guardians—" Her eyes widened. "Your aunt and uncle are the assholes who—"

"Yeah." Ella nodded. "Uncle Ed and Aunt Evil."

"Why didn't you tell me about this?' Janelle demanded, but her face wasn't angry. "When we first met?"

"By the time I realized for sure, so much time had passed, and I felt so awkward…" Ella bit her lip. "I didn't know how you'd take it. If you'd think I was trying to take advantage of you or pull some backhanded shit to meet them…"

"Is that what you're doing?" Janelle asked.

"*No!*" Ella grabbed her friend's hand and gave it a squeeze. "Please believe me, Janelle. I would never use you like that. I'm so sorry I didn't tell you right away. I was just so confused. I wasn't sure if I *wanted* to meet them. I mean, that's what I came here for, but once I arrived I just..." She sighed. "I got scared."

"Well, you're meeting them now," Janelle said with a laugh, "whether you want to or not."

Ella looked down at her lap, enjoying the feel of Janelle's warm, steady hand in her own trembling one, even if she felt half-insane with shock. The mead was making her head spin. Louie's joints were starting to seem very appealing. *Numb.* That's what she needed, to numb her loud, spinning brain. "I'm afraid," she confessed, not able to bear looking at Janelle right now, with her warm, green-flecked eyes and confident spirit.

Janelle's voice was kind. "I'll be right beside you, godsister." She leaned closer, her voice soft in Ella's ear. "You don't have to tell them tonight if you're not ready."

Evan came into the kitchen and stood in the doorway. "Pie and coffee, my ladies—" As he spoke, there was a knock at the front door.

"They're here," Janelle said with a bright smile, hoisting Ella up by an arm. "Ready?"

"Definitely not," Ella said weakly, not wanting to let go of Janelle's strong, steady hand.

"You got this," Janelle said. "Go meet Kat and Ramon."

FOURTEEN

KASEY wasn't used to her phone's new ringtone. She'd decided that Amy Winehouse's "Rehab" was no longer funny, so she'd changed it. The phone rang five times before it finally registered that someone other than Fallon, who was checking in a maddening amount lately, was calling her. She jumped up from where she'd been rummaging through the box—again, it seemed like she'd gone through the items and lovingly ran a hand over each one at least a dozen times in the past week—and ran over to grab her phone off the coffee table. It was an unknown number, which she'd normally screen, but today, she decided to answer. Something told her it was someone she wanted to hear from.

"Hello?" she said breathlessly, just as she heard a voice on the other end say, "She's not answering."

"No, no, I'm here!" Kasey exclaimed, noting the voice on the other end of the line. It was male, and he sounded young, around her age. She could hear noise—a video game or maybe an action movie—in the background. Her heart started to thud in anticipation.

"Is this Kasey Newton?"

"Yes," she said. "Who is this?"

"Oh, sorry. This is Scott." Kasey's heart fell a little, then lifted when he said, "I'm calling on behalf of my best friend—Andy Bradenton. You emailed him? Or DM'd him on Facebook or whatever?"

"Yes, that was me," Kasey said, sitting down on the couch, suddenly feeling a little weak. She added stupidly, "He's my…uh, well, I think he's my brother."

"So he said," Scott replied in a warm, clear voice that put her at ease. "I hope you don't mind me calling instead of him… It's just that I've known Andy since we were kids. He's like *my* brother, and he was anxious. It's a lot to take in, you know, finding out you have another sister that you never—"

"Another sister?" Kasey cut in. "Wait, so I have a sister, too?"

"Well, um, no. I don't think so," Scott replied, and Kasey heard another voice muttering in the background. "No, I mean, Glitter's dad isn't Louie, so… Auntie J. was with another guy when—"

"Glitter? Who's Glitter?"

"Andy's little sister," Scott said, sounding confused himself now.

"I'm sorry, this is all so confusing," Kasey said with a laugh.

"No, no, it's me. I'm doing a shitty job as secretary," Scott replied, and they both laughed. "Should I start over?"

"Okay," Kasey said, full-on smiling now. Confusion or no, she liked this guy. He was all ease and friendliness.

"Andy's feeling a little weird about all of this," Scott went on. "He's been going back and forth about calling you for the past two days. It's not you at all; he just isn't sure how to tell his dad. I think he's settled on getting to know you better first, before he says anything to Lou." Scott's voice dropped to a whisper. "He just left the room so I can tell you... Andy has an anxiety disorder. That's why I'm calling instead of him. He thought it would be easier if I talked to you first."

"So I can cuss you out and hang up on you instead of him?"

"Basically."

Kasey laughed. "Well, I don't have any plans to cuss anyone out today. Least of all him. I mean, *I* reached out to Andy, so..."

Scott said, "He does have some questions. About who your mom is, and how she came to know Louie...that kinda stuff."

"I have questions, too," Kasey said. "Lots of them. You said Andy wanted to meet?"

"Yeah, if you're down. I think he'd really like that. A lot."

"I would too," Kasey said honestly. Her brain began ticking. She had no money for a plane ticket to Seattle, much less a hotel room... And with her only a few days into her new sobriety, and having lost her job...no car...her cane, which she was becoming more and more dependent on... "I'd love it if we could talk about all of this in person. It'd be so much easier than on the phone." Kasey hated talking on the phone. She gathered her new brother did, too, since he'd gotten his best friend to do his dirty work.

"Great. Sounds like you guys are on the same page," Scott replied.

"The only problem is," Kasey said, already embarrassed, "as much as I'd love to fly out of here for a few days, funds are super tight right now and I can't manage it. And I can't ask you to come to me. I'd hate for you to have to make the trip to somewhere so boring." She sighed. "We might just have to make do chatting on Facebook until I can save up." She was already beginning to feel disappointed. She wanted to talk to her brother in person *now*.

"Well, we can figure all that out," Scott said easily. "I think more than anything, Andy just wanted to feel you out." His voice was warm and low, and oddly comforting, and Kasey felt as if she knew him already.

"I'd love to!" Kasey exclaimed. "Look, you get back to Andy, and tell him to text me or hit me up on Facebook and we'll chat— however, he's most comfortable. We'll iron out the details." Maybe she could talk to Ricky...she dismissed the thought as soon as it came to her. She couldn't ask her stepfather to fund a trip to see her biological family.

"Wow," Scott replied. "You already totally get him. That's awesome."

"Oh, I don't know about that. I'm just so happy to hear from him. Or rather, you." Kasey could hardly contain her grin.

"I'm glad," Scott said in his warm voice. "I'll make sure he knows. I'm glad you reached out to him. I know he is, too. I'll let you go for now, Kasey. It was nice talking to you. I hope to meet you soon."

"Same here," she said, and hit the "end" button on her phone, heart racing. It might take some time to figure out the logistics, but she had a brother, and he wanted to meet her. Now she just had to work on staying clean and figure out a way to reset her life before this new part of it began.

FIFTEEN

BOBBI - WASHINGTON, D.C. - APRIL 3, 1968

IT was standing room only in the tiny office building that served as their headquarters. Bobbi had made her way to the middle of the throng before giving up and staying where she was, craning her neck to see Ramon on the makeshift stage, which some innovative person had built quickly with milk crates. The heat didn't work, and there was a huge hole in the ceiling that was letting in a cool, late-winter draft, but luckily the swarm of bodies, cramped together and sweating, provided a bit of insulation.

Bobbi could see Kat at the front, her curly black hair coiffed into a beautiful afro, standing front and center. She held a brown clipboard with a fountain pen attached by a small string, and in her other arm was a stack of pamphlets advertising their latest political meeting to take place the next day. They were trying to get a group together to travel around and help Bobby Kennedy in his bid for president. The young senator, whom Bobbi still dreamed of meeting again one day soon, had only just announced his candidacy a month before, after what seemed like years of playing coy. Kat and Ramon—who had met him, briefly, the previous year, much to Bobbi's extreme envy—wanted to help him in any way they could, and Bobbi was anxious to assist. They all felt he was the best candidate, especially after how he'd conducted himself in Mississippi and with Cesar Chavez. Bobbi would lay down her life to help RFK become president, and not only because he'd bring her brother and Landrum back from Vietnam.

How they had agonized over those pamphlets, taking turns at designing, rewording, and typesetting them, and throwing together all their meager savings and wages to pay for them. They'd sent Bobbi into the printer to order them— "They won't try to fleece you as hard as they would us," Kat had said with a slightly bitter laugh—and she'd ignored the look of outright hatred on the clerk's face as he'd handed them back to her. The right side of the print had been cut off, and when she pointed out the mistake, he'd shrugged.

"Machines don't always get it perfect," he said in a surly tone, daring her to argue. He took the money she offered and tossed her change back to her. "Tough break." He turned on his heel and disappeared into the back before she could demand he re-print the flyers.

Bobbi, face flaming, had moved toward the door when another employee emerged from the back, rubbing his ink-stained hands on his shirt. "Aw, don't sweat it, sweetheart," he'd said, noting her anger with a flirtatious wink. "Tom ain't a big fan of libbers, that's all. Say, how 'bout you forget all that politics for an afternoon and let me buy you a cream soda down the road? Or better, a wine spritzer?"

"How 'bout you kiss my fucking ass," she spat, her eyes widening at her own gall, and she'd run out of the print shop, ignoring the sound of his surprised laughter.

When she'd told the story to everyone afterward, she'd expected them to be proud, or at least amused by her story. Ramon had sighed and disappeared into the back, and Warren had been angry. "You should have held your tongue and asked them to re-do these," Warren had said. "Lord knows we can't afford to print more, and you can't fully see the address at the bottom. Someone could probably guess it, but this isn't exactly the area where we should be cutting corners."

"He was a racist," Bobbi said furiously, defending herself. "He ran to the back as soon as he took my money; I didn't have a chance to even ask. And the assistant hit on me. It wasn't even subtle. I wasn't about to stand around and take—"

"We're not saying you should've let him do that," Warren said as Kat entered the room, watching them curiously. "But they have our information now. And you went and insulted the guy, and if the boss already has it in for us... It could put us in a vulnerable position, Bobbi. You could have just said no and left it at that."

"I'm sorry," Bobbi said, shame flooding her. As Warren left the room with a sigh, she turned to Kat. "I didn't think. I was just so offended."

"I get it," Kat had cut in with a kind smile. "I hate it, but you're gonna see more of that kind of disrespect if you keep marching with us. Warren isn't wrong about learning when to swallow your pride. If we got bent out of shape about every single little thing, we'd never get anything done." She sighed, picking up one of the flyers. "But at the same time, he could have gone and done this himself. They probably wouldn't have given him the same guff they gave you. He really doesn't have the right to bitch at you about it."

Kat was right, but Bobbi was still ashamed of herself for losing her cool. Hadn't she lectured Amelia on the very same sort of thing just a few short months ago? That drive from Broad Street to the Greenway, when Amelia had been fuming about the smug man who provoked her, seemed like a lifetime ago now, though it had only been about six months. Amelia had since moved down to South Georgia to be with Sam, who had transferred to SCAD. Bobbi was still getting over her shock that Amelia would move to be with Sam, who she'd always been lackluster about, and that either of them would move to backwoods South Georgia—and both Landrum and Guy were gone, off to Vietnam. Everybody she loved was gone. She was lonely and sad and letting her emotions turn her bitter and angry, and it was affecting her in bad ways. She had raised her chin and told Kat, "Still. I shouldn't have lost my cool. I won't let that happen again, I promise."

Now, from her vantage point in the middle of the crowd, Bobbi could see the botched flyers everywhere, in people's hands and hanging out of bags. She felt ashamed of herself all over again. She shouldn't have made a scene at the printer; she should have politely demanded they re-do the flyers. It was the least she could have done with her privilege, and instead, she'd had a tantrum.

God, how she missed Landrum. She thought of him so often, and wished they could sit and talk, pouring out their hearts, sharing the things they'd been through since they parted. She'd written to him, letting him know her latest address, advising him that this would be her home for the next couple of months, but she'd received no response yet. In fact, she'd received no letters from him at all since he'd been gone. She'd gotten his address from Mrs. Walton, who she'd broken down and called one day, desperate for news. Mrs. Walton had been weird on the phone—but then, she was always weird—sniffling and low-voiced, as though she were revealing secrets and someone might be listening in.

"I only heard from him the once," Irene Walton had said, "just before he was getting ready to deploy. I haven't received any letters from him. I've got his last address, but Lord knows if he's even still reachable there. I wish to God I'd hear from him." She sniffled again. "Bobbi, are you sure you ought to write to him?"

"Why shouldn't I?" Bobbi had asked.

"He told me that the two of you busted up," Mrs. Walton said, her voice getting even lower. "And he's in a war zone... It's dangerous where he is... I just wouldn't want any distractions, anything upsetting him while he's in that place."

Bobbi had lost her temper then. "You're a fine one to talk, *Irene*," she'd spat hotly into the phone, "as if you didn't *distract* my family for years, no matter what we were going through at the time. I had a plan; Landrum and I could have gotten out of here. But he chose to go on and fight, even though it was the last thing he wanted. He said he had to do the right thing so he could come home and take care of you."

"Bobbi—"

"How's my brother Ed? I'm sure you've seen him recently," Bobbi had sneered, then hung up the phone before Mrs. Walton could answer.

Yes, her anger was getting the better of her lately.

She heard the way she talked to people, and it made her ashamed, but she couldn't seem to help herself.

Even while missing Landrum, and even with the white-hot rage that seemed to burn within Bobbi all the time now, there was another feeling worming its way into her. A feeling of freedom, of visibility, that she'd never had before.

Oh, the clerk in the print shop really could go to hell; she had no use for sneering, entitled white boys who thought they could paw at her and ply her with scraps. But there had been other boys—men— that she'd seen and couldn't help casting an appreciative eye toward. Bobbi had kept her head down, her mind on the cause, unable to shake her loyalty to Landrum even though he'd ended things—but she couldn't help but notice, and she wondered if there might be some night soon when she got lonely enough that she might allow someone to keep her company. There was no shortage of suitable candidates; when you weren't looking for love, it certainly widened the pool. And when you did meaningful work, stood for important causes, you were thrown together with other like-minded people, people who cared and worked hard for others and sacrificed themselves for the greater good. It was very attractive, she had to admit to herself. Very attractive indeed.

And Ramon is the most attractive of them all, Bobbi thought as she watched him grab a megaphone and clear his throat. *Kat is a lucky woman.* She bit the thought off quickly, glancing toward her friend, who was beaming from the front row. She admonished herself. Having illicit thoughts about her friend's boyfriend—who was also the leader of their little group and therefore deserving of the utmost respect—was not cool at all. Kat had been good to her, and Ramon was hers, through and through. He was off-limits, even if he was the most handsome man she'd seen in a spell. Handsome and charismatic and charming and well-read and poised and furious and determined and—

Stop that right now, Bobbi Newton.

"Bobbi, come quick. Robert F. Kennedy's speaking in Indianapolis!"

Bobbi jumped out of the dingy, tiny shower and threw a towel around her long hair. She was in desperate need of a trim—the bottom three inches of her blonde hair was all dead ends—but she couldn't afford it, nor did she have the time to do it herself. She groaned as she dried herself and threw on a pair of linen bellbottoms and a Jefferson Airplane t-shirt; Bobby wasn't supposed to be speaking yet, was he? She'd thought she had plenty of time to shower and grab a bite before his speech. She was running behind. Her afternoon guest—a nice, if a bit quiet, young man named Sheldon, who she'd met the night before at the pool hall—had been surprisingly bad at taking hints, and Bobbi had finally had to ask him outright to get going. She remembered the hurt look on his face and felt guilty. But what had he expected, a long-term relationship? Sheldon had only just snuck out the back, and Bobbi hoped none of her friends had seen him because she didn't feel like explaining. She finished toweling her hair and emerged from the bathroom in a cloud of steam, running down to the makeshift lounge where her friends were crowded around the television.

"Hurry up," Kat said, inching over to make room for her on the couch. "He's about to talk."

"What's he doing?" Bobbi asked, peering at the TV, confused. "He's not on a podium, is he? The lighting is all weird and the cameras aren't filming him from the front."

"He's standing on the back of a flatbed truck," Ramon said, his eyes glued to the screen. "They didn't have time to finish setting up the podium, they just cut to the press conference without a word beforehand." He swallowed hard. "Something's wrong."

"I'm sure there's not, hon…" Kat said, putting her hand on his arm. "He's always doing that, standing on the back of cars and stuff. It's his thing; you know, how he likes to seem 'of the people.'"

"No…" Ramon said, turning to look at Kat, his eyes bright with worry. "This isn't the same. I have a bad feeling, baby."

Bobbi said nothing; there was a weird gnawing feeling taking root in her belly. Ramon was right. The wrongness was a tangible feeling, thick and heavy in the air. Everyone in the room fell silent with tension.

After a couple of minutes of uneasy waiting, the sound of the crowd dimmed just as Senator Robert Kennedy muttered something in a low voice to the man beside him. Bobbi and her friends were crowded around the television in an uneasy silence. "Did you hear what he said?" Kat asked, craning her head to listen.

"Yes," Ramon said in a low voice. He turned to her, his eyes full of dread. "He said, 'Do they know about Martin Luther King?'"

"Oh no…please no," Kat moaned softly, and Bobbi felt her stomach drop to her feet as the Senator took a deep breath and began to speak, the crowd going mostly silent with respect. Bobby

Kennedy seemed smaller than usual—shrunken, meek. There was something else in his face, too, something she'd never seen there before: shame. Bobbi grasped at Kat's shoulder, the two of them both shaking.

"Could you lower those signs, please?" Kennedy began. The crowd grew further silent, the air thick with dread. Bobby wasted no more time. "I have some very sad news for all of you," he began, his voice thick with nerves and sadness, "and that is that...Martin Luther King was shot and was killed tonight in Memphis, Tennessee."

The crowd began to scream. It was loud and piercing through the old television speakers, and Bobbi clapped her hands to her ears, then moved them to her eyes and back again. She suddenly had no idea where to put her hands. She realized the screaming wasn't just coming from the television, but from those crowded in front of the TV: Kat, Ramon, herself.

"God in Heaven, no!" Kat cried, and Bobbi moved to put her arms around her friend, pulling her close. But Kat pulled away, reaching for Ramon, her rock, where she collapsed into his chest, her shoulders shaking with silent sobs.

Mr. Kennedy went on, his voice heavy with despair, and beneath it, purpose. "Martin Luther King...dedicated his life to love and to justice between fellow human beings. He died in the cause of that effort..." He went on talking, but Bobbi's eyes were not on the Senator, or the crowd in Indianapolis who had given way to tears and cries of anguish, or even to her friend Kat, whose entire body was shaking with sobs, but who hadn't made so much as a peep. Her eyes were on Ramon, who sat still as a sculpture, staring at the

TV, his face like stone, holding Kat in his arms but not noticing her, immovable as a mountain, the only evidence of the pain he felt a single tear that ran down his dark, handsome cheek, landing on his collar as Robert F. Kennedy began to read a poem by the ancient Greek Aeschylus.

Bobbi supposed Robert F. Kennedy read the poem because he did not know what else to do. Nobody did. Not anymore.

"Even in our sleep
Pain which cannot beget
Falls drop by drop upon the heart
Until in our despair,
Against our will,
Comes wisdom through the awful grace of God."

SIXTEEN

ELLA - 1995

ELLA was baked out of her mind, in addition to the alcohol that hadn't quite worked its way out of her system, sitting in a state of quiet disbelief on Janelle's threadbare, scratchy couch, with an older woman holding her hand. She wanted to pull away, to run outside into the night, find a bench in a quiet space and think about the story she'd just been told—but the woman's face was so kind and open, so full of joy, her hand so warm and soft and maternal, that Ella couldn't bring herself to leave.

So instead, Ella sat and listened, nodding at the right times, smiling and pretending her entire world hadn't just been blown to smithereens. Looking over at Janelle, who was nursing yet *another* glass of mead (How did she keep from being shitfaced? And she just drank comfortably in front of her parents? God, their lives were so, so different). Her head spun and shrunk and expanded and seemed to shrink again. She could have killed Janelle for letting her get so drunk, though it certainly wasn't Janelle's fault that Ella had kept such a secret; how was she to know her own parents were Ella's godparents?

It's a wonder all three of them didn't tell me to go fuck myself, considering what I kept from them, Ella thought to herself as her godmother Kat squeezed her hand again, mistaking her state of discombobulation for upset. Ella caught Janelle's eye, who winked at her, and threw her curly dark hair back. As she tipped the glass back again, her red lips curled around the rim in an almost smile. *She really is so beautiful,* Ella thought to herself, feeling a pang of something she couldn't identify. Jealousy?

After all, she'd just been told that the seemingly charmed life Janelle had led could have been hers, too.

Ella couldn't believe it. Any of it.

That her godparents had sat so calmly while Janelle explained—Ella couldn't seem to make the words come out of her mouth—that her new friend and employee Ella was, in fact, Ella Newton, the long-lost daughter of their best friend Bobbi. That Kat had turned to Ramon with a sweet, calm smile, and said, "Ah, of course. We should have guessed you'd find us." And then they'd both turned to her and began to talk so warmly of her parents, the parents she'd never known, her godmother's soft, smooth hands clasping hers as if they'd spent every day together for the past twenty years. That they'd just accepted this news as though it was the most normal thing in the world.

That they'd immediately begun telling her the whole story; the story she'd never once heard from Ed and Grace.

Ella had never been under the impression that Uncle Ed and Aunt Grace were saints. She'd lived with them, knew their secrets, knew who and what they were. But under the aspirations, the philandering, the unhappy union with Grace, one thing she had always known was that they loved her. How could they have kept so much from her?

"I just can't understand it," Ella said finally, careful not to slur her words. "Uncle Ed and Aunt Grace...they had lives, full lives; he had a busy career. I was often in the way. I was a nuisance to them, really..." She shook her head. "If there was a chance for me to go somewhere...to be with people who loved my mother and honored who she was...who *wanted* me... Why wouldn't they let me go?"

"Do you need to ask?" the man across from her on the loveseat asked quietly.

Ella took a good look at this man, who had introduced himself as Leon, but who Kat called Ramon, who had shaken her hand warmly but spent the rest of the time watching her with his soulful, intuitive dark-brown eyes as his wife told the story. She'd taken him at first to be one of those quiet, unassuming husbands who let his wife rule the roost and didn't say much. As Kat had been talking, she'd allowed herself the fantasy of what having him as her father might've been like. Now, she realized he was a different kind of quiet; a worlds-simmering-below-the-surface type of quiet, the kind that *contained multitudes.* She wondered, drunkenly, where she'd read that phrase.

This was a man who did not say much, because when he did speak, his words carried real weight. When he did speak, you *listened.*

She looked into his deep, warm brown eyes and felt herself grimace with shame. "Because you're Black?" The words came out as a whisper.

He nodded, his dark eyes bright, and Katherine squeezed her hand again.

"He's right, but that's not the whole story," Kat said, her voice warm and "Oh, their prejudices played into it, especially that Grace." She spat the name *Grace* like it tasted foul, and Ella began to love her. "But there was more to it. Your uncle Ed, from what I heard, had his issues, lots of things he and his sister argued about, but he and Bobbi loved each other very much. From what she told me, she idolized him as a child, well up into her teenage years. And he doted on her. They were very close. It was only after their father—your grandfather—died, and then Guy—"

"Guy?" Ella asked. "Who's that?"

"Ed never told you about Guy? Your other uncle?" Kat looked surprised.

"I've never heard of him."

"Jesus Christ," Ramon muttered, looking down at his hands. He shook his head. "Disgraceful."

"Why... Well, he was the middle child, I think, between Bobbi—your mom—and Ed," Kat said. "I never met him. He was already in Vietnam when I met your mama. He..." She shut her eyes, remembering. "He died."

"I never knew," Ella said bitterly. "I've never heard his name spoken a day in my life."

"I imagine there's lots you haven't heard," Ramon said, clasping his hands tighter in front of him.

"Daddy," Janelle warned, and he looked at his daughter, his face softening. "Let's just ease her in, okay?" She laughed. "Daddy's...a little intense, in case you hadn't noticed."

"He is not," Kat said with a laugh. She was still holding Ella's hand, and Ella was beginning to find it comforting. "He's a teddy bear if he loves you." Ella found herself hoping that one day he just might.

"Just so I have this straight," Ella said, clearing her throat. "My parents died, and I was put in Ed and Grace's care. But you guys wanted custody of me, because Bobbi—my mom—had named you as my godparents."

"Yes." Kat nodded. "She sent me a letter when you were first born and asked us to be your godparents. There was no christening or anything, nothing official, but we had the letter. And the moment we heard that she'd...that she'd passed... We got down to Georgia as fast as we could. We had every intention of honoring her wishes; we didn't think twice."

Ella closed her eyes. She couldn't imagine a friend loving her so much that they would do the same for her. "And they wouldn't let me go?"

"They wouldn't even let us *see* you," Ramon said with quiet anger. "Wouldn't even let us in their *house.*"

Kat continued. "Grace said that Bobbi had left you with *her,* that she'd clearly meant for her and Ed to care for you. She talked a lot of mess about blood, and family, and God and Jesus and a bunch of white horseshit. Excuse my language." Her hand was still squeezing Ella's. "I wasn't without sympathy. The woman clearly loved you very much. But I told her I had written proof that Bobbi wanted us to have you. I even suggested some type of split arrangement...and she laughed in my face. I remember exactly what she said. 'See if any court in the state of Georgia will honor that paper,' she said with this smug look on her face, 'considering what color you are. See what judge will take your part. Y'all go ahead and try.'"

"That's horrible," Ella said glumly, wishing she could be surprised by her aunt's callous racism. "I guess she was right, since Ed's a judge himself."

"He wasn't a judge then," Ramon said. "But he had plenty of clout all the same."

"We hired a great lawyer, one that had represented us in other things," Kat said, and Ella wondered what kinds of things those might be. "Our organization took up a collection for us, to help pay the legal costs. So many people who loved Bobbi wanted to help. They knew we'd raise you the way she'd have wanted." Her face looked sad. "But Ed fought us hard. He dragged our names through the mud, brought our protests and rallies into it, accused us of being Black Panthers. Nobody would bat an eye now, but back in the early seventies, that wasn't looked on so good by conservatives. Grace was right; we didn't stand a chance. No judge was going to allow us—two Black activists with arrests under our belt—to take a white baby girl home with us to Alabama." Her eyes were glistening with tears. "We tried so hard. We argued that we had Janelle to keep you company, to be your sister. I showed them Bobbi's letter. I told the judge what Bobbi had said about Grace, her temperament, Ed's infidelities, and raised questions about how they'd treat you. But none of it mattered. We lost."

"I've seen that woman arrested a dozen times, beaten, spit on…" Ramon said quietly from the loveseat, but his voice was brimming with fire, "and never in my life have I ever seen her so upset. She sat in that courtroom and sobbed. I had to drag her out, down those cold marble courthouse steps and onto the street, practically had to throw her in the car. Her just a-fighting and crying, because you see, to us, you were our baby. Your mama wanted us to have you, to take care of you. She'd thought ahead..." He cleared his throat and continued. "She had a plan for you. And we tried our best to honor her wishes. But it just...couldn't happen. They weren't gonna let it."

"I'm so sorry," Ella said, aghast.

"We're sorry for *you,* honey," Kat whispered. "Before we left, your Aunt Grace gave me a box—a box of Bobbi's things." Her voice broke. "A consolation prize, I suppose." She looked at Ella. "If I'd known you were here, I would have brought it for you."

"What's in it?" Ella whispered back.

"Dresses, some magazines, maybe?" Ramon answered for Kat. "We put it in the attic for safekeeping. Kat found it hard to look at... the memories and all. Hard to think about."

Kat said softly, her voice pained, "Before we left Athens, I went to the gravesite and paid my respects to your parents. I said I was sorry. We tried, but it was always stacked against us."

Ella didn't know what to say. She could imagine it all very well—Grace's cruelty, Ed's apathy, the both of them fighting tooth and nail for a little girl they didn't even want, partly out of spite, and partly due to good old-fashioned racism. It made her feel sick, and very sad.

"If you think I'm upset or something," she said, looking into Kat's eyes. "At you guys, I mean...don't be. I didn't know Bobbi... my mother. I didn't know anything about her, or you. I had no idea what I was...what I was missing, I guess you'd say." She shrugged.

"And that's probably a good thing, you know?" She swallowed hard, tears threatening to fall. "I'm not angry that you lost the fight. I'm just grateful to hear that you tried."

"Oh, honey." Kat's warm brown eyes lingered on her face, and Ella could see that she was remembering her mother, picking out the features she recognized. Kat was a striking woman for her age, with smooth, dark skin and wide eyes, and a smiling, pillowy mouth. Other than her hair, which she wore in a beautiful, high afro, she could have been Janelle's twin, or at the very least, older sister. "You may not be angry. But we certainly were, for a long time." Her dark eyes brimmed with fire as she squeezed Ella's hand. "But that's done now. The hour is late, but finally, we found you." She smiled. "Or, rather, you found us."

"Maybe fate found us all, and put us in the right spots," Janelle said, and she and Ella exchanged a long, meaningful look. "Ella, you're where you're meant to be now. With us." Ella felt her heart begin to beat fast. "Your family."

"I think we've all had enough surprises for one night, haven't we, hon?" Ramon spoke up from his spot on the loveseat. "We're in town for two days, so we'll have time to visit again." He, too, was handsome, and looked much younger than his fifty-something years. He was lighter-skinned than his wife, with perfectly straight white teeth and large, muscular arms. But it was his eyes that really lit up his face—they were round, a deep brown, and full of something electric and purposeful. Ella almost saw copper in them, though maybe it was just the light from the room. She found herself suddenly desperate to keep these three people in her life. She wanted nothing more in the world. She'd die if she couldn't have them.

Ramon's voice was soft, but commanding. "Let's let these kids get to bed. It's late."

"I really like your parents," Ella said with finality after Ramon and Kat had left. "They're wonderful."

"Oh, sure," Janelle said as she pulled a fitted sheet down over the mattress. Ella was far too inebriated, not to mention so shocked from meeting Kat and Ramon, that she was in no state to go back to her own apartment. She barely had her bedroom unpacked and hadn't even gotten around to buying a sheet set; she was using a t-shirt as a pillowcase. Janelle had been nice enough to offer up her bed. Louie was staying, too. Ella had asked him. She wanted to be surrounded tonight, to feel comfortable and safe with people she knew and loved.

"You didn't have to change the sheets," Ella said, embarrassed. "I would have slept on the couch."

"Fuck off." Janelle laughed. "So long as you don't mind if I crawl in here with you. That couch is uncomfortable as hell. It has this hard-ass beam that digs right into your back."

If Louie, who was standing in the corner smoking a cigarette, minded Janelle crashing their night-time reverie—not that he really *could,* since it was Janelle's apartment—he didn't show it. In fact, he hadn't said much or made so much as a weird facial expression all night. Ella wondered what he was thinking and wished she could talk to him alone. But Ella found she wanted Janelle with them, under the circumstances. It was just so much to take in, she wouldn't be likely to get much sleep, anyway.

"Drink this." Janelle had finished making the bed and handed Ella a small cup filled with amber liquid.

"What is it?" Ella groaned. "Janelle, I've had my share of booze tonight—"

"It's tea; chamomile. It'll help you sleep," Janelle said with a gentle smile. Ella hadn't even noticed her making tea. She rummaged in her nightstand, and Ella averted her eyes, noticing the sleeve of condoms in the drawer. She felt suddenly childlike, and embarrassed. She used to worry about it so much when they'd all first met, but now Ella often forgot that the two of them—Janelle and Louie—had once shared a romantic life together. They were both so wholly themselves, and selfish though it may be, Ella thought of them both as totally hers now. She loved them both so much, in different ways. Even if she felt so much younger than them, so immature compared to their adult lives. The old flicker of jealousy she'd once felt began to worm its way back into her belly, and as she watched Janelle hand Louie his own steaming cup, she felt a pang of something else she couldn't immediately identify.

The three of them changed soundlessly, Ella pulling on a pair of threadbare cotton boxer shorts Janelle had rummaged from her closet. Louie was in boxers, and Janelle pulled on an oversized nightgown that came to her knees, gauzy and white. It would have looked matronly on anyone else, but with her coloring and figure, she looked like a bedroom model from the 1950s, or one of the beautiful, frail heroines on the cover of a Southern Gothic ghost story. Ella laughed to herself. This was the weirdest sleepover—to cap off the weirdest night—she'd ever had.

The three of them climbed into bed, Louie and Janelle flanking Ella like something that needed protecting, like a treasured child. Louie took one more puff on his cigarette and put it out, releasing the smoke in a long stream.

"A lot to take in, I guess," he said, staring at the ceiling. But he was talking to her. "A lot for you to think about. Are you okay?"

"I'm fine," Ella lied, resting her head on his shoulder. He put his arm around her and pulled her close. "I mean, considering. It is a lot, for sure. But I already knew my aunt and uncle were assholes. It'd be easier if I wasn't drunk. God, you guys really tried to fuck me up today."

"That's just the baby stuff," Janelle said with a laugh. "You're such a lightweight." With that, she reached over and flicked off the light.

The room was quiet and dark. Ella couldn't make out anything except the smoke, still lingering from Louie's put-out cigarette, floating through the room. She took a deep breath.

"I just wanted to say..." she said in a quiet voice, her heart hammering. "That I love you both." She paused, then added, "I've never said that to anybody before. Other than my family."

"I love you, too," Louie said, pulling her into his arms. He placed a kiss on her temple, then one on her lips, folding her into his body, safe and warm. Ella had just begun to drift off when she felt him pull away.

"I drank too much; I've got to pee." Louie kissed her again, feather-light, on her forehead. "And I think I might actually take a shower, if that's okay, Janelle. I didn't realize how much I reek. I don't want you girls to have to smell me all night."

Ella watched his retreating back in the darkness, the dimples in his lower back she'd already memorized, his muscular thighs and thin calves, the warm, loving feelings crashing over her like a wave; yet there was another feeling, too—a sadness, a knowing... that something had irretrievably changed tonight. Things had gotten real; they'd gotten heavy. A sliver of light hit Ella's face as Louie opened the door, and she sighed with relief when he closed it.

The sound of him turning on the creaking faucet filled the silence of the room, and Ella settled into the warm spot Louie had left, trying again for sleep.

"I love you, too," Janelle said, her voice almost a whisper beside her. She'd been so quiet, Ella had almost forgotten she was there. "You know that, right?"

"Yes," Ella said, suddenly feeling shaky. "I guess I do."

"But I mean," Janelle's voice had an urgency to it. "I love you different than you love me, I think."

"You do?"

"Yes," Janelle whispered. "I shouldn't say it, but I worried if I didn't tell you now, I never would. And I can't go another day without telling you."

Ella's heart began to roar in her ears. She could hear Louie in the shower, the thud of a shampoo bottle being dropped, the rhythmic thrum of the water hitting the shower curtain. She swallowed, her mouth dry, deciding to speak before she lost her nerve. "Are you sure?" she asked.

Then Janelle's hand was on her face, pushing her hair back, moving it behind her ears, gentle. The mead, the pot, the tea, had all warmed Ella's blood, moving through her veins like slow-burning fire, and she felt her arms and legs awaken with a pleasant thrum. Suddenly it seemed like the most obvious thing in the world, what should happen next, and as she leaned forward to kiss Janelle's warm lips, she placed her hand over Janelle's, and moved it downward, toward her collarbone.

"Girl..." Janelle's voice was low in the room, with a hint of warning, but there was laughter in it, too. Janelle's lip ring was cold and sharp against her mouth, and it felt good. She'd never paid it much attention before, and now she hoped Janelle never removed it. The room seemed to be filled with sounds—the fan, the low hum coming from Janelle's throat, the shower, the sound of the TV in the living room—and all of it was like music. Janelle kissed her deep, her tongue probing in Ella's mouth, her hand moving from Ella's stomach up to her chest, her fingers grazing the tender skin there, back and forth until Ella moaned against her.

For a brief moment, Ella wasn't sure if she could do this—Louie had been her first, and she'd barely known what to do with him. He'd been understanding and gentle and she'd found that their natural chemistry did most of the work for them. But with Janelle, it was somehow different. Other than the obvious, there was something about Janelle that felt bigger, more momentous. It felt *real*. Ella was horrified at the realization, what it meant for her and Louie, but she put it to the back of her mind, unable to focus on anything but the feel of Janelle's body pressed against hers, the soft nightgown pleasant against her skin, the warm weight of Janelle's delicious body beneath it.

Janelle was kissing her, touching her, tasting her—and nothing in Ella's short life had ever felt so *right*.

The shower turned off with a now-familiar squeak. Ella figured Louie had to have been in there for at least twenty minutes. She could hear him rummaging in the cabinet for a towel, then the sound of the electric toothbrush. That he still felt comfortable enough in Janelle's apartment to take a shower; that he still had a toothbrush here; these thoughts filled her with a placid envy, though she wasn't quite sure which of the two she begrudged for this familiarity.

"Why did you do that?" Janelle asked her after a pause. She was lying next to Ella on the pillows, her dark curls spread out in an almost angelic fashion.

"What?"

"Why did you kiss me?" Janelle asked. There was something in her voice, something sad and defensive. "Is it because you're drunk? I worry that I pushed you into…"

"No, Janelle," Ella said in a whisper, surprised. "Maybe it made me feel a little bolder, but…" She was glad the room was dark; she could feel her cheeks burning. The pleasant thrum was moving throughout her body still. She felt a lightness she wasn't sure she'd ever felt before. And an urgent desire to pull Janelle to her again. "I don't know, I just…I just wanted to. I wanted you." She felt embarrassed now that the warm buzz was wearing off. "Did I do something wrong?"

"No," Janelle said. She reached out and pushed Ella's hair out of her face. "It's just…Louie and I have a history, and we closed the book on it. You know that. I meant what I said, Ella, how I feel about you. I just don't want to be…you know…a guest star in you guys' hot fuck-story or whatever."

"It had nothing to do with Louie," Ella whispered, worried he might burst through the door. It almost seemed as though he was taking his time on purpose. "If anything, I feel guilty, but Janelle… I wanted you because I wanted *you.*" She remembered back to earlier in the day, sitting on the couch with Janelle's mother, thinking about how beautiful her friend had looked in the room's warm glow. That feeling hadn't been jealousy. She knew that now.

It had been something else.

Janelle didn't reply, just kept puffing on her cigarette.

Ella listened to the sound of the water running in the bathroom. "Do you want *me?*" she asked timidly. "Still? Now that we…"

Janelle's voice was quiet in the darkness. "Yes," she said softly. "I do want you, Ella. I love you. I think…I think we belong together." She met Ella's eyes, her own brimming with heat and something else, something deeper. "But things are so complicated. My parents, us working together…and Louie. If you feel the same way…then you need to talk to Louie."

"I will," Ella said, reaching out to touch Janelle's face, marveling at how soft her skin was. "I promise." But as the bathroom door began to open, she pulled her hand away and sank down into the pillows, pretending to be asleep as Louie climbed into bed, nestling her between them.

SEVENTEEN

KASEY - 2018

KASEY sat out back by the pool, smoking a cigarette, looking longingly at the half-empty beer sitting on the ledge. Ricky had been cleaning the pool all afternoon, but he'd run inside to catch the kickoff. Georgia was playing Auburn, one of their rivals, and she could hear him and Fallon screaming blue murder at some call or another. Ricky, Fallon, and even Mom before she'd left had all loved their football. It was just one more way Kasey was an outsider.

The beer was being poked at by a large dragonfly, and Kasey moved to stand up and get it. She was curious if it was old, left out here weeks ago before they'd had their talk, or if Ricky was still drinking. Surely he wouldn't have just left it there for her to see, after the promise he'd made?

Kasey sat back down, staring pointedly at the cigarette in her hand. It didn't matter if it was old or new; she knew full well from experience that quitting an addiction was hard, and she wasn't about to make Ricky's life harder by nagging him or nosing in his business. And even if the beer was brand new and icy cold, she wouldn't go near it. Cigarettes were the only vice she would still allow herself, and she'd quit that too, eventually. Besides, if she was going to drink, it'd be something a damn sight better than rancid

Natty Lights. Ricky's taste in booze ran to the cheapest possible case at the convenience store. To her, Natty Lights tasted like piss and smelled even worse.

She moved to pick up her glass of sweet tea and took a long sip as her phone buzzed in her lap. Without looking, she flipped it over. It was most likely Caden. She felt a well in her throat as the phone buzzed on her leg, ignored, but made no move to answer it. It was best this way to just let things float on, drift apart. The alternative would be much more painful.

Caden wanted to have it out. She knew she owed him that much, but if she sat down with him to have the inevitable talk, to look him in the eye and break up with him face to face, she worried the pain would be so great that she would fall off the wagon. She knew it in her shitty, broken-and-repaired bones. Caden deserved more than this cowardly approach, this ghosting that she'd always swore she'd never do to anyone. She puffed on her cigarette, hating herself, thinking about her friend Bailey who had ghosted her last year, just stopped calling and texting with no warning, even going so far as to turn on her heel and walk out of the store when Kasey had run into her at Walmart—but here she was doing the same thing. Caden didn't deserve it, he really didn't. Even with all his problems, he was a good guy deep down, and he loved her. And hadn't he been by Kasey's side, devoted and loving, since her accident?

He tried, and he failed. He failed after two days. And I can't let him drag me back down with him.

It had been just a little slip. Kasey wouldn't even have known if she hadn't been walking by on her way to the bathroom, when

SO LONG, BOBBY

Caden's phone lit up with a text message. Instinctively, she glanced down at it, reading the text from his friend Kevin: "Did you get the mail from the porch? Let me know if you left my bill so I can drive by at lunch and get it."

Mail was code for pills. Bill was code for money. Had Kasey never seen the message, she might not have known. She'd considered saying nothing, letting Caden get away with it, giving him just this one, since she'd sprung it all on him so quickly. But the voice in her head had said *no, cut this loose, you'll never kick it if you keep following these old patterns.* And she knew the voice was right.

Wanting to avoid confrontation at all costs, she'd waited until Caden left that night, given him time to get home, then sent him a short text. *"I saw the message from Kevin. I'm not mad. But I think for the sake of my well-being, I can't be around you for a while. Please don't contact me, okay? Sorry. I love you."* She'd attached the emoji with the single crying tear to the end and hit "send." Caden had immediately started blowing up her phone and hadn't stopped for the past two days.

At first, he'd lied, said that the deal had been an old one and that he'd planned to back out. That he'd never picked anything up or paid Kevin. Then he'd apologized, admitted to everything, and swore to never do it again. He'd begged and pleaded. His voicemails and texts broke Kasey's heart. At 2:00 a.m. the night before, as she'd lain awake staring at the ceiling, sticky sweat covering her extremities, her leg throbbing, he'd left a tearful, desperate voicemail: "I wanted to marry you, Kasey. I thought we were forever. I wanted to have babies with you. I'd do anything for you. I'll stop using, I swear to God. I'll go to rehab tomorrow. Kasey, you're the only person who loves me, the only person who has ever seen anything in me. Without you, I'm alone. Please don't do this. I don't want to live without you. *Please.*"

She'd waited to listen to the message until the morning, and when she'd heard it, she'd lost her appetite and thrown her bagel in the trash. She'd been crying on and off all day. So far, she hadn't caved and answered the phone, but she couldn't find the will to block his number, either. She'd asked Ricky not to let him in the house if he showed up. "Please," she'd pleaded, "Don't be mean to him, Ricky. He's really hurting. He's—he's not in a good place. But don't let him in, okay?"

"I won't, sugar booger," he had said, patting her lightly on the back, a little awkwardly. "I'm proud of you. He will be, too, one day, when it stops smarting."

She'd wanted to ask Ricky what he'd felt like when Mom left, if he had called her to beg and plead the way Caden was doing. How he'd managed to go on with his life, his responsibilities, with his heart ripped out of his chest. But she couldn't ask him that. She was afraid of the answer.

Kasey had been sitting out on the back porch for the past two hours with the intention of reading a brand-new book from the library, but all she'd done was chain smoke and ignore her phone and cry. She stared at the rippling water in the pool, which was a little green, despite Ricky's strident cleaning—Georgia pollen never let up—and sighed. She was finding it harder and harder to fill her days. She needed to find a job, one that distracted her and kept her too busy to think about using or Caden. She supposed Caden himself was a drug of a kind, and kicking him might be just as hard. Maybe harder.

Because she loved him.

She stubbed out her cigarette and groaned as her phone began to vibrate again. She sat it face down on the little glass table by the patio and stood up, stretching. She'd finish cleaning the pool for Ricky; it'd be good exercise and would keep her from staring at the phone, waiting for it to stop ringing. She grabbed the pool sweeper and, looking back toward the pool ledge, flung Ricky's half-drunk beer onto the ground, where it landed in the grass with a *thonk*. She watched the amber liquid leak out on the grass—there was no fizz, which meant it was old and flat—and sink into the dirt. Kasey sighed with relief.

Just as she rolled up her pant legs and ascended the ladder, slowly and carefully, so as not to injure her bad leg, she heard the patio door *whoosh* open. "You have company, Kace," she heard Fallon say behind her.

"I can't deal with Caden right now, Fallon," Kasey called, her voice wavering. "Please, can you tell him to go? Tell him to go, okay?" She didn't turn around, not wanting Fallon to see the tears in her eyes. "Nicely."

"It's not Caden, sis."

Kasey turned around, almost falling into the pool. "Who is it, then?"

Fallon shrugged. "Two guys. I think one of them said his name was Andy?"

"Oh, shit," Kasey exclaimed, panicked. She brushed at her hair, which had been whipping around in the wind for the past two hours, and was a tangled rat's nest. She descended from the ladder carefully, her legs trembling, a sudden pang from her hip making her wince. "They just showed up at the front door?"

"He said they'd been calling," Fallon said with another shrug. "And texting. I guess they didn't want to just turn around and go, because apparently they came a long way." She smiled and lowered her voice to a whisper as Kasey came toward her. "And they're *cute*. Who are they?"

Kasey grabbed her pack of smokes, then put it down again and paced in a circle for a moment. "Andy...Andy is my..." Kasey swallowed, wondering how to break the news. "I think he's my brother."

"What?" Fallon's eyes widened in shock.

"I just found out not too long ago," Kasey explained, stammering. "I didn't realize he'd come here so soon—"

"You found out we have a fucking brother and you never thought to *tell* me?" Fallon demanded, tears springing to her eyes. Her face had gone red.

"No, no, he isn't *your* brother, just mine. His, uh... My biological dad and his dad are the same guy," Kasey hastened to explain. Fallon looked like she might puke. "I was going to tell you. I just needed time to think about it, and I didn't realize he was coming here. I swear."

"That doesn't make me feel any better, Kasey." Fallon wiped furiously at her eyes. "I can't believe you kept this from me. I mean, finding out you have a long-lost brother is kind of a big deal, the kind of thing you might want to tell your sister, like *immediately*, don't you think?" She sniffed. "Sisters are supposed to tell each other everything."

"Fallon, I've kind of been dealing with a lot lately," Kasey said, impatience creeping into her voice. Andy was in there *waiting*, and Fallon was pouting like a child. "Can we talk about this later? Please?"

"Don't bother," Fallon said, brushing at her reddened cheeks with a pale hand. "I wouldn't want to pry into your private business. I'll leave you to your *family*."

Kasey sat in the lawn chair, staring across the fire at the two young men, awestruck. Ricky had come out just long enough to start a fire as the night cooled and offer to grab some takeout. Kasey barely remembered what she'd ordered. Her brain was whirling. She held an ice-old can of Coke, and the two young men were holding Creature Comfort beers. She was grateful her stepfather had offered them something a little nicer than his usual silver-can piss water and noted with proud pleasure that he did not take one for himself. She wondered if Ricky knew about her exchange with Fallon, who had not shown her face again since her outburst. Oh, well, Kasey couldn't worry about that right now. She'd deal with her sister later.

Andy was talking, but she could scarcely hear what he was saying over her own loud thoughts. He was *here*! Her brother! A brother she'd never even known she had until a few days ago. Kasey sat memorizing his features—his dark, beautiful brown hair, his wide brown eyes, so like her own, his wide smile—and marveled at how much he looked like her, and yet so totally different. She saw things in his face she'd seen in her own, had once assumed came from her mother, but now she knew better. Andy was handsome, and tall, at least 6'3", with a lean frame (he had told her he played basketball and ran track) and long, thin fingers (he was also a musician, taught by his—*their*—father). His hair was in beautiful locs down to his shoulders and pulled back with a tie. He wore a denim jacket and Airwalk shoes that looked to be from the nineties—Ella wondered if he had pilfered his—*their*—father's closet. Or did people in Seattle still dress like grunge kids? So many things about him were interesting; she scarcely knew where to begin. As her brother talked, his long, thin hands were clasped in front of him, the fingers working themselves over, and Ella was oddly charmed to see how nervous her little brother was.

Andy had asked her so many questions about herself. How old was she? What sports did she play? Did she play music? Was she married, seeing anyone? Kasey's heart had hurt a little at that last question. But then he'd had more questions. What was her mother like? Why was she gone? Had she ever mentioned their father? Had she never tried to find him before? She gathered intuitively that Andy asked her so many questions because he was anxious, and because it kept Kasey from asking questions about *him*.

Kasey had answered as best she could, but there had been moments when she'd been unable to answer, or had given half-truths, not wanting this shiny new brother to see her pain, or to know her entire sordid story yet. There were things that embarrassed her.

That she was an addict, for instance. That she was unemployed and struggling because of those addictions, that she'd been stunted since the age of sixteen due to an accident. That her mother had abandoned her and the rest of her family for god knows what reason. That she had chronic pain. That she'd just broken up with someone she loved. That she was totally and utterly lost, and that she'd never once wondered about her biological father until she'd hit rock bottom. She did her best to wrap things up with a shiny bow, so her new brother wouldn't hate her, or worse, pity her. Kasey supposed being cagey was one thing she had in common with Mom.

Andy didn't look like the type of guy to hate anyone, so she was probably worried for nothing. He was friendly, open, and warm. His brown eyes locked on her as she spoke, and the smile that turned up the corners of his handsome mouth seemed genuine. He couldn't be more than two years her junior, but he felt so young to her, so fresh and full of promise, which made her both happy and sad, considering that she often felt her own life was dried up.

"Can I get you guys anything?" Kasey asked, standing up. She could smell food wafting through the patio door from the kitchen and knew that Ricky had returned with dinner. "Another beer? Food? Should we go inside or stay here?"

"Let's stay out here," Andy said with an eager smile. "You always hear about the humidity in the South, but it feels great right now."

"That's because it's the beginning of summer," she said with a laugh. "Come back in late July or early August and see how much you love it." She turned to the young man beside Andy, his best friend, Scott. As chatty as he'd been during their one phone call, he hadn't said much this evening. "Can I grab you another one?"

"I'm driving, so I think I'm good," he said with a crooked smile, his large brown eyes crinkling at the corners. "But if you're eating, I'm eating."

Kasey flashed him a smile and went inside. Kasey liked Scott on instinct. He was handsome, with dark, shaggy brown hair and puppy dog eyes, and what he lacked in stature he made up for with a crinkly, crooked smile that made her think of Blaine in *Pretty in Pink*. He was a little wary, she could tell, but she could feel the warmth beneath. This was a guy who had flown all the way across the country to support his best friend in a truly weird endeavor, and she had to admire that. Kasey couldn't imagine what it must be like to have that kind of friend, someone who loved you that much. They had told her they'd been best friends since they were five, and it showed. Kasey felt a pang of jealousy—her own best friend was gone, and she'd never had anyone else as close to her since, not even her sister. Whether that was her fault or that was just part of life, she didn't know, but it hurt.

Kasey returned with three barbecue sandwiches and a container of hushpuppies, as well as a large container of fries. "It doesn't look like much, but the place down the road has the best barbecue ever."

"This is great, thanks." Scott sidled up beside her and grabbed a paper plate. "And hey, if you want us to get out of your hair at any point, just say the word. We rented a room a couple of miles from here."

"Where?"

"The Lazy Dawg Inn," he said. "You know it?"

Kasey made a face. "Uh yeah, I know it. I wish you guys would've gone a little further into Athens. That place is a dive." Kasey had been there once or twice herself, and never for good reasons. "You can stay here if you want. Ricky won't mind. In fact, if he hears you're at Lazy Dawg Inn, he'll probably insist."

"We've already paid for the room—" Scott said, just as Andy said, "We'd love that." Kasey laughed.

"I'll let you work that out among yourselves. I'm just sayin', they have *bedbugs.*" She put some food on her plate and headed back toward the folding chair, breathing in the crispness of the night and ignoring the pains in her leg. Andy was right, it was a beautiful evening. It was unseasonably cool with a light breeze, and all the stars were on full display. The only sounds were crickets and the gentle hum of the pool filter. She watched as the two men sat down across from her, catching herself as she admired the dark sweep of Scott's hair falling over his forehead as he bent down to swig his beer. He was every bit as handsome as her brother was, with large, dark eyes, such a soft, dark brown they almost looked black, and that sweet, disarming smile. He might not be tall like Andy, but he had a confident posture about him, a self-assuredness that was disarming and cool. She imagined he was the type of person who made you feel really safe, no matter where you were.

"Oh my god," Andy said with his mouth full of food. "This is amazing. What is it, pork?"

"Chicken, I think," Kasey said with a smile. "Haven't you had barbecue before?"

327

"There's a couple of places in Seattle," Andy said, popping a hushpuppy in his mouth. "But not like this."

"Well, there's more where that came from," Kasey said, massaging her hip. It was beginning to throb from sitting in the same position for too long, but she found she could bear it, and that she didn't even want a pill. She took a swig of Coke and smiled.

"What happened there?" Andy asked, gesturing to her leg, and Kasey realized with horror that her scar was visible below her denim shorts, which had ridden up her thigh. "If you don't mind me asking."

Kasey felt the color rise in her cheeks and self-consciously crossed her legs in the other direction. She'd gone upstairs while Ricky was talking to Andy and Scott to change into shorts earlier, since her pants were covered in grass stains. Now she regretted it. The scar was mottled, raised and bumpy, and she hated people noticing it. Normally she took pains to keep it hidden, but she'd been so excited to see Andy that she hadn't thought about how short her shorts were, and what they'd reveal. But this was her brother; he should know. "Remember that car accident I told you about? My leg got pretty messed up."

"Is it hurting?" Andy asked innocently. "I noticed you keep touching it."

"A little." Kasey didn't say that it actually ached; deep, to the bone, to the point that sometimes she'd wake up crying, or that she resorted to a cane, or a wheelchair on the days when it was really bad.

"Well, it's a pretty baller-looking scar," Scott said with a grin.

"You're a tough chick."

Kasey grinned back at him and raised her can in a gesture of cheers. Andy raised his beer back at her, and they laughed, his dark eyes flashing with mirth.

Kasey liked her little brother. She liked them both. A lot. She hadn't felt so happy in a long time.

The lights went off inside the house; Ricky and Fallon had gone to bed. Inwardly, Kasey blessed Ricky for giving her privacy, letting her have this moment. She'd talk to Fallon later, smooth things over. She turned to Andy and Scott. "So," she said. "What on earth gave you the idea to fly all the way here on a whim? When I talked to Scott, we mentioned meeting up sometime, but I never expected you'd come all this way so quickly."

Andy shrugged. "Honestly? I needed to get away for a while. I just finished college, and I was climbing the walls, looking for a project. My band just broke up, and I'm between jobs and my grandparents gave me money for graduation," he said, looking sheepish, "and I figured I could lie around and watch TV all day, surf, fartass around, or I could use some of it to do something really cool. And I kept thinking about your email. And I just...I dunno, decided." He looked at his friend and grinned. "Scott may've had something to do with that." Kasey was smiling too. She was glad Andy felt comfortable enough to be so chatty.

"I had a lot to do with it, actually." Scott laughed. "I didn't want to see him waste three grand on pot and breakfast burritos, not when we could take a road trip. And honestly, it was selfish on my part. I'm a huge Athens music fan and I've always wanted to come here.

When I heard you lived right outside of Athens, it felt like fate. I hounded him for days."

"You're from Seattle." Kasey giggled. "And you wanted to come *here*? For the *music scene*?" She was incredulous.

"Athens, Georgia, has a great music scene; it can rival Seattle any day." Scott answered. "I'm sorry, was that mansplaining? I didn't mean to. But I'm really into the Athens sound, mainly nineties stuff. The Elephant Six stuff, the B52s, Pylon, Widespread Panic, Drive-By Truckers, REM. I love it all. I've always wanted to come here, and when Andy told me you lived here, I could not let it go."

"I'll have to take you to a show then," Kasey said.

"I'd love that." Scott's face glowed with excitement, and Kasey could see Andy chuckling from the corner of her eye. "Andy's mom is the one who got me into most of it, actually. She used to listen to this song by Neutral Milk Hotel. It had the coolest lyrics, full of this tender, vulnerable hope. It was so sad, but so…I don't know." He took a sip of his beer, then sang out a few lines in a strong voice. He paused, his face flushed with happiness. "And there was this part that said something about 'Anna's ghost.'" He smiled. "But she'd always change 'Anna' to 'Ella' at that part for some reason."

Kasey stared at him, blinking. "Ella is my mother."

Scott's cheeks colored. "Oh…right. Of course."

"Your mom knew my mom?" Kasey turned to Andy.

"I think she did, yeah." Andy looked uncomfortable. "I mean, she didn't like, talk about her often or anything. But Scott's right—she did change that lyric. So did my dad, come to think of it." He took a swig of his beer. "They both really liked that band, and they'd play that song from time to time when they got together. You know, reminiscing or whatever."

Kasey swallowed, a strange dawning feeling coursing through her. "What is your mom's name?"

"Janelle." Andy said. "Janelle Hawks."

Janelle. Realization hit her with a thud. The letter Kasey had found in the box had been from Janelle. Janelle, who she now knew, looking at her younger brother's fine features, was the woman in the portrait that her mother had tried so hard to get Ricky to throw away. It always seemed to come back to Janelle—who was this woman, and how could she have been so significant to her mother without her ever saying a word about her?

Kasey moved to stand, but her hip cried out in pain and she sat back down, panting.

"Are you okay?" Scott and Andy were both on their feet in a flash.

"I'm fine," Kasey said, a little too quickly. "There's something... I'd like to show Andy. But my hip is being an asshole. Gimme a minute and I'll go get it." She needed her cane, but she didn't want to say that in front of them, didn't want them to see. She was deeply embarrassed that this would happen now.

"Let me help," Scott said. "Just tell me where it is."

"Hard to explain," Kasey said. "If you, uh...if I could just maybe lean..."

"Of course." Scott helped her to her feet and wrapped an arm around her waist, and together the two of them walked inside. Over her shoulder, she saw Andy staring off into the woods, his face a mix of curiosity and sadness. *He's probably wondering what the hell he's gotten himself into,* she thought, trying not to lean on Scott too hard. He smelled woodsy, and clean, like soap and rosemary. It was pleasant, but she couldn't allow herself to enjoy the sensation… She was too embarrassed. She hated looking weak.

"Just down this hall is a closet, and the box is in there," she said as they made their way from the kitchen to the hall. "Thanks for helping me. My hip acts up sometimes before a rain. I think a storm's on the way tomorrow morning."

"No worries at all," he said cheerfully, his hair falling across his forehead.

"I'm sure I sound like an old woman," she said, forcing a laugh.

He gave her arm a squeeze. "No, you don't. But just say the word if we're tiring you, okay? Andy's so excited to spend time with you, but he's high-energy. He can be a bit much, especially if he hasn't smoked. If you're in pain and want to rest, we'll go."

"It's fine, Scott. I promise." She made a point of turning to him, look him in the eye, and smile. The last thing on earth she wanted was this guy—or her brother—to think she was some kind of sickly, weak person, but it seemed as though they understood her quite well already, without any judgment.

"Just here," she said as he opened the closet door for her. "The box right in front. If you open it, you'll see an envelope lying inside that Army hat."

"Cool hat. I'd love to hear the story about that later. This it?" He held up the envelope with the slanted script and peered at it. "Hey, that return address, I know it. That's the co-op where Andy works.

His mom owns it."

"That's the letter, then," she said. She suddenly had the sensation of multiple cogs clicking into place. "Can you grab that painting, too? The one propped up in the back? Come on, let's go show him."

"They were clearly very close," Kasey said, propping her sore leg up on the other chair Scott had pulled up for her, holding her can of cola. She was joshing for a cigarette, but she'd already had two. "She talks about loving my mom several times. Which is so weird because Mom literally never mentioned her."

"Well, maybe..." Andy trailed off. "They were really close friends, I think." He seemed to be holding something back.

"You said your mom never talked about her?" Kasey asked. "Except for those song lyrics?"

"Not really," Andy answered, still turning the paper over in his hands. "I've heard her talk about Ella once or twice, but not often. She seemed sad about it, and for a long time I thought your mom must have died or something. She never mentioned you. In fact, I don't think she knows you exist."

"You didn't tell her about me?"

Andy shrugged. "I thought about it, but...well, not yet. I thought maybe that'd be a conversation for her and my dad."

"He'll get around to it a couple of years from now when he's explored it from every angle," Scott said with a grin. "And started an Excel spreadsheet of pros and cons."

"Shut the fuck up, man," Andy said, laughing. "Seriously though, I will. It's just weird because...like, I don't know what she'll think. My dad being *your* dad…like…I don't want her to be mad at him, you know?"

"Oh." Realization dawned. "You mean your mom and dad were dating when my mom was in the picture? Like, he cheated?" Kasey swallowed. "I just assumed that he dated my mom before he dated yours."

"I don't think so," Andy answered. "My parents met when they were still in high school and dated on and off for several years. They broke up for good after I was born and decided to co-parent as friends. At least that's what they've always said. But you're older than I am by a couple of years, so that means…"

"Either they were 'off' when he was with my mom, or he cheated," Kasey finished for him.

"It's probably the former," Andy said with a reassuring smile. "They were broken up more often than not. Mom and Dad love each other, but my mom's more into women. My dad is the only guy she ever loved." He laughed. "After nearly twenty years, he can almost say it out loud."

"All that time she tried to reach out to my mom," Kasey said, hating her mother a little more, "and she never got a response, never even knew that *I* existed."

"I'll tell her," Andy said with a smile. "I just wanted to meet you first, that's all. And I think it'd only be fair to talk to Dad about it before I talk to Mom, you know?" His face flushed. "After all, he has a daughter he doesn't even know about. And he can fill in the blanks for me before I go to Mom."

Kasey shook her head. "I don't understand this. How my

mom could… Why she wouldn't tell him that he had a daughter? We struggled when I was a kid—so just in terms of child support alone…" She bit off the thought, feeling guilty. "That's not what I mean. I'm sorry. I just can't wrap my head around why she wouldn't tell him." Her mom had plenty of faults, but Kasey couldn't reconcile her fun-loving, opinionated mother with a cowering, shamefaced woman who wouldn't tell a man that he had a daughter somewhere. It just didn't make sense.

"I'm sure she had her reasons," Andy said affably, but she could sense his discomfort. She had a father out there: a handsome, surfing, musician father who had raised a son and lived a *life*, and she'd been robbed of it all. It wasn't fair that she'd grown up never knowing him, never able to experience his love. Then she thought of Ricky and all he'd sacrificed for her and felt guilty.

"God," she said, swallowing. "I can't imagine how he'll react. I can't imagine how anybody would react, finding out they have a grown child. I wonder if he'll even like me."

"What?" Scott said incredulously. "Of course he'll like you. He'll *love* you."

"Totally," Andy agreed. "Dad's going to be over the moon. Seriously, Kasey. He's going to be so happy."

But Kasey wasn't so sure.

EIGHTEEN

BOBBI - MAY 1968

BOBBI craned her neck, staring out over the throng, hoping to catch a glimpse of someone notable. The strap of her knapsack cut into her neck, and she absently rubbed at the raw spot. She'd had to throw the strap over her shoulder diagonally after two different men had attempted to snatch it. It would have been hilarious if she hadn't known the reason for it. She was clearly poor. If her bedraggled appearance hadn't given away that she had nothing to her name, the fact that she was at a planning meeting for The Poor People's March on Washington made it obvious—they were targeting her because of the company she was with. Well, let them try to snatch it again, she thought defiantly, holding the bag close to her. She didn't have anything of monetary value, but she had other things she would die before she let go of. She'd be perfectly happy to wallop someone a good one, if it came to that.

The bruise on her arm, from where the last kid had knocked into her, was turning from a faint purple to blue. Kat had insisted she go see a medic—there was a tent set up near where the speakers were gathered—but Bobbi had shrugged it off. She wanted to hear Dr. Ralph David Abernathy, who had been a good friend of the now-late Martin Luther King Jr. and was becoming famous in his own right, for championing the causes of the poor, Black and disenfranchised. He was one of the main reasons they'd come to the planning meeting today—they'd all transitioned to solely working on Bobby Kennedy's campaign, at least until after the Democratic Primary—and Bobbi wasn't going to miss it. She wished Kat, who had run off in search of a porta-potty, would hurry up and get back, so she wouldn't miss him, either.

Kat and Bobbi had pooled their money to rent a hotel room for the night. Just one night away from their dingy little headquarters, with its miniscule, uncomfortable cot, was a luxury that Bobbi was looking forward to, the perfect cap-off to what she hoped would be a wonderful day.

"Where you from?" Bobbi turned to face the man who had appeared at her elbow, clutching her bag in anticipation. His open, friendly grin implied he wasn't here to steal or otherwise harass her, but you could never be too careful. He was short, with pale skin and a smattering of freckles below amber-colored eyes. A tuft of white-blond hair emerged from his beret. He was wearing a Simon & Garfunkel t-shirt under a distressed army jacket, which was covered in a number of holes and patches. Bobbi gave him a polite smile; he was obviously a veteran, and she had nothing but respect for those guys, no matter what some of her peers said. One day, her brother Guy would be a veteran. So would Landrum.

"Georgia," she said in a quiet voice, her eyes moving back to the front of the crowd, hoping to catch a glimpse of someone she knew.

"I'm from Milwaukee," he said in a friendly tone, and then chuckled. "Wisconsin. So, you're a Georgia Peach, huh?"

She bristled. "I don't—" she began, but he cut her off with another laugh.

"Hey, hey, I'm sorry. I didn't mean anything by it. Look, I haven't been back in the States long, and I'm a little short on manners. I don't know anybody here. I was just trying to, you know, make conversation." He smiled, a faint blush on his cheeks. He reminded her a little of her brother Guy, and she felt herself soften toward him.

"It's okay," she said with a laugh of her own, then added, "Just don't go around calling women 'peaches.'"

"Aye-aye, Ms. Steinem," he said with another smile. "Shit, that's offensive, too. I'm batting a thousand here." His friendly eyes crinkled. "So…when are they kicking off the speeches?"

"Any minute now, from what I hear."

"I'm excited," the man said. He still hadn't introduced himself, but Bobbi didn't mind. Nobody needed to be on a first-name basis here. Their group had picked up so many volunteers by this point that she didn't know half of them; they were all a big, happy, semi-anonymous family. "I was still in 'Nam when the news came over that Dr. King was shot. I've never been so fucking heartbroken in my life. Been trying to find a way to pick up the pieces ever since."

"It was a terrible day," Bobbi agreed. That was an understatement, but she hadn't found a way to vocalize the utter heartbreak and disappointment that she—and everyone else—had felt when they'd heard the news. "One of the worst," she added.

"Things like that, you never forget exactly where you were when it happened," the young man said. "It imprints on you. You think about it, and you're transported right back there. Me, every time I think of Dr. King, I'm back at Can Tho, in the barracks, that tinny little radio crackling and spitting the news out that my hero got killed. Even though it's been two months, I still feel that pain in my gut. It stays with you. They say bad news, trauma, it makes a bruise, but on the inside."

Bobbi shifted on her feet, uncomfortable. He wasn't wrong. Her own aches kept her awake at night, kept her on edge, always wondering when the next shoe would drop. She still hadn't heard a word from Landrum, and it had been a long time since there'd been a letter from Guy.

"Just ignore me," the man said after a moment with another laugh. "I haven't been stateside long and I'm still coming out of the doldrums, that's all. I'm sorry to be such a downer."

"No, it's alright. I understand," Bobbi said. "It's only that my brother is over there. And my uh…friend."

"Everybody's over there," he responded, then asked, "Whereabouts are they? Do you know?" Vets always asked that, as though fighting in 'Nam was a small, exclusive club where everybody knew each other. Not one person who had asked knew her brother or Landrum, but they all wanted to know, just the same. Bobbi supposed after coming from a place like that, even strangers—if they'd been through the same experiences—came to feel like family. She supposed it was a way of coping, of not feeling alone. A band of brothers, as it were.

"My brother is near Saigon," she said, "At least according to his last letter. As for my friend…I don't know. He hasn't written."

"Don't sweat it," he said kindly. "A lot of guys over there don't have the time to write, or if they do, they don't have the heart for it. It's depressing as fuck and they don't want to bring anybody down back home. I had a bunch of friends who didn't want to talk about it, just decided to soldier on through. I'm sure he's just fine. You woulda had a telegram otherwise."

It would be Mr. and Mrs. Walton that had the telegram, but Bobbi nodded in agreement. There was no sense in trying to explain the drama that was Mrs. Walton and Ed. And besides, they were gone from her life now. For good, she supposed. She could only hope that Mrs. Walton might reach out to Ed somehow, someway—if she was able to—if there was news, and that Ed would reach Bobbi. That was all she clung to; the hope that silence meant that Landrum was still alive.

The mic switched on and someone fiddled with it, feedback sounding through the speakers. Bobbi plugged her fingers in her ears until the feedback subsided and tried to ignore the sadness that had washed over her the moment they'd started talking about 'Nam. It wasn't the veteran's fault, and she knew she was privileged—she wasn't fighting over there, and she wasn't about to silence anyone who had—but every time she thought of her brother and Landrum in that faraway place, a cold icy fear staked her heart. She'd had a bad feeling about Landrum lately—he wasn't dead, she didn't think, but something still felt off—and she didn't want to think about it. She tried, most days, to put it out of her mind completely.

She'd broken down and called Mrs. Walton again a couple of weeks ago, and found, to her surprise, that the number had been disconnected. She then called Ed, who had told her, much to her shock, that the Waltons had up and moved two weeks before. "Irene took a bad turn," he'd said, his voice sounding unusually calm, as though he were trying to convince himself he was. "Nervous breakdown, they said. They up and moved without telling anybody where they were going, but I heard a rumor that that asshole Johnny was having her committed."

"What happened to her?" Bobbi had asked, her voice full of dread. "The last time I talked to her, she sounded fine. Well, considering. You didn't do anything to her, did you, Ed? Don't tell me that you two—"

"No, Bobbi, it wasn't me this time," he'd said, irritable, but then his voice had softened. "Look, I wasn't gonna tell you this because I didn't want to worry you and Irene asked me not to, but… Well, last I heard from her, before they took off." He'd paused, as if collecting his words, and Bobbi's heart had begun to pound so hard she thought she might pass out. "Landrum's been taken prisoner over there. I don't know any details, but he went P.O.W. a few weeks back. They had a telegram." Bobbi had let out a strangled cry, and he'd sighed deeply, then continued. "Irene's been real shook up about it. She'd been acting real strange, stranger than usual, and then that happened and I guess…I guess her bastard old man decided he'd lock her away and get the hell away from this street in the bargain." He sniffed. "He packed her up and had her gone in the span of two days. No idea where they went or how she is."

"But…" Bobbi was aghast. "How will anyone get in touch with them about Landrum if they've moved? That doesn't make any sense! What if he's injured, or worse—how will they know? What if he comes home to an empty house and has no idea where his parents are? How could they do that to him?"

"I don't imagine Johnny much cares," Ed said bitterly. "Never got the impression he cared about Landrum *or* Irene, but that's just my two cents." Bobbi supposed he was right, though it made her want to throw up thinking about it. Landrum had never said much about his father one way or the other, and when he had, it had been through a haze of bitterness.

Landrum a P.O.W. And now, with no home to come back to, if he came back at all. His poor mother possibly locked away in some mental institution. Bobbi had cried on the phone, her brother listening silently, not offering her hollow words of comfort. He'd asked her—as he had several times now—to come home, and she'd refused. When they'd said their goodbyes, his voice had been choked with emotion. Bobbi hadn't called home since then.

The freckled young veteran was leaning toward her, breaking into Bobbi's thoughts. In a soft voice, he said, "When the meeting is over, you want to go get a cup of coffee with me? We could do some organizing. I haven't had coffee with a pretty girl in a long, long time." The desperation and loneliness in his voice was painful.

"I'm sorry," Bobbi said, turning to him with a kind but conciliatory smile. "I should have mentioned—my friend—the one in Vietnam—he's actually my fiancé. So I'm afraid I can't." She'd made a vow to herself that she wouldn't go home with anyone tonight. The hotel she'd sprung for loomed in her mind as an incentive.

"Why'd you call him your friend if he's your fiancé?" the guy asked.

Bobbi sighed. "It's just that—"

As she tried to explain, her eyes flitted over to an iconic figure—Dr. Abernathy, who was engaged in impassioned conversation with Ramon, resplendent in a dark black jacket, fitted black jeans, and heavy work boots—and she forgot what she'd been saying. As she stared at him, feeling pride and admiration surge through her veins, she became very aware that her freckled friend was watching her—watching and seeing and picking out the lie.

"What'd I miss?"

Kat appeared at her side, and Bobbi swallowed and pasted on a smile. "Nothing. Just chatting with one of our new volunteers," Bobbi said brightly, looping her arm through the young veteran's. As Kat turned to watch Ramon, Bobbi turned to him and said in a low murmur, "Hey, you know what? About that coffee. I changed my mind."

"Nice of you to finally turn up," were the first words out of Kat's mouth as Bobbi pushed open the hotel room door. She'd hoped to sneak in before the sun rose, while Kat and Ramon were still asleep. No such luck. She should have known that Kat would be up; her friend always complained about her insomnia and that staying in hotel rooms and caravans made it worse.

"Sorry," Bobbi muttered in a whisper, and went straight to the bathroom to wash her face and brush her teeth. Her mouth tasted like cheap wine and cigarettes. She could smell the vet's—his name had turned out to be Oliver—cheap cologne all over her clothes, and she rummaged in her small knapsack for a pair of shorts and a t-shirt, trying not to catch her own reflection in the harsh bathroom light. She didn't want to catch a glimpse of how haunted her eyes were behind the smudged makeup and messy hair. She brushed her teeth quickly, ran a cool cloth over her face, and emerged from the bathroom, pulling her hair into a quick ponytail as she walked over to the twin bed by the wall. She pulled down the covers and tried to ignore Kat's piercing stare. She could feel it burning into her back as she settled into bed, hoping to grab a couple of hours of sleep before Ramon woke up and another day of work began. She could *still* smell the cloying, musky scent of strange cologne on her as she drifted off into an uneasy, hungover sleep.

Later, at headquarters, she and Kat were flitting around in a frenzy, setting out what meager refreshments they had managed to scrounge together—cold cuts, crackers, and tiny chocolate chip cookies—along with a pot of hot coffee, for the impromptu guests they'd only just heard might be arriving.

Ramon's face had been jubilant when he'd burst into the kitchen, holding a stack of flyers. "I was just at the NAACP," he'd exclaimed, grabbing up Kat and whirling her around. "I finally got 'em, Kat. I got 'em to agree to come here and see what we're doing!"

"Who?" Kat had asked, puzzled and giggling. "Put me down, you goof!"

"John Lewis and Ralph Abernathy!" Ramon said excitedly. "I always invite them whenever I happen to run into them, but today they actually accepted. They said they would come by for a few minutes before they catch their flight."

Bobbi was incredibly nervous. She'd always been insanely

jealous of Ramon and his connections, that he rubbed shoulders with the people she admired so much, but was somewhat relieved that she could stay anonymous and in the background. Well, today that would all change. She was about to meet two of her heroes! She hoped she didn't do anything embarrassing or inappropriate. Gosh, what if they brought Bobby Kennedy along?

She bit that thought off quickly, arranging the cold cuts on a platter. The senator was far too busy with his presidential campaign. In fact, he was likely not even in Washington at the moment. But a girl could dream, couldn't she?

"So—are we going to talk about it?"

"What?" Bobbi busied herself with fanning crackers on the plate in a fishtail pattern.

"That hot, haunted young vet you went home with yesterday," Kat said, reaching out a hand to stop Bobbi's fidgeting. "Girl, you know I don't care if you get laid, but you told me you wanted to cool it. You said you wanted to stop picking up these random guys. You said—"

"I know what I said," Bobbi answered, pushing Kat's hand away. "But look, Oliver was just some harmless fun." She thought back to the evening before, how many beers she and Oliver had drunk, and hoped they'd used protection. She honestly couldn't remember. And she'd gotten up, dressed, and snuck out of his tiny apartment before he'd woken up, hoping that he'd be embarrassed enough to not seek her out. If he did, she'd just have to tell him she wasn't interested. She hoped their night had cheered up the sad, handsome young man, but she wasn't interested in seeing him again.

"Anyway, it's not the guys I'm worried about," Kat said. "You're smart enough to weed out the creeps. It's that you're using them as a distraction, as a way to numb your pain. *You're* the one who told me you wanted to stop, who asked me to intervene."

"I know I did," Bobbi said, biting her lip. "Look, can we talk about this later?"

"I'm done lecturing," Kat said, wadding up the empty cracker bag. "I'm just saying I can't help you if you won't let me."

Bobbi sighed and pulled out the coffee filters. Kat was right. Over the past month or two, she had found herself seeking out the company of men several times a week. She was hardly the only single organizer who spent time with guys, passing the time and enjoying a little R&R in the off hours. And she met so many cool, politically-minded young men who were smart, savvy and handsome. She was young, so what was the harm?

Except Bobbi wasn't just out having fun, enjoying being young. She was parading an array of young men in and out of her room to distract herself. To try and forget about Landrum. And in her haste to forget, she'd put herself in compromising situations more than once, which blessedly, Kat did not know about. Several times Bobbi had found herself fleeing from a guy who turned out to be an abusive jerk, or doing drugs when she hadn't intended to. Bobbi knew she was being reckless; half the time she went home with guys she didn't even *like,* wasn't even attracted to. One wrong choice and she could end up assaulted, traumatized, or dead. But she couldn't seem to stop. It was true that she'd asked Kat to help her hold herself accountable, yet every time Kat tried, Bobbi cut her off.

"I'm swearing off guys, I promise," Bobbi said, turning to her best friend with a smile. "I got it out of my system and now I'm done. I won't go out with anyone else until I meet a nice guy who I really like." *I won't go out with anyone else but Landrum when he's back home, safe and sound,* she added to herself silently, hoping she was telling the truth.

"If you say so, B." Kat giggled. "I'm not sure you have the self-control. There's so many fine men in Washington these days. If I didn't love Ramon so much, I might be pulling the same shit."

"Yeah," Bobbi agreed with a laugh, thinking to herself that if she was lucky enough to be with Ramon, she'd never look elsewhere. But Kat wasn't wrong. There were smart-looking men everywhere you turned. "If John Lewis asks me for a date, you can bet I'm not turning him down; I don't care *what* I just said."

"Bobbi, do not even go there," Kat cautioned, her face turning somber. "I'm serious."

"I was just joking," Bobbi said, stung.

"You've flirted with plenty of organizers who have come in here," Kat went on, "and that's fine most of the time, but... Mr. Lewis is too important, Bobbi. It'd be disrespectful. Be on your best behavior, promise me."

Bobbi felt her color rise. "Fine. I promise." She turned her burning face back to the crackers, ashamed.

JUNE 5, 1968

The television was turned up so loud Bobbi could hear it from down the hall. She was in the kitchenette, making ham and cheese sandwiches for everyone watching. It was their own impromptu viewing party, to hopefully see Bobby Kennedy declare a victory in the California primary. Resources were low, and money scarce, so it was ham sandwiches, brownies, and Tang. There was no liquor or even any beer, but from the smell wafting down the hall, somebody had brought along some grass. Bobbi busied herself with working, humming a happy tune. Her low mood from earlier had abated somewhat, though she still felt embarrassed from the talk she'd had with Kat. And she was so worried about Landrum and Guy that she felt sick with it; the bad feeling she'd had all week was worse than ever. But she was determined to enjoy this evening, to enjoy what she knew would be *good* news for a change.

Meeting the young John Lewis and the esteemed Ralph David Abernathy had certainly helped. When Ramon had ushered in the two men, both handsome and impeccably dressed in slim, dark suits, shiny shoes, and fetching hats—Mr. Lewis wearing his signature tan trench coat—Bobbi hadn't been able to control the grin that had broken out on her face. The two men had taken the time to shake hands and chat with every person there, all twelve of them, and John Lewis had been especially interested in hearing that Bobbi was from Georgia. They'd chatted for quite a while about the South, him regaling her with a tale of how he'd once preached to a congregation of chickens in his childhood home of Alabama, and he had listened, really listened, as Bobbi told him about Guy, Landrum, and how worried she was. The charming young activist had told her to keep up the good work. "Keep making trouble," he'd said in his deep, songlike voice, clasping her hands with his own, warm and strong. "Good trouble. Necessary trouble." Bobbi knew she'd be coasting on his sincere, motivating words for days. She could hardly believe he was only in his twenties and had lived through so much pain, adversity, and violence. Lewis had such a strong, purposeful presence, such a clear vision—Bobbi knew he was destined for great things.

Kat had been so busy talking off Ralph David Abernathy's ear that Bobbi hadn't had a chance to say much to him, but he'd nodded at her and given her an encouraging smile. That alone had been enough to make her tremble, she admired him so.

Bobbi shook her head to clear it—she was still shaking a little from all the excitement—and set about making more sandwiches, a few without ham for the vegetarians among their group. They wouldn't be any good; the American cheese she was using was half dried-up, tasteless plastic—but at least they would be on offer. She cut each sandwich in half, organized the brownies on a tray, along with the pitcher of Tang and a handful of thick paper napkins, and set off down the hall to the TV room.

The communal space that Ramon and his organizer friends had rented for them wasn't much more than a dilapidated office building with four big rooms, one of which served as their rec room, one that served as an office/strategy room, the kitchenette, and a large space that had been divided into sections with curtains and propped up boxes. Those areas were first-come-first-serve for anybody who needed to crash. There was a much smaller room off the kitchenette that held a cot and a window offering a view of the street above them, but Ramon and Kat had refused to take it, insisting that it wouldn't be fair for them to have a private room when nobody else in their group did. Instead, they all took turns. Tonight was Bobbi's turn, and she was looking forward to sleeping on a semi-real bed and having private time to think and reflect. She hoped she'd be going to bed with a happy buzz, either from the reefer she smelled or from Bobby's victory, or hey, she wasn't picky—maybe both. Either way, she was determined that she'd be going to bed alone.

Bobbi entered the rec room and set the tray down on the wooden table in front of the TV with a flourish. "Food!" she declared happily, perching on one of the office chairs crowded around the television. It looked to be a live view of the Ambassador Hotel, crowds milling about in various stages of excitement, a combination of men in slim-legged black or brown suits, women in fancy dress, waiters in their white and black livery, and even a few women dressed up as suffragettes, with flat-topped hats, sashes and pictures of Kennedy splayed all over their person. It was a lively, happy, and adorably strange crowd, full of merriment and jubilation.

Kat grabbed a sandwich and settled back on the sofa, where she had a book curled under her legs. She had been reading *The Feminine Mystique* and picking out choice passages to read and chuckle over all week. Bobbi would never admit it, but she thought Betty Friedan, with her gruff, aggressive manner, was somewhat charming. "Thanks for the grub, Bobbi. I'm guessing this was all that's in the fridge?"

"Looks like nobody has put a thing in it since you and I went grocery shopping two weeks ago," Bobbi answered, raising her voice a little so people heard. She and Kat had pooled all of their money to stock the fridge when they'd first taken up lodging, and while everybody had helped themselves, nobody had felt the need to throw them a buck or chip in to replenish supplies. "All we had was ham and cheese and an ancient bunch of grapes that are well on their way to raisins."

"Why don't you assholes buy some groceries?" Kat demanded, but she didn't look angry. She leaned back on the couch and took a bite, her eyes closed. "Bobbi. Tonight feels…I don't know…big. Significant. Do you feel it?"

Bobbi had a sudden lump in her throat. She nodded in agreement, taking a deep breath, allowing the enormousness of the moment to wash over her. She had been obsessed with Bobby Kennedy since she was a pre-teen; the term hero worship didn't really cover it. For her, he was an icon, a larger-than-life example of not only what she wished for her country, but for herself. They had all worked so tirelessly, had marched the streets, organized, rallied, sweat, and bled for this. She and Kat had jokingly begged Mr. Lewis to take them with him when flew to be with the campaign. Had he agreed, they would have gone readily. And tonight, they all stood on the precipice of history. Bobby Kennedy might really become President of the United States! It was almost too joyous to imagine.

The fact that the last time they'd all gathered here to watch TV was when Senator Kennedy had announced MLK's death—well,

Bobbi wouldn't allow herself to dwell on that. She hoped her friends wouldn't either, though she knew they must be thinking about it. *Tonight's a new night,* she told herself, squaring her shoulders. *A new beginning.*

Warren, who sat beside her, his chin resting on his hands as he craned forward to hear the TV, nodded. "I think they'll announce it any time now. According to the polls, he's way ahead. There's no contest."

"Polls have been wrong before," his girlfriend Hanna piped up from the corner of the room where she was knitting. She was a beautiful Hungarian woman with glossy black hair and pretty green eyes. "Don't count your chickens before they hatch."

"Anybody want Tang?" Bobbi asked, and everyone shook their head.

"Nobody wants Tang," Kat said with a laugh as Ramon entered the room. "Do they, honeybunch?"

"Tang?" he said with his nose wrinkled. "Does anybody still drink that shit?"

"Probably somebody else left it behind," Bobbi began, affronted, but Ramon handed her a small silver flask.

"Forget the phony OJ and take a swig," he said with a wink. "And let's watch your boy."

Bobbi hesitated, then took a long drink, unable to refuse an offer from Ramon, the whiskey running like fire down her throat. It warmed her chest, and she took another swig, handing it back to Ramon, who shook his head. "One more," he said with a laugh. "For the woman who stayed up all last night working. Don't think we didn't notice. You deserve it."

She started to protest, but then took another long swig and handed the flask back, already feeling lightheaded. She hadn't drunk much alcohol in her life—Daddy had never kept it in the house, and she'd only ever had a glass of champagne or two with her brothers. But it felt good, warm and soothing in the back of her throat, her head full of a nice, fuzzy warmth. When the flask came back around to her, close to empty, she poured a glug of the whiskey in with her Tang, ignoring everyone's laughter. She sipped it as they watched the newscast, everyone on pins and needles.

"He's got it in the bag, I'm telling y'all," Warren said, and Hanna leaned forward, punching him lightly on the arm.

"We'll see," she said with a wink. "I'm just sayin'... Who was it that said, 'what we must always foresee is the unforeseen?' We don't want to get our hopes up too high."

"Ugh, stop being such a downer, Hanna," Warren rolled his eyes. "And I'm pretty sure it was the guy who wrote *Three Musketeers* or something."

"Actually, it was Victor Hugo," Kat said, looking up from her book, fixing Warren with a smirk. "Alexandre Dumas wrote *Three Musketeers.*" Warren shut his trap, and Bobbi grabbed a sandwich, hiding her smile. Kat was the most well-read person she'd ever met, and anybody who went up against her was a fool.

Just before midnight, a flushed and surprised-looking newscaster announced, "It's official: Robert F. Kennedy has won the California Democratic Primary!" Bobbi was gloriously drunk. As they all jumped to their feet, bellowing and whooping with happiness, she almost fell and bumped into Kat, knocking her sandwich out of her hand.

"Get a hold of yourself, girl!" Kat laughed, but there were happy tears on her cheeks, and she pulled Bobbi close for a crushing hug. "We did it, Bobbi. He did it!"

Her own happy tears drying on her face, blissfully drunk and clutching her paper cup of spiked Tang, Bobbi inched her seat closer to the television and listened to her hero make his speech, a speech ten years and a lifetime in the making.

"I believe…what has been going on in the United States over the period of the last three years—the division, the violence, the disenchantment with our society…the division, whether it's between Black and White, between the poor and the more affluent, or the war in Vietnam—that we can start to work together. We are a great country, and a selfless country, and a compassionate country. And I intend to make that my basis for running in the period of the next few weeks." Bobby's voice was calm and measured, but his proud smile was hard to miss.

Kat gave Bobbi's hand a squeeze. They both sat on the edge of the couch, riveted, Bobbi scarcely breathing.

There was a frenzied energy in the room, something large and looming, and she felt as though the entire world was put on pause, listening to what was actually a rather unremarkable speech. It was full of thank yous and humble politeness, the very essence of Kennedy. But nonetheless, for how mundane it was, it seemed to hold their very futures within each syllable. She watched as he turned to his wife with a bit of a nervous laugh, as he pushed his hair back from his face in his signature gesture, taking a moment to give eye contact to the many supporters and campaigners clustered in front of the podium, never forgetting to make everyone feel seen. He was deliberate and calm, but behind his eyes there was something else—disbelief, perhaps, or maybe he simply felt the magnitude of this moment, the weight of his future, as he spoke to the crowd. The train had meandered down the track so far now; there was no turning back. Bobbi swallowed hard, waiting. This slow-burn must surely be leading up to something explosive and exciting. Life-changing.

"So—my thanks to all of you, and on to Chicago, and let's win there!" Senator Kennedy exclaimed, a bright, shy smile lighting up his face as he flashed a peace sign, pushed back his hair in that same impossibly endearing, boyish tic, and exited the podium, flanked by his beaming wife. Bobbi felt something in her heart clench, then give way.

The crowd inside the hotel lobby was thinning, but the news broadcast stayed on them. Hearing their spirited chants of "RFK USA!" and "Kennedy, Kennedy, rah-rah-rah, Kennedy, Kennedy, siss-boom-bah" was making her happy. Her Tang was almost gone, but the heady buzz she felt in her veins was still very much there.

"I've never seen you so happy," Ramon said to her with a warm smile, and Bobbi's insides fluttered.

"I am," she answered. "I just can't believe—"

"Wait, what's going on?" Warren interrupted, sitting up straight and staring at the TV.

Bobbi stared, but couldn't see anything amiss. It was the same crowd they'd been watching all night, loud and chaotic, chanting away for their hero.

But wait.

Bobbi squinted, wishing her head wasn't quite so fuzzy. Everyone seemed to be moving in hurried time, clustered like a herd of cattle, toward the podium. The chants had given way to frenzied yelling, and she couldn't make out any distinct voice, yet the panic was suddenly clear.

"It's probably nothing," she said, hearing the slur in her own voice. "I'm pretty sure Bobby's already gone. He usually exits out the back, right?"

"Whatever happened, happened in the back, I think," Kat said, her eyes on the TV, her voice low. "That's why everybody is crowding around."

"I heard a popping sound," Warren said. "Just before."

"More than one," Hanna piped up from her knitting.

"I didn't hear anything," Bobbi argued, but then a man appeared up on the podium, distressed and sweaty, his eyes wild with alarm. The crowd surged toward him, a mixture of revelers, campaign workers, reporters, and cameramen, as he raised his hand for silence.

"Is anyone here a doctor?" the man demanded into the microphone, his voice frantic and high-pitched. "Can you please clear the floor, give us some space? Can a doctor please come to the front? Please!"

Bobbi put down her cup of Tang, which had been drained to just powder, stood up, and fled the room before she could hear any more.

The knock was so quiet, Bobbi almost didn't hear it. She was curled up in a ball on the cot; the door locked behind her, looking through the items in her knapsack. Over the past several months, she'd been collecting buttons from RFK's various pit stops whenever she could, banners and flyers and anything else with his visage. She ran her fingers over her latest trinket, a Poor People's Campaign button that John Lewis had pressed into her hand just before taking his leave.

Bobbi was a coward. She hadn't stayed to find out more, couldn't bear to. To think this giant of a man—small in stature, but big in heart—might be at the end of his journey, after working so hard... He had to be okay, he just had to. Anything else was unthinkable.

The knock came again, and Bobbi opened the door. Warren was standing there.

"You okay, sis?" he asked, pushing his way inside. He sat down at the end of the cot, his hands clasped in front of him. She'd never paid much attention to Warren, finding him kind of annoying. His brown hair was messed up, as though he'd been tugging at it. His blue eyes were bloodshot. He'd been crying.

"I guess," Bobbi answered. She didn't want to ask, but she had to. "So...do they know what happened or—"

"Senator Kennedy was shot, Bobbi," Warren said plainly, and she sunk into the cot, feeling her knees go weak. "At least twice; once in the head. Maybe more, we don't know. He was taken to a hospital in L.A. and he's in grave condition, last they updated."

"But not dead." Well, at least they had that.

"No, not dead," Warren said, looking her in the eye. "Yet."

Her cheeks flushed. "He might make it—"

"He won't, Bobbi,"

"How can you say that?" she demanded.

"Why do you think, Bobbi?" Warren asked, and his voice was not unkind, but his face bore the expression of someone who had seen death one too many times before; someone who was no longer shocked by it. "Look at what they did to MLK, just two months ago. Do you think this is any different? They're saying some immigrant shot Bobby, but they can't even tell us how many shots were fired or who else was hit. It's the same thing all over again." His voice was bitter. "Anybody who is an ally to us, who stands for what's right, who dares to open their mouth to speak truth—they die." He shook his head. "Even if he does make it—and I don't think he will—he won't ever be president. Mark my words, they'll try it again, too. Sorry to say it, sis, but better he dies now. There's a mark on his head."

"There's still hope…" She was flailing. "Don't be cruel, Warren."

"I'm not being cruel, sis," he said. "I'm being realistic. I could lie and coddle you or I could talk plain. It's time to wake up and smell the coffee."

He was right; Bobbi knew he was. It was all but over. Even if Robert Kennedy survived, it was over.

She watched as Warren put his head in his hands, his mussed brown hair sticking up in the back. All this time she'd been attending rallies and protests with him, she'd never really *looked* at him, never considered that he cared just as deeply about all of this as the rest of them. A shudder of sadness went through her.

Bobbi collapsed into tears, and Warren put an arm around her. "I'm sorry, sis," he said in a cajoling voice that was full of his own tears. "I don't mean to make you upset. I know he's your number one, your hero. I get that. It's only just—I've already lost all of mine. I guess I don't have any shock and despair left in me."

"I'm sorry," Bobbi said, her voice wavering. "I didn't realize you cared about him so much."

"I care about a lot of things," Warren said, his voice close to her ear, close enough that she could feel his breath on her skin. "I care about you."

His arms were warm and strong around her, and Bobbi sunk into him without realizing it. He smelled like weed, whiskey, and sandalwood, and his soft, messy brown hair tickled her forehead. "I can't bear for him to die," Bobbi cried into his shoulder. "I don't know what I'd do. I don't think my heart could take it."

"Oh, you're a sweet girl," Warren said in a soft voice, rocking her slightly. "You're so young. You don't have the first idea. Bobbi, you'll lose so many people before it's all over. And you'll carry on each time, with a little less of your heart, because that's what we've got to do. You gotta bear up. Bear up or join 'em before your time."

She looked up at him, her eyes blurry with tears. Their gazes locked, and she could see the empathy in his bright blue eyes and a tenderness that she'd never noticed before. As she stared back, she became aware that she could feel his heartbeat thrumming hard against her arm as he held her. "Thank you for checking on me," she said, looking down at his soft lips. "And letting me know."

Warren pulled back suddenly, as though he'd felt a shock, and stood up. "Of course," he said, clearing his throat. "I'm going to go back and join Kat and Ramon and the rest of 'em. See where Hanna got to. Come out and watch with us if you want. You'll regret it later if you don't." He moved to go.

Bobbi stood up too, realizing too late that she was still drunk. She was woozy on her feet and unsteady. "No, wait," she said, her voice a whisper. "Warren. Wait."

"What is it—" Warren began, but she cut him off, putting her hands on his chest and pushing him toward the wall, wrapping her arms around his neck and pressing her lips to his, doing it in one quick movement so he couldn't push her away. Warren stiffened for a moment, then reacted as if on instinct, craning his head down toward hers, resting his hands softly on her waist, his lips tentative beneath her own.

For a moment their bodies pressed together, and she could feel the hardness of his chest and legs, no spare ounce of fat anywhere— he'd been marching and burning the candle at both ends for a long time, she knew, just like the rest of them. How could she have never noticed how sexy he was? Her body ignited, moving her lips against his softly, as she tasted the salt of his mouth and felt his breath mingling with her own. Then she became aware that he was no longer kissing her back. She pulled back slightly, inches away from his face, and tried for a smile.

"What?" Bobbi said a little breathlessly, letting her fingers trail down his neck. "What's the matter?"

"Sis, this ain't right. I know you're upset, but this ain't right."

Warren took her hand and moved it away from him, gently pushing her back. "Whatever it is you're doing... It can't happen. It won't happen."

"I just thought..." Bobbi began, feeling stupid. "There's something there between us, isn't there?"

Warren shook his head, but his eyes shifted to the side. "No."

Bobbi's eyes widened and her face stung as though he'd slapped her. "But you said...you said you cared about me. The way...the way you touched me..."

Warren's face was uncertain. "I do care about you, Bobbi," he said, putting a hand to her face, touching her cheek gently with a finger. "Maybe if things were different, I might... We might... I don't know. There's so much going on..." His face loomed in front of hers and the next thing Bobbi knew, their lips were barely touching, his mouth against hers again, his hand still on her face. Then, maddeningly, he pulled away again.

"We can't. You're drunk and upset. We both are. Let's just forget about it, okay?" He walked out the door, then turned to her again. "I'm sorry." Warren disappeared down the hall, not looking back, Bobbi's lips still burning from their kiss.

Bobbi's eyes trailed after him. She hadn't imagined that he... *had* she? Warren had come on to her first. He'd said a bunch of patronizing shit, but he'd been flirting with her, too. And he had kissed her back; she hadn't imagined it! And then rejected her. Fresh tears started. She didn't know, couldn't tell anything anymore. She watched Warren's retreating back, feeling ashamed and embarrassed, and very, very alone.

"Did I really just see what I think I saw?" The voice was full of quiet anger in the darkened hall.

Bobbi jumped and turned to see dark-haired Hanna standing in the corner, eyes blazing with fury. "Hanna, it wasn't what it looked like—"

Kat stepped forward, the hall light illuminating her like a halo. Her eyes blazed. "I saw it, too, Bobbi."

"Guys, it wasn't what you think—"

Hanna's voice was like acid. "I was worried Warren would only make you more upset. He's not so good at comforting people. Instead, we find him trying to comfort you, and you taking advantage of the situation by sticking your tongue down his throat."

"Hanna, Kat, I can explain. I—"

"You don't need to explain," Hanna spat. "I've been watching you bed anything that moves for months. Only I thought you'd know *my* boyfriend was off-limits. I guess I was wrong."

Bobbi reached out a hand to her friend. "Please, if you'd only let me—"

Kat put a hand on Bobbi's arm. "Bobbi."

"It was only because he—"

"I don't care. I should have known you'd try it. I thought you were my friend. But you're just another privileged, rich little bitch who uses the *work* to get accolades and male attention and then high-tails it back home to your privileged life. None of us never meant shit to you. You're a fake." Hanna shook her head. "And what about your precious boyfriend, the one overseas, trying not to get his head blown off? What would he think about the way you've been slutting around town? Sounds like he made the right call, getting rid of you before he deployed."

Bobbi stared at her, aghast, ashamed, her eyes filling with tears. "Hanna, I'm sorry—"

"You're a coward, a phony," Hanna seethed. "You said Bobby Kennedy's been your hero for *years and years,* since you were a little kid, huh? Then he gets shot and you run out of the room because you can't even watch, you won't even bear witness as it all crumbles, as a good man dies, because your precious feelings are more important than the rest of us watching the last of our hope crumble to ashes."

Bobbi stared at her, tears streaming down her cheeks, as Hanna turned on her heel and stalked off down the hall. Kat stood there for a moment, staring at Bobbi, her eyes full of sadness. She shook her head, gave a deep sigh, and turned, following Hanna down the hall. The door to the rec room slammed behind them.

Bobbi awoke the next morning with a crick in her neck, her head pounding, and the artificial sweetness of Tang slick on her tongue. She sat up and dressed silently, then packed her knapsack, careful not to look at the pins and flyers, not wanting to remind herself of the night before. She felt delicate, like she was made of glass. One swift movement and she'd shatter into pieces. And yet, she did not deserve to feel that way. Hanna had been right. About all of it.

She made her way to the kitchen, averting her gaze from everyone's eyes as she entered, wishing she hadn't come in at all. Warren and Ramon were sitting at the table, a platter of bacon in front of them. Bobbi could smell fresh coffee and her dry mouth watered. Then she remembered Warren's admonishment from the night before—*wake up and smell the coffee*—and her stomach churned. They were listening to the little radio by the window, and Bobbi could hear two men speculating about a man called Sirhan Sirhan, who had allegedly shot Bobby Kennedy, though they still didn't know why, as the man wasn't talking.

Hanna was in the corner, pouring herself a cup. She fixed a steely stare on Bobbi. "You have some nerve coming in here."

"I went out and got bacon and coffee," Warren said to her cheerfully, seemingly oblivious to the tension in the room. Ramon didn't look up from the stack of mail he was sorting through. "It'll make us all feel better. Why don't you help yourself, Bobbi?"

"Thanks, but I'm okay," Bobbi said, even though she was dying for coffee. "I just came in for water." She inched by Hanna, who stood by the glasses, and eased one out of the cabinet, trying to stay out of her way. She filled it from the tap and grimaced as it went down her dry throat. It tasted like metal and rust. The air in the room was thick and muggy. "I'm leaving today."

"Bye," Hanna said, turning her back on her and staring out the window.

"Hanna..." Bobbi began, staring at her friend's tense back, when Warren made a noise.

"I think it's a press conference," he said, jumping up from the table to turn up the volume, just as a bleary-eyed Kat entered the room and headed toward the coffeemaker.

"Senator Robert Francis Kennedy died at 6:00 a.m. at Good Samaritan Hospital in Los Angeles."

Bobbi clutched at the counter, her legs going weak. Beside her, Kat stiffened, and Bobbi ached to grab onto her, to hold her friend, to comfort her and be comforted, but instead she stood there, gripping the counter so tight her palms hurt, watching as Kat and Hanna held each other. In silence, they all listened to the remainder of the press conference, but none of it mattered anymore. Nothing mattered.

Bobbi forced herself to stay, remembering Hanna's words, standing vigil, paying homage, accepting their fate. The dream was dead. It was over.

Bobby Kennedy was gone.

As the press conference ended, Warren stood up and switched off the radio with a trembling hand. "Well, what the fuck do we do now?" he asked helplessly, wringing his hands.

"What do you think?" Kat said bitterly from over by the window, her voice flat and toneless. "Keep trying to save the world, one less person at a time."

The next bus wouldn't arrive for another hour, so Bobbi sat outside of headquarters on a bench, her knapsack beside her. She didn't want to go back to Georgia, not yet, because she knew that Robert F. Kennedy would be interred in a day or two at Arlington. She'd like to find some way to say her goodbyes. And the truth was, a large part of her just didn't want to go back to Georgia. It no longer felt like home. But she couldn't stay here, not any longer. She swallowed hard. She had nowhere to go, nobody to be with. Her hero was dead. She thought back to that afternoon when Ed had taken her to see Bobby at the UGA Law School, the only time she'd ever seen him speak. With as many rallies and events she'd gone to, with as active as she'd been over the past few years, she'd never come in such close proximity to him again.

Where would she go? What would she do now? She wished she had Landrum. But if he knew how she'd behaved with Warren, he'd hate her, too. He'd broken up with her, so she knew he wouldn't judge her for going around with men, for seeing people. But he would judge her for lusting after Ramon for months, for kissing Warren, and for using sex to fill the void he had left. Some of the men she'd been with, she hadn't even known their last names. She hadn't been careful. She'd been so reckless and thoughtless, hurting people, hurting herself. And for what? Not having to spend a night alone?

Guilt rolled in her belly, mixing uneasily with her grief. She had no tears. She had not cried a single drop since the night before. She supposed they had dried up.

The screen door opened, and Ramon called out, "Bobbi, there's a telephone call for you."

Bobbi didn't bother to turn around. "It must be a mistake. Nobody knows me here. Nobody would be calling me."

"He must have tracked you down," Ramon insisted. "He said it was important. Said his name's Ed."

Bobbi got up and walked slowly, as though underwater, back into the kitchen, where she grabbed the receiver and held it to her ear, the cold plastic hard against her skin. "Yes?"

"Bobbi." Her brother's normally smooth, self-assured voice was cracked and pained, and cloaked in tears. "You've got to come on home."

"But why? Did you hear about—"

"Bobbi. I've just had a telegram," Ed choked out. "Guy's... Bobbi, he's been killed. He's gone."

NINETEEN

ELLA - 1995

ELLA leaned back onto the pillows, the now-familiar feeling of euphoria washing over her, waiting until the moment her eyes would close involuntarily and she'd be swept off into a sea of bliss. She could hear the strums of Louie's acoustic guitar as he played beside her; he'd been writing a lot lately. All of his songs were sad and dreamy, and absolutely beautiful.

Ella didn't realize she was singing along—just humming nonsense since she didn't know the lyrics—until Louie began to sing with her. Their voices rose together, a sweet, natural harmony that seemed to crest and fall all on its own.

"We make a good team," Louie said in a soft voice, placing a kiss on her nose. Ella's eyes began to close; she was so sleepy. "You should join my band."

"I don't play," Ella said sleepily.

"Your voice is instrument enough," Louie answered, still strumming. "But I could teach you if you wanted. Bass maybe? Wouldn't take you more than a few months to pick up the basics."

Ella licked her lips and folded her hands in front of her, grateful to be drifting off. She had come to Louie's apartment today with the intention of breaking up—she had put it off long enough—but when he'd answered the door, just back from a midday surf, his hair impossibly cute, dripping wet and curling over his shoulders, she'd lost her nerve. When he'd broken out his bag of "goodies" and offered to share, she'd accepted without a moment's hesitation, eager to ride a wave to euphoria rather than face the music. Well, figuratively, anyway.

Off in the distance, her pager vibrated. Ella knew it was Janelle. They were supposed to meet up for dinner; Janelle was cooking for her tonight. Ella had been dreaming about it for two days—an entire evening alone, just the two of them. She wouldn't have to pretend Janelle was just a friend or try and sneak around Louie. Just her and beautiful, wonderful Janelle.

Now that she was here, though, blissed out on Louie's couch, Ella considered reaching for the phone and canceling. She couldn't go to Janelle's fucked up like this. Janelle would be furious. She had a strict no-junk policy, having already been through the battle and won the war herself, and Ella knew it was a dealbreaker for her.

Dark thoughts loomed, threatening to break Ella's sedated reverie. She had been living on credit, she felt like, carrying on with both Louie and Janelle for so long that she no longer knew where she ended and they began. It seemed impossible, and nobody sane would believe it, but Ella loved them both. She loved them so much it made her heart clench.

But even as Louie bent over her and placed another gentle, sensual kiss—this time on her lips, tasting like strawberries—Ella knew the truth. She *did* love them both so much. But while Louie was wonderful—sweet, handsome, talented, funny—he wasn't

Janelle.

Janelle was the one. Hadn't Ella known it from pretty much the beginning?

So why did she keep putting it off?

Looking at Louie, listlessly strumming his guitar, Ella almost wanted to laugh. She'd come to Seattle to follow her dream of grunge and had ended up dating a musician. The ultimate dream, and she'd accomplished it, but the funny part was, she'd never once seen Louie and his band play a single show, not in all this time.

Was this the big dream? Was it really?

"Can you stay the night?" Louie asked her in a soft voice, putting his guitar on the floor and trailing his hand down her shoulder to her stomach, winding under her shirt. His skin was very warm. "I don't want to let you go."

Ella let out a soft sigh. "Let me just make a phone call," she said, her voice so quiet it was almost a whisper.

TWENTY

BOBBI - 1968

THE tinny radio was blaring in her ear—that song by Status Quo that seemed to be everywhere for the past year—but Bobbi barely heard it.

She was sitting in the kitchen, at the table that had held Ramon and Warren just minutes before. They'd scattered, giving her privacy, knowing from the way she'd slunk to the floor, the phone tumbling out of her hand, what news her brother Ed had borne. It didn't matter, anyway. She wanted to be alone.

The idiocy of the night before came rushing back to her, and she winced, putting her head in her hands. All she wanted was Landrum—the feel of his arms around her, his signature scent invading her senses, the warm familiarity he exuded—how could she have ever sought comfort in anyone else? Perhaps this was her karma for the way she'd behaved, she thought to herself, then bit off the thought with reproach. What a narcissistic thing to think, when her own brother lay dead on foreign soil, alone and cold. *Hanna's right,* she thought, licking her dry lips. *All I think about is myself.*

Just an hour ago, she'd thought nothing could hurt worse than the death of her hero Bobby Kennedy. Now she knew better. She lay her head in her hands, wishing for tears that didn't come. Her eyes were as dry as her heart.

After a time, a cup of coffee was placed in front of her. "Bobbi."

She raised her head, wiping at her tired eyes, and saw Kat standing there. Her face was pained. "Drink that." She put two white pills on the table. "And take these. The last thing you need right now is a hangover."

Bobbi dutifully knocked back the aspirin, chasing it with the hot coffee. It was black, but she didn't bother to ask for cream or sugar. Such indulgences seemed almost sacrilegious at a moment like this, and besides, they likely didn't have any. The coffee was hot and strong, and delicious. The smell of Warren's bacon still clung to the kitchen, and Bobbi's stomach rolled over.

"Thanks," Bobbi said, her voice coming out scratchy. She cleared her throat and said again, "Thank you."

"No problem."

Kat sat down across from her, and Bobbi could see she was wringing her hands in the nervous way she did. Before, she'd only ever seen Kat do that when Ramon was out on some dangerous mission, at a rally or protest where white supremacists—or worse, the government—might be involved. She looked at Bobbi with her wide brown eyes, running a hand absently through her soft, tight curls.

"Bobbi, I'm so sorry about your brother," she said simply. "I'm sorry I didn't come to you right away—I didn't know what to do. We thought you wanted to be alone."

"That's okay," Bobbi said dumbly, wondering how much time had passed. It felt like hours—and less than a second—had passed since she'd woken up and had her entire world implode.

"It's not okay," Kat insisted, then pushed the coffee cup toward Bobbi again. "Is there anything we can do?" She didn't wait for Bobbi to answer. "Ramon and I will drive you down to Georgia for the service, so you won't have to worry about taking the bus or scraping up airfare. We can leave this morning. Warren's insisting that he's coming, too, but we told him he should hold down the fort here. I know the last thing you want is him yapping at you the whole trip. Especially after, um—"

"There won't be any service," Bobbi said quietly, wiping a tear from her cheek. "At least not right away. Guy's, uh" —she choked up for a moment, then recovered herself— "remains…won't arrive for a few days, and Ed's having him cremated. He said we'll have a memorial service on Guy's birthday." She coughed. "His birthday was his favorite holiday, ever since he was a kid. We always teased him about that. His birthday is September 7th." She knew she was babbling, but she couldn't stop.

"Still, you might want to go home, just to be with family… I'm sure they're expecting you to."

That was true—Ed had asked her at least five times during their short phone call to come home—but Bobbi shook her head. "No. I don't think I can stomach Grace just yet, and Ed's probably going to be run off his feet. He doesn't need me there, making things more complicated." She didn't know how to explain to Kat that she couldn't deal with being home in Athens right now, not without Landrum by her side, holding her up. Not when Guy would never be there again. The thought of staying in that bloodless, loveless house with Grace, while she felt like this…she couldn't face it. She hoped Ed would understand. "It's for the best," she said, taking another sip of scalding, bitter coffee. "Honestly. It's probably easier on him if I stay put."

"If you say so," Kat said, but she looked unsure. "I just think… being near family at a time like this is important."

"You're more my family than they are," Bobbi said, meeting Kat's eyes. "Especially now that Guy's gone."

Kat didn't reply, only stared at Bobbi with her thoughtful brown eyes.

Bobbi swallowed. "So, thank you for the offer, but you and Ramon don't need to drive me anywhere." She sighed. "After last night, I imagine that's the last thing you'd want to do anyway."

"Oh, Bobbi," Kat said with a sigh.

"You have every right to hate me," Bobbi pressed, wiping at her eyes. "You all do."

"Nobody hates you," Kat said evenly, looking back at her friend. Her eyes were wide and clear. "I'm disappointed. I hate seeing you do this to yourself. But I'm not entirely convinced that Warren wasn't to blame —in part, at least—for what we saw. I know what he's like."

A rush of gratitude swept over Bobbi, and she swallowed, trying to dislodge the lump in her throat. "You have to know that I—I never meant what happened…" she said. "I just misread the signals… I was drunk… When I heard the news about Bobby I felt so alone, and I wanted Landrum…" She shook her head. "It's no excuse, and it's all my fault. I don't know what the hell I was *thinking*. I'm so sorry."

"You've been spiraling for a long time," Kat said quietly. "I worried, from time to time, that you'd make a play for Ramon. I know you have a crush on him." Bobbi swallowed hard and looked at her lap, ashamed. Kat went on. "I guess when I saw you and Warren, my fears about that took over and I just… I followed Hanna's lead." She took Bobbi's hand. "But look, Bobbi, it's been a hard couple of days. We're all distraught."

"So you forgive me?"

"I have nothing to forgive you for," Kat said, her voice tender. "Hanna, that's another story. I imagine she'll put it behind her for now, considering what you're going through. As for Warren, well, Ramon and I have agreed that it'd be best if he moves on, finds somewhere else to stay. We'll talk to him about that later."

"I'm so sorry," Bobbi whispered again, and Kat stood up from the table and put her arms around her, squeezing her tight. "About all of it. I don't deserve you as a friend."

"Maybe you do, maybe you don't," Kat said with a chuckle, "but either way, I'm not going anywhere."

TWENTY-ONE

ELLA - 1995

"**ARE** you high?"

Ella stared at Anita, buying a few moments before answering. She rolled over from where she'd been lying on her belly on the worn futon and sighed. "I smoked a joint with Louie before he left," she answered, reaching for the Slurpee that was laying just out of her reach on the floor. "Why?"

She had MTV on, cranked to the highest volume. They were doing a metal/grunge rock block, and she was hoping to catch a glimpse of Alice in Chains, whose newest single, "Grind," she'd yet to see the video for, or maybe "Black Hole Sun" by Soundgarden. It was her new favorite afternoon activity—getting high as a kite and watching rock videos all afternoon. Sometimes, when she was really inspired, she'd dig out her art supplies and throw a little paint on the canvas. More often than not, though, she just laid on the futon and zoned out.

She had so much to think about. Just this week alone, she'd had a call from her uncle Ed. "Just to check in," he'd said, but there'd been a hidden agenda. A few of their church friends had started asking where she'd got off to, he said, and would love her to consider coming back home and enrolling in UGA, where a spot was all but guaranteed for her. The day after that, she'd gotten an email from an old school friend—Ricky, an upperclassman who had taken her to his senior prom. He'd found her by chance and wanted to say hi, ask how she was. Ricky, who had always been cute and sweet, had grown another foot and grown a beard, too. Ella hadn't written him back yet, though, or given Ed an answer. Because there were also the things she had to think about *here*.

"I don't mean pot, and you know it," Anita said, hands on her hips. She was getting ready to go out, as usual, a knockout in her shin-length slinky black skirt and Mudhoney t-shirt that she'd cut the collar out of and laced up the sides with ribbon. She wore a shade of almost-black lipstick and thick, darkeyeliner. Ella continued to be jealous of how both she and Janelle possessed the kind of effortless beauty that allowed them to dress like total crackpots and still look chic and sexy.

"You look gorgeous," Ella said honestly, sitting up and grabbing at her Slurpee. "You going out with Tad?"

"No, I told you the last time I dumped him, it was for real this time," Anita answered, her eyes narrowing. "Stop dodging the question, Ella. Did you use?"

Ella sighed. Her silence told Anita all she needed to know.

The relationship with the three of them—Janelle, Louie, and Ella—had gone beyond complicated into total clusterfuck territory, and Ella had begun to wonder just how much Louie knew, and what they were all going to do about it.

"Don't bring that shit around me, Ella," Janelle had warned. "I have too much to lose. So do you, in fact. So does Louie. I think you guys are being fucking stupid." They hadn't talked about it again—Ella didn't want to do anything else to upset her, considering the foolish game she was already playing. Janelle's patience was understandably wearing thin. Janelle was Ella's boss, to say nothing of their relationship, or who Janelle's parents were. So Ella kept her using at a minimum, careful not to start up a habit, telling herself that she was going to quit for good, very soon. She and Louie were discreet, and they kept it light. Still, it appeared that Janelle had talked to Anita about it, and now Anita was barking at her.

"I don't do it that much," Ella said defensively, slurping the green apple slush in the bottom of her cup. "It's barely a blip. Don't worry."

"I don't want a junkie roommate," Anita said, fixing her with a steely glare. "For one thing, it's too uncertain. Junkies don't know how to act and they certainly don't pay their fucking rent. And anyway, haven't you paid attention? Louie never gets gigs. Look at how Andy Wood died. Look at Kurt Cobain. Look at Lanegan. Isn't Alice In Chains your favorite band? Layne Staley looks like *dogshit,* Ella—"

"I know, I know." Ella groaned, waving a hand, wishing Anita would stop. As if she was a saint. She was drunk every day and Ella had seen her doing coke in the bathroom at the last house party they went to. "Look, I'll scale it back if it makes you more comfortable. I can take it or leave it, anyway. It's mainly Louie's thing."

"If you have to use drugs to keep things good between the two of you, maybe it's time to move on."

"What does that mean?" Ella sat up straighter, feeling defensive.

"Things are great between Louie and me." She considered telling Anita about the marathon sex session they'd had just an hour before, making Louie late for work; he'd had to skip showering and the sexy kiss he'd placed on her neck before rushing out the door still burned there like a brand. "We're hot as ever."

"Oh, really?" Anita's brows rose to her hairline. "Then why are you sleeping with Janelle behind his back?"

Ella's mouth dropped open. Apparently Janelle had been discussing more than heroin with Anita. Ella's sudden anger was second only to her jealousy that Janelle would confide in Anita without telling her. "What makes you think that?" she said, trying for innocence.

"Oh, drop the act, Ella. Everybody knows. Well, everybody except Louie, I guess." She snickered. "Though I suspect he knows it too, and it either makes him hard or he doesn't care because he's too stoned." She shook her head. "Janelle thinks the two of you are in love. But what it looks like to me is that you want to have your cake and eat it too, while getting high the whole fucking time."

"Anita, you're starting to piss me off—" Ella retorted angrily, but Anita cut her off.

"Look, it's none of my business what you do with either of them. I love all you guys, and that's the only reason I even said anything. You still have a chance to quit that shit and get back on track. Stop the junk if you want to keep your job, your boyfriend, and your friendships." She opened the door and stepped out, then turned back to Ella. "But especially if you want to keep Janelle. You may not realize it, but she's already slipping away. That girl doesn't play second fiddle to anyone—whether it's junk or a dude."

Anita walked out into the hall and slammed the door, leaving Ella to stare open-mouthed behind her.

There was a painful ulcer on the inside of her lip, and Ella poked at it with her tongue as she waited in the bathroom. She was perched on the toilet seat, leaning up against the cold porcelain, her back bare, only wearing a pair of Louie's flannel pajama pants and her bra. She hadn't managed to dress yet, though she'd meant to after Anita had stormed out, intending to get up and clean the house and do something productive. But she was so exhausted. Nausea roiled around her belly, making her groan.

She'd been feeling queasy, tired, and achy for days, as well as dizzy and hazy, as though her brain were in a fog. She'd been attributing her symptoms to the junk, but what she'd told Anita was true—she didn't use often enough to have such adverse effects. It wasn't a "problem," not yet. Still, Anita was right. It wasn't worth it to feel this way, to piss off the people who were important to you, to waste your time and money on something that had harmed so many. She made a mental note to tell Louie she was off the stuff, not to bring it around her anymore. She hadn't come to Seattle to become a pitiful, washed-up junkie—she'd come to start a new life. Broke and hooked on heroin wasn't new, and it wasn't a life, either. Louie would understand. Whatever problems he had of his own, deep down, he was a good guy. The best of guys, actually.

Ella didn't deserve him.

She didn't deserve Janelle, either. What a mess she'd made of things.

Ella took a deep breath and squared her shoulders. The three minutes had long passed, and truth be told, she'd seen the little window on the plastic tube start to change colors the moment she'd finished peeing and set it on the side of the tub; she just hadn't brought herself to look at it yet. Instead, she stared at the ceiling and thought to herself, *why DID I come to Seattle? What was my grand plan? To play happy families with Kat and Ramon and Janelle? I could have that, and yet I'm sabotaging it. Why do I suddenly have no idea what I'm doing or why?*

She heard someone knocking on the front door. Ella sighed, pulled on a dirty t-shirt from the hamper, and, taking a quick glance at the plastic tube on the tub, swept it into the trash and left the bathroom. She opened the door to see Janelle standing there.

Ella's brow furrowed. "I thought you were still out of town, at your parents'," she said. Janelle being gone from the co-op for a few days had made it much easier to call in sick.

"I came back late last night," Janelle said, pushing past her and coming into the apartment, where she turned around to face Ella with a grimace. "It stinks in here. When was the last time you washed that shirt?"

"I'm sick."

"You definitely look it," Janelle said, not unkindly. She was holding a large brown box taped at the top with purple duct tape. "I was worried when Rachel told me you'd called out."

"I'm okay," Ella said, and Janelle leaned over to kiss her on the temple, her lips sending a spark of heat through Ella. She longed to pull her closer, loving how it felt to have Janelle near, but she didn't want to be too clingy. Every time Janelle was close to her, it was all Ella could do not to touch her. She craved her, more than she craved anything else in this life, even the junk. But bigger than the craving was the fear. The fear that Janelle could drop her at any time, could lose interest, say it was all a mistake. And so Ella held back and didn't let it show.

"Where's Louie?" Janelle asked casually, sitting down on the couch.

"He's at work," Ella answered. "I think he gets off at four, but I probably won't see him tonight. He has band practice." She moved to sit down in the chair opposite Janelle, but Janelle gestured for her to come closer. Ella sat down on the floor in front of Janelle, her stomach rolling and rolling, clutching at the carpet with her fingers.

"Want me to stay, then?" Janelle asked her, pulling Ella's head back toward her, her fingers gentle as she began to braid her hair. Ella leaned into her touch, sighing with pleasure, then abruptly pulled away, another wave of nausea rolling over her. She didn't deserve Janelle's kind touch, her empathy. Being around Janelle felt so damn good and yet so awful at the same time. Yes, she wanted Janelle to stay, of course she did. But she couldn't say the words.

"I'm worried about getting you sick," Ella responded, glancing backward, then looking away quickly, ignoring the hurt in Janelle's eyes. "Seriously, whatever this is, it's awful. I'm nauseated and I have the chills, and I'm so sleepy. I ache all over." The last part wasn't true, not in any real sense, though she was beginning to feel a dull ache in her throat from the rising panic there.

"Oh sure, okay," Janelle said after a moment, then she added quietly, "This can't go on though, can it?"

"What do you mean?"

"Don't play dumb, sweetie," Janelle said, reaching around to put a finger on Ella's lip, silencing her. Ella found herself leaning into her again, loving Janelle touching her, her recoil from the moment before forgotten. But Janelle took her hand away. "This…thing… between you and me and Louie. I can't keep doing this. It's not fair to him. He's my best friend."

"I thought I was your best friend," Ella joked, trying to deflect.

"You're more than that and you know it," Janelle said, her voice serious. "I told you from the beginning how I felt. But Louie—he actually *is* my best friend — and we've been rolling together for a long time, longer than either of us has known you. This… It's a betrayal. I doubt he'd ever forgive me if he knew what we've been doing."

"He was there the first night," Ella argued. "He had to have known what we—"

Janelle cut her off. "Maybe he knew, maybe he didn't. It doesn't negate the fact that this is wrong. Have you talked to him at all?"

"No," Ella said. She felt defensive. "But it's not like I've told you about every time I've fucked him, either."

"That's supposed to make it somehow better?" Janelle laughed, and Ella bristled. "If anything, that makes it worse. I don't want to share you. I told you, I love you. Ella, this isn't just some fun thing for me. Whatever it means to you, if anything, I don't know. But Ella, the way I feel, it's—"

"Have you been talking to Anita?" Ella asked, recalling the conversation with her roommate from earlier and wondering if it had something to do with Janelle's sudden questions.

"No, I haven't heard from her in a few days," Janelle answered, sounding puzzled. "Why?"

"No reason."

"Ella…"

Ella's pager began to vibrate., and Janelle abruptly stopped talking. They both glanced at the coffee table. With a sigh, knowing she was breaking some unspoken rule, Ella grabbed the pager and looked at the number. "Louie," she said softly, putting it back down. "What were you going to say?"

"Nothing that needed to be said, probably," Janelle said. Her expression had turned sad. "He wouldn't be paging you if it wasn't important. I bet his car broke down again." She stood up and gestured at the box on the floor. "I brought that back from Mom and Dad's. Mom said to give her a call if you want to talk about what's in there. It's the box they told you about; stuff that belonged to your mother. They wanted you to have it."

"I don't want it," Ella lied, feeling suddenly sullen. Who cared about all that crap from the past? It was Janelle she wanted, Janelle she couldn't let go of. When she was away from Janelle, she felt lost and adrift. She missed her so much it ached. Even when she was with Louie, she missed Janelle. Even when the three of them were together, she missed her. Janelle could be standing right in front of her, and Ella craved her, wanted her.

"Stop being a fucking child, Ella. That stuff is your legacy, what's left of your mom, and my parents have held onto it for almost twenty years. Take it and be grateful if you can manage it."

"Why are you so angry?" Ella asked her, hot tears forming in her eyes.

"Don't do that, sweetie," Janelle responded, walking to the door. "Look, I've gotta go. I hope you feel better. Try not to miss too much more work. I can't give you any special treatment. And Ella." She turned and gave her a soft look. "You're going to have to decide soon. This isn't fair—not to any of us, including yourself." She shut the door quietly but firmly; it might as well have been slammed. Ella winced.

She could hear Janelle's footsteps retreating down the hall. She shuffled back to the bathroom, where she fished out the little plastic tube from the trash. She sat back down on the toilet seat and stared at the pregnancy test, trying to swallow down the acid and the bile that had been creeping up her throat ever since she'd glanced at it the first time.

You're going to have to decide soon.

Janelle had no idea how right she was.

After Ella had peeled herself off the bathroom floor, she went back to the living room, sat on the floor in front of the coffee table, and pulled the taped-up box Janelle had brought toward her. She picked at the tape with a fingernail, finally easing enough up to pull it from the box, opening it and breathing in the old, musty scent of long-ago packed up things. There was a hint of a fragrance there; something like sandalwood or incense. Musky, exotic, and old.

SO LONG, BOBBY

She rummaged through the box, pulling out dresses; they must have belonged to her mother. Her mom had apparently had great taste and was svelte to boot. Ella gingerly laid the dresses in a pile, almost afraid to touch them. The lovely fragrance was coming from them, and she longed to put one on and swish about the room. But she hadn't even showered today. Her guts were rolling, and she felt unworthy of these beautiful things. Maybe she'd try them on later (and do it in her room, where there was no chance of Anita stumbling in and laying claim to anything).

Below the dresses was a cigar box filled with political buttons, banners, and pamphlets, most related to either Robert F. Kennedy or various Civil Rights causes. She recognized a young John Lewis on one button, and a few with MLK and the NAACP, but there were more of Robert Kennedy's toothy smile and shock of strawberry-blond hair than anything else. Ella put these aside; she knew next to nothing about Robert F. Kennedy save for he was President John F. Kennedy's brother and had lived in his shadow. She didn't care much about the Kennedys—she'd grown up hearing Ed revere Ted, and that told her all she needed to know.

A hat sat in the box; felt maybe, hardly worn, a deep army green and emblazoned with a delicate gold pin. It dwarfed Ella's head when she tried it on. As she held it, a feeling of deep despair seized her, something desolate and bereft. She clutched it to her, feeling a momentary deep grief that seemed to have no bottom, then placed it gently on top of the dresses.

The box was nearly empty now, save for a few ancient, dried-up cosmetics, a Rolling Stone magazine from 1972 announcing

Jim Morrison's death (she would definitely have to show that to Louie; he'd die), and an envelope. She pulled it out and opened it, extracting a letter.

Kat,
Sorry it's been a few months since I wrote. I've been run off my feet with this baby. Landrum helps as much as he can, but with his disability, it's hard for him to pick her up when she gets to wiggling and having a tantrum, which is pretty much all the time. So I have to do most of the washing, cooking and tending to her. But oh, he loves her so. Ella is a daddy's girl, through and through. Just like I was at her age.

Ella felt her heart clench painfully. She didn't remember her father, or her mother for that matter, but their love was coming off the page, a real, tangible love. She wished she could picture her father, wished she could remember him holding her in his arms.

Just between you and I, I wish he'd see someone. He has such dark days, days where I know he's remembering things. Not just things from the war, but from his childhood. He's so unhappy, and he tries to hide it. He drinks too much and he chain smokes and it's like he tries to blot out everything but Ella. Sometimes I think he even tries to blot me out. Not that it would take much. I feel less and less every day, seems like. Like a stiff breeze could just blow me away. Ever since I had the baby—honestly long before that, because I think something that started long ago came to a head that day in 1968—I've felt myself slipping away. That day I lost myself, lost your trust, then I lost Bobby, and my brother, worst of all. It hasn't been the same since then, Kat. I think I sealed my fate that day, and nothing, not even Landrum and I, will ever be the same. We used to love each other so much, were on fire for each other, and now...neither one of us has a flame left to burn.

What was that writer, the poet, what was it he said: "Things fall apart; the center cannot hold"? You would know; you're the smartest woman on the planet and you've read every book there is to read.

Enough about my troubles. How boring. How is your sweet, dear baby girl? I wish I could get to Seattle to see you and Ramon and meet the little darling, but it's just so dear. Landrum and I are counting our pennies until we can fly out. I promise you then I'll smother my goddaughter with kisses and make up for lost time. I love you all so much and sometimes just thinking of the three of you, happy and settled on the west coast, with your adorable house by the ocean, after all you've done for others, makes me so happy I could explode. It gets me through.

Here's a little picture of our family for your wallet. Excuse the poor quality; we can't afford one of those fancy photographers. This was taken by Grace (the devil).

I love you,
Bobbi

A picture had fallen out from the creases of the letter to the floor while she was reading. Ella picked it up and held it in front of her face and peered at it. The little girl in the photo had to be no older than a year old. She had wispy, light-colored pigtails and big eyes, and she was wearing a gingham dress not unlike Dorothy's in the Wizard of Oz. She was sitting on her mother's lap, a woman who looked like a grown-up version of the girl—light blonde hair, big blue eyes, and a faraway look on her face. Her mouth was pinched in a forced smile, but there was something else in her expression, something dreamlike and hopeful. Her arm was linked through a man's, who was standing off to the right of them. He stood very tall, in uniform, wearing the very hat that Ella had just put on her own head. He was handsome, with an open, friendly face but a haunted look in his eyes. Ella couldn't tell if they were gray or blue. The woman's arm linked in his clutched at him, and his hand rested in her long blonde hair.

Ella stared. The girl in the photo was undeniably her—she recognized the arch of her eyebrows, the beginnings of what she thought was a too-big nose, her dotting of freckles on her high cheekbones—but she couldn't remember having been so light blonde. For as long as she remembered, her hair had been what Grace called "dishwater"—no doubt it had turned at some early point in her life. To think her mother had been nearly platinum blonde, and so had she as a youngster—made her feel oddly emotional.

The haunted looks on her parents' faces filled her with sadness. And yet, there was love there—she could feel it coming off the photo in waves. The way their arms were linked, the way his hand twined through her hair, the way her mother's other arm was wrapped around her little girl's waist in a squeezing hug—there was love, lots of it. Her parents had loved her, and they had loved each other, despite whatever haunted them.

She felt desolate, and ashamed, suddenly, that she didn't know. She didn't know anything about them, had never cared, really. Oh, she'd asked a few questions here and there when she was young, but she'd taken note of the way Grace's lips would purse and the pained expression on Uncle Ed's face any time she'd asked, and by the time she was eight or nine, she'd stopped bringing them up. And, after a while, it seemed to no longer matter, anyway. She didn't know Landrum and Bobbi Walton. Her parents were Ed and Grace Newton.

I have no idea where I come from. I have no idea who I am. They kept it from me.

Her stomach gurgled, and she looked down at her lap, blinking back tears. Shame and regret washed over her in a flood.

They were so in love. And they loved me so much. Perhaps I was all they had. They died, and I forgot them.

Another knock on the door, a soft one. Louie. She'd completely forgotten to answer his page, and now he'd come back to make sure she was okay.

Ella rose to her feet, gingerly putting all the items back in the box, closing the lid, and scooting it behind the couch. As she walked to the door, she slid the photo into her pocket. One of two secrets she had suddenly decided to keep.

393

Two days later, Ella hummed along to the last notes of R.E.M.'s "Orange Crush" as she slipped on the mustard-yellow A-line. It was a bit tight, especially around the waist—her mother had been slimmer than she by a measure—but she was able to button it up with little trouble. She pulled on the thick black stockings she'd bought at Maurice's recently, then the patent leather boots. She cinched a black belt around her waist, wondering how long she'd be able to wear these types of clothes before she was a swollen balloon, and pulled her hair into a messy braid. She sat on the bathroom counter sideways, peering into the mirror as she carefully applied eyeliner, smudging it the way Anita had taught her, caked on a powdery, thick white eyeshadow, and applied nude gloss to her lips. With a quick spritz of Exclamation! perfume, she was done.

Another wave of nausea rolled over her, and she did her best to ignore it. Ella had no idea if it was the pregnancy or withdrawals making her sick. Maybe both. Either way, she deserved it. She hoped the layer of gloss she'd put on would disguise her misery, at least for the trip, so nobody would bother her. Later, it wouldn't matter.

As for the junk, she was one hundred percent done with that. The little plastic test had cemented that much.

Ella made her way to the kitchen and grabbed a bottle of Josta from the fridge, making a mental note to leave a twenty on the counter to pay Anita back for the stuff she'd consumed throughout the past week. Her paycheck wouldn't arrive until Friday, and by then, she'd be long gone.

She took a big, sweeping look at the apartment—she'd gotten up early that morning and deep-cleaned it from top to bottom, everything from mopping the floors to scrubbing out the bathtub, and she'd even dusted the light fixtures and taken out the trash—taking note of the packed bag by the door, and the sealed box she'd left by the kitchen table. She'd gotten everything, or at least everything that mattered. Only one thing left to do.

With a shaking hand, Ella grabbed a piece of stationery and scrawled out a quick note to Anita. *"Here's twenty bucks for the sodas and stuff. Would you please give the box by the table and the accompanying envelope to Janelle and/or Louie? Either one of them is fine, if you can give it to them together, even better. Thanks for everything. Good luck with the music career. Love you, Ella."*

The CD had stopped. Ella paused, carefully extracting the R.E.M. disc from the changer, putting it in its case, and switching it to Neutral Milk Hotel. She skipped to her favorite song, closing her eyes for just a moment as the lyrics washed over her.

When Ella was finished, tears had streaked through her heavy makeup, leaving a track of mascara on one cheek. The song had skipped to the next track. She started it over.

She laid the envelope on top of the box, which contained a few things she'd decided to leave behind for them—the Jim Morrison *Rolling Stone* for Louie, a couple of dresses she knew would look amazing on Janelle, and a few other trinkets—addressed simply *"To my loves."*

Soon, they would hate her. But Ella knew in her heart that this was the right choice. She loved both Janelle and Louie too much to turn them against each other, even if by accident. And she simply couldn't imagine raising a child on her own—even with the help of her friends, who'd she come to see as her chosen family—so far from home with so little resources, a love triangle complicating her life. It had only been a few short months since she'd sat on Janelle's couch, praying to the heavens that she'd never lose her or her parents, but now Ella knew it was time to leave of her own volition. It was time to go home, to get away from the forlorn, lonely drizzle of Seattle, a place that dazzled but held no future for her, to rid her friends of the pain she'd no doubt cause. Her baby deserved a chance at normalcy, family, love—the things she had missed out on. Might she have had that here, with Janelle and Louie and Anita, had she not botched things so terribly? It was too late to fix it now.

It wasn't all her fault, she knew. She was damaged, she'd been orphaned. She had no idea what it was like to feel the love of a mother and father, to rely on someone and be reliable.

But that was all the more reason she must try.

Another wave rolled over and Ella ran to the bathroom, getting sick over the toilet, carefully dabbing at her face and mouth with a tissue when she was done. She flushed and stood over the sink for a moment, waiting for the misery to pass, then stood and took a deep breath, regarding herself in the mirror. She didn't recognize the person she saw there, with her sad, haunted eyes, the bags under them despite the makeup, the smeared lipstick from where she'd been sick.

Ella had just one more thing to do. She stepped over to Anita's computer, typed in the password, and signed onto the internet, waiting patiently, dabbing again at her streaked makeup and blotting it with the pad from her compact as the modem whirred and buzzed.

"You've got mail!" the friendly robot voice said. Ella clicked into her Yahoo account and opened up the chat feature. She prayed her friend was online; he usually was. He was an internet junkie, spending most of his days reading up on serial killers and mechanics tutorials while smoking pot.

Biting her lip, she began to type in the little chat box. "A/S/L?"

"LOL", he typed back. He was there. She was relieved.

"Hey Ricky," she typed.

"Hey Ella-Bell. ☺"

"I need a favor."

"Anything for you, Ella-Bell."

"Got a place I can crash for a while?"

Just as she knew he would, Ricky said yes. "I'm on the next bus," she typed. "See you in two days."

Everything else was already in order. She had called her aunt and uncle the day before. "I'll come home on two conditions," she'd said before Ed had a chance to talk over her. "I'm not coming home to live with you guys. Those days are over. I'll enroll in school, though—*if* you guys agree to tell me, once and for all, about my parents. I want to know about them. I deserve to know." Ed had protested a little to her terms, but ultimately had agreed. It seemed most of the fight had gone out of him; he sounded tired, cowed. Then Ella had asked to speak to her aunt, who had come to the phone, surprise in her voice.

Ella had told Grace about the pregnancy. She'd been surprised when Grace had not reacted in anger or judgment, but rather had said, "Just come home. We'll figure it all out." What had happened to change the two of them so, Ella wondered, in such a short time? Maybe people could change. Or perhaps life had finally beaten them.

Maybe, just maybe, they had missed her.

Ella logged off the computer and grabbed her bag, taking one last longing look at the apartment, and walked out the door without looking back. She left the CD in the player on repeat and took a cab to the bus station. Janelle, Anita and Louie were all at work and would not even know she was gone until she was a third of the way home.

TWENTY-TWO

BOBBI - ARLINGTON, VIRGINIA - 1968

IT was sweltering out. Bobbi stood among the crowd that had gathered near the train tracks, a mix of various ages, genders, and races; a few with makeshift signs, a couple wearing uniforms. Barefooted children ran around in the grass and dry dirt, playing obliviously, not understanding the implications of why they were gathered there. Bobbi stood in the back of the throng, wishing she could be blissfully unaware too, her hot, itchy dress clinging to her skin. It was the only black dress she owned, and her stockings had long ago bitten the dust, covered in runs and snags from the various rallies she'd attended since leaving home. She was bare-legged, in uncomfortable black boots with a hole in the toe, and a wool dress that was far too hot for the month of June. Her black hat was perched atop her hair, damp with sweat, which she'd pulled into a messy bun on the bus, not bothering to ask anyone for a mirror.

So far, nobody had spoken to her, which was a relief, since she wanted to blend in, be invisible. This was a solemn crowd, save for the children, who seemed to belong to a sphere all their own. Bobbi preferred it that way. She was afraid if anyone spoke to her with a word of kindness, or said so much as a "hello," she might burst into tears.

The late-afternoon sun glinted off the metal of the tracks; it flashed in her eyes and made her head ache. The train was late by more than three hours. The crowd had been gathered there more or less—some people had milled out, while others had stumbled in—for that entire time. Bobbi had overheard one woman, crouched on a crocheted afghan, say that she'd been there since the night before. She was an older woman, in her late fifties, Bobbi guessed, who had shown up in her housecoat and curlers, with light blue slippers on her feet. She held a small white sign that said, "So Long, Bobby."

"I lost three of my sons to that *business* in Vietnam," Bobbi overheard the woman say, tears in her voice. "I only got one son left, and he's sixteen. He'll be old enough soon, and they'll draft him over to die, too. Bobby was my last hope, and now that's gone. What'll become of us now, I wonder."

Bobbi wondered, too. The future was a chasm. She could see no possible outcome; it was clouded in shadow. They all left, in the end, left and took hope with them.

MLK. Bobby Kennedy.

Guy.

And so would Landrum, she worried, squinting in the hot summer sun. He was now a prisoner of war, and whether or not he'd ever be returned to his family, his country, seemed almost irrelevant. Because he might live, yes—but would he *survive?*

Bobbi's work was done with Ramon and Kat. Not because they'd kicked her out—Kat's heart was big, and she'd forgiven Bobbi for the stunt with Warren. And Ramon, well, he'd given her a stiff, one-armed hug and told her, "Put one foot in front of the other, and just keep going. There's work to do here. Focus on the work. It'll get you through." It was good advice, the same advice given to countless others who had lost comrades, friends, heroes and lovers to the fight. But Bobbi could find no solace in it, and her energy was depleted, leaving her a husk filled with nothing but shame. For a brief, shining moment, she'd been part of something bigger, something meaningful. Something with purpose. She'd felt useful and good. Now, it was all ashes in her mouth.

The dream was dead. And hope was gone.

The night before, Bobbi had invited a young man back to her motel room. She'd met him at a bar; he'd been shooting pool with some buddies and giving her the eye while she tried to nurse her gin and tonic. Bobbi had made an effort not to look over, even as they'd begun to catcall her, but as she grew drunker, her loneliness and grief began to edge out her discomfort. She found she had no more cash for another drink, so she'd called the man over. "Hey," he'd said as he sidled up to the bar, his breath full of stale cigarettes. "I'm Ed."

She'd stiffened at his name, suddenly overcome with a bad feeling. But she'd accepted the free drink anyway, and when she left a little later, she'd found that he was flanking her, walking out of the bar as though they were a couple, and she did not protest. He followed her to her motel room, helped her with her room key, turned on the light and turned down the covers as though he was in charge, and so she let him. It was a scene that had played out so many times in so many motels and dodgy, dirty rooms over the past few months and Bobbi was so sick of it, and yet she said nothing, only watched the young man through blurred eyes as he began to unbuckle his pants dispassionately, not even looking at her. He was watching the TV.

After a beat, he'd dragged his eyes away from *Gunsmoke* and looked at her expectantly, his bushy blond eyebrows raising slightly. "Ain't you gonna get undressed?" he'd asked, his thumbs hooking into his splotchy white undershirt. "I ain't got all night."

For a moment Bobbi had just stood there, her vision still fuzzy, swallowing down the acid that was creeping up into her throat. She tried to speak, and it came out a croak. She cleared her throat and tried again, her voice finally emerging.

"Get out," she said, pointing a trembling finger at the door. "I don't want you here."

"Now honey, I bought you that drink, so's the way I figure it—"

"Get out right now." Her voice came out strong and clear, stronger and clearer than it had been in months.

"I ain't goin' nowhere—"

Bobbi had reached into her bag and before she knew what she'd done, the young man named Ed had a face full of pepper spray and was flailing and cussing his way out the door, then Bobbi was locking the deadbolt with shaking hands and crawling under the covers, fully clothed, pulling the pillows over her head, drowning out the sound of the screaming man, pounding and kicking the other side of the door. Let the motel call the cops; she wasn't answering. Bobbi was shaking like a leaf, but she'd done it.

Now, in the hot, blistering light of day, Bobbi fingered the little vial of pepper spray in her bag, certain she could smell the lingering reek of beer from the young man's clothes, the stale cigarette stink of his breath. Kat had given her the pepper spray when they'd first met. Would she be proud that Bobbi had used it?

Oh, Kat. I miss you so much already.

"Miss." Bobbi's thoughts were interrupted by a teenage boy in coveralls and no shirt beneath. His feet were bare, dirty, and his dark skin was covered in a sheen of sweat. He held a folding chair tucked under one arm. "My ma said you been standing all this time, and in that heavy dress," he said with a shy smile. "She said to bring you my chair."

"Oh no, I couldn't take your chair…" Bobbi protested warily, then caught the look on his face. It was the same look that was no doubt on hers. They were peers in grief, in hopelessness. She wondered if he felt the same as her, that he was no longer useful, that there was nothing that could be done, and it wouldn't matter, anyhow. Perhaps this one small gesture might bring him a bit of comfort.

She took the chair. "I… Thank you," she said, fighting back tears. "Be sure to get this back from me…you know, after."

"Yes'm," he said, then started away. The boy turned and met her eye. "It won't be long now."

"How can you tell?" Bobbi asked. She couldn't hear any sign of the train. It had already been hours.

"I can feel it," he said with a grin. "I lived here all my life, next to these tracks. My house is just thataway." He gestured to a block of ramshackle apartments. "You can feel the vibration in the ground and in the walls. I say he'll be passing through in oh, couple minutes or so. Just you wait and see."

"I hope you're right. And thank you for the chair."

"Yes'm."

Bobbi sat down reluctantly, feeling as though she didn't deserve the luxury. The sweat ran down her legs in rivulets, and she adjusted her dress, trying to let in a bit of breeze on her sticky thighs without being improper. Not that anyone was looking. Everyone was staring at the train tracks, as though the train would materialize any moment. The air was thick, muggy, and oddly quiet. Save for a few murmurs and the laughter of the children playing, everyone was silent.

People were gathered everywhere today, Bobbi knew, in towns and cities all over the east, to catch a glimpse, pay their respects, say goodbye. Folks of all types: every race, religion, age, status, clustered together in their desperate, bottomless grief. Bobbi knew that this was history being made right now, that this searing, unbearably painful reality she was forced to participate in, might one day be an abstract thing, something people would look back on and recollect with deference. But she couldn't allow herself to think about that. Because Bobbi couldn't imagine the future at all, really. For the entirety of her almost two decades on the green earth, she'd looked to the future with hopes and dreams, plans and ideas. Law school. Marrying Landrum. Having a family. In an instant, they'd all dried up, and now the only thing Bobbi found herself hoping for was the strength to go on through the thick bleakness that consumed her, the yawning void that had become her heart.

After a couple of minutes, Bobbi felt the vibration through the soles of her boots, a slight rattle in the arms of her chair. The boy had been right. She sat up, putting a hand over her eyes as she squinted, wiping a bead of sweat from her collarbone with the other hand, and watched.

A man standing off to the side of her, in full uniform, took off his hat slowly, and cupped it to his chest. As Bobbi watched, several other men followed suit, removing their hats, placing them over their hearts, standing at attention with perfect posture. Bobbi followed in kind, taking off the heavy black mourning hat and holding it tight against her sweating chest, trying to squash the ball in her throat.

As the crowd watched in silent reverence, the sleek black train appeared on the tracks, as if materializing from thin air. As it careened around the corner, metal-on-metal screeching into the quiet summer afternoon, Bobbi forgot how to breathe. She'd expected a slow-moving train, a quiet, slow tribute, reminiscent of a time gone by—but the train burst down the track at a breakneck speed that surprised her, the cars bouncing heavily, loudly, the hazy afternoon sunlight glinting off the windows, onlookers wincing from the noise and the glare, making it impossible to see inside.

The boy who had given her the chair was beside her, then, and as she glanced over, she saw him raise a skinny arm in a gesture of salute, his eyes glistening with pride and tears.

The woman in the housecoat and curlers, who had lost three sons in Vietnam, began to sing, her voice loud and off-key, carrying over the sound of the train bustling down the track.

"Glory, glory hallelujah,
Glory, glory hallelujah,
Glory, glory hallelujah, His truth is marching on..."

Others began to sing along with her, their voices carried high on the summer breeze, and Bobbi wondered if the grieving occupants inside—Bobby's family, staff, and friends—could hear them, could see the makeshift signs, the salutes, the gestures of honor and respect.

The last car was approaching; she could see it from her vantage point, as the train rounded the bend and started out of sight, to its end—Arlington Cemetery, where Robert Francis Kennedy would be buried beside his murdered brother. *A fitting end,* Bobbi thought. *That Washington should be the end of the line for you, one way or the other. It was always going to be, wasn't it? And you knew.*

The maroon train car passed by quickly, with little fanfare, the crowd silent and watching. An open window in the car caught the breeze; a black curtain fluttered. Bobbi caught the brief sight of a box, a flash of red and white. The heavy sadness within the car floated out in the breeze and settled on the crowd. Bobbi could feel it, the grief, the desolation, so thick and *heavy.*

Bobbi heard someone say behind her, "Oh, bless her, that gal is running after the train," and as she looked down at her pumping legs, Bobbi realized it was her.

Her dreams were on that train. Dead and gone. The train held the last remnants of the life Bobbi had thought she'd have, the life she thought she'd wanted. Her future. She could not let it go.

So Bobbi ran, ignoring the sweat pouring down her legs, wetting the bodice of her tight black dress, ignoring the soft dirt beneath her old boots, ignoring the knapsack that fell off her shoulder into the mud, ignoring the cries of the people behind her, running, out of breath, trying to chase the train that was moving much too fast, the very last car with the billowing black curtain and the flash of red and white, disappearing around the corner and into the abyss, on to Washington where bills were written, but dreams died every day.

She ran, ran long after the train had left her in the dust, after the vibrations were gone from the ground. She ran until she heard a kindly old man say as she passed him, "You can't catch him, doll. You can't catch him; he's already gone."

She collapsed in the dirt, her face in her hands. Finally, the tears came. The tears became sobs, and the sobs became wails, her hands sticky with tears and snot, uncaring even when she felt a kind arm around her shoulders. She cried and cried, until she felt spent of tears, until she could no longer feel the sun beating down on her back, the sweat on her legs, the dirt in her hair; she cried until she could no longer feel anything at all.

After what seemed like a century, she uncovered her face, wiped at her swollen eyes, and looked up. The crowd had mostly milled away. The kind old man had his arm around her, and he said nothing now, just looked at her with understanding, deep sadness and wisdom in his own eyes, waiting.

Bobbi got to her feet, holding onto the man's elbow, and thanked him through her tears. He tipped a hat to her, a gentleman from a time gone by, and shuffled off into the afternoon. Bobbi felt emptied and hollowed out. She cast her eyes to the train tracks once more, to the train that was now far off in the distance, a tiny black dot of metal containing her fallen hero, now nothing more than a memory, a dream. She raised her hand and flashed a peace sign. "So long, Bobby," she whispered, pushing her dirty hair out of her eyes, blinking the tears away. Then, with a thankful smile, she turned her back to the sun and began the walk back.

She would find her bag and the chair, which she would return to the boy. Then she would go home. Back to Athens, to the one member of her family that remained.

There was nothing else left to do.

TWENTY-THREE

KASEY - 2018

KASEY looked longingly at the gin and tonic in Andy's outstretched hand, but she smiled at the flight attendant and shook her head. "None for me, thanks. I'll just have a Coke."

The flight attendant smiled back. "Sure. I'll bring you some pretzels, too. Can I get you a blanket, or anything else? Are you comfortable enough?"

Kasey nodded. The trip had gone surprisingly smoothly so far. She hadn't planned on bringing her wheelchair—she only needed to use it now and again, and she also had a cane—but Andy and Scott had insisted. She'd worried it would hold them up at the airport, and that the plane wouldn't have the proper accommodations. She'd heard plenty of horror stories about people with disabilities and flying. But everything had gone off without a hitch. Her chair was safely stowed away, where it would be retrieved for her upon landing, and she was sitting in an aisle seat, her brother Andy beside her and Scott at the window, gazing out at the clouds. She could still hardly believe it—she was on her way to Seattle.

To meet her father. Her father, who didn't yet know she existed.

"I'm very comfortable, thanks. Just the Coke will be fine." Kasey gave the flight attendant another smile and turned to Andy, who was gulping back his drink. "That looks so good," she admitted. "I'm jealous."

"Does it make you uncomfortable to see us with drinks?" Scott asked. "If so, we'll toss 'em."

"Nah," Kasey replied. "I'm not an alcoholic or anything. It's just...I guess I associate my pills with booze. You're not supposed to take them together, but I did sometimes. And if I'm trying to kick those, maybe I ought to take it easy on drinking, just for a while. Until I feel stronger. I don't want to replace one vice with another, you know?" She didn't add that it was also for Ricky's sake—his affairs were his to share.

"I get that," Andy said, cocking his head. "You know, I probably shouldn't be telling you this, but you come by it honestly."

"What do you mean?" Kasey asked.

"My dad," he replied with a shrug. "Our dad, I mean. When I was a kid, he went to rehab for a while. He had a drinking problem and...well, a drug problem, too."

"Oh." Kasey didn't know what to say. "Was it heroin?"

Andy grinned. "Stereotyping Seattle much?"

"Hey, I just—"

He laughed and put up a hand. "I'm just teasing. Actually, it *was* heroin."

"But he's clean now?"

"Yep. Has been for years. I was about seven when he went to rehab. And as far as I know, he's been clean ever since. He doesn't drink either. The only thing he's addicted to now is surfing."

"Wow," Kasey said. "That's...that's really refreshing. That you guys were so supportive of him, and that you talk about it so openly, without any judgment. It isn't usually like that where I'm from." She sighed. "That's part of the reason I've had some trouble... There's just so much secrecy... It's like everybody is doing *something*, but everybody pretends they aren't. Folks smiling at each other in church, pretending not to know what they all got up to the night before. And if you *do* admit you have a problem, people just judge you. They all say 'get help,' and yet when you ask for it, they say you're just wanting attention."

"Seems like that would make it hard for anybody to get better in that kind of atmosphere," Scott said from the window.

"It is," Kasey said glumly. "I've been ashamed for so long that I don't know any other way to be. And shame makes it pretty hard to get anything done, especially in the self-care variety." She was surprised at herself, at how much self-realization she'd been doing since her little brother had come into her life.

"Well, I'm here for you, sis," Andy said with a grin, reaching out to cuff her shoulder.

"Thank you," Kasey said, feeling shy. "So...our dad. You live with him now? When did you decide to leave your mom's and live with him instead?"

"I was about eleven. I felt like the odd man out at home, between my mom and Glitter. And I knew Dad was lonely. By then we'd moved to California to be near my grandparents, and I missed him a lot. And I missed Seattle. It's more my speed than Cali. My mom and sister are happy there, but it's not my thing."

Kasey was still stuck on the name. "Your sister is actually

named Glitter?"

Andy laughed. "Her name's Gennifer, but everybody calls her Glitter. One Christmas when she was about two, Mom gave her these glittery teal tap shoes. She loved those shoes. Wore them everywhere, danced around in them until they had holes. And they left glitter all over the floors. So we started calling her Glitter and the name just stuck." He smiled. "She's what you call a 'hot mess.' When she's grown, she'll take over the world."

"How old is she?"

"Fourteen. She's in eighth grade and she's terrifying."

Kasey laughed. "I feel that way about my sister sometimes, too, and she's twenty."

"Is Fallon your biological sister?" Andy asked. "She's Ella's daughter, too?"

"Yeah," Kasey answered. "But honestly, we've never been super close. I'm the first pancake."

"What?" Scott laughed. "What the hell does that mean?"

"You know how when you're making pancakes, the first one is always messed up—you either burn that one a little or it's misshapen or something. The first pancake is always the one you give the dog. Fallon was the good pancake, the one that turned out right. I'm the throwaway." Kasey's throat clenched. "I always felt like the odd one out. Fallon doesn't understand me at all. And she's super close to Ricky, my stepdad, and he and I have always sort of tiptoed around each other. She's definitely the favorite."

"I'm sure that's not true," Andy said. "That guy seems to adore you. And so does your sister, from what I saw of her."

"They tolerate me," Kasey said, biting her lip. "And they're tired of me. I've done nothing but disappoint them."

Scott shook his head. "You're way too hard on yourself," he said softly. Andy nodded in agreement. "That's not what we saw."

"There's a lot you guys don't know," Kasey said, deciding that now, stuck on a plane for a few hours, might as well be the right time to let it all out. It wasn't like they could exactly run screaming from her, so why not? "Honestly? I'm a total fucking mess. Ricky's fed up with me, and Fallon is, too. I have no idea what the future holds because no matter what I do, I mess things up. I told you about the pills and stuff, but you guys, it got bad. So bad. You have no idea."

"Then tell us," Andy said.

Kasey took a deep breath. "Well, when I hit my pre-teen years, I was resentful that Fallon was the favorite, so I rebelled. Mom had entered her holy-roller phase by then. I refused to go to church and would go out partying with my friends. Drinking, smoking pot... nothing major, but I was only like thirteen, getting into all kinds of stuff. My best friend Amber was a total wild child and her parents didn't give a crap what we did, so I was always at her house, getting shitfaced, calling up boys to hang out, going to places we had no business going." Kasey shook her head, remembering. "After a while, my grades slipped, and I failed ninth grade and had to repeat it. I got kicked off the cheerleading squad, which was one of the only things that gave me any real happiness. I dated a few losers, got my heart broken. Then, when I was sixteen, I lost it all."

Andy and Scott both listened with rapt attention. Kasey shook a shaky breath before she continued. "Amber and I went to a football game. We were drinking wine coolers and smoking weed behind the stadium with some guys. They invited us to a party. I was slightly less blitzed than she was, and she asked me to drive. I said no, because I was texting back and forth with this guy Caden, who I had a crush on. He was joking about finding me at the party to make out with me. I tried my mom and had no luck, so I told Amber that she had to drive. She was in no position to be behind the wheel. Neither of us was. But we got in the car, anyway." Kasey paused, tears welling up in her eyes. "I don't remember anything after getting in the car. We got in a wreck, and Amber died. The driver of the other car, the one she hit… They were revived at the scene, but later died at the hospital. I was the only one who survived the accident."

"Wow. That's…a lot," Scott said softly, and Andy put a comforting hand on her arm.

Kasey wiped at an eye where a tear threatened to fall. "I was in the hospital for months. I was messed up bad. Broken bones, burns, a shattered hip. All these people came to see me—they brought me flowers, books, milkshakes, movies, signed my casts. Caden came to see me almost every day. They were all so worried. But deep down, I knew I didn't deserve their kind thoughts, their support. If I had driven when she asked me to—or if I'd had the good sense to tell her that neither of us should drive—she might still be alive. That other poor, innocent woman might still be alive. It was all my fault… I had nightmares… I'd wake up in a cold sweat, my leg aching. But I knew I deserved it. I was drunk, but less so than Amber. If I'd only driven like she'd asked…" Kasey gulped. She took a shuddering breath and went on. "Then my mom left us. My friends started to fall away one by one. And then Caden hurt his back on a construction job and bummed a few…and that was all she wrote. He started taking them too, and…well, the rest is history."

"How long has it been?" Andy asked.

"I was sixteen at the time of the accident," Kasey answered. "I'm twenty-two now. Almost six years of this…this hell." She started to cry, horrified at herself. She'd never talked about this out loud to anyone. And now she was crying on a plane. "Six years of losing job after job, begging Ricky for money, lying around in a stupor, trying not to think about the people who are dead because of me. Six years."

"You can't take all the blame," Andy stated softly. "*Neither* of you were in a position to drive, and you might've asked Amber to, but ultimately, she made that decision herself."

"Still," Kasey insisted. "I hold some of the blame."

"Some. Not all. You're trying to fix things now. You're getting your life back in order," Scott reminded "Don't you think Amber would want that?"

"No; I think she'd hate me," Kasey said through her tears. "*I* hate me. I miss her every day. I ended things with Caden, and he's the only guy who has ever loved me. He's the only guy who could. Ricky's sick of my crap. Fallon, too. I can't keep a job. I've used up every bit of goodwill from everybody in my life. Even my mom…" She was unable to finish the sentence.

"What about her?" Andy pressed, his voice kind. "I've been wondering where she is, how she could just leave her daughters. What happened with her?"

"I don't know," Kasey answered honestly. "All I know is that a few weeks after the accident, she split." She sniffed. "I guess I drove her away, too."

"That wasn't your fault," Scott said.

"It *was* my fault," Kasey argued. "Why else would she leave? She left me with Ricky without a word and she's barely talked to me since. I don't even know where she lives; only that it's in Canada. The one thing I'm sure of is that I'm the reason she's gone. I always thought it was because she couldn't bear to see what I'd done to my life, my future."

"No." Scott shook his head, his mouth pressed into a hard line. "You can't blame yourself for her leaving. No matter what mistakes you made, you were just a *kid*. If anything, your mom is a coward and a jerk for leaving her child in a time of extreme need. You almost died, and you pulled through. You were traumatized, injured, depressed and scared, and when you needed your mother most, she bailed on you." He shook his head again. "It lies squarely with her. What a shitty thing to do."

Andy nodded. "I agree with Scott, Kasey. I can't imagine leaving my kid after something like that. Just abandoning my whole family." He looked thoughtful. "I've had issues with both my folks over the years, but god, neither of them would have *ever* abandoned me."

"Must be nice," Kasey said, sounding more bitter than she meant to.

Andy squeezed her arm. "I promise you, Kasey, once Dad meets you, he'll feel the same way about you. He'll be there when you need him, forever, unconditionally, no matter what. I swear he will."

"He doesn't even know me," Kasey said miserably.

"Not yet," he said assuredly. "But when he does, he's going to *love* you."

"I hope so," Kasey said, but she wasn't so sure.

"I was thinking," Andy said. "That I'll go on home first, and maybe you can go hang with Scott for a while? I'll talk to Dad, kind of ease him in, before you meet. I think that's best, rather than springing you on him. If that's okay." He smiled at her. "I think it'd be easier on both of you to let me play the go-between. I don't want to do anything that'll make you feel nervous or put on the spot."

"Thank you," she said sincerely. "That's really thoughtful. And a good idea."

"Anywhere in Seattle you're dying to see?" Scott asked.

"Anywhere you want to show me," Kasey said, enjoying the way his dark brown eyes lit up with pleasure.

KASEY - SEATTLE - 2018

"This wasn't what I imagined when I said, 'whatever you want to show me,'" Kasey admitted several hours later as she held onto Scott's arm, the other arm clutching her cane. The park was well-maintained, and they strolled on a paved trail, but after hours on a plane, her leg was hurting.

"What did you expect?"

"I dunno, the Space Needle, or maybe some infamous bar."

Kasey giggled. "Maybe some park bench where an angsty Kurt Cobain sat writing poetry."

"It's the middle of the day and none of the bars are open," Scott said with a laugh. "And the Space Needle is boring. You can see it from anywhere and all the locals hate it. I thought this place might be meaningful to you, because as it happens, it *does* have a connection to Cobain. This park is a memorial to him; the benches, especially." He gestured at a cluster of benches just ahead of them, painted and sprayed with artistic graffiti.

"Did Kurt ever come here?" Kasey asked, walking toward the benches, enraptured by how beautiful some of the graffiti was. It never failed to delight her how talented graffiti artists were—they often just tagged the odd train or side of a building, but the level of talent was astounding. These benches were beautiful. Kasey could imagine a young Kurt Cobain sitting here, writing in his journals, people watching and strumming his acoustic.

"He did, I think. This park is just south of his house, and after he died, this is where all the fans gathered to pay their respects."

"This is *that* park?" Kasey had seen footage of the fans gathered in the park, bringing flowers, teddy bears, t-shirts, and other offerings to leave in a pile after the Nirvana front man had died. She remembered hearing recordings of Courtney Love addressing his fans, her tear-filled voice full of anger and grief. She hadn't even been born then, but just thinking about it pinged something deep within her heart, filling her with sadness. She wondered if her mother had ever come here.

"Yup. Your mom would've been here right after Kurt died,"

Scott said thoughtfully, as if reading her mind. "In Seattle, I mean. I'm thinking she must have been a huge grunge fan to trek all the way out here by herself. She never said anything to you about that? About why she came here, of all places?"

"No," Kasey said. "She never said much of anything about her time here. Or her childhood, or anything else, for that matter. She was really close-lipped about her past." She sighed. "She was a big fan of the music, though. She and Ricky used to play a lot of grunge and alternative, back before she went all Jesus-y."

"Well, I just thought this place might feel significant for you, might make you feel closer to her," Scott said. "You know how in the song 'Something in the Way,' Kurt talks about how hopeless and dismal he feels? Homeless, sleeping under this leaky bridge, with only the fish and the shit on the ceiling to keep him company. Rock bottom, and I mean that literally." He gestured at a pile of smooth stones that were stacked on one of the benches. Kasey understanding immediately that they must have come from under that bridge, from the banks of the Wishkah, and left here by a fan.

"I know the feeling," Kasey said drily. "More intimately than I'd like."

"Me, too," Scott said softly.

Kasey felt an odd sensation go through her; a lonely, desperate sadness, tinged with faint, almost imperceptible hope. Scott's arm felt good linked through hers. She stared at the benches—the rocks, the graffiti—and felt her soul rise a little.

Scott went on. "But…not long after that, Kurt under that bridge, at the bottom of his rope, his band was the biggest band in the

419

fucking world. You can go from nothing to everything in the blink of an eye. It's just how you handle the highs and lows that counts."

"That's a nice sentiment, Scott, but in case you forgot, Kurt still died by suicide," Kasey said, turning to him with a sad smile. "This place definitely has a vibe…and I'm glad you showed it to me. But I'm not sure Kurt's experiences are the best 'how-to guide' for turning your life around."

"No, they are, actually," Scott said, his dark brown eyes boring into hers as he turned to face her. "For me, life's not about the final destination, it's about the journey. It's about *hope*. Yes, Kurt gave in to his demons, to his disease. The point is that he had *hope,* even in the darkest of times. He had hope, and he had joy and he had creativity, and he held onto all of those through the pain." Scott reached over and pushed a strand of hair from Kasey's eyes. "His time on earth might not've been long, but while he was here, he always had those. I feel like we focus too much on our endings and not enough on the in-between. I haven't known you long, Kasey, but I can see you. Plain as day, I can see who you are behind all the pain, sadness, and guilt. That person is still inside you, and that person will do great things, whatever that means to you. You just have to hang onto the hope. Remember joy." He shrugged. "The future isn't guaranteed. The happy ending is bullshit, I guess. But you can live the life you want to live in the meantime."

"You sound like a failed new-age guru," Kasey joked, but the space inside her chest had started to thrum. "Do you have a podcast or a YouTube channel?"

Scott shrugged again, his cheeks flushing red. It was impossibly cute, and Kasey found herself clutching his arm tighter than she needed to, enjoying the way he felt next to her. "It's just something I like to remind myself when things get bad."

"So what's your sob story, then?" Kasey asked as they sat down on one of the benches. She leaned back, massaging her leg, not minding that Scott saw her do it.

"No sobbing for me," Scott said, his face flushing a deeper red. "I haven't cried since I was a kid. I don't know if I even can. I release my pain through other avenues."

"Huh?" Kasey felt her heart thudding in her chest as she realized what he meant. "Oh...you mean like..."

"Like washing my hands until they bleed or putting lit cigarettes against my thigh." Scott's eyes burned into hers; Kasey was shocked he didn't look away in shame as she would have done. "I have OCD. Like an actual diagnosis, I'm not just talking about being anal retentive. I have it for real. I also have PTSD."

"I'm so sorry," Kasey said. She'd often wondered if she had PTSD after the accident—but she'd never gotten up the nerve, or the money, to go see someone. "Do you, um... What caused you...?"

Scott took a deep breath. "When I was in middle school...there was a shooter. A school shooting. A lot of kids died." He tensed, then rolled his shoulders, trying to relax them.

"My god," Kasey said softly. "What a thing to go through. It's no wonder that you have a hard time coping. The survivor's guilt alone..." She trailed off, realizing what Scott had been trying to convey to her. He hadn't been just spouting off platitudes—he intimately understood what it felt like, what she'd been through.

They were both survivors.

Scott nodded. "I'm on medication. I have a therapist. And I have my positive affirmations that I try to use to get me through." He smiled at her. "Maybe one day I'll tell you the whole story. I don't like talking about it, but I'm working on it."

"I would be honored," Kasey said. "I see now why you're so good with Andy's anxiety. And why you're so understanding of me." Kasey gave his arm a squeeze. "How you can be so accepting of my uh—my disability—" She coughed a little, not used to saying the word. "And my addictions, too."

"If I may—and please tell me to fuck off if I'm overstepping—I think you should worry less about your so-called *addiction,*" Scott said, "and more about what's driving it. You have pain; legit pain. If you think you're over-using your meds, that's an issue, and you should talk to your doctor. But Kasey, I think the real issue is just your brain being an asshole. It's okay to admit that you're depressed, that you're struggling with the trauma of what you went through."

"How could you possibly know that?" Kasey asked, her eyes filling with tears, "When I've never told that to anyone?"

"Because I see you," Scott said, breaking into a crooked grin. "The fucked-upness in me recognizes the fucked-upness in you."

"Namaste," Kasey said, laughing despite herself. "Very quaint."

"I saw it on a meme," Scott said with a chuckle, then his face turned serious. "You're more than your pain." He pulled her close and wrapped her in an unexpected hug, his arms warm and strong. "And I'm more than mine. But they're a part of us. That's where we go wrong... Letting people love us in spite of what we see as flaws…when we deserve someone who loves us *for* them. Someone who loves every bit, every part, because it's who we are." He smiled. "Someone who wouldn't change us if they could."

"That's a nice sentiment," Kasey said softly, resting her head on his strong shoulder. "But the world doesn't work that way."

"I reject any other way of thinking." Scott laughed, his cheek pressed against her forehead.

"Maybe one day I will, too." Kasey grinned, leaning up and looking into his soft brown eyes, her own eyes widening in surprise as Scott leaned down, his face inches from hers.

"Can I kiss you?" Scott asked, and she nodded. He placed a soft kiss on her lips. The bitter, clean taste of gin still lingered on his mouth, and when he pulled back, the taste lingered there on hers, fresh and bright.

"What was that for?" Kasey asked quietly, wishing he'd do it again.

"It just seemed right," he said, reaching down to grab a stone from the damp grass. He wiped it against his jacket, polishing it, and held it out to her. "That's yours. A good luck charm."

Kasey pushed it into her pocket, her cheeks warm, nodding in agreement, though she wasn't sure the stone was the good luck charm so much as the man who'd just given it to her.

Back in the car, her phone rang. "It's Andy," she said to Scott as she buckled her seatbelt. "Hello?"

"Hey, Kasey," her brother said. "You guys can come to the house now."

"You told him?" Kasey's heart beat fast.

"Yes." Andy paused. "He's…a bit shocked. But he immediately wanted to know where you were and how soon you could get here. I believe his exact words were 'I need to lay eyes on my girl.'"

A warm feeling filled Kasey's belly, followed by a blast of nerves. She swallowed. "And you're sure it's okay? *He's* okay?"

"Of course. It's Dad. You'll love him. He'll love you, too. You guys have a lot to talk about." Kasey glanced at Scott. "So are you coming?"

"Yes," she answered, pushing her nerves away. "We'll be there." She hung up and turned to Scott. "Can you take me to Andy's?"

"Yep." He shot her a bright smile. "It's go-time."

TWENTY-FOUR

BOBBI - ATHENS, GEORGIA - 1969

"THAT'S…one small step for man…"

Bobbi reached for the thick glass tumbler on the end table and held it to her lips. The ice had long since melted, the condensation pooling on the antique wood, but she paid it no mind. After all, neither of her parents were around to gripe about it. She took a sip of the burning liquor and felt it warm her throat as it went down. This was her second drink, and she was pondering getting up for a third, just as soon as she could wrench herself away from the television.

"What are you doing?"

Bobbi turned to see Grace standing in the doorway, a frown marking her pursed lips. "Watching television," she said casually, turning back to the tube. "They've just landed on the moon. Neil Armstrong. Do you want to watch with me?"

"I don't care a whit for that unnatural, ungodly business," Grace said with a sniff. "If you ask me, our taxpayer dollars ought not to be funding heathen organizations like that NASA. It ought to be going to help our troops in Vietnam."

"How is NASA heathen, exactly?" Bobbi asked. "You'd rather support an unjust war where thousands are slaughtered every day than space exploration?"

"God put us *here,* on Earth. And that's where we are meant to stay," Grace said, sauntering over, hands on her hips. "We've no business venturing beyond this God-given paradise. No business poking our noses where they don't belong. No good ever came of being too scientific. That's where you lose God."

"Oh, shut the hell *up,* Grace," Bobbi said irritably, lazily grazing the tumbler over her lips, letting a few drops of scotch hit her tongue. "Take that holy-roller nonsense elsewhere. I'm excited to see this, and I'm not letting you ruin it." She smirked, then added, "And if you think this shithole is paradise, you're even more delusional than I thought."

Grace ignored this. "Are you drinking, young lady?"

"Can't get a thing past you," Bobbi said, crossing one leg over the other and meeting Grace's dark eyes. "Ed's own bottle of George Dickel. This is actually my second."

"You've gotten water all over my nice antique table; it'll warp the wood. You know I don't allow drinking in my house—"

"This isn't *your* house," Bobbi said vehemently, slamming the tumbler down on the table. "And it's not your fucking antique table, either. It belonged to my mother. You might be married to my brother, but this place is every bit as much mine as his. Especially now that Guy's gone. You don't get to tell me what I can and can't do. Now buzz off. I'm busy."

"Busy getting drunk," Grace countered, hands still on her hips. Bobbi mused to herself that if Grace ever sat for a portrait, she'd be in that exact position. "I'm going to speak to your brother about you. It's time you moved along. You're old enough to make your own way. I don't want you darkening my doorway any longer." She spun on her heel and walked toward the door.

"It's not *your* doorway," Bobbi called after her with a laugh. "Go ahead and call Ed. We'll see who he sides with. We both know he hates your guts."

Grace paused in the doorway, her back to Bobbi. She stood there for a moment, her back rising and falling, then continued down the hall. Bobbi stared after her, feeling momentarily guilty, then shrugged and picked her tumbler back up, her eyes on the television, where a man in a puffy white spacesuit was bouncing up and down on the moon in what seemed to be slow motion.

"You ought not to have spoken to Grace like that. She phoned me at work in tears. Said you cussed her up and down."

"Come off it, Ed. You know how she is. Do you really have any doubt that she started it?"

"She said you were drinking in the middle of the day." Ed put down his newspaper and looked at her sternly.

Bobbi reached for her cup of coffee. Her plate of eggs and bacon was untouched. "I was watching Neil Armstrong walk on the moon. I felt like having a celebratory drink."

"You know she doesn't like drinking in the house. You were just trying to rile her up."

"I don't care what the hell she likes, Ed." Bobbi raised her chin and looked at her brother defiantly. "She's not the woman of the house, not while I still own half the place." Ed's eyebrows raised. "I didn't raise a stink when you two moved in, because I was traveling—"

"Gallivanting around the country like a dirty hippie, meddling in causes—"

Bobbi ignored him. "—but according to Dad's will, this place was to be owned in equal shares by his three children. And seeing as we've lost Guy" —she winced, still feeling a fresh pain— "it's half mine. I haven't asked you to sell it, and I won't. I know you paid a lot of the mortgage. And I don't plan to stay here long; you can live here in marital bliss forever for all I care. Just as soon as I get on my feet, I'm going to get my own place." She stabbed at her eggs with her fork. "But don't you *dare* try to lord that buttoned-up, holy rolling wife of yours over me as if she has any right to tell me how to live my life. She is *not* in charge of me, not any more than she's in charge of *you.*" She met her brother's eyes, a small, wry smile on her face. "Because we both know good and well that you haven't changed a single one of your habits. And I'll be damned if I let her—or you—try and crow over me as if you have a leg to stand on. If you do, maybe I'll just start spilling secrets. Got it?"

Ed looked down at his empty plate, his cheek twitching. "You've changed so much," he said, pushing the plate aside. "You never used to be so precocious, so…hateful."

"I think spiteful is more like it. Anyway, I grew up," Bobbi said, taking another sip of coffee. "And began to see some things for what they are."

"I'll speak to Grace," Ed said, his face betraying his anger, but there was a deep sadness there, too. Bobbi felt a momentary pang of guilt. Losing their father and Guy in such short succession had not been easy for him, either. "But for God's sake, can't you at least try not to provoke her? Just the minimal amount of effort to placate her... It wouldn't take much."

"It's not my job to placate the wife you don't love, so she goes easier on you."

Ed stood up from the table, slamming his coffee cup down on the counter. "Goddammit, Bobbi. Do you have to be such a bitch? Things like marriage, running a household, holding down a responsible job—these are grownup things, mature *adult* things. Something you wouldn't understand because you've decided to stay a child. I thought you had goals, dreams—I tried to help you attain them once. And we were close, once upon a time. I don't even know who you are anymore. It's like you flushed your entire future down the toilet, just because the boy next door went off to war. Well, guess what, sis? The rest of us stayed here and tried to make a go of it, the best we could. We *had* to. I didn't have the luxury of, of—" His face was red, and he sputtered.

"The luxury of what? Get off your high horse, Ed. You haven't given up a thing. You were just barely too old for the draft, you get to live in our parents' house, you've got your socially acceptable marriage with your Godly wife who keeps house for you, and your respectable well-paying job at the firm, and your mistresses and your fancy booze to warm your bed at night when things get too rough. What exactly have you given up?"

"Losing Dad and Guy—and Mama—destroyed me," Ed said in a hot whisper, his cheeks bright red. Bobbi was horrified to see tears in his eyes, but she wouldn't back down. Not now.

"Yeah, well, it destroyed me, too," she bit back. "And I don't have such *comforts* to make me feel better."

"And you're going to throw away your future because you're in pain?"

"Who said I'm throwing away my future?" she demanded.

"I don't see you looking for work or going back to school. I don't see you out making connections or seeing friends or volunteering your time. All you do is sit in this house and mope." Ed grabbed his briefcase. "You can judge me all you want. Lord knows I'm not perfect and never have been. You've always known me better than anyone." He sighed. "I never claimed to be an example for you to follow. If anything, I always thought you'd rise above, do *better* than me. I thought you'd go to law school and become a great political lawyer. I thought you'd marry some fine young man and have an amazing life." The anger had left his face, and now he just looked sad. "You're still young, Bobbi. You've still got time to do those things. Don't throw away your dreams, everything you've worked for, because you're temporarily disillusioned."

"Who says it's temporary?"

Ed smiled now. "You'll wake up one day and realize you're no longer young, and that question will seem so very foolish." He walked over and gave her a kiss on the forehead. His cheek brushed against her skin; it was damp. "I hope you'll think about that. Anyway, I'm late for work. Try to refrain from cussing Grace out today, okay, sis? Love you."

"I love you, too." Bobbi watched her brother's retreating back as he walked out the door, and when it slammed behind him, she put her face in her hands. She'd won the argument for a change, but the guilt she felt made it impossible to relish in it.

TWO WEEKS LATER

The little silver clock buzzed shrilly in Bobbi's ears, waking her from her nap. The sun blazed down hot on her skin, and she rolled over on the blanket, reaching for the timer to set it again. She'd woken up that morning and decided on a whim to lay out in the sun, to try to put a little color back into her pale flesh. She reached behind her and untied the straps to the navy blue high-waisted bikini that she'd had since her junior year of high school, and lay face-down on the blanket, letting the sun bake her. The portable radio beside her was playing The Doors, and she had a glass of icy, fresh-made lemonade beside her. She should be happy.

Bobbi sighed. This was the most content she'd felt in weeks—no, months—and yet, she was still impossibly empty. Nothing brought her joy anymore. She thought back to her high school days, when she'd lay out in the sun with Amelia, who had gone off and married Sam and moved to Savannah for his career. She'd heard through the grapevine that she was pregnant and due any day. Bobbi found she had no interest in getting in touch with her former best friend; she felt light years away now. Then there was Kat and Ramon... She missed them terribly. So many times she'd moved to grab the phone and call their headquarters, or Kat's home in Alabama, just to see if she could find them. But her guilt held her back. The way they'd seen her behave toward the end had been shameful. And she couldn't blame it on the loss of her brother or Bobby Kennedy or even Landrum going off to war. She had nobody to blame but herself. She just hoped that one day she could make it up to Kat, could show her how much she meant to her.

Grace hadn't said much to her, other than a few well-timed sighs and a grimace or two in the past few days. But she could see from the set of the woman's shoulders and the almost aggressive way she went about her cleaning that she was angry. Her every movement said *you're not welcome here,* and Bobbi felt it. The house might be half hers, but that didn't mean shit. Grace had the run of the place, and Bobbi did not belong. It was time for her to go, and soon. She didn't have enough money to put down a deposit anywhere, but she supposed she could borrow it from Ed. She'd just have to find a job waitressing or perhaps as a shopgirl until she could find something a little more solid. Nothing appealed to her, but it was time to grow up and move on, unless she wanted to well and truly have it out with her sister-in-law.

It was that, or give up.

The song switched from the Doors "Soul Kitchen" to "A Whiter Shade of Pale," by Procul Harum, the deejay speaking over the beginning strains of the song. "It's a glorious, sunny morning, ladies and gents," he said in a strong southern accent. "Get out and enjoy this beautiful Athens day!"

"I already am, hoss," Bobbi answered, her forehead resting on her hands. "But you couldn't have played something a little more upbeat?"

She was considering getting up to switch off the radio when she heard the doorbell ring from inside. *Likely one of Grace's church friends,* she thought to herself, not moving. Nobody she knew would visit at ten o'clock in the morning on a random Tuesday, and besides, she was in her bathing suit. By the time she pulled on a robe and got to the front door, they'd be gone. Let Grace get it. She leaned over to take a sip of the tart, cold lemonade and settled back down onto the blanket with a lazy sigh.

After a moment, she heard two sets of footsteps coming toward the deck, and the French doors creaked open. Bobbi groaned, her head still resting on her hands; she didn't feel like seeing one of Grace's annoying, nosy friends right now. "Bobbi," she heard Grace say from behind her, but she didn't look up. Maybe Grace would assume she was asleep and let her be.

"Bobbi!"

"What?" she said irritably into her hands. "I'm sunbathing."

"You have a visitor, if you could peel yourself off the grass."

"Who?" Bobbi rolled over lazily, shielding her eyes from the late-morning sun, and gasped.

Standing there on the deck, beside sour-faced Grace, was a tall man with dark-blond hair tucked under a cap. He was dressed head to toe in a green uniform that looked tattered but neatly pressed. His shiny black shoes gleamed in the sunlight, a wide grin on his face, and there was a bouquet of yellow roses in one hand; his opposite arm, hanging awkwardly at his side, seemed to be missing something, but Bobbi only noticed this absently, because she was too busy screeching as she moved from the grass to the deck in one swift movement.

"LANDRUM!" Bobbi was in his arms before she knew what was happening. His uniform was scratchy, and he smelled exactly the same. His beard was prickly against her cheek as he held her lightly with one arm wrapped around her waist. "Oh, my god!" Her arms were around his neck and she clung to him for dear life, letting him pick her up and hold her there, suspended. *It's him, it's really him. I can't believe it, but it's him!*

"Dear God in Heaven, she doesn't even have a top on," she heard Grace say in disgust behind her, and Bobbi realized that she'd left her bathing suit top behind on the blanket. "Disgraceful. Sinful." She was topless in Landrum's arms, and the yellow roses were being crushed, the petals falling onto the deck. But Bobbi didn't care. Nothing else mattered now. Landrum was *alive*, and he was *home*.

Bobbi's eyes followed Landrum hungrily as he picked up his glass of sweet tea and held it to his lips, his hand trembling a little. She watched as he drank, his lips partially hidden under the sandy-colored beard with just a hint of red, watched the way his neck bobbed as he swallowed. He smiled as he looked at her, but the smile didn't quite reach his eyes, though he was making a valiant effort. The delicate skin under his eyes was a bit puffy, and his cheeks were drawn. He sat the glass back down, his other arm tucked discreetly in his lap, shoved down between his thighs, as if he could make it invisible. A peeled, segmented orange sat on a plate beside him, untouched.

"Well," Landrum said finally, still smiling at her. "What in the hell have you been up to?" His eyes glowed with a warmth that almost disguised the haunted look behind it. "I have to say, I was surprised to find you here. I mean, this was always gonna be the first place I looked, but I did expect you would've high-tailed it out of here by now, gotten a place on campus or something."

Bobbi stared at him a moment, realizing Landrum thought she was in law school… It seemed such a faraway thing now, she almost couldn't believe she'd ever had such a dream.

"I'm not at UGA," she said with a shrug. "I decided I'm not cut out to be a lawyer. Or for college in general."

"With the way you argue?" Landrum teased, then his face turned serious again. "I'm surprised to hear that, Bobbi, but…as long as you're happy."

Bobbi didn't know how to answer that. Instead, she said, "I did get out of town for a while, though. In fact, I just got back. I've been staying with Ed and Grace, but I've been looking for an apartment. It's sheer luck that you happened to show up while I was here."

"I would have found you, no matter where you went," Landrum said with a grin, and her heart did a flip. "So, where did you go?"

"Where didn't I go, you mean," Bobbi said with a proud smile. "I spent a lot of time traveling—Alabama, Virginia, a few months in D.C. I made some friends, activists named Kat and Ramon, who I can't wait for you to meet—working, trying to help people. I went to a lot of rallies, helped with the anti-war effort" —she looked at him carefully to see if he would wince in pain or perhaps offense, but he gave nothing away— "as well as some civil rights rallies, and I even campaigned in a few towns for Bobby Kennedy…" She trailed off, feeling the ache starting in her gut, the way it did every time she remembered that dream was over.

"I was real sorry to hear about him," Landrum said. "We didn't get the news till a few days after, but I thought of you right away. I know that must have devastated you, losing your hero like that." He swallowed. "I bet my mama was tore up, too—you remember how she always loved RFK."

"How is Irene?" Bobbi asked, thinking of Mrs. Walton. She added reluctantly, "And your dad?"

"No idea," Landrum said. "She wrote to me once or twice when I was deployed, before I was captured. Then, nothing. I guess you know they moved? I don't even know where to. When I got back stateside, I tried to get in touch with my aunt, my dad's sister, to see if I might find out, but her phone was disconnected. I'll find them eventually, I guess."

"You don't know where your own mother is?" Bobbi was incredulous. "How could your father be so heartless?"

"I haven't found them yet, but I will," Landrum said firmly. "Once Ma finds out I'm back stateside, she'll find me, I'm sure." His voice burned with quiet fury. "If my dad lets her. I was…I was actually hoping maybe you'd know something." His voice lowered further. "Or…or Ed."

"I'm sorry," Bobbi said softly, "I don't. I don't think Ed does, either." She sighed. "All that's finally, officially over, I think. Grace made sure of that." She cut her eyes toward the house, shaking her head.

"Not getting along with her?" Landrum asked, his eyes showing a hint of their old mirth.

"That's the understatement of the century," Bobbi said. "She's so holier-than-thou; she's on me about everything. Everything I do is a fucking sin. Honestly, though, I owe her, because if it wasn't for her being so terrible, I might not have ever got off my butt and left in the first place."

"And what about Guy?' Landrum asked innocently, reaching for his glass again. "Is he still deployed, or did he run out of here too?"

Bobbi looked at her lap. She swallowed, waiting for a moment when she could speak without her voice giving way to tears. "Um, he…" she began, then found she couldn't continue.

"Oh, no." Landrum was near her in a flash, wrapping his arm around her shoulders. "I'm sorry Bobbi. I didn't know. When did it happen?"

"I don't know the exact day, but I got the call the day after… the day after Bobby was shot," Bobbi said, taking a deep breath. She hadn't talked to anyone about Guy. Not since it happened. She looked down at the arm wrapped around her neck, saw the mottled scars on Landrum's pale skin as his shirt sleeve rolled up a little. "June sixth. It was a…a very bad day."

"Do you know what happened?" Landrum asked. "How he was killed?"

Bobbi supposed Landrum, having been to war, might have an interest in such things. She'd never even asked. It wasn't important to her, the whys and hows. All that mattered was that he was gone. "Ed knows, I'm sure," she answered him, wiping at her eyes, still

437

looking down at his arm. "I'm sure he'd tell you. Honestly, I couldn't bear to know, so I never—"

"It's okay." Landrum pulled her close, and she settled into him with a deep sigh. Though he still smelled exactly the same, the similarities ended there. Even his body felt different—still warm and solid against her, but he was thin and muscular now, almost wiry, his baby fat and innocence gone. Bobbi leaned into him, wondering if the two of them could get back to where they once had been, or if the gulf was now too wide. "I thought," she said in a soft voice, looking up into his eyes, which were the same familiar gray, but with a newfound hardness, "that you might not make it back, either."

"I don't blame you," Landrum said. "So many of us didn't. I had plenty of close calls. When I was captured, I figured it was the end. I didn't expect to make it back out. I know how lucky I am to be here, believe me."

"I'm so glad you're okay."

"Okay," he said, his expression bland. "Okay is relative, I guess."

"Do you want to talk about..." Bobbi said, looking down at the bright, angry red scars on Landrum's arm, and turned her head upwards to meet his eyes. Did he have other scars? Worse ones, visible or otherwise? "About that? About what happened to you... during your..."

"Sometime," Landrum said, pulling her against him with his other, unblemished arm, nuzzling his head into her hair. "Just not today. Today, let's just do this."

"Sounds good to me," Bobbi murmured, warmth coursing

through her. Nothing mattered now, except she and Landrum. She grabbed an orange wedge and tilted Landrum's face up to hers, popping it in his mouth. He smiled, the rind over his teeth; wide, happy, and bright orange.

TWENTY-FIVE

KASEY - SEATTLE - 2018

THE first thing Kasey noticed, stepping into the house, pushing her cane down into the plush, fluffy blue carpet, was the smell of patchouli, cloying and unmistakable. She smiled and turned to Andy and Scott. "Is this a cliché hippie den?"

"Why would you say that?'

She gestured, laughing, to the shaggy carpet and the tapestry hanging on the wall in the foyer. "I mean, given the décor…and the incense…"

"I wouldn't call Dad a hippie, exactly," Andy said with a chuckle, leading her into the living room. "He's what I guess you'd call a naturalist, or maybe just spiritual. He likes a lot of new age-y stuff but he's not like an annoying anti-vaxxer Green party member or anything." His dark brown eyes danced. "I promise you he didn't vote for Jill Stein."

"It wouldn't mean anything to me if he had," Kasey said as she followed him into a room decorated in soft browns, with warm looking suede chairs and a large throw rug. "I didn't even vote in the last election."

Scott grinned. "I'll forgive you this time. Can I get you anything to drink, Kace?" She was touched by the abbreviation of her name.

"Louie's always got tea and coffee. Seltzers, too."

"Do you always serve people in his house like you live here?" Kasey joked.

"Hey, this was my home away from home when I was a kid, and I still consider it that." Andy cuffed him on the head. "I'm the honorary brother here."

"Does that make you *my* honorary brother?"

"I sure hope not." Scott's eyes flashed as they met hers, and she felt herself flush.

Andy was deftly pretending not to see. "Should I go get Dad? He's out back, I think. He just came in from surfing."

"I guess now's as good a time as any," Kasey said, squaring her shoulders and steeling her nerves. Her heart hadn't stopped beating double time since she got in the car, and her stomach was doing somersaults. "Time to face my past."

"And my future," came a voice behind her, and she turned to see a man standing in the doorway.

Louie—her father!—had warm, dark eyes that softened as they fell on her, and Kasey couldn't tell at first glance if they were brown or dark blue. His shoulder-length brown hair was curly, resting lightly on his tanned shoulders. He was naked from the waist up, and he held a threadbare towel to his chest, though he was still dripping onto his black flip flops and the carpet. His smile was wide and sweet, though there was a hint of worry behind his soft eyes. He moved forward toward Kasey in a slouchy, careful way, as though he were a little afraid of her. But the joy and surprise on his face were evident, and Kasey felt herself erupt in a smile as she stood to greet him.

Louie. Her father.

"I can't believe it's really *you,*" Kasey said, and he enveloped her in a hug, his skin smelling of salt and sunscreen and fragrant herbs. "I never dreamed I'd ever get to meet my father."

Louie pulled back from the hug and stood there, looking at her, seeming to memorize her face. They were almost eye to eye; he was just barely taller than her. Andy must have gotten his height from his mom, Kasey thought, staring back at the man who her mother had once loved but never once mentioned. His eyes were indeed dark blue, almost indigo, and full of gold specks that caught in the late afternoon light. There were tiny, almost imperceptible freckles on his tanned skin, and his hair had threads of auburn, which she recognized in her own hair, holding her hand up to her messy bun, suddenly wishing she had taken more care with her appearance. She hadn't expected her father to be so handsome.

"Any first thoughts?" her father asked with a mischievous smile.

"You look like surfer Jesus," Kasey said, then clapped her hand to her mouth in embarrassment. "Oh god, I so didn't mean that as insulting as it sounded."

Her father tilted back his head and let out a joyful laugh. "I'll take it. I was expecting you to say Eddie Vedder. I've been getting shit about that for years, not that I don't lap it up." He gestured for her to sit, and she settled on the soft couch, her father sitting beside her, facing her. He took her hands in his as though it were the most natural thing in the world. Scott and Andy sat in the corner on a dusty piano bench, both of them watching but saying nothing, giving them space. Kasey was infinitely grateful for both of them. *They already feel like family,* she thought happily.

"Kasey, I'm at a bit of a disadvantage here, because until this morning, I didn't know you existed," Louie began, sounding unsure. "I don't want to make excuses for myself, because I know how hard it must have been to go through life without a dad. I did it myself and I was bitter for years. I just want to say how very sorry I am that I wasn't there. Not only to support your needs...financially, emotionally...but just in general. To be your dad."

"It's okay," Kasey said, her tongue feeling too big for her mouth. "How could you have known?"

"I did try to reach out to El," Louie said. "Ella, I mean. A couple of times. I sent emails. I called around... I only got as far as her uncle's house, and the woman I talked to basically told me to go to hell. She wouldn't even confirm or deny that Ella lived there. Janelle—that's Andy's mom—tried, too, several times over the years. I gave up long before she did." His smile was sad. "But we were so young, and Ella and I weren't together for that long. After a while I just...let her go." He swallowed. "But Kasey, if I'd had any idea about you, I never would have given up. I would've flown to Georgia, I would have found you." His eyes glistened with tears. "I'm so sorry. I should have tried harder. I should have guessed that she fled for a reason, that maybe..."

"It's okay," Kasey said again, uncomfortable. "She didn't tell me, either. About you, I mean. Or anything about her life in Seattle." He squeezed her hand, and she squeezed it back. "I guess she had her reasons... I just have to assume they were good ones."

"I was just nuts about your mom," Louie said. "I really was. She was so beautiful, so sweet… She had this naïveté about her, like everything was an unknown mystery. She was very innocent in some ways, but she had a steel spine. She wasn't a cruel person. I imagine she had her reasons for leaving. I just wish she would have told me about you." Guilt was etched on his face. "I have to assume she left without a word because of my…problems…at the time. I imagine she thought I couldn't handle fatherhood, that I'd be a bad influence. That I'd ruin both your lives. She ran from me." He looked stricken.

Kasey swallowed. "Andy told me a little about…about your struggles."

Louie nodded. "Yeah? Well, that's good. I'm upfront about it. You have to be, if you want to stay on top of it. You start getting secretive and lying about things, that's when you fall off the wagon." He looked at Andy proudly. "I got clean when he was born, then I relapsed when he was little. But then I got clean for good. He was all the incentive I needed. I couldn't stand the thought of being a drug-addicted dad… I wanted him to have something better."

Kasey looked down at her feet. His words stung, but it wasn't his fault; he hadn't even known she existed. Still, hearing the love in his voice for his son made her heart hurt.

"I'm sorry, Kasey," Louie said again. "I would have done the same for you. If I had known." He shook his head. "Well, never mind all that 'what if' stuff. The point is, you were robbed of me growing up, and I want to do anything I can to make it right. I'm here for you now, whatever that means for you. And I want to get to

445

know you, to have you in my life, if you're okay with that."

"Of course I am," Kasey said, her voice a little choked.

"Andy tells me you have a stepfather," Louie said. "And a sister. Think they'd be okay with us getting to know each other?"

"I'm a grown woman," Kasey said firmly. "I decide who is in and out of my life. But anyway, Ricky's not like that. He was thrilled to find out I was coming here. He's always been good to me. He raised me as his own—even after Mom split. And it hasn't been easy for him—I, uh, haven't made it easy."

"He sounds like a standup guy."

"He is," Kasey replied, touched. "You'd like him." How nervous she'd been to tell Ricky she was heading to Seattle to meet her real father. She'd worried so much about hurting his feelings, of making him feel unwanted, but as soon as she'd told him, a huge grin had broken out on his face and he'd pulled her into his beefy arms, smothering her with a bear hug.

"So where is Ella, then?" Louie asked after a pause. "If you don't mind my asking. How long has she been out of the picture?"

"Almost six years," Kasey answered, embarrassed. "I was about to turn seventeen when she left." She swallowed. "She's somewhere in Canada, last I heard, but…honestly? I never asked exactly where. I was so angry at her I didn't want to know." She shook her head. "I was in a car accident… A bad one, and it took a long time for me to recover. I don't know for sure because she's never told me but… I guess it was too much for her. The wreck, my recovery… She bailed."

"I'm sure that can't be the reason," Louie said firmly. "Whatever her faults, that doesn't sound like the Ella I knew." His face was stricken; Kasey imagined he was lamenting not being there himself. "I'm so sorry about your accident, Kasey."

"Thank you. She…changed a lot," Kasey said, feeling like she was betraying her mother, but unable to stop talking now that she'd begun. "When I was little, she was so much fun. But as time went on, she got really heavily into the church she grew up in. They're pretty evangelical, very strict about 'secular' things like music and pop culture. She started looking like something out of Good Housekeeping magazine." She tried to smile, but tears were threatening to form. "The more religious she got, the less interested she was in us. Especially me."

"That's rough," she heard Andy say from the corner, and she flashed him a grateful smile.

"She loved us, of course. I'm not saying she didn't. She was just so involved in the church, always flitting off to a baby shower or a revival or whatever, cooking for her church friends at services. She was almost never home and when she was, she guilted the three of us about not going. Ricky's not a religious guy, never was, and he wasn't budging." Kasey wiped at her eye. "I honestly think my accident was just the excuse she needed to be rid of us."

"But why leave town?" Scott asked. "I get if she wanted out of her marriage, or even if she needed a break from her kids, but why move out of town? Why all the secrecy?"

"I don't know," Kasey said, her eyes brimming with tears. "I always figured it was to get away from me and the shame I'd brought her."

"Your mom's a runner," Louie said. "Some people just are. I remember her telling me when she first got to Seattle that she was fleeing from her aunt and uncle. They were super strict—well, at least the aunt was. I got the impression that her uncle maybe just didn't care. As soon as she was legal, she got the hell out of dodge. She just got on a bus and took off. I always thought that took major balls."

"It does," Kasey admitted. "But it's a whole other thing when you leave two kids and a husband behind. Or leaving your boyfriend without even telling him that he's going to be a dad."

"Yes, it is," Louie agreed, squeezing her hand. "A whole other thing."

A silence fell over the room. Kasey bit at the inside of her lips, wondering what to say next. The mood had gone somber. Then her father stood up and gave a little stretch, scratching at his still damp skin.

"Well, I say fuck it," he said with a guffaw, reaching out a hand to help Kasey up. "We can't fix a damn thing, so what do you say we make a big batch of fucking waffles?"

Kasey smiled through her tears. "I think waffles sound fucking great."

TWENTY-SIX

BOBBI - HULL, GEORGIA - 1975

Kat,

First of all, CONGRATULATIONS on your engagement! It's about damned time Ramon made it official. The man worships you. I'm so happy for you both and nobody deserves it more. I'm sorry it's been a while since I wrote. I've been so busy working and taking care of Ella that I scarcely have time to breathe. I spent four years trying to get pregnant, but if you'd told me how exhausting having a baby would be, I might've reconsidered (never tell Ella that; I love her to death).

Landrum tries to help me as much as he can, and he still dotes on her (and spoils her), but I try to handle most of the day-to-day routine, so he can rest. Working in the granite yard in Elberton takes a toll on him. It's almost an hour's drive out there and an hour back, and the work is grueling and risky. And he comes home dog-tired and covered in bruises. He's been to the doctor twice in the past two months for granite fragments in his eye. Yet he picks up every extra shift he can get. And we are still barely scraping by. I have been urging him to find something a little closer to home and easier on him physically—there's work all over in construction, automotive, even retail—but he says it's a good job with steady hours and he needs something physically grueling to wear him out so he can sleep at night.

Not that it's helping much. He still wakes up most nights with the sweats, screaming out in anguish. It would chill your blood if you heard some of the things he yells in his sleep. Poor Ella is so used to it that she can sleep through it, bless her heart. I wish I could say the same. I've urged him to see someone about it. The bags under his eyes are almost purple sometimes, Kat. But he swears he's fine and it would be ridiculous to take the time off work.

He finally did track down his parents, but their phone is always cut off. He's been writing them letters but never gets a reply. It hurts him deeply. I keep telling him we'll just take off and go visit them, but he says he can't 'take the time off.' I think the truth is that he's afraid to see them. Afraid to see what's become of his mother.

He's been home for over five years. And still the nightmares. What's eating at my husband? The stuff with his parents, yes, and the war, but there must be something more. But I don't know, because he won't let me in.

I'm working part-time at Last Resort Grill downtown, waiting tables. I hate it, but the tips are good. Especially if I wear a shorter skirt.

Go ahead and judge me, Kat—I judge myself, believe me. But it's hard to keep my mind on things like equality for women when my baby is hungry and my husband can't sleep through the night. God, you must hate my guts. I'm one of those women now. I hope, just as soon as things get settled down for us a little, I'll be back out there with you, fighting the good fight.

I can't wait for the wedding. I'd be honored to be a bridesmaid. I'll try to start saving now for the dress and plane ticket. I'm so happy for you, Kat.

All my love,
Bobbi

"Bob."

Bobbi snapped back to attention, glancing over at Landrum, who was holding up two cans of peaches. "I can't remember. Does Ella like the ones canned in syrup, or the ones in water?"

"Get the ones in water," Bobbi said absently, looking down at the stroller, where her almost-toddler was waking up from a nap, her face flushed with sleep, her hair in her face. "She likes the ones in syrup, but they have so much sugar and they're ten cents more a can."

"Oh." Landrum frowned at the can, then tossed two of them into the buggy. "Should we get a can of pineapple, too? I wouldn't mind a pineapple upside-down cake for dessert tonight. Mama used to make those, and I've been craving one ever since I deployed."

Bobbi sighed. "I've got a shift tonight. I'm not sure I'll have time to bake a cake, Lan." At the sight of his disappointed face, she added, "But they're super easy to make. You think if I wrote down the recipe you could handle it? It might be something fun you and Ella could do together!"

Landrum brightened. "That's an idea. I think we can handle that, can't we, June bug?" Landrum reached down and tousled his daughter's hair. Ella smiled up at him, her cherubic face covered in a sheen of drool. Bobbi felt a pang in her heart watching the two of them together. Landrum was such a good father.

She reached out and touched her husband's arm. "The pineapple is on sale," she said brightly, not wanting his moment of happiness to end. "Why don't you grab two cans?"

"Are you sure?"

"It's Thursday night," Bobbi said, reaching over and grabbing a can from the shelf. "Trivia night. I always get good tips on Thursdays. We can swing it."

"If you say so, moneybags," Landrum said, then leaned over to plant a sweet, unexpected kiss on her lips.

Bobbi leaned into him, breathing in his warm, familiar scent, before he pulled away and resumed shopping. She felt a rush of blood from her head that traveled from her chest down to her groin. Her cheeks flushed as she watched him scanning the instant coffee, looking for the cheapest variety, inwardly embarrassed at the physical reaction she'd had at such a slight touch. She admired the way he bent over, peering at the price tags, a shock of dark-blond hair falling over his forehead, his hands tucked into the pockets of his well-fitted slacks. His green army jacket, covered in patches and a couple of medals that he declined to talk about when people asked, hung from his broad shoulders. If he lost any more weight, it would be too big. He was too thin by a measure, and his face still had that gaunt, haunted look, but the full beard he'd grown and the muscle he'd packed on from working at the quarry over the past few months had turned him from a haunted young boy to a strong, mysterious man.

Bobbi had heard women joke about how marriage was the fastest way to banish thoughts of lust and sex from your mind, but she'd only come to want Landrum more the longer she had him. She thanked her lucky stars every day that he'd come home, that he was hers again.

Bobbi hadn't minded the shotgun marriage at the courthouse, attended only by Amelia and Sam, back in Athens just for the day (and whom they hadn't seen since), or the small, one-bedroom cottage they lived in between Athens and Hull. She didn't mind that they both had to take every spare shift they could to make ends meet and barely saw each other, passing like ships in the night. Bobbi didn't mind any of those things, because she had Landrum, and he had her, and that meant forever... And he'd given her little Ella, his June bug, and they were a family. She'd lost so much of her family in one fell swoop, and Landrum had given her one back.

Watching Landrum extract a can of coffee from the shelf and toss it into the cart, turning to wink theatrically at their daughter, Bobbi felt her pang of lust and affection turn to wistful regret. If only they had more time to spend with each other. If only their physical love could be more than just a quick, frenzied act in the middle of the night, two bodies fumbling in the dark of their bedroom every few weeks when they happened to both be home during night hours. If only she could express the kind of passion she really felt…

But Bobbi was scared. Scared because Landrum was no longer completely Landrum. Gone was the confident, funny, sensitive guy who had snuck into her bedroom at night to run hot kisses up and down her neck. Gone was the guy who let nothing ruffle him, whose easygoing attitude had put everyone around him at ease. Now Landrum Walton was a man who jumped at sudden movements, who was sullen and despondent, who had night terrors and leapt a mile in the air when she woke him from sleep with the gentlest of touches. He would never hurt her; he'd die before he did that, Bobbi knew. But the playful spontaneity was gone. He was a man who had seen things he would not talk about, who had come back less than whole, a man who took extra shifts at the granite yard not just because he needed the money, but because it was easier than talking to his wife about his feelings.

Bobbi pinched her arm lightly, reminding herself to stop the stinking thinking. It was a bright, sunny day outside. Her beautiful daughter was smiling and giggling in her stroller, and Landrum, whose days off were rare, had chosen to spend his free time with them. It would just take time, that's all. Time for him to…adjust. "I'd rather spend the day at the grocery store with my girls," he'd said that morning over a breakfast of toast with grape jelly, "than spend the entire day with a grand in my pocket at Atlantic City." What a liar he was… But Bobbi's heart had surged with happiness, anyway. He was trying. She wouldn't let her brain ruin today.

Bobbi put a hand on her husband's shoulder and smiled at him. "Why don't you get a can of the real stuff this week, hon?" she asked in a low voice. "I know you'll want a cup of good coffee to go with your cake."

"It's two dollars more, Bobbi," he argued. "I can't justify it."

"You deserve it, as hard as you've been working," she insisted. She gave him a gentle squeeze, and he smiled tentatively. "If you're so worried about the extra two dollars, we can skip the rump roast this week. I've got a whole chicken in the deep freeze that Beverly next door brought me as a thank you for watching her nephews. We'll have that for Sunday roast, skip the beef, and then you can have your coffee."

"Or we could save the cash and put it away—"

"Landrum Walton. I'm putting my foot down. Buy the damned coffee."

"Yes, ma'am." He grinned at her and selected a can of Folgers from the high shelf and tossed it in the buggy, his eyes flashing at her. She felt the warmth low in her belly again. She knew that look. If her shift didn't end too late, maybe he'd still be awake and waiting for her when she got home…

"Excuse me."

They both turned to see a young woman standing there. She had light, feathery hair, pulled back in a messy braid, and round-rimmed glasses. She was holding a stack of leaflets. Bobbi didn't remember her name but recognized her as a girl who'd attended some of their antiwar rallies back before Landrum had been drafted. Back then, she'd been a slight thing, still very young, probably not even in high school. She had tagged along, more in the way than not, wanting to be useful. Now she was a young woman, almost grown, with the self-possessed posture of someone who knew her place in the world. *She looks like I used to.* Bobbi flashed a bright smile. "Hi!" she said to the girl, assuming she'd come over to hand her a leaflet. Maybe she'd try to get involved again…if she had the time.

But the girl paid Bobbi no attention. Instead, she looked pointedly at Landrum, her nose in the air as though she'd smelled something foul. "Nice jacket," she said, her voice louder than it needed to be, her cool eyes appraising him. "Vietnam?"

Landrum opened his mouth to reply, but before he could speak, the girl leaned toward him, opened her mouth, and launched a mouthful of spit into his face. "Fuck you, *baby killer,*" she said, her voice high and bright, then turned on her heel and stalked out of the grocery store, flipping her braid behind her.

Bobbi watched, seemingly in slow motion, as her husband stood there, spittle dripping from his cheek down to his army jacket, his eyes lowered, his body stock still, as though he'd frozen into a pillar of salt. One fist was clenched in front of him, the knuckles white, and the other arm, where, Bobbi knew, beneath his jacket there were raised, mottled scars, hung limply by his side. From her stroller, sensing something traumatic had happened, Ella began to wail. Bobbi faltered, not sure who to comfort, who to help.

After a beat, she fished a handkerchief out of her bag and began to dab at Landrum's face.

"Don't pay that little brat any mind, hon," she assured him, wiping at his cheek. "She's just a stupid kid putting on a show. Jesus,

I thought all those idiots had run out of spit by now." She tried for a nervous chuckle, but the look on Landrum's face stopped her.

"No, Bobbi, leave it," Landrum said, stepping back from her. His face had gone white.

"Landrum, just let me—"

"I said *leave it, goddammit!*" He swatted her hand away and stepped back from her, his expression one of wild fury. "Don't fucking baby me. Don't you dare."

Ella's wails turned to screams. Bobbi felt tears of embarrassment and hurt fill her eyes. She picked up her daughter, nestling her face in her soft, wispy hair. People had stopped shopping, openly staring at the girl's performance and Landrum's reaction to it. There was still spit dripping off Landrum's face as he turned to her, shamed.

"I'm sorry, Bobbi," Landrum said softly, his voice pained. "You finish shopping. I'm going to go wait in the car." He fished his wallet out of his pants and threw it in the cart. "But put the coffee and the pineapple back. I don't know what I was thinking. I'm not going to bake a fucking cake."

Then he was out the door, leaving Bobbi to cry alone into her daughter's hair. After a few moments, she gathered her composure, put back the can of pineapple with a shaking hand, and finished her shopping. She kept the coffee. Nobody came to ask if she was all right, all pretending they'd seen and heard nothing, passing her like planes over an unmanned island.

"Hey, Bob."

"Hey, Lando."

Their eyes met over the kitchen table later that evening. A rare smile was creeping up over Landrum's lips, making him look like the teenage boy with whom Bobbi had fallen in love.

"I'm sorry about today. I should have handled that better. I guess I was embarrassed. I just want you to know how much I love you," Landrum said, leaning over to spoon up applesauce, which he then flew into Ella's mouth, making an airplane noise.

"I love you, too."

They stared at each other for a moment, then Bobbi looked down at her plate, a pleasant flush on her cheeks. The skin on her arms erupted in gooseflesh, an enjoyable sensation, but then a strange feeling passed over her, a sudden cold. She rose to shut the window; the late afternoon sun had cooled, and the breeze was too much for the dining room. As she passed by, she tousled Ella's hair, then Landrum's, feeling the brittle yet soft strands of dirty blond beneath her fingers. She let her hand linger there for a moment, grazing his temple, feeling his pulse under her fingers, needing to commit every part of him to memory.

Then Bobbi sat back down, placed her napkin in her lap, and resumed eating, almost afraid to look at him.

TWENTY-SEVEN

ELLA - VANCOUVER, CANADA - 2018

HER phone was beeping for the third time, this time louder and more insistent. Ella reached over with a groan, not bothering to open her eyes, and tapped blindly at the screen, hitting the "snooze" button. Just another ten minutes… She'd been dreaming such a nice dream…

Outside her window, a seagull squawked loudly, and the neighbor's car beeped, most likely at Layne, her half-feral, ancient orange tabby, who liked to sleep behind the tires. Ella sat up with another groan. She wasn't going back to sleep now. She'd lie there worrying until she was sure Layne wasn't smooshed under some teenager's beater. They were so careless; even though she'd pleaded with them to look out for her mangy devil several times, they never did, and Layne was already down to life number four, at least.

Ella padded downstairs from her small bedroom loft and unlatched the door, stepping out onto the porch. It was cool out this morning, the sun muted by a thin, iridescent fog. She whistled for the cat, looking out over the apartment parking lot and out to the ocean beyond. She could barely see the horizon and gray-blue water through the thick mist. It reminded her a bit of Seattle, though the air here was colder and infinitely more breathable. Here, she felt less closed in, could breathe.

Ella felt a tickle on her bare legs and looked down at her Russian Blue, Jerry, with his wide, clear blue eyes, and smiled. "Good morning, Mr. Cantrell," she said, leaning down to stroke his soft head. "And where is your mischievous brother Layne?" She caught a glimpse of the orange-striped tabby over by the rosebush, inching his back against a scratchy bit of leaves, and grinned. "So long as you aren't behind that idiot's car, we're good," she called to the cat, and sauntered back into the apartment to make herself a cup of tea.

Ella pulled on the light green bathrobe she kept hanging on the peg by the hall closet and grabbed a packet of English Breakfast from the Twinings box on the counter, rummaging through the dishwasher for her favorite ceramic mug. It might be a two-cup morning, the way her head felt. She hadn't been sleeping well lately, had been having nightmares and insomnia, ever since the last time she'd talked to *them*. Even just receiving an email from one of her family put her on edge, threw her out of whack for days. Just talking to Ricky was enough, and Fallon was hard, but Kasey...talking to Kasey was the worst of all.

She knew it was wrong, and she lived with the guilt every day, but it was the only way Ella knew how to go on; to be unreachable, faraway. Invisible.

The kettle was clicking over, a trickle of steam beginning to inch out of the spout, when she heard her phone going off again upstairs. It would keep ringing until she silenced it, so she grumbled her way up the tiny stairs into the loft, throwing herself on the bed and reaching over to the table by the window to grab her phone. As she scrolled to unlock the home screen, she realized it wasn't the alarm—her phone was ringing.

And it was her daughter, Kasey.

A long, shaky sigh escaped her lips. *Again?* She'd just spoken to her oldest daughter last week... A long text exchange where she'd divulged *lots* of information, enough to have kept her mollified for a while. She knew Kasey could not understand the mental stamina it took to talk of these things, to talk at all... She couldn't be expected to understand what it was like, but...

Couldn't she just leave her be?

Ella sat on the edge of the bed, running her thin robe through her fingers until the phone stopped ringing. Waves of guilt went through her, but she tried to shrug it off, heading back downstairs to finish making her tea. She was barely awake. She hadn't had any caffeine yet and last night had been shit. Her therapist was on vacation and she hadn't been able to talk to her in days. She needed time to build her stores back up, to mentally prepare for a conversation. Ella sighed, pouring the boiling water over the tea and reaching for the honey. Maybe Kasey wouldn't call back.

Ella was just sitting down on the loveseat in the studio living room when the phone began to vibrate again. She raised a shaking hand to her lips, allowing herself one sip of the scalding tea, and scrolled her thumb up on the screen, answering before she lost her nerve. If she didn't, it would just ring all day, until she threw herself into the ocean.

"Hello, Kasey," she said, doing her best to put on a voice of calm, confident assurance.

"Mom? Ella?" Her daughter no longer knew what to call her. Ella felt a pang of what might have been regret.

"Yes. Good morning. How are you?"

"I'm...good. I guess." Kasey hesitated. "Listen, sorry to keep calling, but...I have news."

"Oh, really?" Ella took another sip of tea, bracing herself. "Given our last conversation, I assume you found your dad?"

"I did." Kasey's voice came out in an excited rush. "But not only that... Mom, I...I found Janelle."

"Oh," Ella said, her voice coming out a squeak. "I see."

"Come on, Mom." Kasey's voice turned firm. "Can we talk about this?"

"Kasey, I'm very glad to hear you've found your dad," Ella spoke evenly. But her hand shook so hard she spilled her tea, hot and scalding, on her leg. It soaked through the robe and burned her skin. "But I've only just gotten up and I haven't even finished my morning tea, so I'm afraid we'll have to resume this conversation another time when I'm—"

"I'm in Seattle," Kasey interrupted. "Guess who's with me?"

"I...I don't know," Ella answered.

"Everyone," Kasey said, her voice an excited whirl. "I met Louie—I mean Dad—and he's wonderful and kind and immediately put me up in his house and he insisted that Ricky and Fallon come out, too. He paid their fares! And they actually *came*, Mom. They flew all the way here. They wanted to meet him! And did you know I have a brother? Louie has a son; his name's Andy. He and his best friend, Scott... Mom, they're just wonderful. They're this big,

happy family. And Janelle, well, Louie got on the phone with her and told her all about me, and she immediately drove up to Seattle, and she brought her daughter. Her name is Glitter, how funny is that!"

"That sounds…like chaos," Ella said with a nervous laugh, but this was anything but funny to her. In fact, it was the stuff of nightmares. The thought of all those people together, likely talking about her in her absence, talking about all her failings, made her nauseated. *Please God,* she thought, clutching the cup with a trembling hand. *Don't let her ask me to come.* "I'm very glad to hear you're having fun. Seriously though, Kasey, I need to go. My cat—"

"There's just one person missing, and that's you," Kasey said, as though she'd read her mind.

Ella let her breath out in a slow woosh, the cup tumbling out of her hand and onto the floor, tea staining the light-gray carpet. "Kasey, I'm sorry, but there's no way I can come to Seattle…" she said, gripping the phone tight in her hand. *There's no way I'm leaving this apartment. I haven't stepped off the front stoop in years. I left my husband and my daughters and never looked back. What makes her think I can fly to Seattle for a family reunion? And God, what is Janelle doing there? Janelle. Janelle.*

"—I can't force you to come here," Kasey was saying. Ella jerked back to reality. "I know you had your reasons for leaving and you have reasons for not wanting to…to be around us." Ella swallowed hard. "Ricky and Janelle and Louie have all filled me in on things, helped me understand. But I need to talk to you. You're the missing piece. You have the answers I need so I can…so I can move on with my life, make it better. Can't you understand that?"

"I've told you what I can," Ella said weakly, her tea spilled all over her now ruined carpet, forgotten. Her face buzzed, and her left arm hurt; it felt like a panic attack. For the first time in a long time, she wished she had a fix. And yet, she knew exactly what Kasey meant. There had been a time, once, when she'd felt exactly the same, and had no mother to run to.

"I know," Kasey said. "But I just think...if I saw you in person... Mom, you might find that I understand more than you realize. That it might actually help us both. Help you."

"Kasey..."

"Mom, please." Kasey was pleading. "Please. Let me come to you. I need you, Mom. All these people... They're so kind and good and they love me, but you're my *mother.* Please." There were tears in her voice, and it wrenched at Ella's heart to hear it. She couldn't remember the last time she'd heard her daughter cry. Not even in the hospital, frail and sunken in her bed, hooked up to wires and tubes, her face deathly pale, had she cried. "You of all people should know what that's like, to want and need your mom, and not have her."

Ella put her head in her free hand, massaging her temple. Her stomach rolled over. She took a deep breath and said, despite herself, "I... All right, Kasey. But just you. Promise?"

"I promise," Kasey said breathlessly. "Just tell me where you are, and I'll hop on a plane, or a bus, whatever I need to do..."

"If you're in Seattle... Well, you can drive here," Ella said, her voice wavering with uncertainty. "Are you able to drive? Is your passport still up to date? Do you have it with you?"

"Yes," Kasey said, then, "I brought it. Just in case."

"I'll text you my address," Ella said, ignoring the implications of what her daughter had just said. The thought of her planning to visit her ahead of time made her even more nervous. "And...Kasey?"

"Yeah? "

"It will be nice to see you." Ella hung up the phone, staring at the blank screen until the rapid, chaotic beating of her heart slowed down. She stared at the tea stain on her carpet.

Her daughter was coming. Her daughter.

TWENTY-EIGHT

KASEY - 2018

"I'D feel much better if you let one of us come with you."

Kasey stared at the two men standing before her. Ricky, with his white almost-mullet, tall and imposing, his soft blue eyes focused on her, a picture of concern and love. And Louie, standing there in still-damp clothes from his morning surf, his wet brown hair curling below his ears, his own soft smile trained on her. Her two dads. Kasey's heart surged with a warmth she hadn't felt in a long time.

"I think it'll go easier if it's just me," she said. "She sounded so panicked on the phone. If I show up with a crowd, she's going to freak out."

"I just don't want you to leave disappointed or hurt," Ricky said in a gruff voice. "It's been so long since you saw her, Kace, and there were things I didn't tell you…things I kept from you."

"I know." Kasey gave her stepfather a bone-crushing hug. "I know how much you protected me. And I'm grateful for it." She smiled at him. "But I need answers, and Mom is the last piece of the puzzle. I feel like she owes me a face-to-face conversation. And it might do her more good to see me than she realizes."

"It's not just you I'm worried about," Ricky said after a pause, gesturing to Fallon, who was sitting on the porch swing with Andy and Scott. "She puts up a brave front, but when your mom left, it crushed her just as much as it did you, honey. She might not show it, but she misses your mom like crazy. And she sure does love her big sister."

"I know," Kasey said softly. "Neither one of us—me or Mom—has been fair to Fallon. I know that now. I'm going to go see her and try to make things right, to fix this split in our family. I promise."

"Be sure and tell her that we love her, too, Kasey," Louie said, his dark eyes moist with tears. "All the stuff with you... There's no hard feelings on my end, okay? We've got things to talk about, sure, but she doesn't need to be scared...of my anger. If you'll tell her that."

"I will." Kasey beamed at her biological father. "I'll make sure she knows."

"Well, I suppose you ought to be heading on, then," Ricky said, and Louie nodded, opening the car door for her. "Don't want you driving too much after dark. If your leg starts to bother you, stop and rest, okay?"

"I will." Kasey was just easing her way into Louie's Prius—her hip was already aching today; she'd found that the rainy Seattle weather didn't do much for her pain—when Scott came running up to the window. "Heading out without saying goodbye?" he cracked.

She gestured to the passenger seat. "Get in for a second."

He obliged, and she rolled up the windows as he shut the car door. "I wanted to say thank you," Kasey said, smiling as he reached over to take her hands in his. "For being so kind... For helping Andy reach out to me in the beginning, for flying with him all the way to

Georgia, and for…for everything else you've done since then." She looked into his soft brown eyes and smiled. "You're a real catch, Scott. Do you know that?"

He shrugged, looking embarrassed. "This kinda sounds like a kiss off. Should I be nervous?"

"It's not a kiss off." Kasey laughed, squeezing his hand. "But I… Whatever is between us, it scares me a little."

"Why?" Scott's brow furrowed adorably. "What's to be scared of? We like each other, don't we?"

"Yes. I definitely like you. But my life is complicated." Kasey sighed. "I have anger issues, anger toward my mom, the rest of my family…" She gestured at her aching legs. "I'll be dealing with this pain for the rest of my life. I'm okay with that, but I'm not okay with treating people badly because of it. I think you're right, about the pills and the depression and everything. I'm trying to figure out how to climb my way out of this mindset I've become accustomed to." She took a deep breath and marveled at how intently Scott listened to her, his dark eyes full of tender concern. "I just ended a relationship that was codependent and unhealthy, even though I loved the guy." She looked into his warm eyes, feeling that she could get lost in them, never wanting to return. "And if it's possible, I feel an even deeper connection with *you.*"

Scott's face broke into a smile. "I feel it, too."

"But I'm scared. It's hard enough, with you being long-distance. But then you add all these family dynamics that I don't understand, and my disability, and all my baggage…"

"Kasey." Scott's voice was low and soft. "Do you think I don't have baggage of my own? There's plenty of it. What I told you at the park, that's only a small sliver of my story. But isn't that part of being with someone? You accept the baggage?"

"Yes. But…" She swallowed again. "Scott, I'm trying to turn over this new leaf, to be someone who advocates for herself, who accepts her mistakes and flaws but doesn't look at herself like some victim. I want to be with people who take me at face value and don't see my limitations as flaws—"

"I told you before," Scott interrupted. "I don't pity you or feel sorry for you or want to swoop in like some knight in shining armor to 'fix' you. I just want to… Well, I've met someone I think I could maybe love, and that's you. That's it. That's all."

Kasey felt her eyes fill with tears. "Do you mean that?"

"Of course I do."

"Well then…" She blinked, wiping at her eyes. "After I get back, I'll ask you again. After you've had some time alone to think. And if you're sure…"

"I will be," Scott said, not skipping a beat.

"…if you're sure, then we'll see where to go from there. Sound good?"

Scott chuckled and squeezed her hands. "You're something, Kasey Newton. You really are. I like you so much."

"I like you, too." Kasey winked at him. "It doesn't hurt that you're so gorgeous you turn my insides to jelly."

"Ditto, beautiful." He leaned forward and pressed his soft lips to hers, cupping a hand behind her head, pulling her close to him. His stubble tickled her chin, and she sighed with pleasure.

"I wish you could just come with me."

"I think Ricky and Louie would protest, considering you just told them not to come."

"Probably." Kasey laughed. "Well, I'd better head out. They're right about me driving in the dark. I get nervous."

"I'll be here when you get back," Scott said, opening the passenger side door. "With more of those kisses."

"I'll hold you to that."

"Bye, Kasey." He shut the door and walked back up on the porch as Kasey backed out of the driveway, the grin on her face hurting her cheeks.

Kasey sat down awkwardly at the table, trying not to stare too hard at the woman who sat across from her. The ambiance on the back porch overlooking the sea was beautiful and peaceful, and the plate of food she held—biscuits and gravy, a specialty she hadn't had since before her mother left—smelled delicious. But the rail-thin, pale woman who sat before her seemed nervous and wary. So pale she was almost bloodless, and her eyes were so *haunted*. The moment Ella had opened the door and Kasey had taken note of her shrunken appearance, her sad, tired eyes, whatever anger she still held had dissipated and given way to concern.

"Thanks for this," Kasey said, gesturing down at the plate, picking up her fork and taking a tentative bite of fluffy biscuit. "Oh, man. These are just as good as I remember."

"I don't think I've made them since the last time we were at a table together," her mother admitted, picking up her own fork.

"Biscuits and gravy aren't really a thing in Canada. I should have made you poutine."

"Yum. How did you end up here, of all places?" Kasey asked, taking another bite.

"An old friend was from here. Anita," her mother answered after a moment, setting down her fork and taking a sip of water. "We were buddies in Seattle. I met her around the time I met, uh...your father." She sipped her water again nervously. "She was one of the few people I stayed in touch with, so when I left, she was able to help me get a place here."

"That's good, I guess. That you've got friends here," Kasey offered.

"Had. She and I don't speak anymore," her mother said flatly.

"Oh." Kasey resumed eating, the biscuit suddenly feeling like sawdust in her mouth. She didn't want to say or do anything that would upset her mother and alter the course of their conversation, but she couldn't seem to sidestep all the triggers.

But at the same time, wasn't that why she was here? Her mother had to know that. She had to realize it was time to start talking.

"I'm sorry I don't have a glass of wine or anything to offer you," her mother said. Her voice was oddly formal compared to how Kasey remembered. She was talking to her like a stranger. "I don't keep alcohol in the house."

"It's okay," Kasey said. "Neither does Louie, and Ricky stopped drinking. Seems to be a trend." Her mother didn't crack a smile. "I just made the decision to quit myself, for a while anyway. I've had some issues. Since the accident...with um, pain pills and alcohol and stuff. Self-medicating, I guess. It got out of hand. I'm 'cleaning house,' as they say."

Kasey had expected her mother to react to this—the news that Ricky had quit drinking was a big deal in itself, to say nothing of Kasey—but her face was blank. She nodded once, but said nothing. Ricky had already alluded to Kasey's sobriety, so she knew, but Kasey felt stung at her lack of support.

"Both Ricky and Louie send their regards, by the way," Kasey said after a moment, gauging her mother's reaction. "They both wanted to come."

"Really?" Ella chuckled, but it was a nervous, hollow sound. "Ricky doesn't surprise me...but Louie, really? He was going to come along?"

"Yes." Kasey scooped up some gravy on her fork. "He's...he's actually pretty great. I really like him. And, of course, Ricky... Well, I guess I'm really lucky."

"I'm glad you see it that way," Ella said after a pause. "You're a lot less angry than I expected. You have every right to be furious with me."

Kasey sighed. "I am furious. Or was. For a really long time. I can't help but wish I'd known my father. I won't pretend it isn't upsetting, knowing how many years we lost. Why couldn't you ever tell me about him?"

"Because he didn't know you existed," Ella replied. "I didn't want him to know. If I had told you, you would have wanted to be part of his life."

"But why couldn't I?" Kasey asked. "Is it because he was on

473

drugs?"

Ella fiddled with her fork. Her food was largely untouched. "That was part of it. But it wasn't the only reason."

"Tell me, Mom," Kasey pleaded. "Please. No more secrets. I know nothing about my dad, about your life before I was born, about my grandparents... I need to know where I come from." She stared at her mother, meeting her eyes, so much like Fallon's. "I know you don't like to talk about this stuff, but...please."

"Are you done eating?" Ella asked abruptly, gesturing to her plate. "If you are, let's walk down to the shore. The beach is so pretty at dusk." She smiled a strange smile, then added, "I haven't been down there in months. But I think I have the strength to go now."

Kasey stared at her, uncomprehending.

Ella stood up from the table. "I don't leave the house. I find it...hard. I haven't left this apartment complex in over a year. But I think it'll be easier to tell you everything out there, with the water lapping at my ankles." She managed a small smile. "Washing away my shame. Will you go with me? I get...nervous. I might need to hold your arm."

"And I might need yours, too," Kasey said after a pause. Then she got up from the table and followed her mother out the door and into the night.

They sat together on the sand, Ella's pant legs rolled up to the ankle, Kasey's skirt pulled up around her legs to avoid the tide. Kasey saw her mother sneak a sidelong glance at her scar. "Does it still bother you?" she asked.

"Yes. My hip hurts all the time, especially in overcast weather," Kasey answered. "Some days I have to use my cane and there are times I need the chair."

Her mother winced. "They told us at the hospital that you'd make a full recovery." She sighed. "I guess that was a lie."

"No, it wasn't," Kasey said. "I did fully recover... I'm here, aren't I?"

"But you aren't..."

"Healthy? Whole? Complete?" Kasey said. "Mom, I'm all of those things. It hasn't been easy, and God knows I've had trouble adjusting to everything, but I'm living with it just fine. There's pain sometimes but...I'm okay. It took me years to realize that." She paused. "Honestly, it took me until *last week* to realize that."

"It's not easy seeing your child hurt," her mother said, staring out at the water. She'd wrapped her arms around her torso, so tight she looked like a body-distortion artist. Kasey didn't like seeing her so uncomfortable, but there were things that needed saying before they could go back inside.

"Your leaving hurt me worse than any injury ever could," Kasey said quietly, and her mother went tense beside her.

"I guess I deserved that."

"Yes, you did." Kasey sighed. "But I've forgiven you, Mom. I can't forget, but I have forgiven. I just want to know *why*. Why did you leave us? I thought that it was because of my accident, because it was too intense for you to deal with. But now..." She looked out over the darkening horizon, noticing a star that had appeared in the inky sky. "I don't think it was just my accident. You were changing before that even happened. You became so religious and you pulled away from all of us. Not just me and Fallon, but Ricky, too. You were well on your way long before I ever got in that car." She looked at her mother. "So why, Mom? Why did you go? I need to know."

"I doubt there's anything I can say that would make you feel any better," Ella replied in a choked voice. "So what difference does it make?"

"It makes a difference because I'd *know*," Kasey said. "And then I can decide for myself how to feel about it. You've kept so much from me. It isn't too much to ask for some answers now. Let me be the judge of how I handle those answers, okay?"

"I'll try," Ella said, her voice choked. "I'll...do my best."

Kasey said nothing, just stared out at the water, waiting for her mother to speak. She would give her the time she needed to get it out.

Ella took a ragged breath and began to talk, curved into herself like an infant. "As you know, I was orphaned as a little kid," she began, her trembling fingers tracing circles in the sand. "Both of my parents died when I was barely two. My father fought in Vietnam. He was a P.O.W. for a short time. He saw things there that... Well, I honestly don't know *what* he saw, because he wasn't around to tell me. But from what I've heard, he was a funny, sensitive young man before he went to war. His home life was sad—his dad beat his mom, among other things—and my mom, Bobbi, was the only good thing in his life. She was the literal girl next door. They grew up together, were high school sweethearts. She had an idyllic upbringing at first—parents still together, two doting older brothers—but by the time she was eighteen, both her parents had died and her brother Guy, my uncle, had been killed in Vietnam."

"How sad," Kasey murmured, imagining her grandparents, remembering how they'd looked in their picture, both of them bright and shining and *young*.

"After that happened, she took off and started traveling around the country, going to political rallies," Ella said. "She was obsessed with Bobby Kennedy. I think she worked on his campaign a little when he announced he was running for president. And she also did some work with the NAACP, or another one of those groups that did Civil Rights stuff. She met John Lewis through the Poor People's Campaign. I know that because Uncle Ed told me. He hated most of what she did, but he was super proud of that."

"Wow!" Kasey exclaimed. "That explains the stuff in the box… That's what got the whole ball rolling for me. There were pictures, buttons, flyers…and a photo of her wedding to your dad."

Ella nodded. "My godparents—Kat and Ramon—sent that stuff to me. I never looked at it too much. Ed and Grace never talked about them when I was a kid. The only reason I know what little I know now is because I cornered Uncle Ed after you were born and forced him to tell me everything. Then, after, I wished he hadn't. I find talking about it…thinking about it…too painful." She shook her head. "It was easier not to know.

"So, eventually my dad, Landrum, came home from the war… But he wasn't the same when he got back. He and my mom got married, got an apartment together, and had me a few years later.

477

From what I've heard, he spoiled me rotten." Ella smiled wistfully. "I can't even remember him, Kasey. I don't remember the first thing about him. It haunts me. He loved me so much and…I don't remember anything at all."

"Oh, Mom." Kasey felt a wave of pity for her mother.

"And then, well…then I was with Ed and Grace."

Her mother's body was tense beside her. Kasey knew it pained her to talk like this after so many years of not talking at all. "You don't have to talk about that," she said gently. "If it's too much."

"No. You came all this way to find out, so I'll tell you." Ella shook her head as if to say, 'what the hell?' "I know you've heard things about Aunt Grace and Uncle Ed… How awful they were, how strict, how shitty they could be. All of that's true. But when I was a kid, for a time, they were wonderful. Before my parents died, Grace would take me twice a week to give them a break, so they'd have some time alone. She adored me. She couldn't have children of her own, so she'd bring me with her to church, to Sunday school… Sometimes she'd take me out for ice cream. She called me her little buddy. My parents really relied on her, because things weren't great." She swallowed. "They were up to their necks in bills and could barely make rent, even with both of them working 'round the clock. They were too proud to live with Ed and Grace, plus they didn't really get along. They were both free-spirit types, very opinionated, as you can imagine. And Grace was buttoned up and religious and…it didn't mesh. But Grace did help them, in her own way. With me. However things were between us as I got older, she loved me when I was a kid. I'm grateful for that."

SO LONG, BOBBY

"So what happened?" Kasey asked. "Why did it fall apart?"

Ella sighed. "My father took his own life. One night when my mother was at work and I was at Aunt Grace's, he went to his makeshift lounge in the garage, sat in his easy chair, put on a record and shot himself in the mouth." She bit her lip, tears welling up in her eyes. "He was Bobbi's moon and stars, and he didn't even leave a goodbye note. It destroyed her. She was hanging on by a fingernail and after that, after all she'd been through, she was just gone."

"Oh my God," Kasey said softly.

"She'd already lost both of her parents and her brother. She had a young daughter to feed and could barely pay the bills. All of her friends scattered across the country, and she was all alone. And he just up and *left* her." Ella wiped her eyes. "I can't be angry at what he did…what the war did to him… I imagine he saw things that…" She cleared her throat. "And his home life as a kid was so awful. I can only imagine the pain he felt. But I've never been able to fully forgive him for leaving us like that, for doing that to my mom. How different might her life have been…might *mine* have been, if…" She swallowed. "If he could have just hung on. But then I think about the times that I've thought everyone would just be better off if I…" Her voice choked and wiped at her cheek. "I understand him better now. I understand them both."

"What happened to Bobbi?" Kasey asked, almost wishing her mother wouldn't answer her. But Ella did.

"A couple of days after the funeral, my mother packed up my overnight bag and took me to Aunt Grace's. There was a baby shower planned for one of the ladies who taught Sunday school, and

479

lots of other kids were going to be there. It was a standing date and Bobbi didn't think there was any sense in me missing it just because my dad had passed" —she gulped— "or that's what Aunt Grace said, anyway. My mother dropped me with her early that morning and…well, she never came back."

"What happened?" Kasey asked, a lump in her throat.

Ella looked at her, her eyes brimming with tears, her tense shoulders moving upwards in a clumsy shrug. "They found her on the railroad tracks behind the high school the next morning. It was a special place to her and my father, apparently. The caretaker was out on the football field and saw something glinting off the tracks. It was a pin she'd stuck on her coat, attached to a Bobby Kennedy banner." She shrugged again, a strange, sad gesture in the deepening dusk. "She was hit by the train. Killed instantly. We never knew if the conductor saw her and wasn't able to stop and just…didn't say anything, or if he never saw her at all." She wiped her eyes. "He claimed the latter, of course. No charges were brought."

"Mom, was it an accident or was it… Did she…?"

"I don't know," Ella said matter-of-factly, brushing at the sand with her shaking hands. "My aunt and uncle always said it was just an accident, that she was out of her mind with grief and she never would have done something like that on purpose. They figured she stepped out on the tracks and never knew what hit her." She laughed joylessly. "I've been down there to those tracks. I've stood there in that very same spot. Kasey, that train is loud as *hell.*" She sighed. "But it doesn't really matter, does it? She's dead either way."

"I'm so sorry, Mom." Kasey didn't know what to say. "I…I

can't imagine what it was like, growing up like that, without your parents. Knowing that they…"

"I was so young, I barely knew what was going on," Ella said, her voice far away. "They did their best to give me a good childhood. Aunt Grace doted on me, and Uncle Ed was good to me, at least in the early years." She swallowed. "As I got older, though, once I hit adolescence…things changed. I argued a lot with Grace. She had such rigid ideas about propriety and being a lady, and I was basically my mother made over. I asked questions about my parents a lot, and that bothered her. She felt that because she and Ed had raised me, that *they* were my parents, and it hurt her feelings that I was so curious about Bobbi and Landrum." She paused. "By that point, it was obvious that her and Uncle Ed's marriage was hanging on by a thread. He cheated on her all the time. He was abusive. He was climbing up the ladder socially—making all kinds of money, well respected in the community, known for his social causes. And the more successful he became, the more of a jerk he was to Aunt Grace. He saw her as an old fuddy-duddy, a killjoy. He hated taking her to social events because she embarrassed him. But at the same time, he made no secret of the fact that he had mistresses. He rubbed them in her face. And she couldn't do anything about it. She didn't believe in divorce, and however much she was starting to resent me, she loved me, too. She wouldn't have left me. She was stuck."

"That sounds like a terrible situation."

"It was. Uncle Ed was always nice to me, and he tried to intervene a little here and there when she was especially strict. I felt so torn, because he was my blood, you know? And he would talk to me about my parents and defend me to Grace. But deep down, I knew that *she* was the one who cared for me and saw to my needs. In her own way, she thought she was mothering me. We were just so different. She was cold, and strict, and bitter. And Ed used me as a pawn to hurt her." Ella swallowed. "I didn't see that for so long. When I finally figured it out, I felt so guilty."

"It wasn't your fault."

"No, it wasn't, but that didn't change how I felt," Ella said sadly. "I'd already been robbed of one set of parents, and I desperately wanted Ed and Grace to be everything I'd lost. But they...they were just who they were.

"So, I ran away. I left just shy of my nineteenth birthday. I think it nearly broke Aunt Grace's heart, though she never let on. I had a small inheritance from my mother—that she inherited from her own parents—that became mine when I was of age. It was just a few thousand dollars. Nothing compared to the fortune that Uncle Ed had, but I didn't want his money," she said. "I drained my bank account, packed a bag, and got on a Greyhound bus to Seattle."

"Why Seattle?"

"I wanted to go somewhere far away, somewhere on the opposite end of the country from Georgia, and I was a big Alice in Chains fan," her mom answered with a chuckle. It was the same story Louie had told her, and Kasey had to smile. "Plus, Seattle was on my mind because I'd gotten a letter from there a few years before from my godparents, Kat and Ramon. At one time, they'd lived there, and I flirted with the idea of seeking them out. But honestly, I didn't care where I went. I just wanted to be away from the toxicity. Somewhere I could find myself, figure out who I was, without Grace's expectations and Ed's manipulations. I just wanted to be on my own."

"I can understand that."

"I loved Seattle," her mother said dreamily. "Right from the beginning. It just felt like home. The grayness of it, the cool, quiet air, the sense of loneliness and hopelessness that permeated everything... It felt so much like I felt inside. I just...I felt at one with the place right away."

"I see why you've picked Vancouver, then," Kasey said with a laugh. "It's a pattern."

Ella nodded. "You joke, but it's true. I felt like Seattle understood me, and I understood it." She smiled. "And I made some amazing friends right off the bat. Anita, and then Louie, your father..." She swallowed hard. "And Janelle."

"Tell me about them," Kasey said quietly.

Ella sighed, staring out at the water. Kasey thought she might refuse—she had to be exhausted by now, with all she'd already told—but then she started to talk again. "I started dating Louie pretty much right away," she said, her voice almost a whisper. "I was so into him. He was so...so beautiful. He had this long, curly brown hair, and dark blue eyes, almost black... I could get lost in them. You have his eyes." She smiled at Kasey, then looked away. "He was a musician, which was my weakness. We met at a show. He knocked my drink over by accident and he was so flustered and cute, apologizing, that I fell for him right then and there."

"He still looks like that," Kasey said. "Long-haired, intense hippie surfer guy. He says he looks like Eddie Vedder."

"He would say that about himself." Ella laughed. "But he's not wrong. He was my first real boyfriend. I'd dated a guy back in Georgia, but he was super conservative and strait-laced. Louie he was different. He gave me many firsts." Her face flushed, and Kasey smiled. "I really thought I'd marry him."

"So what happened?" Kasey didn't want to allow herself to think about how different life might've been if Ella *had* married Louie. It was too painful to imagine.

"Janelle happened." Her mom took a deep breath and fixed Kasey with a stare. Her arms, still crossed over her legs, were tense and trembling. "This is…hard to talk about. I never have."

"Please try." Kasey reached out and touched her mom tentatively on the arm. She couldn't stop now, not when she was finally learning who her mother truly was. "Please."

"Janelle was one of Louie's friends. I met her around the same time. I was crazy jealous of her because she and Louie had dated before, and she was just so *beautiful*. There was nothing between them anymore. They were better off friends, and she was part of the group. She got me a job at the co-op her parents owned, and she was always around, hanging out. After a while, I stopped being so jealous and intimidated by Janelle, and we became close." Ella took a deep breath. "It was all too good to be true. I should have known that from the start."

"What do you mean?"

"I told you I flirted with the idea of meeting my godparents? Well, they had a daughter. Janelle." Kasey's eyes widened. "I figured it out pretty soon after meeting her. The backpacker's I picked was near the last address I had for Kat and Ramon, so it wasn't all that strange—but the thing is, I didn't tell Janelle." Ella grimaced. "Not until months later, when she brought them around, and I had no choice but to come clean about who I was."

"Wow, that's pretty heavy. But you met them?"

"I did. And they were thrilled to see me. And while I was glad to meet them, it also really freaked me out. I'd built it up in my head for so long, and then once they were there… I didn't know who to be around them. How to act. How to act around Janelle, who I'd just dropped this bombshell on. How to confront my feelings of anger at Ed and Grace while still protecting them—because I did feel loyalty to them, too." Ella sighed. "It was just…a lot. All at once."

"Is that why you left?"

Ella shook her head. "No, but it started the cracks in the foundation. I started dabbling in drugs around that time. Louie brought them around; he was into heroin back then, though I hear he's gotten clean" —when Kasey nodded, Ella looked relieved— "and I started messing with them, too. I never did that much, but enough that I knew if I kept going down that path, I wouldn't be able to stop. And then…well…there was Janelle." She bit her lip.

"What about her?"

Ella took a deep breath and seemed to decide something. "I… This is weird to say. I've never said it out loud. I…I fell in love with her."

Kasey stared at Ella with wide eyes. Her evangelical mother had been in love with a woman? She thought back to the portrait in the garage. How lovingly rendered it had been, every stroke of paint full of love, how desperately Ella had wanted it destroyed..

"God, if I'm being honest, I was in love with Janelle from the very beginning. She and I were… There was this magnetic attraction between us, something bigger than ourselves. I would find myself just staring at her, memorizing the way she moved, trying to freeze her face in time. I'd do anything she asked me. I was always in awe of her, following her around like a puppy." Ella's face was wistful. "I loved her. Just desperately loved her. But I was dating Louie. I loved him, too. I was crazy about him. But it was different with Janelle. With Janelle…it felt right. She was my soulmate."

"Given who her parents were," Kasey mused. "I can see why it felt like fate."

"It did. It felt like she was supposed to be in my life. So, I…I started seeing Janelle behind your father's back. I couldn't help myself; it was something bigger than me. It just felt right being with her. And she loved me, too." Ella dug into the sand again. "But it couldn't last. I was terrified of Janelle, and what it meant to be with her. Everything with her and her parents—it was a lot of pressure. I wasn't ready." Ella swallowed. "I couldn't bear the thought of hurting Louie… And then, in a case of perfect timing, I found out I was pregnant with you."

"So *that's* why you bailed? Me?"

Ella nodded. "I was a coward. The right thing to do would have been to tell Louie. And then to sit down and have a conversation with both him and Janelle, lay my cards out on the table, and figure it out. But I couldn't face it." She frowned. "I didn't want to hurt

Janelle, and I knew Louie was in no position to be a father. I knew he'd freak out, panic… I was worried about bringing a baby into that. More than all that, though, I couldn't choose between them." Ella sighed. "I hadn't talked to Aunt Grace in months, but I found myself on the phone to her, pouring out my heart, telling her about the baby. She said, 'Come home. We'll figure it out, Ella. Come home.' It was the first time in years that I heard love in her voice. So, I bought a bus ticket, and I left, without a word to anyone.

"I was too proud to live at home again with Grace and Ed, so I crashed on Ricky's couch. He'd had a thing for me all through school, and I took advantage of it, I guess. I knew he wouldn't run me off. Grace helped me with money, so I could buy things for the baby. She was so excited about my pregnancy. Eventually, I got a job and started making a little cash of my own. I'd planned to get my own apartment and do the single mother thing, but Grace was pushing me hard to find a man and settle down, get married, all that nonsense. So when Ricky proposed to me, right before you were born, I said yes."

"Did you love Ricky at all?" Kasey asked, afraid of the answer.

Ella's eyes were sad. "I did, yes. Still do. But if you want the truth, Kasey, I didn't love him the way he deserved. I loved him as a friend. Later, that turned to something deeper…but it didn't last. It couldn't have. Because I was—I've always been—in love with someone else."

"With Janelle."

"Yes," Ella answered, her entire body tensed. "With Janelle."

"I understand." Kasey said, and her mother's shoulders

immediately sagged, as though she'd been holding her entire soul in them, as though she'd been afraid of what Kasey might say. It made her heart ache. "And I understand why you had to leave Ricky and live your truth. I get that, but what I *don't* get is why you left Fallon and me? We're your daughters! Did you think we wouldn't support you? Why did you abandon us?"

"Do you remember when I got back into religion?" Ella answered her question with a question.

"Yes," Kasey answered. "You started going back to church, wearing all those floor-length skirts, not letting Ricky bring his beer in the house—"

"I started using again," Ella said bluntly, cutting her off. "I started taking pills. I wrenched my back at work—you remember that pizza restaurant I waitressed at, and they'd always make me dump those huge buckets of ice into the cooler—well, I threw my back out, and the doctor prescribed me Lortabs. I didn't disclose to him that I'd dabbled in heroin as a teenager. Before I knew it, my back was fine, but I was still taking those pills every day." She shook her head. "I knew I had a problem, but it wasn't until Ricky confronted me that I admitted it. I denied how bad it was. I told him he was a hypocrite because he drank. Ricky didn't like it, but he tolerated it until I really fucked up. I cheated on him…with the person I was getting the pills from." She shrugged. "It just sort of happened. Ricky wasn't even angry with me, just hurt." Ella put her head in her hands. "It killed me, how much I'd hurt him. After all, he'd done for me. And for you girls."

"Oh, Mom." Kasey's heart went out to Ricky. How hurt he must have been.

Ella sighed. "After that, I quit cold turkey. I got off the pills. I knew I'd need something to keep me on the straight and narrow so I could fix my marriage. I started going to church with Aunt Grace again. I wanted to cleanse myself, to be a good wife and mother. I wanted to banish my mind of Janelle and focus on my family, stay off the drugs and be a good person. The only way I knew how to do that was through God."

"Did it work?"

"No," Ella said plainly. "But I threw myself into it, anyway. I stayed clean, and even though I knew Ricky wasn't fond of it, at least I was home every night, cooking dinner and helping with homework." She swallowed hard. "Then you got in your accident."

"Yeah." Kasey dug her nails hard into her leg, remembering. She felt a shudder go through her.

Her mother took a deep breath. "The accident was my fault, Kasey."

Kasey looked up sharply at her mother. "What? How do you figure that?"

"The night of that game, you asked me if you could go," Ella answered, rubbing at her eyes. "I told you no, that I had a church meeting and Ricky was working late at the garage, so nobody would be home to pick you up. You argued that the game wouldn't be over until after nine, and that we'd both be home by then. There was some boy there that you had a crush on, and you really wanted to see him."

"Caden," Kasey said, ignoring the pang in her stomach at his name, at the fact that they'd had a six-year relationship and her mom had never really known him.

"I told you that the answer was still no. I didn't feel like picking you up." Ella sighed. "The truth was, Ricky and I had had a fight that morning and I wanted to make up with him. We were having problems, and I was trying to save things. I didn't want to mess up those plans, having to pick you up at some football game." She shook her head, her face full of regret. "You told me you'd just catch a ride back with Amber. I didn't like you riding with her, because she hadn't had her license long, and she was so wild, but you swore that you'd come straight home after, and since we lived right around the corner from the school, there was no way you guys could come to any harm." She sighed again. "You wore me down, and I let you go. And then you got into an accident and almost died, and it was my fault."

"Mom," Kasey said gently, putting her hand on Ella's arm. "There's no way in hell that was your fault. You were just being a mom, saying no. You had no way of knowing that Amber would drink and get behind the wheel. If anybody is at fault, it's me. She asked me to drive, and I said no."

"You were just a kid," Ella argued. "It's the parents' job to keep you safe from harm. I was too worried about my own stuff to do that."

"Mom, it's not your fault," Kasey argued, but Ella had resumed her story.

"When I saw you in the hospital, I almost died myself. I couldn't bear to look at you like that. I couldn't stand the thought of you being in pain. I was so afraid you might die. You looked so frail and pitiful and I just…" Her voice broke. "The doctor asked me if there was anyone else I should call, and I thought of Louie…and the guilt that washed over me was unbearable. The thought that you could be born and then die with him never knowing you existed in between.

"And then, a few days later, I overheard a nurse talking about how they'd put you on Percocet for the pain. My mouth was *watering,* Kasey. My daughter lying in a hospital bed, having barely escaped death, and I was drooling over the thought of your pain pills." She wiped away a tear. "I went home to that empty house, and Ricky's stuff was everywhere, and I just stared at it, stared at this house we'd made a home that didn't feel like a home to me at all… And I realized how much of a lie I'd been living, how I'd imploded my own marriage, almost ruined my kids' lives the way I'd ruined my own." Her voice was full of tears. "And I made a decision. I wasn't going to do that to you all anymore. I couldn't stay, messing things up, living lies, ruining everyone's lives. So I packed a bag and called Anita and made arrangements to come stay with her."

Kasey felt like she'd been punched. "That's all it took, and you just left?"

"No, it took me *years* to get to that point, Kasey," her mother answered. "Years of unhappiness and depression, feeling suicidal and trying to hide it, grieving over everything I'd lost, over all I'd seen in my childhood. I took all those awful lessons and brought them into my marriage and let them poison everything. I had to get away, to try and start over, and I knew you'd hate me, but I thought you'd be better off. Ricky was so good to you. He always treated

491

you like his own. He loved you both so much. I thought you'd be better off with just him. Without me."

"We needed our mother," Kasey said fiercely. "Fallon and me. We needed you."

"You were better off," Ella said stubbornly.

"I imagine Bobbi thought the same thing," Kasey said harshly. "Just before she stepped in front of the train."

Her mother reared back as if struck.

"I'm sorry," Ella said in a small, childlike voice. "I'm sorry. I just...I failed."

"So that's it, then?" Kasey said, standing up, the tide washing over her ankles. "That's your big reason for leaving us? A bunch of sad history and a 'Sorry, I failed?'"

"My whole life, all I've ever known is how to run away," her mother said helplessly, her eyes glassy with tears. She made no move to stand up. "I had no parents to love me and guide me, nobody to hold me and tell me it would be okay. That I would make it through. All I knew was how to run from a mess I created because that's all I've ever been shown. It's the only reality I know."

"Your life could have been so much different," Kasey said, tears running down her face as she looked down at her mother. "If only you'd had a little faith in yourself, if only you'd ever just once in your life trusted in a single person who loved you."

"I know," her mother said quietly. "But the problem was, I never believed I deserved their love. Or anyone's."

But Kasey had already turned and started back to the house, her own tears blinding her eyes, the sand gritty and rough beneath her bare feet.

TWENTY-NINE

ELLA - SEATTLE - 2018

ELLA stepped out of her car and stretched her legs, hearing the crack in her knees, a sign of her impending old age. *The last time I set foot in this place was over twenty years ago,* she marveled to herself as she looked up at the Seattle skyline. She remembered it as vividly as if it were yesterday—the busker on the street corner playing Alice in Chains, the youth hostel that reeked of weed, the cold, drizzly gray sky.

"I can't believe I did this stupid thing," she muttered under her breath as she locked her car and headed toward the street. She'd chosen a parking garage about a block from the house. She thought it would be less awkward to walk there than park in Louie's driveway and draw unnecessary attention to herself. Nobody was expecting her; she'd chosen not to call and announce her impending arrival, just in case she changed her mind at the last minute. Besides, she needed a little time to clear her head and get in the right headspace. It had been literally years since she'd left Vancouver and months since she'd stepped off her own property. Being in a strange place far from home was enough to give her a panic attack, and the thought of seeing all those people from her past filled her with dread.

But she was here, and she supposed she might as well see the thing through. For Kasey and Fallon, if for no other reason.

The only thing more painful to Ella than knowing that her entire world—Ricky, her daughters, Louie and his children, and *Janelle*... lovely Janelle—were all gathered there, waiting to see her, waiting to confront her with her past was the idea of all of them together, *without* her. She'd realized that as soon as Kasey had left.

She walked the block to Louie's place quickly, looking down at the post-it with his address scrawled on it in her daughter's familiar hand at least five times, making sure she went to the right place. When she'd last seen Louie, he'd been living in a squalid apartment on the edge of town, infested with cockroaches, and on the bottom floor of a decrepit building that looked ready to collapse at any moment. Now, if Kasey was to be believed, he had a two-story house right on the beach, with huge bay windows and solar panels. It sounded very much like something a grown-up, successful Louie would obtain for himself, but it was still hard to accept that the poor, drug-addled musician with whom she'd once been enamored had become a successful, well-adjusted music executive who had a big, waterfront property. Someone who was clean and sober and a wonderful father, who surfed every day and whose life was filled with happiness.

How had she let her own life go so horribly wrong?

She hadn't told Kasey—she hadn't had the chance, since her daughter had fled her home that morning after her revelations—but Ella had tried once to reach out to Louie.

It had been a year or so after Kasey's birth. Ricky was working late that night, and in the quiet of the evening, as she nursed her daughter, staring out the window, Ella had begun to think about Louie. About how wrong it was, the way she'd left. He deserved to know he had a daughter. He deserved a chance to be in her life, if that's what he wanted. It wasn't fair, what she'd done.

Ella waited until the next morning when Ricky left for work, and after she put Kasey down for her late-morning nap, she'd picked up the phone and called Louie's old number. Disconnected. She tried Janelle's apartment, then Anita's, but neither number worked. Then, she had an idea: she'd call Janelle at the co-op—*that* number was likely to be the same. They'd put her in touch with Janelle, and she would be sure to have Louie's number. It would be bittersweet, talking to Janelle—Ella still thought of her every day, missed her terribly, even if she'd never tell a soul—but it needed to be done. Louie deserved to know.

An irritable voice answered on the second ring. "Seattle Co-Operative? How can I help?"

"Yes, can I please speak with Janelle Hawks, the manager?" Ella asked, her heart in her throat, her hands trembling.

"She's on maternity leave." Ella heard a crash in the background and the voice in her ear swore. "Sorry. It's chaos in here without her. Nobody knows what they're doing—" She heard another shout, and the voice said, "I'm sorry, who is this?"

"I'm uh—a former employee," Ella stammered, her heart beating hard. Maternity leave? The thought of Janelle being pregnant was impossible to imagine. "I was just calling to check in with her. I'm sorry to have bothered you."

"Okay, no prob," the voice said, and she heard them fumbling with the receiver.

"Wait!" she shouted, and the voice came back on the line, more impatient now.

"Yes?"

"I just, uh—I just wondered... When did Janelle have her baby? And do you have her address? I'd love to send a card..."

"It's been, uh... I guess she had him about two weeks ago now. His name is Andrew—Andy." The voice on the other end brightened. "He's adorable. He's got Janelle's pretty dark skin and curly hair, but he has Louie's eyes. He's the cutest baby I've ever seen."

"Louie?" Ella's felt all the breath leave her at once.

"Yeah. You know, her on-again-off-again. He's over the moon. They both are," the voice said. "Look, I've got to run. We're super busy. But if you want to send her a card, just send it to her house." They quickly spouted off an address. "I'm sure she'd be glad to hear from you. Take care, bye!" And the voice was gone.

Ella sat there, dumbfounded, still holding the receiver to her ear. Through the baby monitor, she could hear Kasey stirring, a tiny little cry in her sleep. Janelle and Louie had a child together. Kasey had a brother.

So much for "there's nothing between us." She should have known.

Life had gone on in her absence, and Janelle and Louie had found their way back to each other. And now they had a child, and their perfect little life was complete. They were a family of their own now, and there was no room for her or Kasey. They had likely forgotten Ella, a stupid blip in their love story. And Ella had nobody to blame but herself because she'd thrown them both away. She could not disrupt the happiness they'd found, not now.

Ella braced herself for the tears, but they did not come. She sat there at the kitchen table for a few minutes, smoking a cigarette, then she picked up the phone again and dialed. "Aunt Grace?" she said when her aunt answered. "I thought Kasey and I might stop by this afternoon. Will you be home?"

Now Ella stood outside the open front gate, staring nervously at Louie's home. The house was a rich tan, with mahogany-colored shutters and a wide, heavy front door. There was a pride flag hanging from a beam on the porch, and a large, colorful tapestry hanging behind a huge porch swing. Ella smiled despite herself; Louie was just the same as he'd always been.

Before she had a chance to second guess herself, Ella stepped up onto the stoop and knocked on the door lightly. She heard footsteps, and then the door swung open.

A handsome, dark-skinned young man stood there, with familiar wide, dark eyes and a friendly smile. "Hi."

"I'm here to see…" Ella faltered. "Kasey. And uh…well, everyone, I guess."

"Well, you're in the right place, because everyone is here," the young man said with a grin, and ushered her inside. "I'm Andy. I bet you're Ella, huh?"

"Yes," she said, surprised. "You've heard of me?"

"Seriously?" the young man said with a laugh. "You're practically a unicorn in this house. He shook her hand firmly. "Not

499

to mention Kasey… She's talked about you a lot this past week."

"Is she still here?"

"Yeah. She and Fallon are out back picking up seashells," Andy answered. "I'll go get them. You can go into the living room, make yourself at home." He gestured at a room to the right of the foyer and made his way out the back. Ella stood there, not sure what to do with herself.

"Ella? Is it you?"

Ella turned, her heart pounding in her throat. Standing there in the foyer, his dark blue eyes flashing, was Louie. Before she knew it, she was in his arms, her head resting on his shoulder as he held her tight, feeling his curly hair tickle her cheek for the first time in over twenty years.

"If you aren't a sight for sore eyes," Louie said with a chuckle, his familiar voice warm and smooth like honey, his hand patting her warmly on the back. "We didn't think you'd come."

Ella looked up into his blue eyes, feeling tears in her own. She hadn't cried in years, not since Kasey's accident, but for the past two days she had done nothing but. "Louie…I'm so sorry. I have so much to apologize for… I know you can never forgive me."

"It's all done, Ella. There's no point in holding onto anger," Louie said, his hands still on her shoulders.

"But I…I kept your *daughter* from you," Ella cried, staring at him in disbelief. "You never even knew she existed. I left you high and dry without a word. How can you not hate me?"

He shrugged and gave her a wry smile. "Probably all the AA." He chuckled. "They're big on forgiveness."

Ella could only stare at him, stricken.

"If you're wondering if I have regrets, of course I do," Louie said, staring down into her face. "When I first found out... I *was* angry with you, Ella. But I sat down and thought long and hard and remembered how it was back then. I loved you like crazy, but I was strung out. Worse, I was getting you into it. And there was the whole thing with Janelle..." At her name, Ella let out a ragged sigh. But if he noticed, he didn't show it. "We were all broke and barely scraping by. I can understand why you panicked and wanted to go home to your family. Why you didn't want me in Kasey's life? I can understand that you thought I" —his voice broke, betraying his hurt— "that I wouldn't be a good father."

"I never thought you wouldn't be a good father," Ella insisted. "There were so many times I wanted to reach out over the years," she confessed, looking down at the floor. "It was all me and my dumb decisions... I've made so many mistakes, treated people so badly. Running and running away from everything and everyone. How you all don't hate my guts, I don't know. Kasey does, and I can't blame her."

"Kasey doesn't hate you," Louie said softly. His eyes darted to the couch, and Ella wondered if he wanted to sit down, to give them more privacy, but she couldn't seem to wrench herself from the doorway. The door, just to her right, was beckoning to her. She could still flee...

"She does. You should have seen how fast she left my house after I'd told her everything." Ella laughed joylessly. "She couldn't wait to get the hell out of there."

"She wanted you to follow her," Louie said in a kind voice. "And you passed the test."

"This is no game, Louie," Ella said, wiping away another tear.

"No, it's not," he said, taking her by the arm and leading her down the hallway. "But we're all still playing, best as we can." He gave her a squeeze. "Come on out back with me. We're grilling and everybody's outside. I'll make you a plate. Kace told me your place was right on the ocean—well, so is mine, so you'll feel right at home. Nobody's going to come after you, I promise. We're all so glad you're here."

"Even Janelle?" Ella asked in a weak voice, but Louie was already halfway out the door.

THIRTY

KASEY stared agog at her mother, resplendent in a long purple dress and black ballet flats, as she sat in a garden chair, raising a veggie burger to her mouth. Beside her sat a cold cream soda, and on the other side sat Louie, strumming away on an acoustic guitar, playing a tune she recognized now as Athens' own Neutral Milk Hotel's "In the Aeroplane over the Sea." Once, she now knew, that had been her parents' song, and Janelle's, too. Andy and Scott had sung it to her on the plane. Now, it was as familiar and comforting to her as they were.

Her parents sitting together. Together, for the first time since before her birth. Kasey watched them, picking apart features and parts, trying to figure out what she inherited from whom. Her father's dark blue eyes flashed, and her mother raised a hand to her dark-blonde hair, pushing it behind her ear. Her slim legs were cradled under her, and when she laughed, the sound was genuine.

It was a homecoming, a reunion. Kasey marveled at how her mother had changed seemingly overnight. She'd been at Louie's for just shy of two hours—had shown up without warning or fanfare—and she'd already sat down with almost everyone, catching up; her own little apology tour. She had greeted Ricky with a flirtatious

smile and an apology, as he'd wrapped her in a bear hug and kissed
her cheek. She'd swept Fallon away to the front porch for a private
talk, and Kasey had found she wasn't in the least jealous for the first
time in her life. Fallon deserved to have their mother, too. Ella and
Andy had had an instant rapport, and her eyes had perked up with
interest when she'd met Scott, who had won her over immediately
with his talk of the Athens music scene. When she'd left him to go
get food, she'd given Kasey a wink, causing her to blush. How had
she known?

Now her mom was sitting quietly with Louie, listening to him
play, looking as though she didn't have a care in the world. But
Kasey wondered… Was she nervous? She had to be, after years of
agoraphobia, of being silent and invisible, alone, to avoid her pain.
And there was one person who wasn't here, who she hadn't seen yet.
Now that she'd heard her mother's whole story, Kasey felt a knot of
dread at the thought of that meeting. Everything had gone well so
far; the last thing she wanted was for her mother to go running for
the hills now that she had her back.

"Penny for your thoughts."

Kasey turned and smiled at Scott, who had appeared at her
shoulder. He was holding her cane. "The way you were leaning
against that tree, I thought you might need this," he said, handing it
to her.

"Thanks," Kasey said, shooting him a happy smile. "And, hey…
Thoughts are worth way more than a penny these days. What can
you actually get for a penny? Pennies are obsolete."

"How can you disparage the honorable Abraham Lincoln like

that?" Scott said with a laugh, putting an arm around her shoulders. Kasey felt her entire body erupt in a warm, liquid feeling as she settled into his shoulder.

"Oh, I don't know. He's just another old white guy on a coin," Kasey said. "Anyway, I was thinking about my mom. Worrying about her, I guess. I still can't believe she came."

"She's beautiful," Scott remarked, looking at Ella. "Just like her daughter."

Kasey felt herself flush and punched him lightly in the arm. "Flatterer."

"Absolutely. I'm buttering you up as much as I can before you go," he said. "I figure I only have so much time to make you fall in love with me before you fly back to Georgia and break my heart."

Kasey turned to look at him, her face turning serious. "Scott…" she said, not sure how to say what she felt. "Did you…did you think about what I said? Before I went to Vancouver?"

"Yes," he said, looking into her eyes. "I took everything you said to heart. I thought long and hard about it. I know things are… weird. And we just met, and you're going through some stuff, and you need time. I get all that. I respect it." He took her hands and smiled. "I'm trying to do the same with my life. I just thought… maybe, while we're doing all this work, we might…"

"Might what?"

"Do it together." He shrugged. "Nothing more, nothing less. I don't have any expectations of you, no pressure… I just want to be with you. If that's what you want." He pressed her hand to his mouth and kissed it. "Kasey Newton, I'm falling in love with you."

Kasey's breath caught in her throat. "Are you sure it's not just because I'm from Athens and you need an in to the music scene?"

"That's definitely a huge plus," Scott said with a low chuckle, her fingers still pressed to his lips. "But no… It's you, Kasey."

Her voice was a whisper. "I think…I think I'm falling for you, too, Scott."

"You are?"

"Yes," she said, looking into his eyes, leaning forward to place a gentle kiss on his lips.

"Well, in that case," Scott said, his lips curling into a grin, "this is officially the best cookout I've ever been to."

"I brought you a veggie burger." Kasey, lost in thought, staring dreamily at her mother and father, turned to see Fallon standing next to her, holding out a paper plate. "Topped with onion rings, barbecue sauce, and mayo, just the way you like it."

Kasey took the plate and gestured for Fallon to sit down next to her. "Thanks. I'm starving."

"No prob. It's good to see you eating," Fallon said. "Even if you do eat some of the grossest concoctions I've ever seen."

Kasey took a huge bite, feeling oddly emotional. Fallon had just been teasing, but it was true that Fallon and Ricky knew Kasey like nobody else, knew her quirks and tastes better than anyone else did. They might have been exasperated with her over the years, but they'd always been there for her, always supported her. Even if she hadn't always been able to see it, she saw it now.

She chewed and swallowed, then turned to her sister. "I owe you an apology," Kasey said, taking a deep breath. "For being such a shit to you these past few years. I was in pain, depressed and grieving, but it wasn't fair of me to take it out on you. I know you were only trying to help."

Fallon's eyebrows raised in surprise, and she brushed her hair behind her ear nervously. "I didn't have to be so hard on you, either," she said finally, looking down at her feet. "I was trying to do the whole tough love thing, but I think I was just picking on you some of the time. I don't blame you, Kace – for what happened. I was just jealous, I guess—you got so much attention after your accident, and then after mom left, Ricky was always trying to make you happy… I felt invisible."

"Me?" Kasey looked at her little sister incredulously. "*You're* Ricky's favorite, Fallon. He thinks you hung the moon!"

"No, he just knows he can depend on me," Fallon said. "That's not the same thing. He knows I'll never do anything to make him worry, so he doesn't bother with me at all."

"That can't be true," Kasey argued, but deep down, she understood Fallon's feelings. She supposed being the dependable sibling came with its own burdens.

"I guess we both felt short-changed," Fallon said, her cheeks coloring slightly.

"Because we both were," Kasey said, taking another bite of her burger. "Speaking of, did Mom talk to you?"

"Yeah." Fallon sighed. "I don't know how to feel about it."

"Me, either."

"Can we start over?" Fallon asked suddenly, turning to face

Kasey.

"What do you mean?"

"You're my big sister," Fallon said, her big blue eyes wet. "You're basically my hero. I want to be your friend—your best friend. But I feel like you *hate* me."

"I thought you hated *me*!" Kasey exclaimed, setting her plate down.

"I don't want to be left out of your life anymore. I promise I won't judge you or boss you around. I just want to be in your life. As your sister. Even if it's messy." She swallowed, looking sheepish. "Can we do that?"

"You silly doofus. Of course we can," Kasey answered, and pulled her sister into her arms for a crushing bear hug. "Nobody can ever replace you. You know me better than anyone else in the universe and you're still here."

"I always will be," Fallon said, squeezing her sister right back. "Even with your gross taste in burgers and pizza."

THIRTY-ONE

ELLA - 2018

ELLA heard the voices inside the kitchen as she stood to throw her paper plate in the trash. She tensed and felt Louie's hand on her shoulder.

"Janelle's back sounds like," Louie said in a warm voice. "I'll go check on her, give you a minute, then you can go and say hello."

"She may not want to..." Ella's voice faltered, and Louie gave her a reassuring look.

"Don't do that to yourself, Ell," he said, calling her by her old nickname. "We're all friends here."

Ella caught a glimpse of Kasey, standing off in the trees with the handsome dark-haired young man she'd talked to earlier, the one who had been adorably obsessed with Neutral Milk Hotel. They were deep in conversation, and she watched as the young man held her daughter's hand to his lips, giving it a tender kiss. Her heart lurched. She'd missed so many of these moments, missed so many things she should have been around for. Kasey was a woman now, and Ella had missed it all. And yet, the tender feeling between the two of them seemed to carry in the air and right into her heart, and she couldn't help but smile as she watched them. *Good for you, Kasey,* she thought to herself, feeling her eyes fill with tears for the millionth time that day. *You deserve it.*

Her eyes fell on Fallon, her second-born, with her pale blonde hair pulled back in a messy ponytail as she played horseshoes with her dad. Dear Ricky, clutching a Pepsi instead of a Natty for the first time in twenty years. He'd lost quite a bit of weight since she'd walked out his front door all those years ago, his hair fully gone gray, almost white, despite only being in his late forties, still handsome and full of mischief. She felt another pang, watching him, wishing she still felt those confusing, exhilarating feelings she'd once felt for him, or convinced herself she did. They'd been a family once, the four of them.

Poor Fallon. She'd spent so much time trying to step into her mother's shoes that she had no life of her own to speak of, not yet. She took care of her father and Kasey. *My little mama*, Ella thought sadly. *We've got to put a stop to that. She deserves to be young and happy.* She smiled as she saw Kasey step over to her younger sister and put her arms around her, Fallon resting her white-blonde head on Kasey's shoulder, somehow knowing it was the first time the two sisters had been affectionate with each other in a very long time.

Sitting by the pool was Andy, Louie's son. Janelle's son. Tall, dark, and handsome, Ella had no doubt that he was a heartbreaker. He was a sweet boy, innocent and funny, and she'd taken an immediate liking to him. He was goofy and silly and had a familiar air of anxiety around him, but there was an inner strength, strong as iron. *He gets that from his mother,* she thought, butterflies flitting in her stomach. *Janelle's the strongest woman I ever knew. And I'm about to be face to face with her, Heaven help me.*

On cue, the sliding door opened and Louie emerged, a gorgeous teenage girl trailing behind him, her eyes glued to her phone. She was about fourteen or so, Ella supposed, and had pretty mahogany skin and large brown eyes. Her hair was pulled back in a high bun and she wore a Mother Love Bone t-shirt that Ella remembered very well. "I'd like to introduce my best girl, Glitter," Louie said, and nudged the girl forward. "It's short for Ginnifer, but we've called her Glitter since she was in diapers."

"I'm very pleased to meet you, Glitter," Ella said, smiling at the teen, who was rolling her eyes in a very endearing teenage way.

"I named myself after my favorite movie," Glitter said, in a low, grown-up voice, as Louie threw an arm around her shoulders. "I've loved it—ironically, of course—since I was a kid. Mariah Carey—I stan a queen!"

"Yeah, definitely. I stan," Louie said awkwardly, and Glitter groaned. "Since she was a *kid*." He rolled his eyes at Ella.

"Good lord, Louie, could you be any more cringe?"

"I assure you, I could." Louie gave her a wink and Glitter went running off toward the table full of snacks, pecking away at her iPhone. "She's full of it, by the way. We call her Glitter because she used to have these shoes that tracked cheap glitter all over the floors."

"She's adorable," Ella said with a laugh. "And she's yours, too?"

"Actually, no," Louie said, watching Glitter dig into a bag of Doritos with one hand and texting with the other. "I could see why you'd think so—she and Andy are clones of each other, and they aren't that far apart in age—but no, her dad lives in California. I love her to death, though. She's family all the same."

"So you and Janelle have stayed close."

"Yes," he said. "We have. We're co-parents, best friends…"
Lovers? Ella wondered as he failed to finish his thought.

"Frenemies." Ella's smile died on her lips at the familiar voice behind her. She swallowed and turned to find Janelle standing there, a bemused smile on her lips. It was as though time hadn't passed. Janelle looked much the same, as though it hadn't been a day… Only a couple of tiny, nearly imperceptible crow's feet around her large, beautiful dark eyes gave away that she'd aged at all. She was wearing a breezy black sundress that billowed around her curvy frame, and delicate black sandals that laced up to mid-calf. She looked like an Egyptian goddess, and Ella felt herself swallowing over and over, her mouth suddenly having gone dry.

"Ella. I can't believe I'm actually laying eyes on you after all these years," Janelle said in her smooth voice. "And after all you've done to try and deflect me."

"I'm so sorry, Janelle…" Ella's voice choked up with tears. "I owe you all so many apologies—"

"Save them, honey," Janelle said, placing a hand on her arm, and Ella's entire body erupted in heat, as if she'd gotten a sudden sunburn. The two of them leaned in for a moment, Janelle's arms twitching as though she might hug her, but Ella stepped back, uncertain. Janelle chuckled. "No apologies right now. We're celebrating, aren't we?" Ella nodded, unable to speak. "And anyway, I have a surprise for you."

"You do?" Ella managed a wry smile, though her heart was

pounding. "You don't have another kid stashed away that turns out to be mine, do you?"

"She jokes!" Janelle gave a short laugh, then pulled Ella toward the sliding glass doors. "No, I don't have any more ill-begotten children, but I *do* have someone for you to see. Come on."

Ella followed behind her, enjoying the feel of Janelle's hand on her arm, trying not to look at the smoothness of her shoulders in the silky dress. It was hard to imagine she hadn't seen this woman in twenty years and now she was standing so close to her. Ella knew without a doubt that she still loved her every bit as much as she ever did. She had never stopped.

Just inside the kitchen, two older people stood by the island, the woman holding a large glass of red wine. They were watching the small, portable TV beside the fridge, a puff piece about the fiftieth anniversary of the assassination of Bobby Kennedy, both of them riveted. "My goodness... That's today, isn't it?" the woman murmured, her hand on her heart. The clip cut to footage of a train ambling down a track, crowds of people milling around with grim faces.

"Bobbi made it down to see that train," she said to the man, her hand on his arm. "Remember? After she left... She was there." The woman was a mirror image of Janelle. The only difference was that her hair was in a beautifully coiffed afro, while Janelle had sleek, long locs.

Janelle cleared her throat, and the woman looked over, her eyes wide and kind, and as Janelle led her over, they filled with tears. "Oh, my," she said, her voice a whisper. As she walked over to look at her, Ella felt the strangest sense of déjà vu.

"Is this really Ella?" she asked her daughter, and Janelle nodded. "After all this time."

"It's her, all right," Janelle said, and the woman pulled Ella into a fierce hug.

"Ella," she murmured into her hair, holding her tight. She smelled of rosewater, and her skin was soft and cool. "I can't believe we're finally seeing you again after all these years."

"Hi, Kat," Ella said, her voice breaking. "It's so good to see you." Kat wrapped her in a soft, gentle hug. The man in the corner—Ramon—held his drink awkwardly, looking at the TV, but Ella could see his eyes were wet, too.

"They were so thrilled to meet you all those years ago," Janelle said as her mother still clutched at Ella. "When you ran away from us, and then you didn't answer all my letters... It broke Mom's heart all over again." Ella closed her eyes in shame, tears rolling down her cheeks. "Your mother meant so much to my parents, Ella. You have no idea. They've loved you your whole life. Since before you were born."

"I'm so sorry—" Ella started again.

"Let's not waste any time on *sorry*," Kat said brightly, mirroring her daughter's sentiments, as she pulled back clasped Ella's hand in her own. "I'm just so glad to lay eyes on your face again. Let's go outside and have some food, shall we? I want to meet your beautiful girls; Bobbi's grandbabies. And I want to see my grandson. I heard he's made it to 6'3" now."

"Why he never wanted to play basketball is beyond me," Ramon piped up behind her, placing a gentle, warm hand on Ella's shoulder briefly as he passed by her. It was a tender, casual movement, but Ella felt her eyes spring with tears again at his touch; a touch that felt like acceptance.

Ella started after them, eager to rejoin the party, but Janelle held her back. When they were alone in the kitchen, she turned to Ella, her dark eyes full of pain. "I don't want to hear a bunch of *sorrys*, either," she said bluntly, staring at Ella hard. "But I do want to know why. Why did you just leave like that? Didn't I deserve a goodbye?"

"I...I guess I couldn't bear it," Ella said, looking down at her feet. "I didn't know *how* to say goodbye. Because it wasn't what I really wanted. But I had to go."

"Why?"

"Because I was pregnant, Janelle," Ella said, taking a deep breath. "And I didn't know what to do. Have a baby with Louie and end things with you? Break your heart, or Louie's? Neither choice seemed possible. So I just...ran."

"We would have made it work," Janelle said. "We would have figured it out. You didn't give either of us enough credit. We're family."

"You guys are," Ella argued. "I was just the new girl, the outsider."

"That's bullshit, Ell."

"No," Ella argued, her cheeks reddening. "I saw it... I felt it. You and Louie...you've always had something. It's undeniable. You both told me that you were nothing more than friends, that the romantic part of your life was over, but...but you had a baby together just as soon as I was out of the picture." She shook her head. "That's why I thought I'd done the right thing. There was no room in your lives for me, not permanently, anyway."

"You are so wrong, Ella." Janelle's eyes flashed. "Andy is our pride and joy, and I thank my lucky stars every day that I had him." Her voice went soft. "But he was an accident, the result of a drunken bang that happened after Louie and I spent an entire night drinking whiskey on the rooftop of his apartment, singing Neutral Milk Hotel and talking about *you.*" She shook her head, chuckling. "We were both head over heels in love with *you*, Ella. You broke *both* our hearts. Yeah, we played around at dating when we were kids, but the thing we bonded over, the thing we've always shared, all these years…other than our beautiful son…is *you*. Our love for you."

"That can't be true."

"Can't it?" Janelle's eyes were soft and clear in the dim light of the kitchen.

"Janelle, I…" Ella's head pounded; she rubbed at her temple. "I was scared of more…more than just the pregnancy. When I ran, I was running from something else, too."

"Yeah?" Janelle was still holding her hand, stroking her wrist. Her voice was tender. "What was that?"

Ella took a shaky breath. "I grew up in small town Georgia. My aunt and uncle raised me, and you know how Grace was… Conservative. And pushy about it. I was a disappointment to her long before I left. Going to Seattle was the most daring I'd ever been. So having to tell them that I'd be a single mother…well, it was a daunting prospect to say the least. Telling them that I'm also…that

I'm…"

"It's okay, Ella," Janelle said quietly. "You don't have to say—"

"—that I'm gay…"

Janelle's arms went around her and held her tight as Ella felt something in herself break free. She began to cry in earnest. "Oh my god," she said into Janelle's smooth shoulder. "I'm almost forty years old and that's the first time I've ever said that."

"Girl," Janelle said, rubbing her back. "It's about goddamn time you let that out."

"I know." She sobbed against Janelle, feeling her tears wet her black sundress. "I've held it for far too long." So many years trying to force herself to be something she wasn't, trying to make relationships work and wondering why they didn't, what was missing, what was wrong with her.

Ella let out a ragged breath, one she felt like she'd been holding for decades. She stood there for a moment, crying into Janelle's shoulder, feeling herself let go as Janelle's strong arms held her, silently, lovingly. After a moment, she took a shaking breath and stepped back, managing a small smile.

"Janelle, I'm gay and I've been in love with you since the moment I saw you," Ella said. "I'm so sorry for running away. From you, and Louie, and…all of it. My whole life has been nothing but suffering and abandonment, feeling lost and alone. When I finally found real love, I guess I just didn't know what to do with it."

"Well, now you do," Janelle said. "You can start by taking me on a date, since—lucky you—I'm single."

"I think I can manage that," Ella said, smiling through her tears.

"No more second guessing," Janelle said firmly, placing a gentle kiss on Ella's cheek. "Life's too short and you've got to grab happiness by the scruff of the neck."

"I will." Ella nodded, resolute.

"Now." Janelle took Ella's hand in her own, her fingers intertwining with Ella's. "Let's go outside and join your coming out party." She rummaged in her pocket with a free hand. "I think I might even have a PRIDE button stashed somewhere."

THIRTY-TWO

BOBBI - 1975

NOBODY noticed the thin, young woman wrapped up in the dark
tan overcoat and bright blue scarf as she scampered up the hill and
into the woods.

It was a late Saturday morning in early May, a rare warm and
sunny weekend. It had been raining for three solid weeks and now,
in the late morning brightness, it seemed that everyone was outside,
soaking up the rays. Lawnmowers sputtered in yards, men shirtless
as they pushed them, holding cans of soda or beer for those who
preferred the hair of the dog, smoking their cigarettes. Women lazed
on their decks and screened-in porches, coffee or sweet tea in hand
as they thumbed through fashion magazines or sat by the window,
talking on the party line. Children clamored about their yards,
playing tag and cops and robbers. Teenagers sauntered down the
road on foot or on bikes, to meet up with friends and cause a ruckus.
In the distance, a loud dog barked; in the corner of the nearby
pasture, a lazy cow, fat with a late-spring calf, voiced her hunger
with a loud *moo*. Everywhere was the sound of birds, with their
trilling mating calls, and the intermittent noise of cars on the nearby
highway, heading south toward Athens or north toward Elberton.
And, far in the distance, the sound of the train as it lumbered down

the track toward Hull.

Everyone was enjoying the late spring morning with its warm sun, soaking up happiness and sunshine, which was why nobody remembered the young woman as she climbed up the embankment and toward the tracks.

She had spent the morning in her kitchen, leaning up against the counter, chain-smoking cigarettes and drinking black instant coffee, Landrum's coffee. Since the young girl had spit on him at the market, he'd only gone shopping once, out of necessity—Bobbi had picked up double shifts at Last Resort Grill and he'd been forced to make his way back to the grocery to stock up on supplies. They hadn't seen each other much that week. She'd missed him terribly, longed for him, and fretted over him as she'd poured coffee for strangers and served up veggie plates for traveling musicians. She'd felt him slipping, felt his disquiet, his pain, knew it was growing larger and larger, and with every absent moment felt him going away from her. From them. From himself.

But there were bills to pay, always bills. Without money, they would be evicted, forced to accept charity and move back home with Ed and Grace, so she picked up every shift. There would be time for her and Landrum. Later. He would get over this; *it just took time*. That's what everybody said, wasn't it? That's what she kept telling herself. So, she picked up shifts, and Landrum went to the store. *Later,* she just kept saying to herself. *Later.*

She hadn't realized it was all for nothing; that there had been an expiration date, that neither "later" would ever come.

That was the worst betrayal of all: not that Landrum had been feeling the way he did, because that she understood... Not that things between them had changed, because she understood that too... Not that the pressures of having a young child and mounting bills was almost too much to bear... They were a team, and who knew that better than she did? All these things Bobbi could understand, and did. Could forgive, and did.

But to leave her without a word, without a goodbye, without wondering, even for a moment, how she might get on without him, after all they had been through. *To leave me here alone, to pick up the shit you've left behind. To leave me here, still loving you.*

This morning was the first time she'd ventured into the kitchen and rummaged through the cabinets. She ran her fingers over the items in the cupboard, things she, a creature of habit and perpetual lists, had never really bought or even looked at—cream of wheat, Cheerios, canned yams, instant coffee. He'd bought a two-pound bag of sugar; didn't he realize there was a full bag in the freezer? She kept it there to keep it free from ants. That was seventy-nine cents wasted.

Bobbi had lit another cigarette, pulled down a bowl from the cupboard, and filled it with cream of wheat, carefully reading the instructions on how to prepare it. She poured in the boiling water, seasoned it with salt and pepper, and sat down to eat, forcing herself to swallow every lumpy, powdery, flavorless mouthful. When the cream of wheat was gone, she poured herself some Cheerios, which she ate topped liberally with the sugar Landrum hadn't needed to buy. She started to open the yams, then put them in her purse instead. She'd never liked yams. Using the remaining water in the kettle, she poured herself a liberal cup, then added in multiple teaspoons of the coffee, one by one. More sugar by the teaspoon full. She drank it down, then made another. Holding her third cup in hand, she made her way to the garage, the garage that had been scrubbed clean of all signs of Landrum's betrayal. Aunt Grace had come in and quietly scrubbed everything; Bobbi didn't know when.

The garage still smelled faintly of bleach, acrid and accusing.

Nothing is ever really clean, it seemed to say.

In the corner was the large monstrosity of a record player Bobbi had bought him as a wedding present, insisting that he needed a space to tinker on his car, smoke the odd joint, and listen to his favorite music to unwind. Landrum had loved it, even while lamenting what she'd spent on it, and called it the perfect gift. Every night for the past three years she'd brought him a whiskey, good stuff supplied by Ed, who knew how broke they were, and generic Coke in a glass tumbler, while he smoked cigars and listened to his records. Jimi, Janis, The Yardbirds, Cream. Landrum had unironically and unapologetically loved his "Woodstock Rock," as he'd called it, having been deployed when the music festival had happened. She'd bought him other albums—the Doors, David Bowie—but Landrum loved what he loved. "It reminds me of how it was before," he'd said to her one night, after two or three drinks, in a rare candid moment, "before the world changed. Before the hope was gone." When she'd stared at him sadly, he'd said, "Don't you remember how *different* it was? How hopeful, idealistic we were? Don't you remember how you felt before Bobby Kennedy was shot?"

"No," Bobbi had lied, not wanting him to dwell on the past, not wanting to give herself away and make it worse. She had run her hands up his arm and smiled, breaking into the Doors' "Light My Fire."

Landrum sang back, a little off-key, tears in his voice, the line about love becoming a funeral pyre.

Bobbi now regretted that particular choice of song.

She reached for the first record in the pile, finding the sleeve empty. The record—the one he'd listened to two nights ago when he'd made his exit—was still in the player. She curled up in Landrum's chair, which thankfully did not smell of bleach but rather his cigars and cologne, since no blood had fallen on the threadbare fabric. She tucked her knees under her and leaned over to the record player. She knew without looking where to place the needle for the correct track. It crackled and skimmed over the vinyl, then the familiar, strained and aching voice of a fellow Georgia man, Otis Redding, washed over her as she put her head between her knees. She only made it through the first couple of verses. Bobbi hurled the china cup holding her third cup of coffee into the wall and watched it shatter, black coffee spilling all over the drywall, just as dearly departed Otis, another man gone far before his time, began to whistle.

After a time, Bobbi had gotten up and packed a bag of clothes for Ella, then put her still-sleepy daughter in the car. She was late.

By the time Bobbi got to Grace and Ed's house in Athens, she'd wiped away evidence of her tears and managed to paste on a smile. "I'm sorry I'm late," she said as she bounded up on the porch, holding Ella in her arms. "I know you said you had to leave by eleven-thirty. Someone didn't want to get up from her nap."

"Yes, well, it's only a baby shower," Grace said with a pinched mouth, though her lips hinted at a smile as she took Ella from Bobbi's arms. She had been softer lately; Bobbi didn't like to think about why. Probably Grace pitied her. "I would've gone on, but you know how those mothers all crow over me, feeling sorry for me when I show up on my own. I simply can't stand it. At least if I have Ella with me, they dote on her and stop hovering over me like I'm a dried up, infertile crone."

"You ought to tell them all to go to hell," Bobbi said, and Grace gave her a look.

"There's no excuse to speak so vulgar, Bobbi," she said, but her face had softened even more. "What time will you be back for her?"

"Whenever you like," Bobbi said, pressing her hand to her eyes. She was beginning to get a headache.

"She's never any trouble. Ed and I adore having her. If you'd like the night to…gather your thoughts… Get some rest… Get the house in order…" Grace trailed off, trying for sympathy and coming up just short. "She's welcome to stay overnight with us. You could pick her up in the morning."

Bobbi pressed at her eyes again, trying to think. It was hard with the migraine beginning to pound in her temple.

"We just adore having her," Grace repeated, and Bobbi stared at her daughter in Grace's arms. She'd never seen eye to eye with the woman, had hated her ever since she married Ed. But the fact that she loved little Ella was undeniable.

"All right," Bobbi had said finally, then leaned over to give her daughter a kiss on her powdery forehead. "I'll see you soon, June bug. Mommy loves you." She lingered for a moment, relishing the feel of her lips on her daughter's warm, soft skin, marveling at how much her little girl smelled like her father. Then she turned and went to the car without looking back. By the time she'd buckled and started the ignition, Grace and Ella had gone inside, but Bobbi waited until she'd backed the car out of the drive before she'd given way to tears. Her head pounded the entire way home. She'd have done just about anything to make it stop.

Later, nobody noticed Bobbi scrambling up the patchy hill, close to noon, plucking a dandelion from the patchy ground and holding it to her nose, taking a deep whiff. Finding it had no scent, she tucked it into her pocket, pulling out the one item she'd brought along— an old banner, mounted on a little wooden stick, emblazoned with the faded words *RFK IS A-OK*. Landrum had given it to her that spring afternoon in 1961—god, had it been almost fifteen years?— standing by the UGA Law School steps, when she was barely a teenager. Bobbi ran her fingers over the faded light cloth, then took a bobby pin down from her hair, pinning the cloth banner to her lapel. She shoved her hands back in her pockets and walked on; the birds singing overhead, a tickle of pollen in her throat. She passed by the school unnoticed; the only people on the grounds this time of morning on a weekend were the janitors and yard crew, who worked in the flowerbeds and ag gardens without taking notice of her as she took a shortcut through the soccer field, down onto the football stadium, and through the trees to a little bank with dirty sand.

Bobbi hadn't been to this spot in years, not since homecoming, the one she'd almost skipped. She remembered how awkward she'd felt, how angry. To think being dumped by some high school boy had been enough to make her feel so low. She could laugh at the shallowness of it, the sheer ludicrousness of it all. To think that had happened less than ten years ago, when it felt like she'd lived twenty lifetimes since Landrum had brought her to this special spot, and they'd sat on the sand and listened to the bullfrogs and the trickle of the cool, reddish water on the muddy rocks.

In the distance, Bobbi could hear the approaching train, old faithful, the sleek metal monstrosity lumbering down the track as steadfast and reliable as death itself. She leaned back against a tree and sighed, remembering. Remembering how the boy next door had pushed her against this very tree and kissed her as the locomotive had clamored over the track, drowning them in sound as they kissed.

She remembered how soft Landrum's lips had been. How his strong arm had felt around her waist. How her feelings had taken flight on the soft breeze; a tender, fragile love affair emerging under a clunky old bridge just outside of Athens. After that kiss, she'd known she'd never love anyone else in her life, other than the gray-eyed Landrum Walton.

And she hadn't.

The creek was deserted, the sand devoid of footprints. There was nobody there to notice or care as Bobbi Newton-Walton pulled the tan coat tighter around herself, with no hope of keeping warm, and climbed up the tiny hill with slow, deliberate steps, grabbing onto roots as she pulled herself up the steepest part of the hill, to come standing at the top, looking out over the empty forest. The approaching train was louder now, closer; Bobbi both heard and did not hear. The memories washed over her, bittersweet.

Memories of kissing Landrum as the train rolled overhead, loud enough to drown out the heavy beating of her heart.

Bobbi pulled herself up to the top of the hill, damp dirt crusted over the palms of her hands, and smiled.

She smiled as a beam of light pushed its way through the tall, skinny pine trees and came to light on the train tracks, the dull, old metal glinting in the late morning sunshine.

Bobbi took a step, and then another, her mind far away with her memories.

She remembered that fateful, scorching hot day in June of 1968, when, every last hope dashed, she had run after the train, trying to catch it, trying to catch them again; her life—everything she had lost—as it rushed down the track and away from her.

Today she would catch it, by God.

From the football field, the caretaker looked up from the mower to light a cigarette, and thought for a moment he saw a woman standing at the top of the hill, the sun lighting on her blonde hair, a tan coat pulled around her like a security blanket...

Then the train crested over the tracks, lumbering and loud, and when it passed, the caretaker looked again and saw there was nothing there. Assuming he'd imagined her, he lit his cigarette and went back to work.

THIRTY-THREE

GRACE - ATHENS, GEORGIA - 1975

ED hung up the phone, his face set into a scowl. "That's the third time that Kat woman has called *today,*" he said to his wife, sitting down in his easy chair and picking up his tumbler of bourbon. Grace didn't like her husband drinking in the house—which he very well knew—but she said nothing. He'd been under a great deal of stress, dealing with the arrangements for his sister. She had died so unexpectedly, so tragically, right on the heels of her husband, and everyone in town was wagging their tongues about the scandal. Ed had his faults, plenty of them, but Grace's heart went out to her husband for having to go through this. And there was nobody else to help him, with his parents and brother also gone.

He's the last of his line, Grace thought sadly, adjusting the little one on her lap and sniffing at her powdery blonde hair. *I'll never be able to give him any children, and Bobbi's baby is the closest thing either of us will ever have to family.* Ella gave a squawk in her arms and gestured wildly. "Are you hungry, little buddy?" she asked the little one, juggling her on her legs. "Shall I get you some nice chicken and applesauce?"

Ed's gaze softened as he watched his wife and niece. "I just don't know how much more I can take," he confessed with a sigh.

"Do they really think we'll just roll over and allow them to take her? She's all I have left now."

"All *we* have left," Grace corrected.

"I sympathize with them, of course. It's an admirable thing, to honor a friend's wishes, if that was really what she wanted," Ed went on, staring into his drink. "But I never heard tell of any such wishes. Did you?"

"No," Grace said, pressing her face into the baby's hair.

"I don't know this Kat and Ramon from a hole in the ground. They're strangers. To think they actually suppose they have a *right* to just come and swoop Ella away when she's my *blood*." He took a long sip, holding it in his mouth. "And they're…they're…well, you know I don't see color, but what would folks *think* if…"

"No sense in dwelling on it, dear," Grace said, popping Ella's pacifier in her mouth. "Would you hold her, please, while I get supper on the table?"

Ed drained his drink and held out his arms. Grace placed Ella gently in them, leaning down to give her a kiss on the head. "Everything will be on the table in ten minutes. There, there, Ella, you just play with Uncle Ed now. He's got you, love."

In the doorway, Grace turned, smiling as she saw her husband place a kiss of his own on Ella's tiny forehead. His arms squeezed her tight, and she could tell that he was crying. She left the room and headed toward the kitchen, her heart full for the first time in years, with hopes for a future that might expand for something like family. Grace had given up on that dream so long ago—had let it dry up and rot on the vine—that this new, emerging, tender shoot of hope was almost painful as it expanded through her. *A daughter.*

Ella's overnight bag sat, still packed, in the pantry. Grace supposed she ought to go ahead and unpack it, put Ella's things in the guestroom. They'd have to work to turn it into a room for the little girl, but that was no matter. She'd enjoy doing it—decorating, picking out furniture, painting—all things she'd been looking forward to doing for her own child. She couldn't wait to begin planning with Ed, who she suspected might enjoy the experience, too. She'd already picked up a few paint samples. She'd show him after supper, perhaps, if his mood had improved.

Maybe having Ella might be the thing to save their marriage, to bring them closer together. If anything could salvage it, it was Ella. Ed had many faults, but he set a store by family; that was the key to his heart. Grace began to set places at the table, her heart brimming over with hope as she set an extra place instead of the usual two.

Her eyes fell again on the little diaper bag, and quickly, she walked over and unzipped the front pocket, extracting the piece of notebook paper she'd found that fateful morning. She opened it and scanned the hastily scrawled message there once more, breathing rapidly.

If anything should happen... Please call Kat and Ramon Hawks. They are my best friends, Ella's godparents, and they are wonderful people who will give her a lovely, happy life.

Tell my June bug, Ella, how much I love her, how much her daddy loved her. She was our moon and stars, our sun and sky. The sun shines in her eyes and I hope she will be happy all the days of her life.

Bobbi Newton-Walton

Grace wiped at her eyes as she refolded the note with a trembling hand. In the other room, she could hear Ed and Ella making their way toward the kitchen for their supper. With a quick, furtive movement, Grace walked over to the furnace and threw the note in, watching it catch flame and sizzle into black, feathery ashes. She swiftly shut the door to the furnace and pasted on a smile just as Ed, cradling Ella, came into the room.

"Who's hungry?" she asked her little buddy with a bright smile.

EPILOGUE

KASEY - ATHENS, GEORGIA - 2019

KASEY threw her keys down on the coffee table, pushed her cane up against the couch and eased onto the soft cushions, sighing in relief as she sunk in. It had been a long day; she'd had two classes starting at the crack of dawn, then she'd picked up an extra shift at Applebee's. Her co-worker Jana was sick with the flu, and even though her hip had been sore all day, Kasey couldn't turn down Thursday trivia-night tips.

She pulled her phone out of her bag and scrolled through her notifications, ignoring Facebook and Twitter and swiping over to her messages. She smiled as she saw another text from Caden, who had been harassing her for days, wanting to know if she had asked for next Saturday off. She kept forgetting to write him back. She'd do that now, before she inevitably fell asleep in front of Netflix again.

"Hey Cadee, I checked and YES, I have next Saturday off. I'm all yours. Wouldn't miss it for the world," Kasey typed, a grin lighting up her cheeks. She hit "send," then turned on the TV, scrolling to "Big Bang Theory." More nights than not, she fell asleep on the couch, watching her comfort show, and woke up sometime around midnight with a crick in her neck and her mouth tasting like crap.

And Kasey had never been happier. This mundane routine, this normalcy, this boring adult crap...it was everything to her. She'd worked so hard to get here.

Since she'd come home from Seattle, Kasey had enrolled at Athens Tech, where she'd go for two years, and if she could keep her grades up, then transfer to UGA to get her degree in history. She hoped, one day, she might be a professor at that same university. For now, she was trying her best at the core classes, working and saving as much as she could, and attempting to control her pain and her impulses so she could stay straight on the path to her dreams. This was the second month in her new place—hers and hers alone—a duplex just on the outskirts of Athens, but close enough to Ricky that she could still pop by every day and check on him to make sure he was handling the empty nest okay.

Fallon, who had begun dating a guy from Watkinsville named Greg, had also moved out. She was blissfully happy, and Kasey figured she'd be married within six months, if not before. Her sister had never been shy about who she was or what she wanted. And she deserved happiness, after years of helping take care of Kasey, something she could finally admit without shame. The sisters were slowly, carefully rebuilding their relationship, though Kasey knew she had a lot of work to do. Next week, she planned to take Fallon out for a girls' night, complete with chocolate martinis and cheesecake. They were going to sing karaoke, and Kasey planned to invite her sister back to her place for an old-fashioned sleepover. She'd already bought popcorn.

Kasey's phone pinged, and she picked it up, opening the text from Caden.

SO LONG, BOBBY

"I'm so glad, dude! I would have died if you missed my wedding. I can't wait for you to meet Kennedy. You'll love her."

Kasey smiled, her eyes misting over. She was so happy for Caden. He'd gotten clean, had a great new job working at a construction firm, and he'd met his fiancée not long after Kasey had gotten back from Seattle. From what Caden said, it had been love at first sight. Kasey was thrilled for him, and it felt like a serendipitous coincidence that her name was Kennedy, of all things. Kasey would always love Caden, always be grateful for what he'd meant to her in those dark years, thankful that he'd stuck by her side when she'd needed him most. But they were better friends than lovers; she knew that now.

Kasey typed out a response, a happy tear rolling down her cheek. *"I can bring a date, right?"*

As she waited for his reply, Kasey settled further into the couch with a sigh, her gaze falling onto the opposite wall where she'd hung a cluster of pictures in sleek black frames. The frames had been a gift from her father, Louie, who had told her, "I hang pictures everywhere I go. Pictures are the closest things we have to holding our memories. Constant reminders of who we are, and what we want to remember." Hanging them was the first thing she'd done when she moved into her new place.

On the wall were the memories she held most dear: the silly photoshoot with her, Fallon, Ricky, and Mom; the wedding picture of her grandparents, Bobbi and Landrum, that she'd found in the box; a framed picture of Kat and Ramon at the Poor People's March on Washington that they'd kindly sent her; a picture of Ed and Grace at a judicial dinner; an Army photo of her great-uncle Guy, who she'd never known; a picture of her and Amber at cheerleading practice; and her favorite of all, taken at Louie's house the year before, at their impromptu reunion: a group of smiling, ragtag folks, clustered in front of a choppy Seattle ocean, smiling big and awkward and large as life. Kasey with all the people, both new and old, that she loved. Fallon, Ricky, Louie, Andy, Scott, Janelle, Glitter, Kat, Ramon, and Ella, her mother.

Her *family.*

Soon, there would be another photo for the wall. Her mother and Janelle were currently on a road trip, headed to Ohio, where one Irene Ella Walton, a spitfire in her late nineties, was staying in an assisted living facility. Kasey could scarcely believe it—her mother had tracked down her Grandma Walton, alive and well and desperate to meet her long-lost granddaughter. From what she'd heard, the woman had decades' worth of stories to tell. Kasey could hardly think about it without crying from joy. Landrum's mother— her great-grandmother—was still alive, and Kasey would get to meet her one day soon.

Not only that, but when the trip was over, Ella would be settling back in Athens—in the home she'd inherited from her Uncle Ed and Aunt Grace, a home Kasey hadn't been to since she was a child. A family home she never knew her mother even owned. And Janelle, her soon-to-be stepmother, was coming to join her.

Kasey wiped a wayward tear from her eye—it felt like she'd done nothing but weep since the day she'd found that now-infamous box; a box that held a legacy of pain, a pain for which generations of orphaned women had not possessed the coping skills to heal from—but that was all right, because Kasey knew that pain would end with her. The box, a gift from Bobbi and Landrum, had saved Kasey's life, and the lives of many other people, too.

Kasey stood up, typing out a message to Scott as she walked to the back door, sliding open the glass to the patio. *"Get packed—you're my date for a wedding next week."*

Scott wrote back almost immediately. *"You got it. Why don't I just stay for good this time? These fares are costing me a fortune."*

It was a running joke between them. Scott and Kasey had agreed to take things slow. Every time he asked, "Why don't I just stay?" Kasey would laugh and say, "When the time is right," and he'd acquiesce and fly home to Seattle until the next time. Neither one of them wanted to jeopardize a good thing, and a damn good thing it was. The *best* thing.

And yet… Life was so short, and time was fleeting. If you found love, Kasey had learned, you did not run from it.

She stared at the phone, ready to type her usual response, then grinned and typed, *"Okay. You wore me down. Stay this time."*

The response was immediate. *"OMG, Kasey, are you serious?"*

She stepped out onto the patio into the cool autumn night, breathing in the crisp, quiet air. She stood there for a moment, just breathing it in, staring up at the murky, cloudy sky, then smiled and typed, *"Yes. I love you. I want you here, with me."*

Kasey slid her phone into her pocket with a smile. It was starting to drizzle. She leaned down, pressing her cheek to the cool wrought iron of the porch railing, closing her eyes, letting the long day go as the peaceful nighttime rain washed over her. After a moment, she stood, cleansed, and blew a kiss into the air.

As she moved to go back inside, raindrops mingling with the happy tears on her cheeks, Kasey heard the unmistakable sound of a train off in the distance, running down an old, familiar track into the dark, moonless night.

ACKNOWLEDGEMENTS

My deepest thanks go to:

As always, my faithful and supportive beta readers, Beth Tankard and Jennifer Babineau; you guys are the best. Thanks for taking on my rougher than rough drafts and helping me turn them into something beautiful.

To my friend, fellow author (now publishing house sister!), and '90s aficionado, Lauren Emily Whalen; thanks for all the book talk, critiques, gab sessions and writing advice. I'm so glad we're on this journey together!

Thank you to the team at Sword & Silk Publishing—especially MaryBeth Dalto, Laynie Bynum, Jennia Herold D'Lima, Kristin Jacques, E.M. Wright and Asterielly Designs—for bringing this novel into the world!

Additional thanks go to Jessica Campbell, Ellen Burke and Amelia Ross, who have kept me sane in the "Covid Times," Daryn Cash, Cate Short, Cydney Flanigan, Micah Hudson, Nicole Hensley, Jennifer Fisher and the Madison County Library, Flagpole Magazine, UGA Arts & UGA Willson Center, UGA Historical Archives and Hargrett Library, Madison County Historical Society, Josina Guess, Larry Alexander, Bill Shipp (for more information about the murder of Lemuel Penn, please read his book *Murder at Broad River Bridge*), *Sassy* Magazine (I miss you so!), *The RFK*

Tapes podcast, Classic City Vibes podcast, Juliet Rose, Peter Fenton, Aunt Jean, Jonathan Lawson, Christopher Drake, Sam Veal, Chadd Knight, Kelley Lawson, Erin French, and Nathan Rodriguez (rest in peace, my dear friend).

Thanks to my grandmother Anita (Nonna), whose brain I picked thoroughly as part of my research; thanks to my parents John (who always laughs when I call myself the "first pancake") and Teresa (who got me started on histfic), for always encouraging my writing career and relaying your memories of growing up in this place, in that time; and last but not least, thanks to my husband, Blake, and my son, Callum. Living with a writer is not always a walk in the park, but they handle it with aplomb.

In loving memory of Aunt Nina Mae, who would have loved this book. She always supported and encouraged my writing and made the best chocolate cake this side of the Mason Dixon. We miss you terribly!

How many people can one novel be in memory of? I guess the beauty of being a writer is that it's up to me! So last but not least—I dedicate this book to the memory of my three grandparents who have passed on: Clark and Julia-Ann (Shelton) Drake, and John Newton Lawson, all of whom encouraged me to follow my dreams and continue to inspire my love of history and genealogy. And, also, to the memories of Lemuel Penn and Lent Shaw (murdered in Colbert, Georgia, thirty years apart) and to another one of my heroes, Georgia's own Congressman John Lewis.

I'm sending a few last thank yous into the ether to my personal favorite "grunge gods," Layne Staley, whose soaring vibrato and sad, searching lyrics provided the soundtrack to my angsty youth, and Mark Lanegan, whose sandpaper-and-honey voice makes me want to crawl inside it and go to sleep. They were the constant soundtrack as I wrote.

Lastly, to the best president who never was, Robert Francis Kennedy: *"The purpose of life is to contribute in some way to making things better."*

CPSIA information can be obtained
at www.ICGtesting.com
Printed in the USA
BVHW041834140423
662390BV00007B/27

9 798986 599823